D0971512

WITHDRAWN

The
INCORRIGIBLE CHILDREN
⤳ *of* ⤶
ASHTON PLACE

Book 6: *The* LONG-LOST HOME

Also by Maryrose Wood

THE INCORRIGIBLE CHILDREN OF ASHTON PLACE

The
LONG-LOST
HOME

by **MARYROSE WOOD**

illustrated by **ELIZA WHEELER**

BALZER + BRAY
An Imprint of HarperCollins*Publishers*

Balzer + Bray is an imprint of HarperCollins Publishers.

The Incorrigible Children of Ashton Place Book 6: The Long-Lost Home
Text copyright © 2018 by Maryrose Wood
Illustrations copyright © 2018 by Eliza Wheeler
All rights reserved. Printed in the United States of America.
No part of this book may be used or reproduced in any manner whatsoever without
written permission except in the case of brief quotations embodied in critical articles
and reviews. For information address HarperCollins Children's Books, a division of
HarperCollins Publishers, 195 Broadway, New York, NY 10007.
www.harpercollinschildrens.com

ISBN 978-0-06-211044-2

Typography by Sarah Hoy
18 19 20 21 22   CG/LSCH   10 9 8 7 6 5 4 3 2
❖
First Edition

For Katy

THE FIRST CHAPTER

Beets are very hard to grow.

To PUT IT IN A nutshell: Plinkst was nothing like Ashton Place.

This was the sad and unavoidable conclusion reached by Miss Penelope Lumley, who had recently—and oh, so reluctantly!—joined the household of the Babushkinov family in the unhappy town of Plinkst, in Russia, somewhere south of Saint Petersburg and north of Moscow.

Or was it east of Moscow and west of the Volga? Penelope's grasp of Russian geography was shaky at best. During her years at school she had dutifully memorized the capitals of midsized European nations, but Russia was hardly midsized. On the contrary, Russia was vast. If Russia were a person with both arms outstretched, hugging the earth as if it were an extra-large beach ball, the left hand would lie upon the eastern rim of Europe, and the right hand would reach all the way 'round past China. If Russia were to stretch to its full height, its head would be in the frozen Arctic tundras of Siberia (wearing a warm hat, one would hope), and its toes would be wiggling happily in the golden beach sand on the shores of the Black Sea.

Penelope gave a slow spin to the makeshift globe she had fashioned out of a roundish potato and a long birch twig that had been whittled to a point. Russia! Imagine! It was enough to make a person feel no more than a speck, a scrap of flotsam or jetsam tossing in the waves, to be cast willy-nilly into such an unimaginable expanse. (As the sailors among you know, flotsam and jetsam both refer to items found bobbing in the sea, but they are not the same thing. Flotsam means the leftover bits and pieces of a shipwreck, while jetsam means items thrown overboard on purpose. Whether Penelope was better described as flotsam or jetsam at this point was hard to say. She had been rudely tossed from her former life, which technically made

2

her jetsam, but she felt rather like a shipwreck at heart, which was more of a flotsam state of mind.)

Either way, she had been set adrift. And to wash up in Plinkst, of all places!

Now, to be fair—and Penelope always tried to be fair—Plinkst was not wholly to blame for her misery. Under normal circumstances she would have been thrilled to visit Russia, a fascinating place where the tops of important buildings were shaped like onions and everyone's favorite soup was made of beets. Russia was known for its stormy classical music, its tormented poets, its mournful novelists and bittersweet playwrights. And the Imperial Russian Ballet in Saint Petersburg was not to be missed! That is what Penelope had heard, at least. Plinkst was nowhere near Saint Petersburg, and, disappointingly, the Babushkinovs had not yet proven to be frequent balletgoers.

But, oh! England! How she missed her native land, with its fertile soils and mild climate, its love of good manners and passion for good tea, its comedic operettas, stiff upper lips, and a postal service that was swift and efficient as a sparrow in flight! Penelope had not willingly left England; quite the contrary. Though only sixteen years old, she was an experienced and capable governess, previously employed at Ashton Place, where she had cared for the three wards of Lord Fredrick Ashton.

However, through some terrible legal trickery (the details of which are best saved for later, for Plinkst is unhappy enough as it is), her contract with the Ashtons had been sold to the Babushkinovs without her knowledge or consent. Now her job was to instruct the eldest children of the Babushkinov household: twelve-year-old Veronika and the eight-year-old twin boys, Boris and Constantin.

So far, Penelope's attempts to instill this unpleasant trio with the virtues of her own upbringing had fallen upon barren ground, much like the rocky, thin soils of Plinkst, in which little seemed to grow, not even the beets that Plinkst was inexplicably famous for. The twins were as bad-tempered and cruel as Veronika was vain and insincere. In Penelope's view, only Baby Max, who was a robust toddler and no longer a baby (though everyone in the family persisted in treating him like one) might yet have any hope of growing into the kind of truehearted person worthy of the name of Swanburne.

Dear old Swanburne! She gave her globe another half spin and gazed upon the eye of the potato that gamely stood in for the town of Heathcote, where she had spent so many happy years at school. That Plinkst and the Swanburne Academy could coexist on the same planet seemed as unlikely as pigs taking flight, hens growing teeth, very hot places freezing over, and other such expressions of the impossible. Her heart filled with emotion until she began to sing, under her breath, slowly and in a minor key:

All hail to our founder, Agatha!
Pithy and wise is she.
Her sayings make us clever,
And don't take long to tell.
When do we quit? Never!
How do we do things? Well!

It was there, at the Swanburne Academy for Poor Bright Females, that Penelope's character had been formed. A Swanburne girl was truthful in matters great and small. She was industrious, which is to say she did the work that fell to her without complaint, and to the best of her ability, too. A Swanburne girl was slow to anger and quick to forgive. She was a loyal friend, calm in a crisis, resourceful in a pinch, and optimistic to a fault. In a word, she had pluck.

Penelope was Swanburne to the core, and that is

why, despite the injustice of her situation, not to mention some other pressing and—*unusual* concerns, she felt obliged to do her best at her new position.

"After all," she thought, as she spun the potato globe in the other direction, thus causing time to go backward on the Planet Spud, as she had come to think of it, "one could scarcely find a place on earth where the influence of a Swanburne girl is more urgently needed than here, on the failing beet plantation of the unhappy Babushkinov family and their badly behaved children, the spoiled, rude, selfish—"

There she stopped herself, for "horrible Babushka-woos" was the next stop on her train of thought, and a Swanburne girl did not call people names.

"Savages!" Veronika hurled the insult at her brothers, who had just done something dreadful. The exact nature of their misdeed is unimportant, as Boris and Constantin did dreadful things all day long. Only if they stopped would it be worth mentioning.

"You smell," Constantin retorted.

"No she doesn't," said Boris. "She stinks. Stinky stinky!"

Penelope sighed with such deep melancholy one might have easily mistaken her for a native. Name-calling was one thing, but facts, alas, were facts. Spoiled,

rude, and selfish was precisely what these children were. They were horrible, and as for "Babushka-woos"—well, that was what the Incorrigible children had called them, fondly and in friendship. (The three Incorrigible children were Penelope's much-loved and much-missed former pupils. Their reasons for adding "awoo" to people's names will be made clear soon enough, for those of you who do not already know.)

Veronika shrieked and wept and chased her brothers 'round the room that passed for a nursery in the Babushkinovs' house: a spare bedchamber no bigger than a closet, with uncomfortable chairs and nary a bookshelf to be found, never mind watercolor paints, or puzzles, or an abacus, or any of the other items Penelope would have deemed essential, had anyone bothered to ask her opinion.

"I hate you!" Veronika screeched. "Hate! You! Both!" The boys only laughed.

Horrible, horrible Babushkawoos! This was the third time the twins had made their sister cry since breakfast, and it was not yet time for lunch. Veronika was no better. She mocked her brothers in tones of utter contempt and shamelessly lied to their parents by inventing wrongdoings (as if they needed inventing!), for which the boys were constantly and unfairly blamed.

No one believed a word the twins said, so they felt no obligation to tell the truth, and they were always being punished, so there was no need to behave themselves in the first place. It was all quite backward and unpleasant, but that was how the Babushkinov household ran.

"Enough squabbling, if you please! Let us return to our studies," Penelope said firmly, once she had placed the Planet Spud on a high shelf and corralled the three children back to their seats. "The question is: if Russia were a biscuit jar, and England were a biscuit, how many Englands would fit inside of Russia?"

The Russia/England problem had been inspired by Penelope's homesick mood, but she thought Boris and Constantin might take an interest, as the two boys argued daily over which twin was bigger. In reality they were precisely the same size and always had been; they were the sort of perfectly identical twins whose own parents struggled to tell them apart. And all three Babushkawoos liked biscuits, as most children do.

Veronika arched over the back of the antique loveseat until her long, wheat-blond hair swished across the floor. Countless dance lessons had made her spine limber as a cat's, and she never tired of showing off.

"The question is impossible," she declared from her upside-down position. "Just thinking about it exhausts me!"

"Before giving up, you might at least attempt to find the answer." Penelope tried to conceal her irritation, but honestly! It was like pulling the stubbornest donkey uphill to get these Babushkawoos to try anything that was new to them, or that required the slightest bit of effort, or that made them confused or uncomfortable even for a moment. "And mind the furniture, please!" she reprimanded, for Veronika now dangled in a reverse swan dive, knees hooked over the sofa back, with her strong dancer's feet digging into threadbare cushions that were already on the brink of splitting open.

The whole estate was like this: a glance gave the impression of lavish wealth, but closer inspection told a different story. The roof leaked, the carriage horses' ribs showed, and the flower gardens were overgrown with weeds. Even so, Madame Babushkinov insisted on dressing the family in expensive new clothes in the latest fashions, for she believed in "keeping up appearances," as she put it. Yet just the other evening Penelope had overheard her complain that the dressmaker refused to sew another stitch until paid the money owed her. "Ungrateful woman!" Madame Babushkinov had said bitterly to her husband. "She acts as if we were some common family of no name or reputation, who must pile our rubles on the table in advance of any service!"

Clearly, the Babushkinovs had fallen upon hard times. Penelope was sorry about it, but only because it meant her own meager salary nearly always went unpaid. Then again, there was nothing to spend a ruble on in Plinkst, except postage to write to the Incorrigibles and to Miss Charlotte Mortimer, her former headmistress at Swanburne. These letters she wrote and sent without fail, though she had yet to receive a reply.

But it had been only two months, she reasoned. Who knew how long it would take for a letter to travel to Ashton Place and back again? No doubt the postal workers in Plinkst were as miserable and downtrodden as the rest of the town. In the words of Agatha Swanburne, "The unhappy chicken lays few eggs. If any!"

Penelope would have written to her friend Simon Harley-Dickinson, too—well, perhaps he was more than a friend!—but Simon was a man of the theater, with no permanent home or postal address, and so there was nothing to do except wait and hope that she might soon—oh, let it be soon!—receive a letter from him. For there was a matter of great importance he had promised to send news of, regarding some urgently needed advice from a soothsayer friend of theirs in London, the spookily gifted Madame Ionesco, who was surely the one person on the great spud—globe!—of the earth who might know how to undo the dreadful family curse that had caused so much heartache to begin with, all thanks to that monstrous, unfeeling Edward Ashton. . . .

"Filthy boys, look at your hands," Veronika scolded.

The boys were coughing as if they had just emerged from a coal mine. Miraculously, they had found a dust-covered atlas hidden in some closet. (An atlas is simply a book of maps. As you know, the world is round like a ball, not flat like a book, which is why every nursery ought to contain a proper globe instead of a potato, and why a well-trained governess will not panic if her pupils attempt to play catch during their geography lessons. However, an atlas will do perfectly well for looking up the size of Russia and the size of England, the types of ostriches native to Africa, the average winter temperature in Siberia, and other essential facts. All the maps and globes in the world are no substitute for actual travel, of course. As Agatha Swanburne once advised, "Don't take my word for it. Go see for yourself!")

Penelope roused herself from her bleak mood. Any show of effort by the twins was as rare as a great comet, and she intended to take advantage. "Good work, you two," she exclaimed. "Now, as for the Russia/England problem . . ." But the boys had already lost interest and were trying to pat Veronika's cheeks with their dirty hands. This prompted another screaming chase 'round the nursery.

Penelope used one of her own pocket handkerchiefs to wipe the thick layer of dust from the atlas. "Once you have found the size of Russia and the size of England, you have a choice in how to proceed," she explained, in case anyone was listening. "You might start by guessing, and multiply England's size by various numbers until you arrive at Russia's. Or, if you feel daring, you could divide Russia's area by England's, and find the exact answer at one fell swoop."

"The answer is . . . I don't care, Lumawoo!" Boris threw himself facedown on the sofa, dirty hands and shoes and all. Maddeningly, the horrible Babushkawoos insisted on calling her Lumawoo, as the Incorrigible children had. Each time was like a tiny jab, till Penelope's heart felt as full of pins as the lumpy red pincushion carried by Madame LePoint, the dressmaker at Ashton Place.

Constantin slammed the atlas shut so carelessly that some of the pages tore. "Bah! I have no interest in any of this. Boris, my brother! On the count of three, let us wrestle. *Ah-deen! Dva! Tree!*"

This was how "one, two, three" sounded in Russian. Penelope had not yet learned more than a few words of the language, for the family spoke to her only in English. However, the twins loved to wrestle, so she heard *"Ah-deen! Dva! Tree!"* shouted multiple times a day, and that much, at least, had stuck. (That the children would be taught only in English might seem odd, but among wealthy Russians of Miss Lumley's day, it was the fashion to have an English governess and a French chef, and to speak these languages, even at home. The Babushkinov children had learned English from their former tutor, who was a very odd duck indeed. However, we shall meet Master Gogolev soon enough, so no more need be said about him now, not a word about his bad leg and worse moods, his doomed love for a dull woman, his tin ear for poetry, and his utter refusal to wear a hat, even in the worst weather. All of that and more you will soon see for yourselves.

For now, let us remain in Plinkst, in the meager nursery of the horrible Babushkawoos, for the twins are about to wrestle, and one of them is likely to end up with a black eye before they are done.)

Boris crouched down, Constantin held out his arms, and the two boys flew at each other in a violent whirl of arms and legs.

"Ow!"

"Ouch!"

"You pulled my hair!"

"You split my lip!"

"Cheater!"

"No, *you're* a cheater!"

"What savages you are." Veronika gazed at herself in the hand mirror that was never far from her. "I can hardly wait to tell Mama and Papa!"

"Behave yourselves, please." Penelope bit her pencil stub and frowned, for she had decided to tackle the Russia/England problem herself. As she performed her calculations, the twins beat each other and yowled like hyenas, a sound so commonplace it hardly disturbed her concentration.

Even so, she had to start over several times, and not only because of the tricky sevens and eights of the multiplication tables. It was because the very thought of England made her eyes blur with tears. This made it difficult to read her own writing, and thus she kept forgetting to carry the ones.

"The answer to how many Englands would fit inside Russia," she said at last, "is seventy, more or less."

Seventy Englands to make one Russia! And one homesick, heartbroken governess, lost in the middle of it all!

"You punched my eye!"

"No, you punched *my* eye!"

"Look, Lumawoo!" This was Veronika, as she waved the page ripped from the atlas. "These savages have torn Budapest in half!"

"Hand that over, if you please." Penelope snatched the page from Veronika in a sudden fury. Surely the capital of Hungary deserved better than this! She tried to muster the will to scold her pupils for the hundredth time that morning but found she could not. Instead, she slumped in despair and sighed once more, as deep and melancholy a sigh as one might hear in the most bittersweet Russian play.

"No hopeless case is truly without hope." That was the motto of the Swanburne Academy. Penelope knew it as well as she knew her own name, yet she had all but given up hope for the Babushkinovs. This family was so, well, *incorrigibly* miserable, one might easily conclude that they too were under a curse.

"Just like the Ashtons," she thought, then corrected herself. "That is to say, just like *we* Ashtons—for though I am a Lumley, it seems I am somehow part of that mysterious, curséd family tree as well, and so are my dear Incorrigibles! Oh, if only Simon would write to me with Madame Ionesco's instruction about how to undo this wolfish curse before it is too late! For time is running out, and the Barking Baby Ashton will be arriving all too soon. . . ."

"BLAST!" IT WAS LORD FREDRICK Ashton's favorite exclamation, but for once his outburst had nothing to do with the date of the next full moon. "A baby, a baby, a baby!" he muttered as he paged through his almanac. "Dr. Veltshmerz says the little tyke'll arrive at the beginning of May. Only a month away, and still so much to do. I must hire a new baby nurse, first of all. That mopey Russian girl didn't work out. Just as well! I never liked the looks of her, with those stooped shoulders and darting, shifty eyes. And the baby's room has to be made ready. What sort of wallpaper does a baby like? I've no idea. I'll have to let Mrs. Clarke manage it. Then there's Constance to contend with. Big as a house, but still in good spirits! I'm sure I wouldn't be, if I were waddling about at three times my normal size the way she is. Do you have any children, Quinzy? I don't expect you do. I've never heard you mention them, what?"

His guest slumped in one of the armchairs that faced the row of ancestral portraits in Lord Fredrick's study. The man's face was thin and pale, with raw, weather-scarred patches on his cheeks. A shock of black hair spilled across his forehead like ink.

"My family tree does have a touch of mystery about it," he replied after a pause. "But if I had a child, Fredrick, you would surely know all about him."

It was a sly answer, for the man in the chair most certainly did have a child. "Judge Quinzy" was merely a role he played, as if he were an actor on the stage. In reality he was Lord Fredrick's own father, Edward Ashton! (That a son would not recognize his father may seem hard to believe, but Lord Fredrick's eyesight was notoriously poor. Too, in his current state, Quinzy hardly resembled the stout, silver-haired Edward Ashton who gazed forbiddingly from the portrait that hung not ten feet away. Only the eyes were the same, penetrating and dark, but Quinzy concealed his behind thick-lensed glasses.)

"Yet I approve of children, in principle," the imposter went on. "Without them, who would carry on the line? The day your wife adds a fresh twig to the Ashton family tree will be a memorable occasion, I have no doubt." His voice was cool and even, but his ceaseless finger drumming could not hide the tremor in his hands. Edward Ashton knew what his son did not: that there was a terrible curse on the Ashtons that could only be ended by an even more terrible crime. It was the crime he had spent most of his life planning, and it had to be carried out before the birth of Fredrick's child. Yet here he sat, shaking like a leaf in autumn, with only one moon left and his duty as yet unfulfilled!

"Fresh twig, quite right." Out of habit, Lord Fredrick patted his pockets for a cigar. He found none, for the smell of cigar smoke had grown offensive to his wife's increasingly sensitive nose, and he had ordered Mrs. Clarke, the head housekeeper, to remove all cigars from the premises months ago. "What do you think I ought to name the little fellow? It'll be a boy, of course. We only seem to have boys, we Ashtons!"

"Only boys, eh? Curious . . ." Here again the imposter knew more than his son, for there had been an Ashton girl, once. A secret sister, whose name and existence had been blotted out. Now the memory of her was all but erased, as if it had been written in invisible ink.

"I could name the child after my father." Lord Fredrick was still prattling about the baby. "But perhaps that's a bad idea. The old chap came to a gooey, gruesome end, after all. What do you think, Quinzy? Is it bad luck to name the child Edward?"

"Quinzy" did not answer, for Edward Ashton had sunk into his own half-mad thoughts. Bad luck to be named Edward? Perhaps, but not because of that blasted medicinal tar pit at the spa of Gooden-Baaden, where he had faked his own death so many years before. That was the path he had chosen: to die to all who knew him, and to all he knew—his devoted wife, his bumbling, nearsighted son, his palatial home, his vast fortune. And yet he lived on in secret, under many names and disguises, including "Judge Quinzy." In this way, he could attend to his wicked task freely, anonymously, without bringing more scandal to the name of Ashton.

You are a monster. So the insolent young governess had said when she learned the full, murderous scope of his plan. But was he? Simply because he had vowed to save his family, no matter the cost?

If you want a monster to blame, blame the admiral. He

cast a bitter glance at the portrait of his grandfather, the vain and selfish Admiral Percival Racine Ashton, who wreck'd his ship on an enchanted isle and carelessly murdered a litter of sacred wolflings, as if they were a brace of grouse on his own estate!

Blame the mother wolf, wild with grief for her slain cubs, and the vengeful curse she had unleashed upon the admiral and all his tribe!

Or blame my father. Yes, blame Pax Ashton, for being too weak to resist his fate. The admiral and his wife met gruesome ends, true, but it was their son Pax whose spirit was curdled by the wolf's curse. Overnight he turned cruelly against his own twin. He cast her out and ordered her name never to be spoken and all record of her existence destroyed, as if his own once-beloved sister, Agatha—yes, Agatha Ashton was the secret sister's name!—had never been born at all.

From that day, the family tree had been split in two: Pax and his descendants on one side, Agatha and hers on the other. It was just as the mother wolf had foretold. And now it fell upon him, Edward Ashton, to put things right. He knew what he must do before Fredrick's child was born, and he *would* do it, too. On that point he was fixed and unwavering as the North Star itself.

Only one side of the family can remain, or both will perish from the earth.

Which meant if he failed, there would be no more Ashtons, ever again, never, never, *nevermore*—

"Quinzy, are you listening? I said, how was Switzerland?"

Through sheer will Edward dragged his attention back to his unknowing son. "Switzerland!" He managed a wan smile. "Marvelous country. The Alps are sublime, the marmots endearing. Not to mention the proud ibexes, the flocks of agile goats, the countless rustic villages . . ."

Blasted Switzerland! For two months he had hiked and climbed those snow-capped peaks in the bitterest winter weather, with only his crampons and pickax for company. He had searched every one of those sickeningly quaint villages, with their happy yodelers and endless mugs of hot chocolate, but to no avail. If Switzerland were a person, he would have turned it upside down and given it a good shake to see what fell out of its pockets. If it were a sofa, he would have removed all the cushions and felt his way 'round the edges with his fingertips, the way one might search for enough loose change to pay one's fare on the omnibus.

And what had he found? Nothing.

It was as if the long-lost Lumleys had vanished from the face of the earth.

Still, he did not quit. To learn the habits of one's prey was essential; every hunter knew this. He studied the Lumleys as painstakingly as a poet studies the clouds, or as a birdwatcher studies her warblers and nuthatches. He visited every bookshop that carried melancholy German poetry in translation, and every art gallery that showed sentimental watercolors of mountain lakes and alpine meadows. He had seen so many paintings of edelweiss, that cheerful white flower that dots the Alps each spring, that he sometimes found himself doodling pictures in the margins of his train tickets.

But so far, at least, the prey had eluded the hunter. Exhausted and sick, he had slunk back to England to recover, to think, and to scheme. What had he missed?

"You picked a chilly time of year to visit Switzerland, if you ask me," Fredrick said in a jovial tone. "But to each his own. Next winter I might just do as Constance wants and book us a trip to the Italian Riviera. At least we'll get some sun that way. Of course, next year there'll be the baby to think of. . . ."

If there is a next year, for any of us. Once more Edward Ashton lifted his eyes to the ancestral portraits. His gaze lingered—how could it not?—on his own likeness, that of the "late" Edward Ashton. The governess had figured out his secret, for all the good it had done her. Thanks to him she was trapped in Plinkst, as fitting a place as any to await one's doom. The other three were upstairs, innocent as spring lambs, going about their business in the nursery under the drooping eye of that new tutor, that fool, Gogolev—

"But there were *five* cubs," Edward Ashton hissed, rising blindly from his seat. "Five cubs killed means five to be avenged. . . ."

"Five of clubs, did you say? Afraid I don't have time for cards today, not with this baby of mine chug-chug-chugging 'round the bend. But perhaps you'll take some refreshment before you go? You look a bit peaky, if you don't mind me saying so."

Whereupon the current lord of Ashton Place jumped up to help his wobbly, not-really-dead father back to a comfortable chair. "Easy there, Quinzy, old chap," he said kindly. "You look like you've seen a ghost! This trip to Switzerland seems to have worn you out, what? You'd best stay here at Ashton Place and recuperate. It's much homier than at the club. No, no, I insist! What's the point of having a house with so many rooms if people don't stay in 'em?"

"You are quite right, Fredrick. I am not well." Behind the windburn, Edward Ashton's cheeks were bone white, and his black eyes glittered with fever. Still, an ember of hope kindled deep within him. What could be more perfect than to regain his strength here, at home? For surely Ashton Place was his home, as much as it was anyone's.

"I accept your generous offer," he said, overcome with weariness. "I have always felt at home at Ashton Place. In truth, there is no place else I would rather be."

Fredrick clapped him on the back. "That's the spirit. I'm no medical doctor, mind you, but if I were, I'd prescribe a nice cup of tea, and a biscuit or two to perk you up. Stay where you are, and I'll ring for Mrs. Clarke. We can hear her thoughts on the wallpaper, how's that? *Ahwoof*—pardon me!"

He frowned as he tugged on the bellpull. "*Yap!* Seems I've got a bit of a cold coming on. No cause for alarm. They come and go with me, every four weeks or so. *Arf!* That is to say, *ah-choo!* Hand me the almanac, would you, Quinzy? It tends to wander off if I don't put it right back on the shelf. Why, you'd think the book was cursed, *woof!*"

But Quinzy, or Edward Ashton, or call him what you will, had gone limp in the chair. His eyes roved wildly beneath closed lids, and he did not stir, except to mutter something unintelligible. To a careful listener it might have sounded like *"The fifth . . . where is the fifth . . . ?"*

Lord Fredrick grabbed the almanac himself and squinted at the pages. "Blasted moon! I've mixed it up again. Looks like I'll be laid up all day tomorrow, and with so much to do, *arf!* I'd best get an ad in the paper for a baby nurse, quick."

The Second Chapter

"But what of the Incorrigible children?" and questions of that ilk.

As Agatha Swanburne remarked on the occasion of her eightieth birthday, when presented with a totally unexpected cake, "Well, well! Life is certainly full of surprises!"

As usual, the wise founder was right—but really, what were the odds? The usually optimistic Penelope Lumley was sighing like a Russian in unhappy Plinkst. The usually self-possessed Edward Ashton was muttering and half mad after his failed tour of Switzerland. And the usually gruff and unsentimental Lord Fredrick

Ashton was discussing wallpaper with Mrs. Clarke and cheerily picking baby names, and with a full moon coming on, too!

Even Lady Constance had slipped "out of character," as Simon Harley-Dickinson might say (he was a man of the theater, after all). The usually vain and anxious mother-to-be spent her afternoons waddling contentedly through the new tulip garden. The tulip bulbs had been homely as turnips when planted, but a winter spent underground had worked its magic. Now graceful whorls of green leaves poked through the damp soil, and the stalks had begun to rise, with only a tender green swelling where the flower buds would very soon be.

Mother Nature had planned it all perfectly, for the tulips showed every intention of bursting into bloom four weeks hence, at the beginning of May, just as the Barking—that is to say, Bouncing—Baby Ashton was due to arrive. By then the moon would be full once more.

Truly, it would be a big week for blossomings.

Now, THIS TALK OF TULIPS is all very well—but what of the Incorrigible children?

It is an excellent question. It was the same question

that Penelope asked as she awoke every unhappy morning in Plinkst, and that Miss Charlotte Mortimer brooded upon each evening, in the headmistress's office at the Swanburne Academy for Poor Bright Females. (It should be noted that Miss Mortimer had taken some mysterious trips of her own in recent months. "As Agatha Swanburne often said, 'Mind your business, for if you don't, who will?'" she replied briskly, when the girls dared to ask about her travels. "Now, who among you can name the capital of Sweden? Back to work, please!" *Clap clap clap!*)

Even Simon Harley-Dickinson must have wondered, from his ever-changing position in the theatrical firmament: What had become of Alexander, Beowulf, and Cassiopeia Incorrigible, the three wards of Lord Fredrick Ashton, of Ashton Place, England? Were they safe and in good health? Were they keeping up with their studies? Was Alexander still growing taller by the day, and had Beowulf managed to give up his habit of gnawing on hard objects when anxious, and was little Cassiopeia (not so little anymore!) attempting to read her own Giddy-Yap, Rainbow! stories at bedtime, now that her devoted governess was no longer there to read them to her?

What news of the brave Incorrigibles, indeed?

As is so often the case, there was both good news and bad news to report. The good news was that the Incorrigible children still lived in their well-appointed nursery on the third floor of Ashton Place, as they had done since the day a newly hired Miss Lumley had found them huddled in the barn, wild haired and howling after being caught by Lord Fredrick during a hunting expedition.

How frightened they had been! And how close they had come to meeting a gruesome end in the forest, which only the quick thinking of the coachman, Old Timothy, had prevented! Yet they would rather relive that awful day a thousand times—no! a thousand times a thousand (which equals one million, as Cassiopeia could tell you without even using her abacus)—than endure even once more the cold January afternoon on the pier at Brighton, when dear Lumawoo was shipped off to Plinkst before their weeping eyes, and even the deepest breaths of the good salt air could not loosen the knots of grief in their hearts.

Still, the Incorrigible children had not been raised by a Swanburne girl for nothing. To give in to despair was not their way. All three were in good health and fair spirits, and they went about their days, if not happily, at least without complaint. They took their baths and made their beds and put their toys back in the toy chest before bedtime, for that is what Lumawoo would have wanted. Oddly, her absence made them all the more keen to act as they knew she would wish. Perhaps it was a way of imagining her close by, for unlike the Babushkawoos', their nursery was equipped with an actual globe, and they understood all too well how very far away she was.

Only on rare occasions did their good behavior falter: for example, when peas were unexpectedly served at luncheon. At those times, a meaningful glance from the stronger willed to the weaker was usually all it took to set them back on track.

As for the bad news: their education was now in the hands of the glum Russian tutor, Master Gogolev, who had formerly worked for the Babushkinovs.

Imagine! From Miss Penelope Lumley to Karl Romanovich Gogolev! Penelope could have made a lesson out of it, for Shakespeare had described a similarly unhappy swap in his tragic play *Hamlet*. It is in the scene where the ghost of Hamlet's father returns from Beyond the Veil to discuss his own murder with his son. "O HAMlet, WHAT a FALLing OFF was THERE!" the dead king proclaims, in a spooky iambic pentameter. By this the ghost king means that his murderer,

Claudius, who has married Hamlet's widowed mother, the queen, and thus become king of Denmark himself (as had been his scheme all along, the villain!) is far less qualified as both king and husband than the dead king himself had been when he was alive.

To take a cue from Shakespeare, then, the switch from peerless Penelope to morose Master Gogolev might well make a person say, "O children, what a falling off was there!" But Master Gogolev was too distracted by his own troubles to give a lesson on *Hamlet.* Nor was he interested in being king of Denmark. He had begged for the job at Ashton Place for one reason only: it was because of Julia, the former nurse to Baby Max Babushkinov.

As they say nowadays, Julia was no prize. She was a careless nurse, anxious and self-pitying, with no more brains than an ostrich (as any ornithologist could tell you, the eyeballs of an ostrich take up most of its skull, with only the tiniest bit of room left for brains). Nevertheless, Gogolev was hopelessly in love with Julia, while Julia found him absurd and offered only scorn and mockery in return. It was a rare flash of good sense when he pleaded to be sent far away from the daily torment of her stoop-shouldered, darting-eyed presence. Captain Babushkinov consented, and that is how Gogolev came to replace Penelope, who had already been hired to replace Gogolev.

But alas, poor Gogolev! More woe was in store for him, for at the eleventh hour, Julia was also hired by the Ashtons, who would soon need a baby nurse of their own. (Those of you with poetic licenses know that "at the eleventh hour" is a way of saying "at the very last minute." Also note that the eleventh hour in the morning is the perfect time to enjoy a cup of tea, but the eleventh hour at night is a time when only stage actors and theater critics ought to be up and about. No doubt Miss Lumley would advise all of us to stick to early bedtimes. In the words of Agatha Swanburne, "When the sun is up, so must you be! When the sun is down, so must you be, too!")

That the source of his misery seemed bound to follow and torment him wherever he might go plunged Gogolev into a quicksand of despair. Luckily, Julia's poor posture and lack of intellect proved to be her good qualities. The deceitful girl had no intention of working for the Ashtons, but merely wished to exit Plinkst at their expense. The moment she arrived at Ashton Place, she began plotting her means of escape. Soon enough she found it. She convinced the baker from the village that she was worth wooing, and the two of them ran off together. Rumor had it that they had booked passage on a ship to America, where they planned to open a Russian tea room, perhaps in New York City, and eke out a living that way.

It is a sad and complicated tale, and would make a fine Russian novel, full of heartbreak and irony and thwarted dreams, but it is a tale we need not say any more about, as the fate of Julia and her baker are no concern of ours. However, it does explain why Lord Fredrick was even now writing an advertisement for a baby nurse, and why the village of Ashton was in desperate need of a baker (a fact you would do well to remember, as it may become important before very long!).

Above all, the tragedy of Gogolev and Julia explains how the Lumley/Gogolev problem came to be, and there is no answering the question "But what of the Incorrigible children?" without addressing this unfortunate circumstance in their lives. That is the main reason you have had to endure this melancholy, bittersweet, and thoroughly Russian story, much as poor Penelope had to endure the long, uncomfortable journey from England to Plinkst, and all the unhappy days since.

(Precisely how many Gogolevs it would take to

fill the shoes of one Miss Lumley is another excellent question, but one whose solution will have to wait—for Master Gogolev has finally arrived in the nursery, wailing about a spooky supernatural bird. . . .)

"An albatross!" Master Gogolev cried. "That is what Julia has become! An albatross 'round my neck!" (An albatross is a type of large white seabird. It is also a symbol of an unpleasant burden that one cannot seem to escape. This second meaning we owe to the poetic license of Mr. Samuel Taylor Coleridge, whose famous poem *The Rime of the Ancient Mariner* contained just such a creature. As punishment for killing the bird, the old sailor of the poem's title was forced to wear its gruesome remains as a necktie. To this day, people who have never heard of Mr. Coleridge will speak of "the albatross 'round their necks," which only goes to prove that poets often have the last laugh.)

Master Gogolev ran his hands through his wild hair until it resembled a squirrel's nest. His three pupils sat in the nursery with straight backs and folded hands, waiting for their lessons to begin. It was already late in the morning, for Master Gogolev was not an early riser, and he insisted on drinking an entire pot of strong coffee and reading three different newspapers—one

French, one English, one Russian—before emerging from his bedchamber, still unshaven. That Julia's departure had scarcely put a dent in his suffering is best explained by the words of Agatha Swanburne, who once looked up from a Russian novel she was reading and ruefully announced, "A teakettle that likes to whistle has no need for a stove." So it was with our tormented tutor.

"She is a thorn in my paw, a stone in my shoe, a toothache in my tooth!" Master Gogolev was fond of metaphors. "But why, why, *why* did it have to be a baker? Now I cannot look at a loaf of bread without thinking of her! I love bread," he confided to the children. They nodded in sympathy, for they too loved bread, as most people do. "Yet each time I dream of eating it, it is like a thousand . . ." He made a cutting gesture.

"Bread knives?" Beowulf suggested.

"Yes, bread knives, spreading pain across my soul. Like butter." Gogolev wept. He went through pocket handkerchiefs at an alarming rate; the laundry could hardly keep up. When he was done, he made a trip downstairs to wheedle a snack from the kitchen—nothing to spoil his lunch, just a small omelet and an onion tart, and more coffee, and a pastry for dessert but not a sticky one, as he disliked how a sticky sugar glaze felt on his fingertips. Weeping always left him hungry, he explained to the children upon his food-laden return, and in any case it was already the eleventh hour in the morning, a perfect time to pause in one's labors and enjoy a snack. The children did not mind, for he let them eat all the bread off his plate; in fact he swore up and down he would never touch another slice, despite the telltale crumbs on his jacket.

The truth was that Gogolev did not spend much time teaching. From dawn to dusk he suffered like an animal in a trap, drank coffee, smoked, begged meals from the kitchen, and napped. This left little in the way of time or energy to examine the Poetics of Aristotle, the poems of Mr. William Wordsworth, the techniques of watercolor painting, or any of the other topics that the children would have been only too glad to study.

As far as the Incorrigibles were concerned, then, their tutor's late arrival, bleak mood, and greedy appetite were all signs of a perfectly ordinary morning. Yet it was that very same morning that Miss Penelope Lumley had posed and then tearfully solved the Russia/England problem in faraway Plinkst, and that "Judge Quinzy" had paid an unexpected call on Lord Fredrick Ashton. Even now, as Master Gogolev gorged himself on food and self-pity, son and father sat in Lord Fredrick's taxidermy-filled study only one floor below, speaking of Switzerland, wallpaper, and baby names.

The laws of time and space prevented the children from knowing any of this, of course. Innocent as the spring lambs Edward Ashton imagined them to be, they gnawed on the dense, flavorless bread that was the best the kitchen could obtain (there was no longer a proper baker in town, do not forget!), and waited for their tutor's laziness and disinterest to come to the fore.

They did not have to wait long. After his meal, Gogolev belched, yawned, excused himself for a few hours of "personal reflection," and left them to their own devices.

"Educashawoo!" Cassiopeia crowed when he was gone. Her brothers ran to fetch their notebooks and pencils. Now their school day would truly begin, for what could be more educashawoo—that is to say, educational—than free time and a lack of supervision? The Incorrigibles had become expert at spending their days wisely, all thanks to an invention they called "the to-doawoo list." (The Incorrigibles were not the first to think of the "to-do list," as it is commonly known. The use of such lists goes back to the days of antiquity; for all we know there were well-organized Neanderthals jotting their daily schedules on the walls of caves.

If you have never written a to-do list, you are missing out on one of civilization's greatest achievements. To make one is nearly as soothing as cup of tea, but to tick items off the list when completed is a feeling so delicious one might easily confuse it with actual cake. Consider putting "make a to-do list" on your to-do list for tomorrow.)

The first item on the children's daily to-doawoo list never changed: *letter to Lumawoo.* These were no ordinary letters. Alexander drew clever maps that showed Plinkst and Ashton Place as neighboring towns connected by many short bridges. Beowulf contributed original poetry, written in all his favorite poetic meters. At the moment, he was attempting a villanelle, a poetic form more complex than even the most complicated dance step. Cassiopeia expressed her feelings through the use of math problems: *Four Minus One Equals SO SAD*, for example, or *Three Plus One Equals HOORAY.*

Each day's letter was addressed to "Miss P. Lumley, care of the Failing Beet Plantation of the Horrible Babushkawoos, Plinkst, Russia, Across the Sea So Far Away." Solemnly the children would bring the envelope to Mrs. Clarke, who would pat each of them on the cheek and murmur, "Ah, Miss Lumley! I hope she's getting on all right, poor thing!"

However, on this particular, ordinary-seeming morning, they could not find the good lady in any of her usual spots. She was not in the kitchen, fretting with Cook about the difficulty of finding a qualified baker. Nor was she supervising the housemaids as they dusted knickknacks in the parlor. The children wondered if she might have snuck up to her room on the fourth floor, to read for a bit while nibbling on a piece of licorice. Mrs. Clarke loved licorice and had grown quite fond of the Giddy-Yap, Rainbow! stories, ever since Penelope had introduced these fine books to the household.

With their day's letter to Lumawoo still clutched in Alexander's hand, the Incorrigibles marched upstairs to knock on the good housekeeper's door. But there was no answer, for by this time Mrs. Clarke was in Lord Fredrick's study, nervously answering questions about what sort of wallpapers babies liked, whether a silk or wool carpet would be nicer for a little child to crawl upon, and which room she intended to make ready for Judge Quinzy to move into during his recuperative visit to the household. ("I don't like that Judge Quinzy, and that's a fact! One look at those dark eyes of his and I feel like someone's walking on my grave," she would later confide to Cook over a restorative glass of blackberry cordial. It should be noted that Mrs. Clarke was no ghost and had no grave. She was merely using an expression that means to get a sudden and unpleasantly spooky feeling. Whether ghosts are spooky to other ghosts is a haunting question, but one best answered by those who peek Beyond the Veil.)

The children were disappointed not to have completed their mission, but not tragically so. They simply returned to the nursery and took out their to-doawoo list. *Find Mrs. Clarke* was moved to later in the afternoon, which was all right, as the letter would still go out in the day's post.

Now they could decide what to do next. There was no shortage of pleasant tasks to choose from, for it was all written down on the list.

Visit Bertha was Cassiopeia's first pick. Bertha was the speedy but dimwitted ostrich who had been left at Ashton Place by a fascinating but dishonest explorer named Admiral Faucet, a friend of Lord Fredrick's mother. He pronounced his name Faw-*say*, but he was not French; very likely he was no admiral, either. Bertha lived in a POE—a Permanent Ostrich Enclosure—on the grounds of the estate. She could not fly, for ostriches are flightless birds, but she could run like the wind, and gave the children ostrich rides that were thrillingly fast.

Alexander frowned.

"Paint each other's portraits," Beowulf suggested. As a poet he was not half bad, but painting was his passion.

Alexander shook his head. It was their rule that two out of three had to agree. Clearly the eldest Incorrigible was not yet convinced.

"Latin verbs?" Cassiopeia offered, for it was a school day, after all.

Alexander looked down at the floor and sniffed. (The children had very keen senses of smell, but there was no magic about it. They had simply been raised to use their noses the way wolves do. It was a matter of paying close attention, combined with a great deal of practice. Of course, to focus one's attention and practice is the secret behind most of what people think of as extraordinary talents, like playing stormy Russian music on the piano, or twirling a dozen whip-fast pirouettes in a row without getting dizzy, or shooting an arrow from a hundred paces at a target no bigger than an apple. As Agatha Swanburne said, "To make something look hard is easy; to make something look easy is the hardest work of all.")

"Something smells funny downstairs," Alexander announced, wrinkling his nose. His siblings sniffed, too.

"I smell cigars. And high, cold places," Cassiopeia said.

"I smell snow," Beowulf agreed. "And chocolate. And taxidermy."

"It must be the smell of Switzerland, coming from Lordawoo's study," Alexander concluded, for he knew his geography from the North Pole all the way to the South. "But there is something else, too. Something bad." He sniffed once more, then snorted and shook his head, as if he had gotten a noseful of rotten-egg smell. "Hate and fear, mixed. It smells like . . . hunting."

Cassiopeia started to whimper, and Beowulf turned pale. "Never mind." Alexander playfully cuffed his siblings on the head to cheer them. "Probably it is the smell of a bad dream someone is having. Let's play with Nutsawoo."

"Play with Nutsawoo!" the other two quickly agreed. The unanimous Incorrigibles ran to the nursery window, where the long branch of the elm reached out to them, just on the other side of the glass.

"Nutsawoo!" they called. "Nutsawoo!"

But the little scamp was nowhere to be found.

Cassiopeia gazed longingly out the window. "I miss Nutsawoo," she murmured. Nutsawoo was their pet squirrel, and the children spoiled him with treats and head scratches as often as the furry rascal would let them. But Nutsawoo had been unusually skittish of late, and came by the nursery rarely. It seemed as if the little rodent was preoccupied.

So it was for all the animals of Ashton Place: the warblers and nuthatches and the wee mousies in the fields. They knew that springtime was coming, just as the tulips knew. The wild creatures were bright of eye and bushy of tail, and many were in a romantic frame of mind. All over the estate, nests were being feathered and cozy family-sized burrows dug.

In fact, if Nutsawoo had been able to speak or draw a map, write a poem, devise a math problem, or even perform a *tableau vivant* to express what was on his (or her) mind, the fuzzy-eared scamp might have proudly announced that arrangements for a squirrel-sized nursery in the treetops were already under way.

"THAT NUTSAWOO IS GOING TO be a mother—or a father, for it is hard to tell with squirrels—is all very well," you are no doubt thinking. "And Edward Ashton becoming a houseguest at Ashton Place is worrisome, true! But what happened to all the letters?"

It is a fine question, for, as you know, Penelope had not received a single one of those heartfelt and educational letters from the Incorrigible children, even though Mrs. Clarke dropped the envelopes in the post every day without fail, and paid for the stamps out of her own wages, too.

Nor had the children received so much as a picture postcard from Penelope, though she too wrote to them daily. She wrote her letters in the evening, after she had wrestled the horrible Babushkawoos into their night-clothes and read them a bedtime story. At least, she tried to. The Babushkawoos never listened, but whispered cruel remarks as Penelope grimly plowed ahead. Eventually they grew too exhausted to continue insulting each other and dropped miserably off to sleep.

Then she would return to her tiny room. Letter paper was scarce in Plinkst, but she had found a stack of yellowed sheets in the nursery that still bore the faded trace of Master Gogolev's handwriting. It was all in Russian, but she guessed they were lines of terrible love poetry about Julia. (As it happens, she was correct. However, Gogolev's bad poetry is no concern of ours, not even the stanzas in which he compared the darting, nervous glance of his beloved to the path of a mosquito, or her hunched posture to the caved-in shape of a rotted wine barrel: "The staves are warped, the joints are loose/Yet still perfume'd by former use. . . ." Staves and joints, honestly! Please banish Gogolev's appalling verses from your mind at once. Even the worst poems about shipwrecks and gloomy supernatural birds are a thousand times better—no! a thousand times a thousand times better!—than this.)

Once the candle was lit, Penelope would take out a sheet of this paper, a quill pen with a bent but usable nib, and some ink. The wooden inkpot was carved in the shape of a troika, which is a kind of Russian sleigh pulled by three horses harnessed abreast. (Interestingly, troika is also the name of a Russian folk dance in which one man dances with two women, and can be used to describe any group of three. Troika thus has a troika of meanings, which simply proves that words are slippery creatures in every language. Poets find this useful, but poets are a slippery lot to begin with. Hence their need to be properly licensed, for their own safety and that of the general public, too.)

In England the tulip buds were swelling, but in Plinkst the Russian winter was not yet done. A thin layer of snow had fallen during the early evening, and the sky had since cleared. Now the frosted landscape glittered in the light of a moon that was only one night short of being full.

Penelope had grown used to being cold. She wrapped a thin blanket around her shoulders, dipped her pen in the ink, tapped off the excess, and began. "To my troika of Incorrigibles, the three cleverest pupils any governess could wish for. How go the multiplication tables?" She wrote on, bravely and cheerfully, as was her habit. Not once did she mention how unhappy she was, how much she missed her former pupils, and how truly afraid she was, for all of them—for surely Edward Ashton could read a calendar as well as the next man.

Where was that murderous scoundrel, with his mad plan to save one side of the family tree by doing away with the other? Was he lurking about Ashton Place, plotting against the children? Or had he made good on his threat to seek out her own long-lost parents, wherever they might be?

Or might he even be in Plinkst? The back of her neck prickled at the thought. It was the terrible wolf curse that had set Edward Ashton on his deadly mission, and it was her side of the family tree he was hunting now:

As the wolf has four paws, four generations must pass under this curse. In the fourth generation,

the hunt begins—and ends.
As the wolf has one tail, only one line of your
descendants can remain.
When that comes to pass, the curse is finished.
Otherwise, the house of Ashton, all it has been and
all it might ever be, shall be destroyed, forever.

Poor Incorrigibles! Poor Long-Lost Lumleys! They had no idea of the danger they were in, and here she was, useless, half a world away!

The risen moon was framed snugly in the high, small window of Penelope's room, like one of Mrs. Clarke's fresh-baked gooseberry pies tucked inside a pie box. Moonlight cut a cool blue shaft through the air and landed squarely on the face of the mantel clock, which glowed like an answering moon.

Tick-tock, tick-tock, tick-tock, tick-tock, tick-tock . . .

Restless, she put down her pen and walked the length of her room, no bigger than a cell. As she neared the window, she combed her fingers through the cool blue light and watched her hand turn into a ghostly puppet. If only she might climb that moonlight like a ladder and make a run for it! But it was much too far to run.

"A troika from Plinkst to the train station in Moscow,"

she thought, tracing the journey back to England in her mind. "Then the train from Moscow to Saint Petersburg. From there, some sort of boat to take me 'round Scandinavia"—"The capital of Denmark is Copenhagen!" she paused to note, pleased that she remembered—"and then south to Brighton. Then, another long train ride to Ashton Place."

Blast! All those tickets to purchase, and all those nights spent in hotels, and here she was without a ruble to her name! Truly, travel was a great bother and a great expense, and it was no wonder most people preferred staying at home. "If only there were some way to skip all that moving about, and simply be in the place I am thinking of," she thought miserably.

There is such a way, of course: it is called reading books, for a well-told story plunges us all at once into the sights and sounds and smells of the tale we are reading, and even the slight bother of turning a page now and then cannot persuade us otherwise. Surely most of us know what it is to miss one's stop on the omnibus, or fail to hear repeated cries to wash one's hands and come to supper, simply because one has one's nose, and mind, and heart, buried inside a book.

Penelope knew this feeling well, for she loved a good book more than anything. Alas, Ashton Place was not in a book, and she could not transport herself there simply by reading about it! There was a great expanse of Russia and Europe, and miles of roiling sea, between her and the place she most longed to be.

And that curséd contract she had signed! It meant the Babushkinovs could have her pursued and arrested if she dared leave their estate without permission.

Tick-tock, time flies, the clock warned. *Tick-tock, time flies, tick-tock, time flies. . . .*

The candle on the night table was sputtering, the wick nearly gone. Penelope had always preferred early bedtimes, but in Plinkst she often found herself unable to sleep. She would lie in the dark on her narrow, straw-stuffed bed. Her room was a small one off the kitchen that had once been a pickle pantry, and it still smelled sharply of vinegar, as if a barrel of sauerkraut were hidden someplace nearby.

"Simon," she whispered (as the sailors among you know, sauerkraut was often served aboard long sea voyages to prevent scurvy, and Simon had eaten his share of it during his days at sea). "Simon! Where, oh where is your promised letter? What has Madame Ionesco told you about the curse upon the Ashtons, and how to rid ourselves of it once and for all, but without bloodshed or treachery?"

50

This was the main reason she had not already plotted her escape. Recall that Penelope was a governess, not a soothsayer. She knew which was a metaphor and which was a simile, which a stalagmite and which a stalactite (well, usually). She could play chess, divide fractions, write in cursive, and do a strong-voiced recitation of at least three different Shakespearean sonnets. These skills and more had been part of her education at Swanburne, and she was grateful for every one of them.

But how to undo a curse? Never, not once, had such a thing been mentioned in all her years at school. When it came to the supernatural, Penelope was simply out of her league, as they say nowadays. If she left Plinkst, Simon would have no way to reach her, and she would never receive the urgently needed advice from Madame Ionesco.

If she left Plinkst, she would truly be on her own.

Then again—and the idea pained her sharply even as she thought it, like swallowing something cold too quickly—perhaps she already was.

QUIET AS A MOUSE, SHE padded out of her room. She had some hard thinking to do, and she always thought better while walking.

How she longed for a friend to talk things over with! But Penelope had no friends in the Babushkinov household. Now and then she tried to exchange a few words in French with the chef, to keep in practice, but the kitchen was always in an uproar. The grocery bills had not been paid in months and yet somehow the poor man (his name was Pierre) was expected to provide elaborate meals three times a day. The last time she had stopped in to ask him what he had planned for dinner, he clawed at his face and shrieked, *"De la soupe à l'air, un soufflé à l'air, un rôti d'air, des tartes pochées à l'air!"* which Penelope understood to mean "Air soup, air soufflé, roasted air, and poached air tarts!"

Other than the Babushkawoos, the only person she spoke with now and then was the Princess Popkinova. This ancient woman was the mother of Captain Babushkinov. She knew some English but did not care to use it. Most of the time she preferred not to speak at all. It was Penelope's lack of Russian that guaranteed she would not annoy the old woman with conversation, which is why the princess found her an acceptable companion, and would occasionally send for her in the evenings. They would sit in silence, or play a popular Russian card game called *durak*, which meant "fool." Other times the princess would watch from her wheeled invalid chair as Penelope sewed.

Perhaps from habit, then, Penelope's aimless walking led her to the hall outside the princess's bedroom. The princess tended to doze in her chair for much of the day, which meant she was often awake late at night, playing solitaire alone in her room.

On this night the door had been left ajar, and a soft light flickered from within. Penelope switched to an extra-silent tiptoe, but it was too late. The princess was awake and had already caught sight of her accidental visitor. Her eyes were hooded and sharp, like an eagle's.

Penelope curtsied and said, "Good evening, Princess."

The old woman grunted and used one long, gnarled finger to beckon Penelope inside. Her playing cards were spread out on a tray table set in front of her wheelchair. She swept them into a pile. *"Durak,"* she barked. "We play."

Penelope hesitated. "If you wish—but perhaps it is too late?"

"Too late! Too late!" The old woman repeated the phrase in her creaky, accented English, like an ancient Russian parrot. "Too late for cards? *Nyet.* For life? *Da.* I am older than my life. You understand, yes?"

The Princess Popkinova was a gloomy talking bird

indeed. Then again, Penelope was in a dark mood herself. "No hopeless case is truly without hope," she replied without conviction, and pulled up a chair.

"I hope for nothing." The princess stared, unblinking. "You?"

"I hope for . . . nothing in particular," Penelope said evasively.

"You lie, ha ha!" the old woman exclaimed. "You hope to leave. But is no escape from Plinkst." She counted on three fingers, unfurling each in turn like a claw. "Born. Unhappy. Die. Unless . . ."

"Unless what?" Penelope blurted. The princess smirked and said nothing.

What an irritating old woman! It had been a mistake to come in, and now Penelope simply wanted to get it over with. "Shall we play?" she inquired briskly. Without waiting for a reply, she picked up the deck and shuffled the cards. Then she dealt, six cards each.

The cards were difficult for the princess to hold. The old woman's knuckles were so swollen with arthritis, Penelope wondered if she could even remove the large jeweled rings she wore on each finger, or whether she would have to be buried in them.

Penelope won the first game, which gave her more pleasure than perhaps it should have. *"Ah-deen! Dva!*

Tree!" she counted idly as she dealt the cards once more.

The princess raised an eyebrow. "You learn Russian?"

"Just a few words I picked up from Boris and Constantin."

"Say again," the princess ordered.

"Ah-deen, dva, tree," Penelope repeated, cautious. "I imagine my pronunciation is a bit off."

"Again! Again!" The old woman thumped her fist on the tray in tempo. "Strong!"

"Ah-deen, dva, tree. Ah-deen, dva, tree. Ah-deen, dva, tree . . ." Penelope chanted the words over and over, as the princess demanded. A contented, dreamy look came over the old woman's face. She closed her eyes and moved her stiff hands in the air.

"Dance," she croaked. "Look." She curved one of her gnarled fingers toward the wall opposite the window. There were vines outside, ropy and twisted and moving in the gusty breeze. Their moon-cast shadows formed lean shapes that stretched and folded, leaped and spun and skated across the cracked plaster.

"I was dancer once. For the tsar! How beautiful I was. . . . Ah, Saint Petersburg! I never should have left." Her eagle eyes bored into Penelope. "I will die in

Plinkst. But I was *alive* in Saint Petersburg."

"Saint Petersburg," Penelope repeated, not knowing what else to say.

The princess's eyes drifted shut and her face went slack. Moments later, a soft snore indicated that she had fallen asleep. Her chin dropped to her chest, her clawed hands softened, and the playing cards slipped to the floor.

Penelope gathered the fallen cards. She found a pillow to prop next to the old woman's head and tucked a lap blanket around her legs, but she did not leave right away. Instead, she sat and watched the shadows play on the wall, leaping and twirling to the steady beat of the princess's rattling breath.

"They do look like dancers," she thought. Her brow furrowed, as it sometimes did when she was thinking very hard. "Like ballet dancers, at the Imperial Russian Ballet. In Saint Petersburg!"

THE THIRD CHAPTER

*A thrilling invitation arrives
by post.*

THE NEXT MORNING, FOR THE first time in many weeks, the Babushkinov household received a letter in the mail.

It was found by Svetlana, the grim-faced servant who did more than her share of work around the estate. Whether she would be so grim-faced if she were not bound to the Babushkinovs as a serf is a question only Svetlana could answer, but to be a serf in Russia was a terrible condition, a form of slavery that caused suffering to millions. (Svetlana could not know this, of course, but the tsar would eventually abolish serfdom altogether, saying that it was better to "liberate the peasants from above" than wait for them to seize their freedom from below. But just as Rome was not built in a day, centuries of injustice could not be made right so easily. There would be many years of famine, unrest, revolution, and other difficulties yet to come. Still, as Agatha Swanburne once observed, "Better to take one small step in the right direction than run a mile in the wrong one.")

Penelope had never exchanged more than a curt nod with Svetlana. On the rare occasions when they met, Svetlana looked at her with suspicion, as if wondering why that weak-looking English girl wasted her time fussing over useless children when there were carpets to be beaten, horses to be shod, beet fields to be plowed, and leaky roofs to be patched.

On this particular morning, there was also a walkway to be swept clear of snow (as you recall, a fresh layer had fallen the previous evening). This job, like so many others, fell to Svetlana, and that is how she happened to find an entirely unexpected letter lying on the front step.

Coincidentally—though you may judge for yourselves how much of a coincidence it was!—Penelope

had risen extra early that morning and instructed three groggy, unwilling Babushkawoos to get up and clean the nursery from top to bottom. "We shall have no more atlases covered in dust," she said, in a voice so firm and resolute that, for once, the children found they had no choice but to do as they were told.

"The rest of the morning will be devoted to the study of art," she announced when they were done. The Babushkawoos fussed and complained, and Boris went so far as yelling, "Art is dumb," whereupon Penelope gave him a look that could have thawed Siberia. She marched the trio through the halls until they reached the entryway, where a large, dreary painting loomed.

"Here we have the subject of today's lesson: Overuse of Symbolism in the Unhappy Pastoral," she explained. "Symbolism is when an object is meant to stand for an idea or feeling. Pastoral means having to do with life in the country. Unhappy means—well, I am quite sure you know what unhappy means. Interpretations, please!"

The painting showed an old man in cracked spectacles standing beside a lame horse, in the midst of a homestead that had burned to the ground, so that only the smoking ruins remained. The sky above was thick with storm clouds, and a vulture swooped overhead. Try as they might, the Babushkawoos could find nothing symbolic, pastoral, or even particularly unhappy about the picture. Finally Boris guessed, "I know! The glasses are a symbol that he can't see. Am I right?"

"Quite so, quite so." Penelope nodded. "Boris, your deep insight reminds me of the character of Tiresias in Greek mythology, for though he is blind, he is a soothsayer, which means he sees what others cannot—why, good morning, Svetlana! How do I say good morning in Russian, children?" Svetlana had just finished sweeping the steps. She shook the snow off her broom before stepping back inside.

The children hesitated. "DOH-bruh-yeh OO-truh," they mumbled, with downcast eyes. Speaking to serfs was not something their mother encouraged.

"DOH-bruh-yeh OO-truh," Penelope repeated with a broad smile. (Note that Russian words are properly written in the Cyrillic alphabet, like so: Доброе утро. Cyrillic writing is based on the alphabet of ancient Greece, while the Latin alphabet used by most Western languages is based on that of ancient Rome. Alphabets are a fascinating topic, and there would be no monogrammed pocket handkerchiefs without them, but it is a topic best saved for later, as Svetlana is terribly overworked as it is, and now she has an unexpected letter to deal with on top of everything else.)

"Poochta!" Svetlana grimly replied, for that is how the Russian word for "mail" sounds. She closed the front door and showed the letter to Penelope. A dusting of snowflakes still clung to the envelope, like a sprinkling of white sugar on a cupcake.

"We will help you deliver the mail," Penelope announced gallantly. Truly, she seemed to be in excellent spirits. She extended a hand and smiled once more. Slowly, with a suspicious look, Svetlana handed her the letter.

Penelope whipped out a pocket handkerchief and dabbed the snow off the envelope. "First, let us discover to whom this correspondence is addressed."

"Me me me me me!" the horrible Babushkawoos shouted. They pushed each other and scrabbled for the letter.

Penelope held the envelope high in the air. "Patience, children! This letter might be for your father, the captain, or for your mother, or even for your grandmother, the Princess Popkinova. Why, it might even be for me! How might we find out?"

"Read it read it read it read it!" they yelled.

"I am quite sure I have never seen you three so eager to read anything," she remarked drily. "Perhaps we ought to tackle a bit of poetry before your enthusiasm wanes. Hmm! The penmanship on this envelope is superb. And look, here is the address, plain as the three noses on your three faces . . . why, it seems this letter is intended for . . ."

"Who who who who who?" the Babushkawoos demanded, like a flock of crazed owls.

Penelope lifted one eyebrow and waited until they hushed. "It is addressed," she said, "to Miss Veronika Ivanovna Babushkinova, Plinkst, Russia."

Veronika squealed and spun in place like a top. "But who is it from?" she yelped.

"See for yourself." Penelope held the envelope so Veronika could read it. The girl's eyes grew wide, then wider still.

"The Imperial Russian Ballet in Saint Petersburg!" Veronika snatched the envelope from Penelope. "But why would they write to me? Unless . . ." She held the unopened letter against her forehead. Her eyes fluttered; with a gasp she fell upon a nearby settee. "I can't open it, I can't, I can't," she babbled. "Oh, my heart will give out, someone, please take it from me before I faint!"

Her brothers helpfully seized the letter from her and ran to throw it in the fire. That roused her quicker than even the smelliest smelling salts could have, and she chased the twins 'round the room while screaming, "Mama! Mama!" Svetlana's face grew even more grim, for the out-of-control children were making a mess of the floors she had just cleaned. Silently she slipped away to continue her chores in the fields and barnyard, among creatures far more manageable than three untamed Babushkawoos.

The children carried on at full volume, a cacophony of shouting and taunting and weeping. Meanwhile, Penelope moved near the window to gaze out at the snow-frosted estate—honestly, had Plinkst ever looked so pretty?—and waited.

WITHIN MOMENTS, MADAME BABUSHKINOV'S SCOLDING voice could be heard. "What is all the yelling about? Boris Ivanovich! Constantin Ivanovich! When will you learn to behave?" Then the woman herself stormed in, flushed with annoyance, with one side of her hair put up and the other still hanging loose about her shoulders.

She gestured wildly with a hairbrush. "Savages! I was in the middle of getting dressed! Why are you having your tantrums here, and not in the nursery? Where is the governess?"

Penelope was still by the window. She turned to her employer. "Good morning, madame. There have been no tantrums, I assure you. But there is wonderful news, for Veronika has received a letter. Her brothers are terribly excited about it on her behalf, and are simply trying to open the envelope for her, as any well-mannered gentlemen would. Would you like to read it? It appears to be in English, judging from the way it is addressed."

All three children calmed at once, for the sight of their governess lying so brazenly to their mother was fascinating to them. Madame Babushkinov snorted and tossed her head like a horse. "Bah! If it is in English, you read it, Miss Lumley. To speak the language is one thing, but to read it? Impossible. Those strange letters! They are like the footprints of chickens, dancing across the page."

Penelope gave a meaningful look to the twins, who were still in possession of the envelope. With shuffling feet and downcast eyes, while making sidelong gargoyle faces at their sister, they handed the letter to their governess.

She took her time examining it, turning it over and over again, as if she had never opened an envelope before. Finally, as there seemed to be no letter opener handy, she slit the flap open with a fingernail and removed its contents with care.

"Ah!" she said. "Well! It appears . . ."

"Yes, yes, what is it?" Madame Babushkinov demanded.

Penelope cleared her throat. "Madame, it appears that your daughter has been—well, let me just read it aloud: 'Miss Veronika Ivanovna Babushkinova, congratulations! You have been selected to audition for the Imperial Russian Ballet in Saint Petersburg. Please report to the theater at your earliest convenience, but no later than the eighth of April,' at such and such an address, Saint Petersburg. There are some detailed instructions about what to bring, the proper care of toe shoes, and so on. Veronika, this is quite an honor. What a marvelous surprise!" She offered the stunned girl the letter.

The twins snickered, but their mother silenced them with a hiss. "My heavens!" she whispered, clasping her hands to her bosom. "Saint Petersburg! The Imperial Ballet! What do you have to say, Nikki?"

Veronika let the paper flutter to the floor. She raised her arms in a graceful arch above her head and turned her tearstained cheeks to the sky.

"My destiny calls, at last!" she cried, and folded to

the ground as if bowing before the tsar himself.

"Does that mean we're going?" Boris asked.

Madame Babushkinov cuffed him on the head. In a spirit of fairness, she did the same to his brother. "Of course we're going, foolish child. One does not ignore an invitation from the tsar!"

After that came a great hubbub of excitement. Madame Babushkinov wondered aloud whether new clothes could be ready in time for the trip, or whether they would be forced to travel to the most fashionable city in all of Russia in clothes that were—horrors!— already a month old. The boys practiced challenging each other to a duel, which they felt certain would impress the tsar, should they meet him, while Veronika energetically practiced every dance step she had ever learned.

Penelope sent word for the dressmaker to come at once and take down Madame Babushkinov's instructions. She praised Veronika's pirouettes and grand jetés, and helped the boys retrieve the gloves they kept hurling to the ground as they took turns yelling, "This insult cannot go unanswered! I challenge you to a duel!"

Inwardly she felt a pang of relief, for in all the mayhem no one had noticed her mistake. She herself had only realized it while looking out the window: despite the fresh dusting of snow outside, and the fact that a letter had been found on the doorstep, there was not a single footprint leading to the house.

CAPTAIN BABUSHKINOV DID NOT LEARN about the invitation until later, as he spent the day out riding, inspecting the beet fields. This put him in a foul mood, for the beets' first tender sprouts had been nipped by the snowfall. Much of the crop was ruined and would have to be replanted.

It was near dinnertime when he stormed into the house. He stank of horses and left muddy boot prints on the floors that poor Svetlana had so recently scrubbed. His wife made soothing remarks and proposed that he enjoy a sauna, followed by a cold bath and a vigorous massage with a *venik*, which was a kind of handheld broom made of long birch twigs.

To go from a piping-hot sauna to an ice-cold bath only to be beaten with a broom might not be everyone's idea of relaxation, but Captain Babushkinov found it invigorating and did as his wife suggested. (The daredevils among you may be eager to try this for yourselves. If so you are in luck, for the traditional *platza* massage using a *venik* is practiced in Russian baths to this very day. Bear in mind that a *platza* is not for the faint of heart. It requires a thick skin and a high tolerance for agony. Afterward, one is expected to complain that the sauna was too cold, the ice bath too warm, and the *venik* too soft, but this show of pluck is simply part of the experience. A good *platza* will leave one parboiled and beaten half to death, yet woozy with gratitude to have survived. This, perhaps, is the true benefit of the practice, and it is not to be sneezed at.)

Once the captain was suitably refreshed, the family sat down to dinner. Penelope joined them, as she often did. After all, someone had to mind the Babushka-woos at the table while their parents argued. However, tonight Madame Babushkinov was on her very best behavior, full of warmth and charm, while the children ate in fearful silence. They had been ordered with terrifying strictness to say *not one word* about Veronika's letter or any other topic until their mother decided the moment was right to spring the news on the captain.

That moment did not come until after dessert, when the family moved to the drawing room. They pulled their chairs in a half circle 'round the fire while Svetlana made tea in the samovar, a large brass urn filled with water and quite pretty to look at, with a chimney running through the center. A fire burned in the chimney to heat the water, using pinecones as fuel, as they were easily gathered and burned more slowly than coal. They lent the room a wonderful piney scent, too.

Once the samovar began to "sing" (this was the sound it made as the water inside came to a boil), the tea was prepared and served in small glasses with metal handles. Only then, with the captain well fed and drowsy by the crackling fire, did Madame Babushkinov casually mention that there had been news, such wonderful news, nothing short of a miracle! She then proceeded to tell her husband what it was.

Minutes passed, but the captain said nothing. His silence was nerve-racking, for no one knew whether to prepare for an explosion or a celebration.

"Saint Petersburg!" he finally exclaimed. "A trip to Saint Petersburg!" He tugged at the heavy whiskers that ran down both sides of his jaw. "I am due to report to maneuvers next week. How am I to explain my absence to the army?" (To go on "maneuvers" is how the army practices being at war during times of peace. Whether it would be more fruitful to practice being at peace during times of war is a question for philosophers to take up. For now, recall the words of Agatha Swanburne, who once said, "Spend one-tenth preparing for the worst; spend nine-tenths reaching for the best." As you see, the wise founder was both a deep thinker and good at fractions, two skills that remain useful to this very day.)

Madame Babushkinov's self-control began to fray. "The army has hundreds of captains, Ivan," she snapped, "but Veronika has only one father."

"But the expense! There are train tickets and hotels . . ." His great black eyebrows drew together in a single bristling line. "No new clothes, Natasha. *Nyet!* Not one sock, you hear me?"

"Nonsense! We cannot go to the capital dressed in rags. This is no time to be cheap! Think of your daughter. Her whole future depends on this trip. It is her one chance for happiness, her only chance, and it will never come again!"

Through all this, Veronika sat pale cheeked by the fire, curled in a chair with her arms hugged 'round her thin chest. Her feet anxiously traced little dance steps on the carpet, as if they could not help themselves. At her mother's words she began to moan, soft and high-pitched, but it sounded just like the singing of the samovar, and no one paid her any mind.

Penelope sat a ways off with her sewing in her lap, although she had not taken a stitch in several minutes. However, one could hardly accuse her of eavesdropping, as the heated words between the captain and his wife were as public as newspaper headlines: PARENTS ARGUE ABOUT CHILD AS IF CHILD CANNOT HEAR THEM, for example, or GROWN-UPS COMPLAIN ABOUT MONEY, AND SUN CONTINUES TO RISE EACH DAY!

The captain shook his great head back and forth. "Impossible! There are taxes to pay, not only this year's but last year's, too. The roof leaks, the horses need shoes, the crops need land, the land needs serfs, the serfs need food. . . ."

"If it is a question of money," his wife said in a low voice, "then I suggest you ask your mother."

"Ah ha ha!" His deep bass laugh boomed, three shots of a cannon. "You are dreaming!"

"You know she has a fortune hidden away, though it seems we will not see a ruble of it till she dies."

"Nonsense. Her old furs and a few jewels are all the fortune she has left."

Madame Babushkinov's voice grew shrill. "Let her sell some of her gaudy rings to pay for the trip, then! Someone, get me a knife! I will chop off those crooked fingers myself!"

The captain was an imposing man, well over six feet tall, with shoulders strong and broad enough to build on. When he stood, his shadow fell across the room.

"Enough!" he roared, raising a fist in the air.

Baby Max began to cry. Svetlana tried to console him by making grim faces, but to no avail. (Yes, in addition to all her other duties, Svetlana had been charged with caring for the toddler in the evenings, as the household had not hired a baby nurse to replace Julia, due to the expense. Unlike Julia, at least Svetlana had the strength to lift the enormous child, and the attention span to keep watch so that he would not climb out the windows or waddle into the kitchen to play with Chef Pierre's very sharp knives. This was good news for Max, but more work for poor Svetlana.)

"Fine, fine. I do not wish your mother ill. But why must we wait?" Madame retorted. "Why can't the old woman give us a portion of our inheritance now, when we are in such need? Ivan Victorovich, surely she must know how things are with us!"

"My mother's fortune is a fantasy of yours, nothing more. If it existed, don't you think I would know?"

"No, because you are a fool who believes what your mother tells you as if you were a child. You would sooner ruin your daughter's life—"

"Stop it!"

"—*ruin* her life, than ask your mother for a ruble! A kopek, even! You would rather lose the family dacha than stand up to that selfish old woman!" She pressed her hands to her heart. "Ivan, if we lose the dacha, that will be the end of me! Even thinking about it is like the stab of a knife—oh, my heart! Quick, someone! Fetch my children! Bring them to me, so I may say farewell. . . ."

On cue, the three older children dashed to their mother's side, weeping and begging her not to succumb. Baby Max hurled his overheated bulk into her lap, squalling like a siren. This earsplitting scene would last for a good ten minutes. (While it does, you may be interested to learn what a dacha is. Dacha rhymes with cha-cha and is the Russian word for a summerhouse. That a family who lived so miserably on a rundown estate they could scarcely afford would also bear the expense of keeping a summerhouse in the country may seem ridiculous, but to have a dacha was absolutely essential in the Babushkinovs' social circle. If misfortune struck and a family could no longer afford to keep their dacha, the shame was terrible. If they ran into friends in town who asked when they were leaving for the dacha, they would lie and claim that the dacha was being painted or the roof repaired, and that they would be off to the country the minute the work was done. Families without a dacha had been known to hide at home with the shutters closed and speak in hushed voices all summer long, to make it seem as if they were away—but that is enough about dachas for now, for it appears Madame Babushkinov has some life in her yet. . . .)

"The dacha was a gift, Ivan!"

"From the tsar, I know! 'Let no head go uncovered!' How many times must I hear about it?"

This was a rhetorical question and thus required no answer. Everyone in Plinkst knew how the family dacha had been given to Madame Babushkinov's grandparents by the tsar. It was in gratitude for their services as hatmakers to the royal family. To give an entire house as a thank-you gift may seem extreme—a prompt handwritten note is usually more than sufficient—but this is why it is good to be the tsar. A tsar can give houses, or jewel-encrusted eggs, or hereditary titles or whatever he likes. A gift from the tsar was something to brag about, and heaven knows Madame Babushkinov liked to brag about her dacha.

"I won't even think of selling it, Ivan! If you say dacha one more time I'll scream!" This was not much of a threat, as she was already yelling quite loudly.

"We could rent it out for a summer or two, that is all I ask."

"That is what poor people do," she bellowed. "We are the Babushkinovs!"

"If only we were the Rubles! Then I could pay taxes with our name," he roared back. "As it is, we have a name and no rubles. And all because of those beets!" He shook his fist at the ground, and at the sky, and then at the ground once more, as if unsure where the true blame lay: in the barren earth below or with the cruel beet gods above, who summoned catastrophe at every turn.

"Fine! If that is what it will take to get my precious girl to Saint Petersburg, then go ahead! Rent out the dacha! For the sake of my daughter's future"—the woman was near hysteria—"rent it, Ivan! Sell it! Burn it to the ground, I don't care!"

A near silence descended; the only sounds were the singing of the samovar, the crackle of the fire, the gasping sobs of the lady of the house. No one else dared breathe or move except Baby Max, who was sweaty and panting like a racehorse, as he was always terribly overdressed and had crawled too near the fire before watchful Svetlana lured him away.

Captain Babushkinov blinked and wiped a manly tear from his eye. He strode across the room and took his wife in his arms. They wept and trembled; tenderly he kissed the top of her head. When he spoke, his voice was thick with feeling.

"My love, if you would be willing to sacrifice the family dacha for the sake of this trip, then I am wrong. It will be as you say. We will keep our dacha, and we will go to Saint Petersburg! We leave in three days!"

This, of course, was the answer Madame had been seeking all along. She wept afresh, with joy this time, and embraced her husband once more. The twins wiped their noses on their sleeves and fell to the floor, where they commenced to wrestle in celebration. By now Baby Max had turned red as, well, a beet, and Svetlana hurriedly took off several of his many layers of clothing and dabbed cool water on his face.

As for Penelope, she had found the whole business utterly exhausting, but she was glad of the outcome, for of course it was precisely what she had hoped and schemed for. Still, now that the matter was decided, she realized her heart had been pounding in her chest the whole time. What a frightful drama the Babushkinovs made of everything! Even Leeds' Thespians on Demand, the famed English acting troupe known far and wide for their loud voices and shameless overacting, could not hold a candle to this family.

"Mama! Papa! There is something I wish to ask."

Like those of the girl in the fairy tale who cannot remove her curséd red shoes, Veronika's feet had done nothing but dance for hours. Now she tried to stand up, but her legs buckled beneath her, and she nearly fell into the samovar.

"Careful, you clumsy child, you will set yourself on fire." Madame did not sound terribly concerned. "Didn't you hear? You are going to Saint Petersburg to audition for the Imperial Ballet! What else is there to know?"

Veronika's feet pointed and flexed of their own accord as their owner struggled to speak. "It is just this: I wonder how they heard of me."

Penelope sneezed, loudly and suddenly. "Excuse me!" she exclaimed to no one in particular. "What a terrible cold draft I feel! One of these windows must be open. . . ."

Madame waved away the girl's question. "What difference does it make how they heard of you? They did; isn't that enough?"

"The tsar's imperial nose can smell your smelly toe shoes from Saint Petersburg!" Constantin teased.

Boris pinched his own nose between two fingers to make a nasal, honking duck voice. "Smelly toe shoes!" he honked. "Smelly toe shoes, smelly toe shoes!"

The captain frowned. "But how *did* they hear of her?"

"Ah-choo! Ah-choo!" Penelope jumped to her feet, sneezing with gusto. She was prepared to make a speech about the dangers of going without a hat in cool weather, the native ferns of Russia, or even how to prepare tarte Phillippe, the most indescribably delicious dessert ever invented—whatever distraction was needed to prevent the Babushkinovs from thinking further about the sheer improbability of the letter their daughter had received.

Fortunately, there was no need for such heroics. Madame Babushkinov had already made up her mind, and mere facts could not sway her opinion. "Perhaps her dance teacher has powerful friends," she replied with an impatient wave. "Who knows? Who cares? We are going to the capital, and that is that. But Ivan, hear me! We cannot possibly set foot in Saint Petersburg dressed like beggars. Not if Veronika is to take her place in the tsar's own ballet troupe!"

"We want to go, too!" The boys fought to climb back onto their mother's lap, but Baby Max had escaped Svetlana and was already there.

"Hush, don't worry, my pets." Madame stroked the boys' identical heads, which they rested on her knees in compromise, since her lap was full. "We are all going. Even Miss Lumley is going."

"Boo! Lessons!" the twins moaned.

The captain scowled. "Why the governess? It is one more ticket to buy."

"She must come, Ivan. It says so in the letter. Read the part about the education of the dancers, Miss Lumley."

Obediently, Penelope extracted the letter from her pocket and read: "'Auditions may not interrupt the dancers' educations. Therefore, all lessons are to continue as usual during the audition period. Failure to comply will disqualify the applicant.'"

The captain said, "Hmm."

"Personally I find travel tiresome, but of course I will be glad to come with you, since my presence seems to be required." Penelope sat with her hands folded, stone-faced. Thank goodness she had thought to add in the sentence about education! Now that her scheme had been launched, she needed only to stay out of its way, like a clever rider who knows when to loosen the reins and give a pony his head, so to speak. She added, "I expect Saint Petersburg will be a highly educational place to visit."

"Educational! I should say so. It is the most fashionable city in Russia." Madame Babushkinov returned to her chair and closed her eyes. "I wonder what the officer's wives are wearing this season."

"Officer's wives, bah! Not one kopek is to be spent on clothes, do you hear me?" The captain sounded cross, but now that the thing was decided, he was feeling better by the minute. Officers' wives, of course! How clever of Natasha to think of it! Surely a trip to Saint Petersburg was an excellent idea, for there he could meet the senior officers and perhaps put in a good word for himself. He was long overdue for a rise in rank, but for all his size and bluster, the captain disliked nosing about for promotions and salary increases. It wounded his pride to have to ask, and he much preferred going about his business and letting his superiors notice for themselves what a dedicated soldier he was. Perhaps this would be his chance.

And there were some fine gambling establishments in the capital, let it not be forgotten! As was true of many men of his circle, gambling was a favorite pastime of the captain's: cards, dice, horse races, roulette wheels, all of it. One stroke of good fortune and his financial woes would be over! Or so he told himself, as he sat there contemplating the trip. Yes, this summons to the capital was good news, wonderful news, nothing short of miraculous, just as his brilliant wife had said;

an unexpected opportunity that could solve all their problems with a well-placed word to a general, or even better, with a lucky roll of the dice!

What a strange evening it had been! It was like a violent storm that ended quickly, leaving the mildest sunshine it its wake. The samovar had cooled and was silent, and Svetlana had taken Baby Max away for a diaper change. The exhausted Babushkawoos looked questioningly from one parent to the other. A moment ago these mysterious adults had been in a screaming argument, but now they seemed satisfied and self-absorbed, as if each had privately declared him- or herself the winner. Little did any of them know it was Miss Penelope Lumley, who sat placidly sewing in her corner, who was the evening's true victor.

Madame paused to rearrange her skirts, now that the smelly baby was gone from her lap, and drew her three eldest children close to her. "Don't pay any mind to your father's grumbling! He has already said yes, and there is no turning back. We will borrow; we will steal if we must. But in three days—or perhaps two, if we make haste!—we leave for Saint Petersburg!"

THE FOURTH CHAPTER

*The Incorrigible children are
given a job to do.*

MADAME BABUSHKINOV WAS BEING OPTOOMUCHSTIC
when she said they might leave for Saint Petersburg in
two days. This means there was too much optimism
in her thinking. Optoomuchism was a rare occurrence
in the Babushkinov household; in Plinkst it was nearly
unheard of. One was far more likely to encounter its
opposite, which is pessimax, the maximum degree of
pessimism one can endure before sinking into full-on
weltschmerz. (Bear in mind, it is never accurate to fix
one description to a group of people, but it is also true

that ways of thinking can be as contagious as a yawn. One person spreading pessimax can easily plunge a dozen acquaintances into despair. In the words of Agatha Swanburne, "Swim in a tar pit and you'll come out sticky.")

However, Captain Babushkinov knew how to move troops and supplies from one stronghold to the next, and he had it right: even working at full tilt, it could not have taken a minute less than three full days to prepare for the trip. Svetlana was given enough chores to occupy a regiment, from polishing all the family's boots to making sure the horses that would pull the troika were properly shod. These tasks she did grimly, in keeping with her unfortunate circumstances.

From morning till night it continued: the choosing of outfits, the practicing of pirouettes, the making of to-do lists. None of this need be gone into in detail, for the point of any journey is the taking of it. What comes before is boring, dull, tedious, and frankly uninteresting. "Anyone can pack a suitcase, but only the brave set sail," as Agatha Swanburne also said. Truly, the wise founder had a pithy saying for most, if not all, occasions.

During these same three days, however, events elsewhere—that is to say, in England, on the estate of the notoriously wealthy, hopelessly nearsighted, and increasingly worked-up father-to-be, Lord Fredrick Ashton—were as far from uninteresting as the frozen tundra of Siberia is from the balmy beaches of the Black Sea. Fortunately for us, and unlike Miss Penelope Lumley, we can return to Ashton Place simply by reading about it, and so we shall. Thanks to the tireless efforts of Mrs. Clarke, the baby's room is nearly finished, and surely that is well worth a look. . . .

"HOLD ON NOW—I'VE ALMOST GOT it. There!" Mrs. Clarke was not a small woman, nor a young one, but she scurried down the ladder as nimbly as a squirrel. After several tries, the painting she had been trying to hang on the wall was now perfectly centered between the windows of the sunny bedchamber that was being readied for the new baby.

She gazed at her achievement with satisfaction, hands planted solidly on hips. "A bit of art is just what the room needed. As our dear Miss Lumley would say, it's never too soon to begin a child's education! That picture of yours is a perfect example of—what did you say the style was again, dear?"

"Ominous Landscape," Beowulf explained. "But not too ominous. Baby Ominous."

It was true: If the Baby Ominous Landscape style of painting had not previously existed, Beowulf had surely invented it now. The painting he made especially for the Barking Baby Ashton's room portrayed a dense wood, but not a spooky one, as broad beams of yellow sliced through the trees to make cheery patches of sunlight on the mossy forest floor. Animal eyes glinted from the shadows, but they were the eyes of friendly bunnies. The birds perched in the trees were not vultures but gentle cooing doves, with a few comically roosting chickens mixed among them.

As for the figures who occupied the foreground of the work—well, yes, they were wolves, but they were happy, gentle wolves and featured a mama wolf tenderly playing with her cubs. Overall, a perfect balance of light and shadow had been struck. One could say the painting had gravitas, but not gloom. (Gravitas, gravity, and even the word "grave" all come from the Latin word *gravis*, which means heavy. If something has gravitas, that means it is serious and possesses dignity. Beowulf was the sort of artist who liked to put a bit of gravitas in his work, but he knew that a painting for a baby's room ought not to cause bad dreams, either. As you see, his present for the baby was both handmade and chosen with the recipient in mind, which is the best kind of present there is.)

Mrs. Clarke propped the ladder by the door. "It's lovely, dear. I can't imagine the baby not liking that picture, especially since it's from one of his . . ." But her words tapered off, for what relation were the Incorrigible children to the new baby, exactly? Obviously they were not siblings. Companions? Housemates? "Fellow children," she concluded. "It's a gift from one of his fellow children, and that will surely please him. And look how perfectly it matches the wallpaper!"

As she had nervously explained to Lord Fredrick and his haggard houseguest just the other day, she had chosen a nature theme for the baby's room. Lord Fredrick had quite a chuckle over it. "Nature, quite right! As if the child were napping in the woodsy woods, among the wild animals, what? Har, har!" The wallpaper was a leaf pattern in a pale green, and the ceiling had been painted a bright sky blue, with loopy clouds in shades of white floating here and there.

The crib itself was an elaborate wicker swinging cradle that squeaked when it rocked. Cassiopeia could not resist giving it a push every now and then, so she could listen to the way the *skaweek*ing slowed and faded as the crib stopped moving. She did it once more. *Skaweek, skaweek, skaweek, skaweek* . . .

"Oil can?" Alexander suggested.

Mrs. Clarke shook her head. "Best leave it be. That's the same crib His Lordship slept in as a baby. We never fixed the squeak because it meant a person could hear when the little scamp was climbing out in the middle of the night, as he liked to do every so often."

"Sure he did! Every four weeks, on the night of the full moon." Old Timothy leaned in the doorway, hands shoved deep in his pockets. He had carried the ladder upstairs and was waiting to take it away when Mrs. Clarke was done with it. "No need to mince words, Mrs. Clarke. Young Freddy was a, well—*unusual* child, and that's the truth."

Mrs. Clarke gave her apron an irritated tug. "I'm not mincing words, you strange old man. I'm minding my own business, and you should mind yours."

The enigmatic coachman jerked his head in the direction of the Incorrigibles. "It's too late for keeping secrets, Nell! As if these three cubs didn't know how stirred up the moon can make a person feel. Wild and lonesome inside, and restless as the wind, till the only thing to do is throw back your head and let loose. *Ahwoooooo!*" He crooned a long, soft howl, so wolflike it made the skin on the backs of the children's necks prickle. "And soon we'll have a wee little moonstruck

Ashton on the premises. Imagine that! Let's hope he's not the last of the line."

"What a thing to say about a child who's not even born." Mrs. Clarke placed a pile of clean folded blankets in the crib, jostling it. *Skaweek, skaweek* was the noise it made as it rocked from side to side. *Skaweek, skaweek*. "Poor lamb," she murmured, as if the baby were already in there, nestled among the blankets. "He'll be an odd one, if the past is any guide—Oh, there it is again!"

Her eyes widened and her shoulders drew back sharply. "It's like a sliver of ice rubbed down my spine. It's been happening nearly every day lately. Just like when Mr. Clarke passed! For weeks afterward I'd be going about my business in a sad fog. Then all at once I'd get the strangest notion he was standing just behind me, looking over my shoulder. I'd spin around to see—but there'd be nothing, nothing at all, and then I'd get that same icy shiver, like I just had now."

"Sounds like ghosties," Cassiopeia said, unafraid.

The housekeeper flinched. "In a baby's room? I hope not!" She stilled the crib with a hand, as if it might move again of its own accord. "Then again, who knows what sort of mischief goes on Beyond the Veil? I'd like to think we just shimmy out of our old worn-out bodies and float calmly to the realm invisible when our time comes, but perhaps that's not always the case."

Old Timothy snorted. "I'll say. There's a world of difference between being dead and being at rest."

"'O HAMlet, WHAT a FALLing OFF was THERE,'" Alexander proclaimed. His siblings nodded in agreement. *Hamlet* was one of the better ghost stories they knew.

Mrs. Clarke turned to the coachman and wagged a finger. "Now don't you say anything else frightening, Old Tim! You've got the children spouting nonsense. I'll barely sleep tonight as it is, after all this talk of you know what."

Beowulf cocked his head to one side. "Shakespeare?"

"Rhymes with toasties, my boy! I'd rather not speak the word again." Mrs. Clarke began folding the basket of cloth diapers and comically miniature baby clothes she had brought to fill the dresser drawers. "Lord knows a new baby ought to be a joyful occasion, but this icy shiver of mine leaves the most peculiar feeling when it's gone. Like something dreadful is on its way. Like time is running out."

Her voice dropped, as if she were speaking mostly to herself. "I haven't felt right since Miss Lumley's been gone, that's the truth of it. This big old house isn't the same as when she was here, dancing through the halls, pilfering books from the library and spouting words of wisdom from that school of hers! Poor thing! Poor Miss Lumley! I hope she's all right."

The Incorrigibles looked grave. Cassiopeia emitted a small, high whimper that made Mrs. Clarke remember where she was. "Whoops, silly me, running off at the mouth! Of course she's all right—there's no one more brave and clever than our Lumawoo, is there, children? I'm sure she's managing just fine." She grabbed one of the clean cloth diapers and used it to blow her nose.

The children ran to console her, though they could have used some consoling themselves. Old Timothy rolled his eyes. "Enough bellyaching. There's work to be done," he grumbled. He tipped the ladder sideways and edged it through the door.

As he did, Lord Fredrick and his wife turned the corner at the end of the hall. "Don't fret, my dear. The advertisement will be in Thursday's paper. I'm sure we'll have dozens of ladies to choose from," he said as they approached. "One of them's bound to be suitable. Whoops! Easy, there, Tim! Mind your ladder, unless you want to try your hand at a bit of jousting." Lord Fredrick chuckled and played at jousting for a moment.

"Awfully medieval, jousting. A man could get hurt. I'll stick to billiards, what?"

Old Timothy grunted enigmatically and propped the ladder in the hall. Lady Constance paid him no mind as she sailed into the room. "Suitable is not good enough, Fredrick! The baby nurse must be perfect. Strict, but not too strict. Kind, but not too kind. It is far too easy to spoil a child with affection, one must beware– *Eek!*" The lady's shriek was so sharp and sudden that everyone looked down to see if a wee mousie was scurrying about, but her round, doll-like eyes were fixed on the Incorrigibles. "The wolf children! What are *they* doing in here?"

Alexander snapped a salute. His two siblings did likewise. "Baby Room Inspection Service reporting for duty, your noble ladyness," he said. "This room has been deemed acceptable for the young heir-to-be."

"Aye aye, sir!" Beowulf added. He and his brother clicked their heels together for emphasis. It was a habit they had picked up from Captain Babushkinov. The children's memories of their former friends in Plinkst were bittersweet at best, heartrending at worst, but the heel-clicking gesture was both invigorating and enjoyable, and they saw no reason to give it up.

"You are very big, Lady Globe." Cassiopeia curtsied

93

and spread both arms wide, as if to embrace the earth itself.

"Lady Globe?" Lady Constance's expression soured. "Does she mean I look like some sort of planet?"

Mrs. Clarke stammered an explanation while the children volunteered to name all the planets, but Lord Fredrick interjected, "Nonsense, dear. You're sleek as a racehorse. I'd never believe you were with child if Dr. Veltschmerz hadn't said so."

That made his wife beam. She perched her hands on either side of her enormous middle as if showing off a tiny wasp waist. "It's true that we Barbeys are known for never losing our figures. And I am still wearing all my favorite dresses, so it must be so!" As you may recall, Miss Constance Barbey had been her name before she married Lord Fredrick. However, the seamstress Madame LePoint had been letting out all of Lady Constance's dresses for months, and the lady was none the wiser.

"I hope you like how the room's coming along, my lady," Mrs. Clarke said, for she was rightly proud of it. "It's not finished, of course! But we're getting closer by the day. Why, I've already put some diapers in the drawers."

"Diapers!" Lady Constance shivered in distaste.

"What an awful word. I hope I shall not have to hear it again." She walked around the room, inspecting. "I am not convinced about this wallpaper, Mrs. Clarke. It is very leafy."

"It's symbolic," Beowulf offered. "It symbolizes leaves."

"Leaves, yes . . ." Lady Constance chose a book from a small bookshelf that had been placed beneath the window. "*Giddy-Yap, Rainbow!*" she read, and confidently declared, "This story is about a pony. I can tell from the picture of the pony on the cover. But babies cannot read." She frowned. "Can they?"

"Not at first, my lady," Mrs. Clarke explained. "But even very young children like being read to. Our own Miss Lumley taught me that." (It was Mrs. Clarke who had placed these books in the baby's room, for, as previously mentioned, she had grown fond of the Giddy-Yap, Rainbow! tales. She sometimes read them aloud with great feeling when she was alone in her room, between bites of licorice. If caught, doubtless she would have blushed and said it was just practice for reading to the children, and that may have been true in part—but mostly she did it because she liked to. She liked saying the words and hearing them, and she liked imagining herself, a plump, widowed housekeeper with more of life behind her than ahead, as a wide-eyed young girl astride her first pony, learning to ride and having adventures and growing up all over again. It was like having a time machine and a fountain of youth rolled into one, and all between hard covers!)

Next, Lady Constance stopped in front of Beowulf's painting. "What a strange picture," she said. "It is gloomy, but not entirely so. One might say it is both gloomy and cheerful. But oh, my! Wolves! That will never do. It ought to show a bowl of fruit, or a queen with a dog in her lap, or some cut flowers waiting to be put in vases. Isn't that what the best paintings have in them?"

Beowulf growled, just loud enough for his siblings to hear. This was quite out of character for a well-mannered Incorrigible, but not entirely out of character for an artist whose work has been so rudely unappreciated. Alexander pinched his brother's arm in warning, and the younger boy covered his mistake with a bit of theatrical throat clearing. But Cassiopeia could not resist defending her brother.

"It's art, you big Globe," she said to the lady, none too respectfully.

Lady Constance looked around, suspicious. "Symbolic

wallpaper? Books and art? What sort of a baby's room is this?"

"Well, it's not quite finished yet, as I said! And this painting is a present for the baby, isn't it, Beowulf, dear? All three of the children made presents for the baby. Isn't that lovely?" Mrs. Clarke said, trying make peace.

Judging by the look on her face, Lady Constance remained unconvinced.

IT WAS TRUE THAT THE Incorrigibles had made presents. They were generous by nature, but in this case their motives were complex. Frankly, there was something nerve-racking about not knowing how the burping, crying, diaper-wetting new arrival might change things at Ashton Place.

This is a perfectly ordinary way to feel about the arrival of new babies, of course. In such situations, kindness is all that is truly required, but "A present couldn't hurt," as Agatha Swanburne had often advised. In that spirit, Beowulf had made his painting, and Alexander had built a clever toy called a kaleidoscope. It was made from one of those newfangled telegraph tubes that the postman had given him as a curiosity, with some bits of broken mirror and a handful of sequins and sparkly beads cadged from Madame LePoint.

After a nudge from Mrs. Clarke, Alexander now offered his kaleidoscope, but Lady Constance waved it away without even looking at the glorious display within.

Cassiopeia had had a harder time thinking of a gift. She herself would not have minded having a rocking horse, but a rocking horse was not a good gift for a baby who could not yet sit up in the saddle. She thought of carving a teething ring out of wood, but the baby would not have teeth for a while, either. Stumped, she had asked the young housemaid, Margaret, for advice about what babies did for fun, but the girl only laughed her squealing, high-pitched laugh and said, "New babies don't do much of anything, love. They sleep and eat and cry and mess their diapers, and believe me, that's enough."

Cassiopeia found this answer unhelpful. In the end, she had made a hand-stitched pillow. It was a baby-sized pillow, too small for even a pithy nugget of wisdom, so she had settled on a simple greeting.

"Go ahead, dear." Mrs. Clarke spoke in that overly sweet, up-and-down singsong tone grown-ups sometimes use to steer children past awkward moments. "Show her ladyship the pretty present you made for the baby! Why, you sewed it all with your own sweet hands, didn't you, dear?"

With a distinct lack of enthusiasm, Cassiopeia showed Lady Constance the pillow she had made.

"'Hawoo, Baby'?" Lady Constance read. "What on earth does that mean?"

"Hawoo," Cassiopeia explained, with infinite patience. "What you say when you meet someone."

"Hawoo!" Lady Constance spun 'round to face her husband. If her globe-shaped tummy had been a real globe, she would have gone from sunrise to sunset, just like that. "Did you hear that, Fredrick? Hawoo!" Her voice dropped to a loud whisper, which everyone could hear. "I told you these howling wolf children ought to be sent away! Imagine what sort of influence they might be!"

Now, Cassiopeia was a bright and hardworking student. She could multiply fractions, turn a cartwheel, and recite entire stanzas of "The Wreck of the Hesperus," a marvelous poem about a shipwreck by Henry Wadsworth Longfellow. However, when it came to spelling, her own name was so difficult to get right that she had given up on the subject altogether. Her hand-stitched *Hawoo* had not been intended as a howl at all but was merely her own way of writing "hello" so that the word would sound the way she liked to say it. (The professional educators among you will note that Cassiopeia had unwittingly invented what would later be called "phonics," a boon to teachers and students to this very day.)

"Not ahwoo," she protested. "Hawoo."

Her brothers understood perfectly, and tried to clarify by alternating a howling "ahwoo" with a friendly "hawoo." "Ahwoo, hawoo!" they demonstrated. "Ahwoo, hawoo! Ahwoo, hawoo! Ahwoo, hawoo!"

Lady Constance turned pale and pressed her hands to her ears. "Wild, untamed creatures! Now I cannot hear myself think, not that I much care for thinking." She moved her hands to her belly, as if trying to cover the baby's ears. "Do not listen, little future person! Behaving like a wild animal is all very well for your father's wolfish wards, but it will never do for the heir to this great estate!"

Lord Fredrick's good humor seemed to leave him all at once. "All right, you three, that's quite enough of that," he said sharply. Like well-trained cadets, the children instantly stopped making noise and pressed their lips shut, in three straight lines.

Lady Constance looked smug. "Much better! Fredrick, let us go. I wish to finish our walk, have a chocolate, and then lie down, and perhaps have another chocolate while I am lying down. That would settle my nerves perfectly. Dr. Veltschmerz would surely approve."

"Mrs. Clarke, have some chocolate brought to my wife's chambers," Lord Fredrick commanded. Mrs. Clarke jogged to ring the bell pull, but Lord Fredrick interrupted her by adding, "Do it in person, please."

"As you wish, sir," she said with a worried glance at the children. "I'll go to the kitchen and see to it myself." Reluctantly she left.

The mere promise of chocolate had already done wonders for Lady Constance's mood. Expectantly, she slipped her arm through her husband's, but Lord Fredrick turned to the door. "Timothy, are you still there? Don't pretend otherwise, I know how you like to eavesdrop."

The old fellow appeared in the doorway. "I was just waiting until the missus was done with the ladder," he explained gruffly.

"Never mind about the ladder. Take Constance to finish her walk, if you please."

"Aren't you coming, Fredrick?" she exclaimed.

"In a moment, dear." Gently Lord Fredrick steered

her toward the door. "I'd like to have a closer look at this wallpaper. You may be right; the symbolism could be a bit much for a baby. I'll catch up with you and Old Tim shortly. We'll have some chocolate together—how's that, what?"

Before she could form a reply, her arm had been smoothly transferred to the coachman's. "This way, my lady," Old Timothy's voice took on an irresistible cooing tone. "We'll have a nice walk, we will. Come along now."

Lady Constance was easily persuaded as a rule, but the soothing sound of Old Timothy's voice could make even the most high-strung horse step calmly into a rushing stream. Obediently she went with him down the hall.

"What an enigmatic fellow you are, Old Timothy," she remarked, cheerful once again. "I sometimes wonder about you, you know! I wonder what you must have been like as a child, and whether you have ever been in love, or made and lost a great fortune, or traveled to distant lands."

"Distant lands, my, my," he cooed as they walked.

She laughed. "Well, there must be more to you than simply being our coachman! But don't tell me, please. It is ever so much more entertaining not to know. And how tedious it is to listen to stories about other people! Honestly, they put me right to sleep."

LORD FREDRICK WAITED UNTIL HIS wife's prattling voice had turned the corner. Frowning, he gave the antique crib a sharp push. *Skaweek, skaweek.* "Still squeaks—imagine that," he remarked. "I'll have to tell Old Timothy to get it fixed—or I suppose I could find someone to fix it—blast, I'll just take an oil can to it myself."

He turned to the Incorrigibles, who stood in a line as if awaiting inspection. "Now, listen up, you three," he said. "I know you mean well. But I won't have you reading books and painting pictures and making clever presents for the baby. That will never do."

Shock and disappointment was written on all three faces, for had they not tried their very best to be welcoming to the new baby?

"But why not?" Alexander mustered the courage to ask.

"It's much too civilized." Lord Fredrick shook his head. "What I need for you to do is to bark and howl as much as you can."

The children were flummoxed. "But not around the baby?" Beowulf asked, trying hard to understand.

Lord Fredrick dropped down to his knees so he could speak to the boy face-to-face. "No! I mean—yes, howl around the baby! Especially around the baby! You must carry on like wild cubs, just as if you were trying to teach the baby to yap and bay at the moon."

Cassiopeia tugged on Lord Fredrick's sleeve. "Lordawoo, wait. You *want* us to act like woofs around the baby?"

"Precisely, little girl." He gave her an awkward pat on the head. "That's your job, and a very important responsibility it is, too. I need you three to woofy up the baby." He smiled the rubbery, doggish Ashton smile that all the men in his family shared, wide and toothy, with the canine teeth on full display. "Don't be shy about it! I know you've got it in you."

The Incorrigibles batted at their ears in puppyish disbelief, an old habit that only popped up at moments of extreme confusion. "Excuse me, Lordship, sir," Alexander said, after giving his head a shake. "So you *want* the baby to woof?"

"I do indeed! To woof and bark and howl and scratch, like a proper little Ashton should." Lord Fredrick rubbed his hands together. "This way, when the full moon comes, and the baby starts to act like a pup, Constance will think it's because of you three. She'll never suspect there's anything, well, *unusual* about the baby, and that's how it's going to stay."

"She will be mad at us," Cassiopeia declared solemnly.

"She is already mad at us," Beowulf corrected. "She will be madder."

"Mad, madder, maddest," Alexander offered. The Incorrigibles had been studying comparatives and superlatives. (This was no thanks to Master Gogolev, who was not only lazy, but lazier than most tutors; in fact, he was the laziest tutor imaginable. If you ponder that for a moment, you will know all you need to know about comparatives and superlatives. This ought to make you quite proud, or at least prouder than your friends, or possibly the proudest member of your entire family.)

Lord Fredrick nodded. "She'll complain, no question, but never mind about that. I'll handle Constance. She has a good heart, really. You three just keep doing your job."

"But we already learned *not* to be woofy," Cassiopeia insisted, for she had worked particularly hard at this and had not quite mastered it yet, either. "From Lumawoo."

"Lumawoo, yes! Talk like that! Put your little awoos

everywhere. Woofy it up, that's the spirit! It'll be our secret game, and I expect the baby will be extra clever and catch on right away, no doubt by the very first full moon." He stood up again with a grunt. One might almost say he looked cheerful, or at least relieved. "That's all. I'm relying on you three, remember that."

LORD FREDRICK'S INSTRUCTION TO "WOOFY up the baby" puzzled the Incorrigibles at first, for of course Lumawoo had gone to great pains to teach them to be less woofy, not more. There had been much practice, a Squirrel Desensitization Program, and many tasty treats employed to this end, and it seemed a giant step backward to give it all up now, after so much time and hard work. But then they remembered that Penelope had also taught them the meaning of irony, and that made the situation perfectly clear.

(If you have forgotten, irony is when what happens is the opposite of what one has been led to expect will happen. When people say the opposite of what they truly mean, that too is irony. And there is a special kind of irony called "dramatic irony," which is when the audience of a play knows more than the characters onstage do. For example, you know far more than Lord Fredrick does about the curse upon the Ashtons, for he thinks it is merely going to make his baby embarrassingly wolfish during the full moon. Alas, the truth was much more dire, a fact that had been concealed from him his whole life by that imposter of a houseguest who was even now sleeping the sleep of the dead in the Egyptian Room, a lavish guestroom on the far side of the house.)

As soon as Lord Fredrick left, the Incorrigibles made a beeline back to the nursery. *Woofy up the baby*, Alexander wrote on the to-doawoo list. All three children gazed thoughtfully out the window, past the branches of the elm to the dark forest beyond.

Alexander turned to his siblings. "Do you remember how to act woofish?"

"I think so," Beowulf said uncertainly.

"I do! I can give lessons." Cassiopeia growled fiercely and showed her teeth, to prove her point. Truth be told, she had always been the wildest of the three. Now she seemed ready to plunge wholeheartedly into her former ways.

Her brothers did not feel lessons would be necessary but thanked her sincerely for the offer.

She dropped to all fours and scampered along the floor, just as she used to. She stopped and sat up on her haunches, her head cocked to the side. "How woofish should we be?" she wondered aloud. "Maximum mayhem? Or just barky?"

Alexander considered the question. "Medium barky to start," he decided. "We can always adjust."

Beowulf gnawed anxiously on the back of his chair. "Can I still make paintings?" he asked. It was a reasonable question, as even highly unusual wolves did not typically paint. Yet Beowulf was dedicated to his art and would be heartbroken to give it up, even temporarily.

Alexander gave his brother a reassuring swipe of his paw—that is to say, hand. "You may paint, but woofishly," he said. In that instant, the Woofish School of painting was born. (Critics still marvel at this brief but dramatic swerve in the history of portraiture. Why a few painters in a remote part of England would suddenly decide to depict their subjects with long noses, rough whiskers around the muzzle, tapered ears, and long pointed canine teeth, all rendered in a confident but childlike hand, has been a mystery that art historians have long tried to solve.)

The children continued to discuss how to best go about returning to their old habits, and pondered the ethical dilemmas that might pop up. On one point they were in firm agreement: they would happily howl at the moon, chew on expensive leather shoes, climb the furniture, and wreak havoc in any number of wolfish ways, but under no circumstances would they go back to hunting squirrels.

Nutsawoo was a twitchy little scamp and a bushy-tailed menace (and, unbeknownst to the children, a soon-to-be-parent—another fine example of dramatic irony!), but the dim-witted rodent was simply not a potential meal.

The Fifth Chapter

*The capital of Russia is
Saint Petersburg!*

Saint Petersburg, Saint Petersburg! Back in Plinkst, the packing was nearly finished. The trip to Saint Petersburg was happening, would happen, *must* happen. The sheer unlikeliness of receiving such an unexpected invitation was mentioned by no one. Even Veronika had the sense not to repeat her plaintive question, "I wonder how they heard of me."

Not that it would have mattered. The Babushnikovs were in the grip of a kind of faulty logic that psychologists nowadays call "confirmation bias," but that the rest of us might simply think of as being Babushkinov, through and through: when new facts threatened to upend their opinions, they simply chose to believe what they wished was true, and ignored all evidence to the contrary.

For, really, what were the odds of finding a letter from the tsar's own ballet company lying on the door-step? Such an obvious trick would not have worked on most people, but as Edward Ashton himself observed, to know one's prey was essential, and Penelope knew the Babushkinovs. She had gambled on the family's foolishness and self-delusion, and she had won by a length, as they say at the Derby.

Or so she believed. There were two members of the household who had their doubts about the letter. One was the Princess Popkinova. The evening before the family's departure, the ancient woman sat in her wheel-chair in a dim corner of the drawing room, watching through half-closed eyes as the family quarreled. A blanket of exquisitely soft fur, an ink-black sable, was wrapped around her shoulders, and another just like it was tucked around her legs. In the shadows she looked like a disembodied head.

"Saint Petersburg!" the old woman said. She drew the word out with profound sarcasm, a tone that requires no translation. "Saint Petersburg!" One crooked finger emerged from the sable folds and waggled from side to side, as if it were too much trouble for the princess to actually shake her head in disbelief.

No one paid attention. They were too busy arguing about whose possessions would go in which trunk, whether it was necessary to tip the driver, who would sit in the front of the troika and who in the back, and so on. There was a great to-do about leaving Baby Max, for the captain flatly refused to hire a nurse to come along on such a long and expensive trip, and Svetlana had far too much work to do at the house. Madame pretended to be heartbroken, but she had no interest in caring for the child either, and so the boy would have to stay home. He screamed till he was red in his little round face, though he could hardly have understood what the fuss was about.

The princess waggled her finger. "Saint Petersburg, Saint Petersburg!" With each exclamation it was if she was saying, "Are you all complete idiots? What fool would believe that my simpering granddaughter would attract the attention of the greatest ballet company in the world? She is an overdressed country bumpkin, a spoiled child, and a mediocre dancer at best. If she dares put one smelly toe shoe in Saint Petersburg, she will end up a laughingstock, nothing more!"

But all the old woman said, or needed to say, was "Saint Petersburg!"

The other person, interestingly, was Svetlana. Shortly after dawn the next morning, on the day of the family's departure, Svetlana appeared in the doorway of the nursery and stood there, blank faced and still as a post.

Penelope was surprised to see her. It was unusual for her to be out of her room herself at that hour. But she had awoken in the dark and could not get back to sleep, and so had decided to tidy that sorry little nursery, one last time.

"Alas, poor spud!" she had just done intoning, Hamlet-like, to the withered potato, which was now furry with mold. "Into the waste bin with you! For you will soon begin to stink, and I would not leave such an unsavory item behind for someone else to get rid of. No doubt the task would fall to Svetlana, and surely that poor woman has enough to do as it is."

It was at that moment Penelope turned and saw the woman herself, as if her very words had summoned her. She had to blink a few times to make sure the sight was real, much as Hamlet might have done at the sight of his father's ghost appearing on the ramparts of the castle.

"Svetlana! My goodness, you startled me! That is to say . . . good morning." She was not sure if Svetlana understood, and she gestured for her to come in.

Svetlana did so and closed the nursery door behind her.

"Spasiba," she said grimly.

It meant "thank you"—that much Penelope knew, from her failed attempts to get the children to say it—but what could Svetlana be thanking her for? She followed the woman's gaze to the rotten potato in her own hand.

"Ah! I understand. You are thanking me for throwing Planet Spud into the dustbin," she said. "Well, it is no trouble. Dear, moldy old spud! It was not a very good globe, but it was all the globe we had."

Svetlana stepped closer. *"Spasiba,"* she repeated with feeling. Apparently this had nothing to do with the potato. She glanced furtively at the closed door and lowered her voice. *"Duraki!"*

"Duraki?" Penelope repeated, intrigued. "There is a card game called *durak* I have sometimes played with the princess. Do you mean that you want to play

114

cards?" She put down the potato and mimed shuffling and dealing a hand of cards.

Svetlana shook her head. *"Duraki!"* she repeated. She sprang into motion, and danced comically around the nursery like a broken puppet. It was a surprising show of animation. Whatever she was trying to say must be important.

"Yes," Penelope replied, nodding. "Yes, I remember. *Durak* means fool. *Duraki* must mean fools." Penelope did an even sillier puppet dance to show she understood.

"Duraki, da!" Now Svetlana pretended to write a letter. With great theatricality, she dropped the imaginary correspondence on the ground. She shivered with pretend cold and wiggled her fingers downward through the air to indicate snow falling.

Fully in character, she grabbed Planet Spud from Penelope and held it by its twig. "Babushkinovs," she said, and tapped the top of the wrinkled, shrunken potato. "Svetlana," she said, tapping the bottom. Slowly she rotated the potato, so that what had been on top was underneath, and what was on the bottom was now on top.

"Babushkinovs, ha ha!" she concluded. She flicked the bottom of the potato with her index finger, a gesture of clear contempt. *"Duraki. Da?"*

"Da." Penelope nodded. *"Da, da, da."* Yes, now she gathered Svetlana's meaning quite well. Someday, those on the top of the potato—the selfish land owners, like the Babushkinovs—would be on the bottom, and those currently stuck on the bottom, meaning Svetlana and her fellow serfs, would be on top. That day had not yet come, but in the meanwhile Penelope had made *duraki*—that is to say, fools—of their employers by tricking them with that absurd invitation to the capital, and now Svetlana's heart was filled with the bitter joy that only a serf in Plinkst could feel, mixed as it was with misery and resentment, rage and gloom and an abiding hatred of beets.

It was a lot to glean from a round of charades. Then again, Penelope had always excelled at the game. She wanted to show she understood. She rose on tiptoe and performed a single, wobbly pirouette. Then she bowed to Svetlana, reverent and low, as if she were bowing to the tsarina herself.

Like a ray of sunlight breaking through dense fog, Svetlana smiled broadly—her teeth were excellent, for she had never eaten a piece of candy in her life—and she took Penelope by the shoulders and kissed her on each cheek.

Svetlana's face was transformed by the smile, and Penelope realized she was quite a young woman, scarcely older than Penelope herself. It was her grimness that made her seem older. But then the smile faded. Wordlessly, Svetlana left the nursery. She took the Planet Spud with her, to toss in the kitchen scraps that were fed to the pigs. Or perhaps she would trim away the rot and make a secret, thin soup out of it, one that she would not have to share with anyone.

Penelope felt somber after Svetlana was gone. She would have liked to sit for a while, to wonder what might become of the girl, and to wish her well, but there was no time. The sun had risen; the troika would be leaving soon, and she had to pack with care, for she would not be coming back.

BEFORE LONG THE FAMILY WAS up and fighting. When it finally came time to leave, Madame Babushkinov swirled her fur cape to and fro like a matador to coax her three older children to the door. The captain carried the weighty, unhappy Baby Max tucked under one arm, like a squalling bedroll.

"Kiss your grandmother good-bye, my dears!" Madame said brightly. "After all, she might be dead by the time we get back."

"Dead? Ha!" The princess had asked to be wheeled out of her room to see the travelers off. Now she endured the indifferent kisses of her grandchildren as if she was being pestered by mosquitoes. "I do not fear death. But I am in no rush, either. Maybe I will live forever. For spite, ha, ha! Wait."

She clutched one hand with the other and wrestled them together. With all the strength she had, she twisted off one of her large jeweled rings and offered it to Madame Babushkinov.

"Take this with you," the old woman said. "My emerald. My favorite! A gift of great value, from an admirer, long ago. If I die, you can sell. Pay for funeral! If I live—too bad! Ah ha ha!"

The cackling of the princess continued until the travelers were outside. After that, Max's howls of dismay at being left behind drowned out every other sound, until the door had been firmly shut behind them.

The recent snow had melted, but the air was cold and the ground was slick with mud. A team of porters loaded the Babushkinovs' trunks and luggage onto the troika. Penelope carried only a carpetbag. It held a change of clothes and a flannel nightdress, a pen and some letter paper (in case a thank-you note or other urgent correspondence was called for), and a papier-mâché seashell the Incorrigible children had made during their winter holiday in Brighton. It was her only keepsake of them and weighed little, and she would not leave it behind.

"And why are we not on our way? The tsar's own palace could be built in half this time!" Madame Babushkinov began complaining the moment she was seated, but the troika driver would not be rushed. Patiently he checked all three horses, the fit of their harnesses and the condition of their hooves, before he climbed into his seat and gathered up the reins. He had the grumpy, reticent look of a person who preferred animals to people. Penelope thought of Old Timothy and held back a smile. The enigmatic coachman was hardly her favorite person at Ashton Place, but how her heart would have leaped with joy to see him now!

"Heya, heya!" the driver called, and they were off. The twins immediately tried to stand and turn around, though they had been told a hundred times to stay in their seats. "Good-bye, house, good-bye!" they yelled. "If we are lucky, Veronika and her smelly toe shoes will never return! Finally, we can be happy!" At this Veronika sobbed. The captain growled at the boys and cuffed their heads, while Madame Babushkinov tried to comfort her daughter with promises of new dresses and plots of revenge against her brothers.

Penelope did not turn back even once to look at the ramshackle estate, but kept her eyes fixed on the road ahead. Was she giddy with joy to finally bid the barren fields of Plinkst good-bye? One would expect so, but her time in this unhappy town had taught her that it was possible to find the gloom in nearly any situation. "Even to leave a place one dislikes is bittersweet," she thought, "for it reminds us that time gallops in one direction only, and there are places we have been and people we have known that we surely will never see again."

But then she caught herself. She sat up straight and took a deep calming breath. What she needed now was not Plinkstian melancholy but pluck; yes, pluck of the most Swanburnian kind. Her plan to get back to Ashton Place and the Incorrigible children was in no way foolproof. It would require a great deal of good luck and not one spoonful of bad, and what were the odds of that happening? Only an optimistic—no, optoomuchstic!—person would have dared take the first step, and now she was on her way at last but still a very, very, *very* long way from home.

"No hopeless case is truly without hope," she reminded herself, then soothed her nerves by repeating under her breath, "The capital of Russia is Saint Petersburg!" over and over again.

THE TROIKA WAS FAST, EVEN in the muck. The drumming of three sets of hooves, along with the ceaseless ringing of the bells that hung from the *duga*, the part of the harness that arched like a rainbow over the center horse, created a hypnotic, complicated rhythm, as if all the poetic meters ever invented were being tapped out at once. It made Penelope drowsy, and when the driver shouted and pulled the troika swiftly and hard to the rutted edge of the road, it startled her into a yelp. She had been dreaming that she was on a train, en route to her first job interview. . . .

"Bandits!" yelled the twins, and readied themselves to fight by punching each other, for practice.

Bandits! The *clip-clop, clip-clop, clip-clop* of hooves grew louder by the second. A wagon approached from the other direction. It was pulled by a pair of heavy-boned workhorses, with broad chests and sturdy, thick-furred legs that churned like pistons.

"It is not bandits, you ridiculous children," Madame

Babushkinov snapped. "It is the mail sled. Finally! I am glad we are not home to receive any. Bills and more bills!"

Even with the Babushkinov's troika dragged halfway into the gully at the road's edge, the mail sled came so close that it splattered mud on them as it passed. The sled was piled high with burlap mail bags, all stuffed to bursting.

"The mail sled?" Penelope repeated dumbly. She twisted 'round to watch the sled continue down the narrow road they had just traveled, gouging a fresh set of tracks in the mud.

"The grocer. The butcher. The man who sells feed for the chickens." Madame was still going on about the bills. "Those are the true bandits, demanding our rubles or else! 'You are out of credit,' they say. The nerve! We are the Babushkinovs! Our name ought to be credit enough."

"Grocers must eat too, my darling," her husband interjected.

"They will get paid when I say so, and not a moment before. As far as I am concerned, the more they ask, the longer they must wait. . . ."

Penelope could not tear her eyes away from the receding sled. There it went, bound for Plinkst, piled high with sacks of mail. Surely one of them held her long-awaited letter from Simon Harley-Dickinson! For all she knew, there were dozens of letters in those sacks, from him and the Incorrigibles, and perhaps from Miss Charlotte Mortimer, too. But it was too late to turn back now.

"The mail is so slow," the captain observed. "It is worse than a strike."

"Strike? You mean like this?" Constantine struck his brother to demonstrate. Calmly the captain picked up the boy by the back of his coat and moved him, arms flailing, to sit on his mother's other side, uncomfortably squeezed between his parents.

"Forgive me for asking," Penelope said, keeping her voice steady, "but why is the mail so slow?"

"It is the fault of the beets," the captain said. "Plinkst has no beets. No beets means no rubles. No rubles means no pay for postal workers. No workers means no mail."

"Beets! I curse them, roots and stems and all." Madame Babushkinov sneered. "Beets have been our ruin, Ivan! We never should have left the hat business."

The captain shrugged. It was an argument he had lost long ago.

Left without a twin to punch, Boris was forced to

pull Veronika's hair to get his parents' attention. She shrieked in outrage, an earsplitting noise that made the horses' ears pin back and their tails lash. The troika driver grumbled under his breath as he coaxed the nervous animals back onto the road.

"But then how did Nikki's letter arrive?" Boris asked.

"Yes, how?" his brother parroted.

Beneath her lap blanket, Penelope's hands curled into fists of fear. On the other hand, this show of logic by the twins was impressive, and she wondered if she had taught them a little something after all.

Madame Babushkinov smacked Boris, then Constantine, then both boys at once. "Do you think the tsar cares about the problems of Plinkst? About our failed crops and lazy postal workers? No! If he wants a letter delivered, you may rest assured it will be delivered, no matter what. *That* is what it means to be the tsar!"

THE JOURNEY TO SAINT PETERSBURG was long and dull and cold and wet. The rain mixed with sleet that felt like needles against the skin, and the troika had to go slowly over the muddy roads, which were beginning to freeze. Veronika was so nervous, she could only wring her gloved hands and weep. Boris and Constantin alternated saying, "I'm bored!" and "Are we there yet?" until they forgot whose turn it was to say what and quit in frustration. For entertainment, they pinched their sister to make her scream, while their parents snarled and blamed each other for things that could not be helped: the poor weather, for example, or the long wait when the troika driver had to stop and have one of the horses reshod.

Lips chapped and tempers frayed, and the ceaseless ringing and jingling of the troika bells grew so wearisome, it was like something out of Poe. (Fans of gloomy talking birds are already well acquainted with Mr. Edgar Allen Poe, who famously wrote a poem about one. He also wrote a poem about bells, bells, and more bells, ringing and clanging and jangling away, from tinkling sleigh bells like those of a troika, to the deep, basso tolling of funeral bells. That poem, aptly titled "The Bells," uses so many different words to describe the sounds made by bells that Mr. Poe evidently ran out and had to invent a new one: "tintinnabulation." Tintinnabulation, honestly! As if further proof were needed of the slipperiness of poets! They make up words willy-nilly and have them mean whatever they like. Thank heavens they are licensed and thus kept somewhat in check. If they were not, could full-blown mayhem be far behind?)

Only Miss Penelope Lumley sat straight-backed and uncomplaining as the time dragged on. She entertained the horrible Babushkawoos as best she could with stories and games, and offered gentle reprimands whenever their behavior grew intolerable. She did all this calmly, without seeming effort, for caring for children in this way was second nature to her and left her mind free to wander. Outwardly, she was steady and efficient; inside, she was full of secrets.

Luckily for her, every few hours the Babushkawoos complained and fussed themselves into exhaustion and fell asleep. Only then did she retreat into her own thoughts, and she had a great deal to think about, you may rest assured.

However, even for patient Penelope the journey was a long one, with many hours yet to go before the troika arrived in Moscow, and then an even longer train ride north. It would be three full days before they arrived in Saint Petersburg. For the moment, then, let us turn our attention back to England, to the grand house known as Ashton Place. That well-tended estate was the very opposite of ramshackle, with no failing crops to be found, only daffodils in bright yellow bloom and the swelling green buds of tulips, full of promise. Yet the mood of the local villagers was not unlike that of the Russian peasantry, for a revolution of sorts was brewing among them. . . .

"Bread! We need bread!" the people cried. As you surely ought to recall by now (for this fact will soon become quite important to our tale!), the village baker had run off to America with fickle, stoop-shouldered Julia, the former baby nurse, and now there was no bread baker for miles.

Lord Fredrick had placed an advertisement for a baby nurse before the full moon curse had come upon him, but bread baking? That was another barrel of flour altogether. As he said to Mrs. Clarke, "Blast! I don't even know where bread comes from, and why should I? As far as I'm concerned, it ought to grow on breadfruit trees, like they have on those islands in the tropics. Perhaps we ought to plant some, what?"

Lady Constance was no help either, and offhandedly suggested that the kitchen serve gooseberry pie to the villagers instead of bread and satisfy the people that way. Alas, there were simply not enough gooseberries on hand to make that many pies. It was a pity, too, as Mrs. Clarke's gooseberry-pie recipe was beyond compare.

Poor villagers! To let them eat pie was not an option, yet it seemed they could not go one more day without bread. Mrs. Clarke and Cook diligently searched for a replacement. They invited bakers from miles around to travel to the bakehouse at Ashton Place and bake samples of their finest loaves.

Many came and took up the challenge. These were all experienced and well-qualified bakers, mind you, but for some mysterious reason, every attempt turned out a failure. Either the loaves failed to rise or else they puffed up absurdly and turned hard as bricks. Even worse, while in the oven, none of these loaves gave off that delicious baking-bread smell that makes the streets of Paris so appealing, as there is a boulangerie on nearly every street in that fair French city. *Au contraire!* These loaves smelled horrible. One gave off the stink of smelly toe shoes the minute it was put in the oven. Another smelled like a pile of wet rope encrusted with seaweed and left to rot in the sun, and a nasty, fishy aroma it was. Even a promising-smelling sourdough soon turned rank. The longer it baked, the more it smelled like a wet dog that had recently encountered an angry skunk, and the terrible odor lingered for days afterward.

It was uncanny, to say the least. If one were inclined to believe in the supernatural, one might even suspect that the bakehouse at Ashton Place had fallen under some sort of a curse!

Now, Mrs. Clarke did tend to believe in the supernatural, within reason. But she was no quitter. Too, she had long been in the habit of having a piece of buttered toast and marmalade at eleven o'clock in the morning and was sad to miss it. Curse or no curse, a baker was needed, and a baker must be found, even if the whole of England had to be searched!

The housekeeper thought hard about who to send on this difficult quest. It would have to be someone quick and close-lipped, for once rumors of those foul-smelling, inedible loaves spread, no respectable baker would dare come to Ashton Place for fear of the dreaded "bakehouse curse." Imagine if such a thing were contagious! That could be the end of bread everywhere, for everyone. BREAD DECLARED EXTINCT, BAKEHOUSE CURSE TO BLAME, the headlines would read.

"Quick and close-lipped . . . I'd say Old Timothy's the man for the job," she decided. The enigmatic fellow was well aware of the estate's predicament, as he himself was a skilled sandwich maker, and the lack of bread had deprived him of his favorite lunchtime meal. Mrs. Clarke gave him strict orders not to return to Ashton Place until he had found a truly excellent baker. By now there were tummies rumbling from one end of the vast estate to the other, and the villagers would not settle for less.

He chose a pair of his fastest horses and a small, swift carriage. "There's only so much soup and boiled potatoes a man can stand at luncheon. I'll find your baker, missus," he declared, "even if I have to go to the edge of the earth, or beyond! Hey-ah!" he called to his team, and off he went.

Three days later he returned, the horses lathered and winded as if they had run the Derby. The coachman said not a word as he walked them 'round the drive to cool them off. Mrs. Clarke chased after him.

"But who's the baker? *Where's* the baker?" she demanded to know, for the villagers were now three days grumpier than they had been before.

"In the bakehouse, where do you think?" he replied crossly.

"What's the baker doing there?"

"Baking, maybe?" he retorted. "What else would a baker be doing in a bakehouse? Now, out of my way—I've business of my own to attend to. This way now, my lovelies. What a good run you had!" He made soft *cluck-cluck* noises to the horses, turned them gently, and headed for the barn.

Mrs. Clarke fretted and paced, but within the hour a thin plume of smoke rose from the bakehouse chimney. Before long, the delicious, unmistakable smell of baking bread was carried on the early spring breeze. Drooling mobs formed as the bread-starved villagers caught the scent. When the tempting aroma reached the open windows of the nursery, it brought Master Gogolev to a near breakdown.

"Bread, bread, bread! I am losing my mind—all I can smell is bread! Ah, why did it have to be a baker?" He babbled in a mix of languages and pounded his fists on the nursery wall until the plaster threatened to crack.

Alarmed, the Incorrigible children persuaded him to sit down. They tucked him in a chair with a blanket 'round his legs and brought him cups of tea and some paper and a pen, so that he might express his feelings by writing bad poetry rather than by breaking things. But they too had been captivated by the tantalizing smell. They quickly added *eat bread* to their to-doawoo list and ran downstairs to the kitchen.

"We volunteer to be bread tasters," Beowulf announced.

"Bread tasters, *woof!*" Alexander interjected, as a reminder that they were supposed to act woofy again.

"Yes, *woof!* I mean *arf!*" Beowulf stepped forward to explain. "We are the Bread-Eating—"

"And Sweet Treats, *grrr!*" Cassiopeia added, in case there was any cake involved.

"*Grrr,* yes—Incorrigible Evaluation Squad. *Yap, yap!*"

"Well, you're just in time, loves. I mean BEASTIES," Mrs. Clarke said, after she had puzzled out the acronym and had a good chuckle. "The first basket of samples has arrived from the bakehouse this minute. What's the verdict? Do we have a baker, or do we not?"

She opened the basket, and the irresistible smell floated up doubly strong. There they were, still warm from the oven: dozens of flat, round cakes in a fragrant heap, nestled in a colorful, wildly patterned cloth.

"Gypsy cakes!" Alexander exclaimed, wide-eyed. He was so surprised he almost forgot to say, *"Ahwoo!"*

Beowulf grabbed a loaf in each fist. *"Mmmf!"* he said, jamming them into his mouth. *"Mmmf mmf mmf!"*

Cassiopeia wriggled with excitement, for there was only one person this side of the veil who baked in this

133

particular kind of way. "That means the new baker must be the semi-soothless toothsayer—the themi-toothless truthsayer—" It was not easy to speak clearly with a mouth full of Gypsy cake. "I *mean* it must be Madame Ionesco—"

"Oh, you must have another!" Alexander interrupted, tucking a piece of his own loaf into his sister's mouth. "The BEASTIES approve of this baker," he said to Mrs. Clarke, in an official tone. "Let the bread-baking commence! *Grrrr!*"

"*Woof!*" agreed Beowulf.

"*Yap, yap!*" Cassiopeia said, making it unanimous.

"Judging from the mouthwatering smell, I agree with your decision, BEASTIES! But it couldn't hurt for me to take a bite, now, could it?" Mrs. Clarke helped herself to one of the little round loaves and nearly swooned. "Ah, now! This is some of the nicest bread I've ever had. But you three are surely in a puppyish mood today! I haven't heard this much yapping and ahwooing in many a month."

She patted them on their heads and gave each of them a Gypsy cake to take with them, plus one extra for Nutsawoo. "It's to be expected, I suppose. Poor Miss Lumley's been gone too long. No harm in it, though, is there? I ought to try a bit of barking myself!"

FULL OF WONDER, THE INCORRIGIBLES raced back to the nursery. Master Gogolev sat scribbling his poems and sobbing in a corner, where he could safely be ignored. The children gathered in the back nursery, the small separate room where their beds were, as it was a place where they could close the door and speak in private.

They arranged themselves in a circle, squatting on their haunches as they used to do. Alexander had some trouble, as his legs had grown so long—how quickly he had become used to sitting in chairs!

They opened the folded napkins Mrs. Clarke had wrapped their tasty treasures in and put all four cakes in the middle of the circle for closer examination. With eyes closed they inhaled deeply, for a good, concentrated sniff was the most foolproof way of knowing what was what.

In this case, there was no doubt. "These," Alexander said, "are Gypsy cakes."

"One hundred percent Gypsy cakes," Beowulf concurred.

"Mmmf, mmmf!" said Cassiopeia, by which she meant "Yum, yum!" She was already eating hers, for it was too good to resist. When she was done swallowing,

she added, "But why would Madame Ionesco pretend to be a baker?"

"That is the question," Beowulf agreed, Hamlet-like. All three grew silent and thoughtful.

"She could be traveling incognito," Alexander suggested. His siblings had studied enough Latin to know what incognito meant: it was simply *in*, which means "not," plus *cognitus*, which means "to know." Thus, to travel incognito means to be "not known"; to use a false identity, or to be in disguise. (Interestingly, the word incorrigible is also made from bits of Latin: *in* plus *corrigible*, which means "able to be fixed." Whether the Incorrigible children were fixable or not would depend on whom you asked. Miss Penelope Lumley would say yes, of course they were; like all children, they simply needed patient instruction on how to behave properly. Lady Constance Ashton might say the opposite: they were *in*corrigible, hopelessly wild and scarcely human, and could never learn to be otherwise. The children never troubled themselves about whether they were fixable or not, as they did not consider themselves broken in the first place. You may decide for yourself what to think about it, but it is worth remembering that often people who are told they need fixing are perfectly fine as they are. It is our own narrow notion of how things ought to be that is truly in need of repair. As Agatha Swanburne once observed, "Narrow minds are like narrow roads: only one idea at a time can pass, and that makes for slow going indeed!")

Alexander's incognito theory made sense, for Madame Ionesco was well known to Lady Constance and Lord Fredrick. In fact, she had visited the estate some months earlier to conduct a séance that did not go precisely as planned. "You can't boss around the dead," as the soothsayer tried to explain afterward, but Lady Constance was convinced the fortune-teller was a fraud, and spoke harshly about the incident for weeks afterward.

Because of this unfortunate misunderstanding, the spooky Madame might not be a welcome visitor at Ashton Place, which gave her good reason to travel in disguise. But why would Old Timothy bring the semi-toothless soothsayer back to the house to begin with?

"If we ask Old Timothy to explain, he will do this," Beowulf grunted enigmatically, and walked away, in a fine imitation of Old Timothy's rolling, bowlegged gait.

"Maybe a crystal ball could tell us," Cassiopeia said. All three children remembered how the fortune-teller had used a crystal ball to summon spirits from Beyond the Veil. It seemed to be a handy and informative item.

The problem was they had no crystal ball. Theirs was a well-stocked nursery indeed, thanks to their former governess, but a crystal ball was not an everyday classroom item, even in Miss Lumley's day.

"Or crystal globe?" she went on, thinking of the items they did have. "Crystal abacus? Crystal *A Child's History of England*, by Mr. Charles Dickens?

"Grrrrr." It was Alexander, growling deep in the back of his throat the way he used to, long ago in the forest, when he was thinking hard and wanted quiet. It had been a long time since Beowulf and Cassiopeia had heard him make this sound. Frankly, it was rather exciting.

"In the words of Agatha Swanawoo," Alexander said, when he had their attention, "let's go to the bakehouse and find out!"

THE SIXTH CHAPTER

Traveling incognito has its
advantages.

WHEN ALEXANDER INCORRIGIBLE QUOTED AGATHA Swanawoo as saying, "Let's go to the bakehouse and find out," he was using a form of poetic license called paraphrasing. In other words, he used other words than the ones she used, but the meaning of his words and the meaning of her words were essentially the same, and that is what it means to paraphrase: using different words to say more or less the same thing. (Those of you who pay close attention already know the wise founder's exact words, which appear earlier in this very tale. As for the rest of you: peek if you must, but be quick about it, for the Incorrigibles are eager to get to the bakehouse and discover if their theory about the incognito soothsayer holds water or not, as the saying goes!)

Paraphrasing is a useful timesaver, as it is not always convenient to stop and look up a quotation when making a point, especially if the situation is urgent, as this one surely was. However, any lawyer, judge, or professional thespian will tell you that there are times when knowing the exact words is essential; for example, when performing the role of Hamlet, or when given the task of ending a wolfish family curse. As Madame Ionesco herself once said, "A curse is like a contract. It's all in the wording." That is no paraphrase. Those were her exact words, and it was the exact words of the curse upon the Ashtons that the fortune-teller had to know in order to undo it—or attempt to, at least.

Through pluck, luck, and a knack for the theatrical, Penelope and Simon had managed to discover those exact words shortly before Penelope was whisked away to Plinkst. Even as they bade each other a heartbroken farewell on that cold January day in Brighton, Simon swore he would return to London, find the soothsayer, and tell her what the two friends—and surely they were more than just friends!—had found out.

Had Simon succeeded in his mission? If so, had the soothsayer solved the puzzle of how the cursèd Ashtons could be uncursèd, once and for all? Was that why she had returned to Ashton Place, traveling incognito as a baker?

These are all fine questions, and you may well ask them, but the Incorrigible children did not, for they did not know nearly as much as you do about the Ashton curse. All that they knew, they had learned from eavesdropping on adult conversations. Like most children who have had that experience (and what child has not?), they understood only some of what they overheard, and they felt no obligation to remember it all or even make sense of it, for it was not their concern to begin with.

No; they were much more interested in the Gypsy cakes! *Visit the bakehouse* was hastily added to the to-doawoo list. If the new baker was indeed Madame Ionesco, it would explain all those dreadful, bad-smelling loaves, for the spooky Madame was not above bending the rules to suit her own purposes. She always charged double to the swankily dressed; at solitaire she cheated like mad. To put a temporary spell on a bakehouse would be well within her capacity for mischief.

Excited, the children ran to get their coats. If they were lucky, they might arrive in time for the BEASTIES to sample the next batch of those delicious-smelling, yummy-tasting, perfectly scrumptious loaves of—

"Bread!" Master Gogolev staggered into the back nursery, bellowing like a giant from a fairy tale. "I smell bread! Where are you hiding it?" Then his bluster left him, and he leaned heavily against the wall, too weak to stand. "Bread, O bread, O wonderful, terrible bread! If there were but a single crust left in all the world, I would starve rather than eat it! Slowly I would pass from this world to the next while inhaling its delicate aroma, and spend my last breath dreaming of less miserable times. . . ."

By now, three of the four Gypsy cakes Mrs. Clarke had given them were in the children's tummies. Cassiopeia had the last in her coat pocket, in case they spotted Nutsawoo on the way to the bakehouse. The little scamp was still being elusive, but she (or he) never refused a treat and would eagerly perform tricks to get one: juggling one acorn, for example, or flicking that bushy tail in time to the Swanburne school song, like a furry gray metronome.

Master Gogolev sighed, and sighed again. He seemed

desperate, but for what? The children exchanged looks.

"If there *were* bread," Alexander ventured, "we would happily give you some. *Arf!*"

Gogolev clenched his fists and tugged at his collar, groaning.

"Unless you would prefer that there was *no* bread," Beowulf added. "In which case, we would make sure there was none. *Yap, yap!*"

"To bread, or not to bread?" Cassiopeia said magnificently. "That is the question. *Woof!*"

"Yes, bread or no bread . . . bread . . . no bread . . ." Gogolev sniffed again. "But there *is* bread here! I feel it in my bones!" He came toward the children, who shrank back until the foolish man dropped to his knees. "If you have some, yes, give it to me, I beg you! Writing even a few lines of melancholy poetry has drained every drop of strength from me. Perhaps a nice thick slice of pumpernickel with a smear of caviar would restore my will to live."

Reluctantly (for she would have much preferred to share it with Nutsawoo), Cassiopeia gave him the one Gypsy cake they had left. He brightened at once, slipped the round loaf into his pocket, and made a bee-line for the kitchen. "It would take a miracle to find decent caviar in this primitive land," he remarked on his way out, "but a plate of smoked herring would do nicely in a pinch."

The children waited to make sure he did not come back.

"Now," said Alexander, "once more unto the bakehouse! Hup, hup, hup!"

"Wait!" Beowulf held up a hand, for this strange interlude with Gogolev had given him time to think. "If the new baker *is* Madame Gypsy Cake, something spooky must be going on. Spooky and secret! Maybe *we* should be incognito, too."

The other two saw his point, for who does not like to sneak about in disguise? The Incognito Incorrigibles they would be. But what sort of disguise would be best? It would have to be something that came in threes, obviously, and that would allow them to keep acting like little wolf pups, for they had promised Lord Fredrick, and a promise was a promise.

"Three little pigs?" Alexander suggested.

Beowulf thought it over. "We would have to oink," he said, "but woofishly."

They tried, but "oinkawoo" failed to convince as either a pig noise or a howl. Anyway, Cassiopeia pointed out, "No one will believe we are pigs."

She gestured to show what she meant: two legs instead of four, pert noses, a telltale lack of little curly tails. The difficulty was clear. To be in disguise was different than mere pretending, for a disguise was intended to actually fool people. It had to be convincing. Since they were, in fact, children, they would not be convincing as pigs, cows, chickens, and the like. Nor could they pass as grown-up humans, as they were simply not tall enough.

"We must travel incognito disguised as children," Alexander concluded.

"Three children," Cassiopeia agreed. "But which ones?"

It was an interesting question: What trio—if they had known the word "troika," they might have said, what troika—of children could they possibly pretend to be?

The troika of Incorrigibles sat with furrowed brows, thinking.

"I know," Beowulf said. He jumped to his feet and clicked his heels together, then pretended to punch himself in the eye.

"Do you mean . . . the Babushkawoos?" Alexander said, aghast.

"The *horrible* Babushkawoos?" Cassiopiea sounded intrigued.

Beowulf shrugged. "Why not? We can be just as horrible as they are."

Alexander considered it. "No," he said. "We could be more horrible."

"We will be the most horrible there is!" crowed Cassiopeia. "And the woofiest, too."

And there you have it: superlatives, in a nutshell. The Woofiest and Most Horrible Incorrigible Babushkawoos they would be.

Speaking of masters of disguise, and all things horrible, more horrible, and most horrible: what was Lord Fredrick's houseguest, the ailing and incognito Edward Ashton, up to during all this?

The Incorrigibles did not know the villain's whereabouts, but they rarely thought about it. Nor did Penelope know, but she thought of little else. That is the difference a few years' span in age can make: one day you see the world as a child does, largely oblivious to its dangers. The next, alas, you do not. Tempus fugit, indeed!

But if *you* must know—and for you to know what Edward Ashton is up to, when Penelope and the Incorrigibles do not, is a case of dramatic irony if ever there was one—you may follow Agatha Swanburne's advice and simply see for yourself, for by now the master of disguise has spent a few days recuperating in the Egyptian room, and is much recovered; in fact, he is well enough to pay a visit to the nursery at Ashton Place.

The good news is that the Incorrigible children are not there, having just left for the bakehouse in their woofiest and most horrible disguises, but the bad news—woe, and more woe! The bad news may prove to be very bad indeed. . . .

"HERRING, HERRING, AND MORE HERRING!" Master Gogolev was quite renewed by the prospect of lunch, and the small round loaf he still carried in his pocket made the excitement nearly unbearable. He maneuvered nimbly through the nursery door, with a large covered platter balanced on one hand like a professional waiter.

"Spin—and spin! Just like the old days," he crowed as he whirled into the room. In his youth, Gogolev had been a dancer until an injury ended his once-promising career, or so he often claimed. In a grand gesture, he placed the tray on one of the children's desks and lifted the dome-shaped cover. He was far too preoccupied with himself and his herring to notice that his students were no longer in the nursery.

"Under no circumstances am I to be disturbed," he announced, "for I am hungry beyond endurance, and I require absolute silence to gain the full enjoyment of my meal."

"I shall do my best to oblige." The curtains rustled, and the man who called himself Judge Quinzy (you know the imposter's true identity, of course!) stepped away from the window and into Gogolev's view.

Gogolev was so startled, he nearly knocked over the tray. This made him doubly upset, for what a catastrophe that would have been! "Who are you, sir, to impose upon my company in this manner? Did you come in the window like a burglar? Is it my bread you want? Or my herring? I warn you, I shall defend myself—and my lunch—with vigor, and no mercy!" Gogolev brandished the cover of the platter like a shield. The poor man had worked up quite a head of steam, but this is what comes of letting oneself get too hungry.

Edward Ashton spoke sternly. "Get hold of yourself, sir! That you failed to notice me is no fault of mine. I entered this room moments before you did, through the very same door, and was standing by the window the whole time. I am no burglar but a friend of Lord Fredrick Ashton's." He stepped closer to the sniveling tutor. "We have met before, in Brighton. Perhaps this will jog your memory: I am a man of the law."

Gogolev flinched. "Man of the law . . . met in Brighton . . . are you Judge Quinzy? Yes, of course you are! Forgive me, your honor! I meant no insult, I swear!" It should be noted that Master Gogolev had a terrible fear of the law, due to a lost library book from childhood that weighed heavily on his conscience still. The mere sight of a police officer or a judge was enough to make him perspire with anxiety. "But it is a strange coincidence to see you here at Ashton Place. The last time we met, you were a legal adviser to my former employers. The Babushkinovs." His eye twitched as he said the name.

"I have many clients," Ashton replied smoothly. "Surely there is nothing strange about that. The simplest explanation is often the best, Master Gogolev. It is the lesson of Occam's Razor. I would expect a professional educator to know that." He made a circuit of the room, peeking into corners and behind the furniture. "Where are your students? That is who I have come to see."

"My students?" Gogolev had forgotten all about them. He glanced around the nursery and shrugged. "They were here a while ago. They must have gone to take their exercise out of doors."

"Unsupervised?" Edward Ashton roared in anger. "The master of this house pays you to keep a close eye on his wards, you incompetent! Do you have any idea how much is at stake should they wander off?" He sniffed. "What's that I smell? Something burning? Something fishy?"

Gogolev's fear of the law was great, but his self-ish desire not to share his lunch was even greater. However, if you have ever tried to hide a large tray of smoked herring in a modest-sized room, you know the aroma is potent, no matter how quickly you slam down the lid you were previously using as a shield, nor how many cozy pillows embroidered with wise sayings you hurriedly pile on top.

"No doubt it is my burning passion for poetry you smell." Gogolev wheeled to face his interrogator. "And my fishing for a perfect turn of phrase! For I suffer from a broken heart, and have spent hours in this very room, writing verse as a balm for my pain."

He grabbed the sheaf of papers he had been working on earlier and shoved them into Edward Ashton's hands. "Here are my latest masterworks! Though I fear they are too groundbreaking to find favor with the general public."

"Is this yours, too?" Edward Ashton removed a

small hardcover book from within the pile of papers. It was bound in leather and much read, from the look of it.

The tutor grimaced. "Bah! No. It is some nonsense belonging to the children. A book of poetry, translated from the German. Pure rubbish, in my opinion."

"'Wanderlust,'" said Ashton, turning the pages. "'I wander through the meadows green, Made happy by the verdant scene.' It seems a harmless little poem. What is your objection?"

Gogolev seized the book back. "Harmless? Look at the cover! *A Collection of Melancholy Poetry.* That is what the title promises. But 'Made happy by the verdant scene'? What kind of melancholy is that?" He flipped through the pages with mounting irritation. "It is the same all the way through. Charming descriptions of mountain goats and ibexes! Blooming edelweiss and cute babies! This is not poetry. Where is the suffering? The torment? The thwarted dreams?"

"Edelweiss and babies. Fascinating." Ashton's tone was quite changed. "You don't mind if I borrow this dreadful book, do you, my good man?"

It was not Gogolev's book to lend, but the dark-eyed man of the law stood before him, expectant. Something snapped within the poor fellow. He turned pale and could not answer.

"Master Gogolev? Are you listening?" Edward Ashton stepped closer to the trembling tutor. "Give me the book, if you please." He extended a hand slowly, like an accusing ghost.

"Ahh! Ahh!" Gogolev stammered and swooned. The sight of a stern judge demanding a book from him had been the stuff of his nightmares since childhood. He rubbed his eyes, but the fearful apparition would not go away.

"Am I dreaming, then? But the herring smelled so real!" In despair and confusion, he let the book slip through his hands. "Take it, spirit! Take it, and be gone!"

Ashton caught the volume neatly as Gogolev sank to the floor. "Thank you, my dear Master Gogolev." He turned the book over in his hands and leafed through the first pages. Something he saw there made him catch his breath. Then he smiled. "Of course I did not find them in Switzerland, for they were not there," he murmured. "Not in Switzerland at all."

But now, thanks to this idiot tutor and a book of mediocre poetry, he knew exactly where to look.

He traced a finger along the book's cover, where the faded imprint of the author's name was pressed into the leather, though the gold leaf had long since worn away. Only a fool would leave such an obvious clue, and sign her name so! But they were all fools. An optimistic, naive collection of fools, bred from the foolish founder of the line. They must be culled, like runts from a litter. This was how the Ashtons would survive.

One more moon. It was enough time, but barely. He would need to leave England at once. Tomorrow he would book passage on a ship, any ship. This time he would not fail.

But to Gogolev he only said, "Mind your students, sir! Make sure they stay at Ashton Place! They must not run off. And keep this conversation to yourself. Tell no one I was here. Understood?"

Still cowering, Gogolev agreed to everything. If only he had never lost that library book in the first place! If only the herring were real! If only he could wake up from this awful dream!

ALAS, AND WOE! IF MISS Penelope Lumley had only known that her book of melancholy German poetry in translation was now in the clutches of Edward Ashton! You may imagine how she would feel about it, for this was the book of poetry Miss Mortimer had given her as a gift, many years before. It had been Penelope's most treasured possession ever since, and when she was shipped off to Plinkst, she had left it with the Incorrigible children as a keepsake of her affection.

But Penelope did not know anything about this plot twist—at least, not yet. She was still with her employers, who had long ago succumbed to that dreaded condition known as travel fatigue. After countless miles by troika and train they were exhausted, queasy, and generally out of sorts. With the new clothes they could not afford now rumpled and covered with grit, the bedraggled Babushkinovs and their quiet but unusually alert governess arrived in Saint Petersburg at last.

Saint Petersburg! Penelope struggled to hide her excitement. Like London, Saint Petersburg was built along a central river, called the Neva. Also like London, this sprawling city was both the nation's capital and the home of its royal rulers. In London, this was Queen Victoria. In Saint Petersburg, it was Tsar Nicholas, a tall, stern military man with a fiery temper and an obsession for order. (Nicholas was an autocrat, which means he was the sort of leader who tries to make his own people afraid of him. Under Nicholas's reign, the Russian national anthem was "God Save the Tsar," and the Russian national opera was *A Life for the Tsar:*

A Patriotic Heroic-Tragic Opera. If any Russian bards had dared write a comedic operetta, it might well have been called *The Tsar on Holiday*, but comedic operettas were not a type of theater one often saw in Russia, a fact that remains true to this very day.)

Saint Petersburg! Saint Petersburg! Captain Babushkinov haggled with the cab driver who would take them from the train station to their lodgings. Penelope felt a pang. To think she had arrived at the home of the Imperial Russian Ballet yet would not have the chance to see them perform! It was a bitter disappointment.

To save money, the captain had arranged for them to stay in military housing. Madame Babushkinov was furious to discover that their "hotel" was really a barracks, a single large hall with cots all in a row, and a washing-up room they would have to share. Luckily, the only other resident was a young artillery officer named Leo. He was visiting the capital while on leave, or so he modestly explained as he helped unload their luggage from the cab.

He seemed a bookish sort of fellow, with a serious face and heavy straight eyebrows that sloped downward over his dark eyes. Penelope saw him several times in the common room of the barracks as she and the children explored their temporary quarters. On each occasion, he was either reading or scribbling in his diaries. (Penelope and the Babushkinovs had no way of knowing this, but the thoughtful young man they were expected to share a bathroom with would prove to be one of the greatest novelists of all time. His name was Leo Tolstoy, and he would go on to write several literary masterpieces about war, peace, families both happy and unhappy, and other important topics that continue to fascinate readers to this very day.)

It was rare that women stayed in the barracks. A curtain was provided to hang like a screen, to give some privacy to the cots assigned to Madame Babushkinov, Penelope, and Veronika. Young Tolstoy generously helped with this task but showed no interest in befriending the captain to boast about his own exploits, or to gossip about wars and politics and career advancement, as one might expect of a junior officer.

Instead, shortly after dinner, he approached Penelope in the common room and asked if he might sit quietly and observe the Babushkinov children. He told her that he had been thinking about the nature of childhood and planned to write about it, and wanted to better remember what being a child was like, as he was nearly twenty-four and it already felt so very long ago.

Gladly she said yes, for she welcomed the company. Together they sat and watched Veronika, Boris, and Constantin at play.

"These children are horrible," Tolstoy shortly observed, thus displaying the deep insight into human nature that would characterize his later work.

"They are," Penelope agreed. She felt immediately at ease with this young man, who seemed to possess a wisdom beyond his years. "The whole family is unhappy, for reasons too complicated to explain." She paused, but her instinct told her it was all right to confide in her new acquaintance. "I once had hope for these children, and tried to teach them as I was taught, but my efforts failed."

"No hopeless case is truly without hope," he said fervently. "What did you try to teach them?"

"Oh . . . to be kind," she stammered. His directness took her by surprise, as did his unwitting use of the Swanburne motto. "To think of others as well as of oneself. To be grateful, not just for good fortune but for all fortune, the good and the bad, for it is life's nature to offer a bit of both. To use good manners, not just with one's friends but with everyone, even strangers."

"Do you mind if I take some notes?" he asked, and

removed a stubby pencil from his coat pocket. Penelope shook her head no, of course she would not mind. "Please, go on," he urged.

She closed her eyes, to better remember all she had learned at school: not only the capitals of nations and techniques of watercolor painting, but the truly important things. "To spend time in nature, and not laze about indoors when the weather is fair," she said. "To be curious about everything in the world, and every person whom you meet. To be a loyal friend and avoid gossip. To always carry a book in case of missed omnibuses or long lines at the grocer's, for no moment spent reading can ever be thought wasted. To keep one's room tidy and strive for early bedtimes."

"And where did you learn all these wise things?" he inquired.

Penelope sat up straight and proud. "At the Swanburne Academy for Poor Bright Females. In Heathcote."

"Poor Bright Females, yes." His eyebrows knitted together in an expression of profound concentration. Then he snapped his notebook shut and jumped to his feet. "Someday I will start my own school for peasant children!" he blurted, and took his leave abruptly, the way people do when they have had a marvelous idea and wish to think it through before it fades.

Penelope did not mind. His intensity reminded her of Simon Harley-Dickinson, and she took comfort in the thought that her new friend and Simon would get along swimmingly, if they should ever have the chance to meet. (Whether the notion of a Tolstoy Academy for Poor Bright Peasants was conceived at this very moment we cannot know, but later in his life Leo Tolstoy did in fact open a school for peasant children. He even wrote little primers designed to teach these children how to read. That he did all this while also penning some of the greatest novels ever written simply goes to show that "Those who do, do much. Those who talk, talk much." That is how Agatha Swanburne once put it, anyway.)

IN SAINT PETERSBURG IN APRIL, the last light of dusk faded quite late in the evening, but for once the Babushkinovs chose an early bedtime, as they were exhausted. Being in the barracks put Madame on her best behavior, for she knew how important the charm of an officer's wife could be to securing his advancement! Yet without the freedom to blame and criticize and order people around, she could find little to talk about. She soon crawled into her cot in silent irritation and turned to face the wall.

The children were likewise worn out and went to bed with only minor griping about the lumpy mattresses and thin, scratchy military blankets. Once tucked into her own narrow cot, Penelope fell asleep in an instant and dreamed she was back at Swanburne. But the illusion did not last, for the captain's rumbling snore from the other side of the curtain was a sound she would never have heard at school. (Her bunkmate had snored with gusto, make no mistake. But Cecily's snores were of the piping soprano kind, and blended nicely with the morning birdsong.)

She awoke refreshed, and quite early, in time to get the very first cup of tea from the samovar in the common room. She sat and sipped and considered her next move. "The Babushkinovs will soon discover that the letter that brought them here was a fake, so I must act quickly," she thought. "If I simply walk out, they will come looking for me. No . . . best to slip away under the pretext of some complicated errand. It will be hours before they realize I have not returned, and that will give me the advantage of a head start. All I need is a window of opportunity." (A window of this kind is no ordinary hole in the wall. Such windows open, but briefly and only once. To dither and dally when the window of opportunity opens means to end up with one's nose pressed against the glass of fate, gazing with regret at what might have been. There is an old saying that advises us to "look before you leap," but to leap without looking is not nearly as bad as to look, and look again, and never work up the courage to leap at all.)

By the time Penelope returned, Veronika had arisen, in a deep crisis of confidence. She claimed to have forgotten not only how to dance, but how to walk. Paralyzed with fright, she lay facedown on her cot, moaning into the pillow.

Madame Babushkinov was ill equipped to console the child, for she was a bundle of nerves herself and chattered nonstop. "I am done wasting away in Plinkst, that is for certain!" she announced. "This is where I belong! The culture! The excitement! Listen to me, Ivan. Once our Nikki is in the ballet, I shall have to stay in Saint Petersburg to supervise her. A girl of her age needs a mother. We will lease an apartment here, in the city. Wouldn't you like that, precious girl?"

Veronika raised her tear-streaked face from the pillow. "Only if the savages stay home," she said heatedly. "Boris and Constantin can live in Plinkst. If they come here it will ruin everything!"

The captain put down his newspaper. "An apartment

in Saint Petersburg?" he said to his wife, incredulous. "You will spend me into bankruptcy!"

"We want to go home!" the boys wailed, for this idea of their mother abandoning the family to live with Veronika did not sit well with them.

"Fine, fine," the captain retorted. "We shall all go home at once!"

Madame snatched his newspaper away and scolded, "Ivan Victorovich, stop tormenting the child!" as Veronika shrieked wildly into her pillow.

"We want to walk outside and throw stones in the river!" the boys demanded.

This was the most sensible thing any of them had said so far. Penelope quickly volunteered to take them, for she was desperate to get away from the quarreling. Her window of opportunity to escape had not yet opened, but in the meanwhile she could at least take a walk and see her surroundings. For she was in Saint Petersburg, home of the Imperial Ballet and countless other wonders, and who knew if she would ever pass this way again?

BORIS AND CONSTANTIN WERE SMUGLY victorious about having an excursion while their sister was left behind. They spent the first quarter hour of their walk gloating.

Then they began planning the lies they would tell Veronika upon their return, about all the wonderful adventures she had missed.

"We'll say we saw an organ grinder with a monkey," suggested Boris.

"And a fire eater," said Constantin.

"A fire-eating monkey! Who does tricks."

"While riding a horse."

"No, a camel."

"Camels stink. A horse is better."

"Idiot, you have never been near a camel. How do you know what they smell like?"

"I know they smell almost as bad as you!"

"As you, you mean!"

And so on. Penelope listened but did not interfere. They were horrible boys, from a horrible family, and they had no wish to change. Trying to stop them from being cruel was like trying to stop the tides.

They walked along the granite embankments of the Neva, past the magnificent Admiralty building and its proud white columns, its countless statues and friezes depicting figures from myths and ancient times. "There are the four seasons," she showed the twins as they walked, "and the four elements, and the four winds. There is the goddess Isis and the Roman god of the sea, Neptune."

By now they had reached the central gate. "Look up," she said, pointing at the tower. "All the way up, at the top of the golden spire. There is a weather vane there in the form of a ship. It is modeled after one of Peter the Great's actual ships." Penelope knew all this from her Swanburne geography class. "The weather vane has a name. *Korablik.*"

"That means 'little ship,'" Boris said, grudgingly showing interest. His brother refused to look up.

"Indeed it does," Penelope said. "Imagine! A little three-masted schooner made of gold, sailing across the sky!"

"Weather vanes don't have names," Constantin said, kicking at the ground.

"This one does." Penelope gazed up at it, awestruck. She wished she had Alexander Incorrigible's spyglass, so she might get a better view.

"Ships don't sail in the sky," Boris pointed out.

"This one does," she repeated. She had to shield her eyes from the harsh gleam of sun along the spire's golden edge. It was like the needle of a compass pointing at the heavens. The shining *korablik* danced on top.

Now, Penelope knew good architecture when she saw it. She had been to Buckingham Palace and the

British Museum, and Ashton Place was nothing to sneeze at, either. But there was something so brave and solitary about this little ship of gold, weaving its way through the air currents. Never had she seen anything so exquisite.

"I'd knock down that golden spire and melt it. Then we'd be rich!" Constantin said.

As if in protest, the *korablik* gave a half spin in a sudden gust, then righted itself. What a highly unusual weather vane! It seemed to whisper words that only Penelope could hear: "Be brave, for you too will weather what is to come, and right yourself somehow, whichever way the wind blows!"

She watched the *korablik* dance, and let its message console her and fill her heart with joy. How full of the unexpected life repeatedly proved to be! Only three years had passed since she was a schoolgirl in geography class at Swanburne, doodling funny pictures in the margins of Cecily's notebook. *Cecily the Great,* she had scrawled beneath a drawing of Peter the Great, to which she had added freckles and two long pigtails. Who could have foretold that she would set foot in the city he founded, even if only for a day?

All those unhappy days and nights in Plinkst might have dimmed her Swanburnian spirit, temporarily. But this new feeling within, this swelling gratitude and simple delight—it was something more than optimism. It was more, even, than optoomuchism. She suspected that Tolstoy fellow would understand right away. It was the true, clear knowledge that no matter what might happen later, for this single hour her eyes were wide open to the splendor of it all, the golden spire against a crisp blue sky, and the mirrored surface of the winding Neva reflecting them both, an even more perfect version of this already glorious world.

And all the while, scampering in circles 'round her, poking each other out of boredom and meanness, the two horrible children who could not stop tormenting each other long enough to see the beauty of any of it. Foolish twins! But they had no model to learn from save the pettiness of their parents, whose heads were too full of worries about money and rank and the opinions of others to appreciate the riches they already had: a family, whole and healthy and all living under the same roof. Imagine how glad the Long-Lost Lumleys might be to possess such a treasure!

It was a great luxury to be unhappy about small things, Penelope realized. All the petty complaints and discomforts of everyday life meant nothing compared to those sudden, unlucky swoops of fate that arrived with no warning, like a hawk that dives from a dizzying height to snatch an unsuspecting rabbit from the ground.

The boys were restless. They raced ahead, turned corners, and paid no attention to where they were going. Penelope followed, but the side streets were narrow and full of shadows. It would be too easy to get lost.

"We have wandered too far from the main road," she said, once she caught up with them. "We must retrace our steps." The twins took this literally and walked backward, exchanging quick punches every time they bumped into each other. Soon they reached the Neva once more, and scoured the banks for rocks to skip along the water.

Penelope watched as they fought over who saw which rock first, and whose rock had skipped farthest, and which of them would be first to touch the opposite bank in a swimming contest, and she wondered, could the Babushkinovs ever retrace their steps to a day when they were not so miserable, and chart a different course forward?

"At least the Ashtons have a curse to blame for their troubles," she thought. "If not for the terrible shipwreck that landed Admiral Percival Racine Ashton and his crew on an unmapped island, and if not for the admiral's selfish desire for a new fur-lined vest, which made him cruelly hunt the litter of wolf cubs whose mother was the sacred animal of the tribe, and who laid her terrible wolf-curse upon him and his descendants, causing all sorts of difficulty and bother, until now there are only a few weeks left for me to get home and sort things out—why, if not for all that, the Ashtons might have been the happiest family in England!"

She gazed across the water. "Of course, if not for the storm at sea, the shipwreck would never have happened in the first place. But one cannot blame the sea for what happens on dry land. Listen to me, inventing such sayings! I suppose I must have the blood of Agatha Swanburne in my veins after all."

The twins had grown bored once more; now they wanted to go back and torment their sister. To return to the barracks, they had to cross Nevsky Prospect, the city's main boulevard that either began or ended at the Admiralty, depending on which way you were facing. The Admiralty was the headquarters of the Russian navy, and all along Nevsky Prospect were sailors in uniform. Naturally this made Penelope think of Simon, who had spent a fair amount of time at sea himself.

Simon! Simon Harley-Dickinson! Repeating his

name was like reciting a very short, very cheering poem. Simon was the best navigator she knew. Give him a sextant and a glimpse of the stars, and there was no chance of getting lost. Yet she was the one who had to find her way back home this time, and on her own, too.

As they walked, she kept glancing over her shoulder at the golden spire of the Admiralty. The *korablik* caught the light, winking with each change of the breeze. Block after block they traveled, but the brave little ship stayed in view the whole time, just as the moon does.

If only she could sail that glittering golden ship across the sky, all the way home to Ashton Place!

THE SEVENTH CHAPTER

A new baby nurse is hired.

SIMON! SIMON HARLEY-DICKINSON! WITH THAT unruly, poetical forelock and the gleam of genius in his eye!

Now, perhaps you too are wondering if we will ever see Simon Harley-Dickinson again. He had always been a difficult fellow to pin down, with his love of adventure and the wide-open seas, his endless search for a fresh plot twist, his yearning to explore Parts Unknown with only his sextant and the North Star to guide him. Whether the job was to jump on a stolen velocipede, win over a band of pirates, visibilize invisible ink, pen a sonnet, or don a disguise, Simon

Harley-Dickinson was the man for it. But he had no fixed address, which made him, if not long-lost, at least easily misplaced.

The Incorrigibles could not help but think about him as they fashioned their disguises, for Simon was a man of the theater, skilled in the art of stagecraft. Putty noses, horsehair wigs, and phony accents were his bread and butter, so to speak. He would have leaped at the chance to transform three clever, well-mannered (if occasionally wolfish) children into the Horrible Incorrigible Babushkawoos.

Luckily, the children had superb imaginations. They simply asked each other, "What would Simon Harley-Dickinson do?" Soon they had scores of ideas. Alexander and Beowulf each blacked an eye with candle soot, for they knew Boris and Constantin fought like two cats in a bag, as the saying goes, and often sported such bruises. They slicked back their hair with pomade and put on matching outfits, thus giving the impression of being twins. Lastly they obtained a pair of tattered men's gloves from Jasper, one of the young manservants of the household staff, who had always been a good friend to them (he was a particular favorite of the Margaret's, too; her distinctive high-pitched voice trilled like a skylark when he was nearby). They

171

each tucked a single glove beneath the belts they had cinched 'round their waists. That it was only one did not matter. These gloves were not for wearing, but for challenging people to duels at the slightest provocation, or for no reason at all.

Meanwhile, Cassiopeia found a length of pink tulle in Madame LePoint's trunk of fabric scraps, left over from a petticoat made for one of Lady Constance's gowns. This she fashioned into a ballerina's tutu. A pair of socks with bows stitched on top served nicely as ballet slippers.

"What is important," Alexander said, when the costumes were complete, "even more important than the clothes—the most important part of our disguise!—is that we are horrible. In the words of Agatha Swanawoo, 'If you wish to be convincing, first you must be convinced.'"

Brimming with confidence, the Horrible Incorrigibles made their incognito exit, thus narrowly missing the fishy arrival of Edward Ashton and the even fishier return of Master Gogolev and his herring. (Note that fishy can mean both "suspicious" and "smelling like fish." Carp is a type of fish; carp also means to complain. Flounder is a type of fish; it also means to be hopelessly confused. And sole, as you may know, is yet another type of fish. Sole also means the only one, as well as the bottom of the foot. If sole were the sole type of fish whose name had multiple meanings, that would be one thing to carp about, but three is enough to make anyone flounder. A fishy business indeed!)

Even as their nemesis prowled the nursery, the Horrible Incorrigibles whined, punched, dueled, and pirouetted all the way to the bakehouse. All that bad behavior was exhausting, and they made frequent stops to rest. They did this by sitting and pouting, having lying-down tantrums, and giving each other the "silent treatment."

No one recognized them, and they felt proud of their disguises. Then again, it was midday and all the household staff were hard at work. The only person who actually saw the children was Old Timothy. He came across them as they lay belly down on the ground, pounding their hands and feet against the earth and blaming each other for their misery. One of the coachman's eyebrows flew up as the other scrunched down, but he simply walked on, chuckling.

Eventually the children reached the bakehouse, a stone cottage that housed a massive brick oven with a double-width chimney. When the oven was in use, the bakehouse grew hot as a sauna, and they pushed the door open with caution. But there was no fire lit. Along one wall was a wooden trough for mixing the dough and metal buckets for adding water to the flour. Tall iron baker's racks held the rising loaves on one side and finished loaves on the other. Wooden paddles had been propped next to the oven, ready to slide the loaves in and out. (Nowadays you might see something similar in a pizza restaurant, although you can be sure that the Incorrigibles had never set foot in such an establishment).

The bakehouse smelled deliciously of bread. All that was missing was the baker.

"Yoo-hoo," the children called, cupping their hands to their mouths. "Yoo-hoo, baker!"

As they waited for an answer, they continued to complain and pick fights with each other. They planned to stay incognito until they knew for certain that the new baker was their old friend, the spooky Madame. But there was no one in the bakehouse at all, as far as they could tell.

Surely the bread was not baking itself! After a brief discussion, they decided to make eerie ghostie noises. These would be likely to intrigue the soothsayer and lure her out of hiding, if she happened to be in earshot.

"Boooooo!" they intoned. "Boo, boo, *ahwoooooooo!*"

Bang! A cloud of ash billowed from the oven. The Incorrigibles jumped back as a tall, slim figure, bloodless and gray as some awful specter from Beyond the Veil, emerged from the chimney itself.

"Aaaaaaaaaaah!" the children screamed, for it truly looked like a ghost.

"Aaaaaaaaaaah!" the figure screamed in return, for he was just as taken aback as they were.

Despite her lack of proper pointe shoes, Cassiopeia rose effortlessly to her toes out of sheer terror. Alexander and Beowulf shakily threw down their gloves.

"I challenge you to a duel, you . . . you—oven monster!" Alexander yelled, to cover his trembling voice.

"Me too, you . . . you—smoky ghostie!" Beowulf added. The boys raised their fists and tried to look fierce. The apparition loomed before them, pale as the moon.

"Say," the monster said, "if I didn't know better, I'd swear you were those three horrible Russian children I once met in Brighton! But that's not possible, is it? I must be dreaming. Or maybe I got some cinders in my eye while I was up there in the chimney—hold on a minute. . . ."

The monster rummaged through his pockets and procured a filthy handkerchief. He rubbed his eyes

and face and looked at the children again. This time he broke into a wide smile. The teeth behind his ash-gray lips gleamed white as a crisp new sail.

"Well, I'll be! I almost didn't recognize you, Cassawoof, in that nifty dancing outfit. And look at you two fine fellows, with your hair all slicked back! Shows what I know about fashion."

"Simon!" the no longer horrible Incorrigibles yelled, and ran to hug him, filthy as he was. "Simon Harley-Dickinson!"

ONCE SIMON HAD STRIPPED OFF the work coveralls he had worn over his clothes, and washed his face and hands with clean water from the pump out back, he looked nearly himself again. Only his hair was left silver with ash. "It would be a fine bit of stagecraft if I'm ever called upon to play my own grandfather," he joked. "Then again, Grandpap's life has been dull and contented as a frog's on a rock. 'Good lives make bad plays,' as they say, but all that peace and quiet surely helps the digestion. So, Incorrigibles! We meet again. I'm glad of it. Any news from our Miss Lumley?"

The children's expressions of joy faded, and they shook their heads.

Simon chewed his lip. "That's too bad. I haven't

heard a peep from her either, and I've sent a letter just about every day." He was quiet for a moment, then shrugged off his mood with ease, the way one might shrug off a coat upon coming indoors. With an open smile, he reached out and tousled the children's heads till they too were cheerful again. "Well! I suppose you're wondering what I'm doing here."

The children spoke at once. "New baker!—Madame Ionesco!—Gypsy cakes!"

"Nothing gets by you three, does it?" he replied, laughing. He leaned close and dropped his voice. "You're not wrong about any of it, but mum's the word. The good Madame is in disguise. Here in the bakehouse we can speak freely. There's no one near and the walls are solid stone. But outside this room, she's Flora the Bread Lady. Understood?"

The children nodded. "We are in disguise, too," Alexander explained. "As the Horrible Incorrigible Babushkawoos."

Simon grinned. "That's a relief. For a minute there I really thought I was seeing things! But why the secrecy?" His tone changed to one of concern. "Say, is anyone following you? Making threats? Causing trouble?"

"We are incognito as Babushkawoos because we

thought Madame Ionesco was incognito as a baker," Cassiopeia explained.

"A regular incognito party, eh? And I expect you didn't want to risk giving her away by being yourselves when she was being someone else?" The children nodded, and Simon grinned. "Clever as always! Anyway, I bet being horrible is fun, and a lot of work, too."

With this the children could not argue. "But why are *you* here, Simawoo?" Beowulf asked, which prompted a jumble of questions. "What were you doing in the oven?" "Why is Madame baking instead of sooth-saying?" "How many Gypsy cakes would go into the tummy of an Incorrigible?" And so on, until Simon raised a hand for silence.

"To explain all that is a tale, all right. It's not a long tale, but a medium one—say, that's not bad! A medium tale about a soothsayer." The children groaned to show their appreciation for the pun, for they knew that "medium" was another word for soothsayer, and that a soothsayer who was halfway between large and small could fairly be called a medium medium. Once they were done groaning, they begged Simon to tell his tale.

Ever the showman, he quickly arranged three upside-down buckets as stools for the children to sit upon, like a proper audience. "To begin with, since the last time I saw you three, I've done nothing but eat, sleep, and look for Madame Ionesco. It's what our dear Miss Lumley asked me to do, for reasons that are what you might call urgent."

"What reasons?" Cassiopeia asked innocently.

Simon looked uncomfortable. "Oh, nothing we need to go into right now. As I was saying—"

"Does it have to do with the curse upon the Ashtons?" she interjected.

"The one that says only one side the family can survive?" Beowulf asked. "Or else both will go extinct, like the dodos?"

Whereupon Alexander mimed the death of the very last dodo, and a tragic, squawking death it was. Apparently the children had understood far more about the family's troubles than the adults in their lives imagined they did. Simon tugged at his forelock, releasing a small cloud of ash.

"Well, as a matter of fact, it does, but don't you three be worrying yourself about curses and whatnot! Let's just say that finding the good Madame was important. Anyway, I searched for the old Gypsy all over London, at all of her usual haunts. Haunts, get it?"

Agreeably, the children groaned at his clever use of the word "haunts." Simon grinned and grabbed one of the wooden baking paddles, which he proceeded to ride like a hobbyhorse 'round the bakehouse. "I checked the occult bookstores, the spooky carnivals, the abandoned cemeteries, and all the obscure and little-trafficked corners of the city. Nothing!"

He dismounted, breathless. "Panic set in! As I said, I'd promised Miss Lumley some answers that only Madame Ionesco could give, and I wasn't making any progress. I even worried that our dear Penny might be cross with me about it, and perhaps that's why she wasn't answering my letters."

The children's eyes grew wide and sad. "Well, never mind that," Simon quickly went on. "Imagine it: day after day, I search for the soothsayer. At night I sleep backstage at whatever theater has left the stage door unlocked. If you don't mind a firm surface, a pile of sandbags can make a decent mattress, you'll be pleased to know."

"But what about Madame Gypsy Cake?" the children begged.

"I'm nearly there, mates!" His voice took on a mysterious tone. "About a week ago, with the moon only one night short of full, I'm pushing a janitor's broom across the stage of the Royale Piccadilly in exchange for a meal"—now the wooden paddle stood in for the broom—"when I hear a ghostly voice calling from the back of the theater. 'Simon!' it moans, eerie as can be. 'Simon Harley-Dickinson!'"

He paused for effect, and indeed, the children were on tenterhooks. "Well, I know how to pick up a cue when I hear one," he continued. "I drop my broom, take a deep breath, and answer back, 'Angels and ministers of grace defend us!'"

"Shakespeare!" the children cried.

"You bet it is." Simon struck a theatrical pose. "It's what Hamlet says when the ghost of his kingly dad turns up at the castle at Elsinore. I know the speech by heart, and would have been keen to play it, too—but before I can spit out another forsooth, the mysterious Madame herself waddles down the aisle and plants herself at the footlights.

"'Madame Ionesco! Where on earth have you been?' says I. She smirks, as if I'd asked the wrong question! 'Never mind where,' she says. 'Now listen. A message has come to me from Beyond the Veil. We must go to the rich man's house, quick! Call us a cab, would you, honey?'" He paused. "By 'the rich man's house,' she meant Ashton Place, in case you had any doubts."

"But what was the message?" Beowulf asked, in thrall to the story.

Simon shrugged. "You'll have to ask Madame Ionesco. Whatever she saw in her orb of prognostication, so far she's kept it to herself. Anyway. 'Aye aye, Madame,' I reply. I dash out of the theater to find us a hansom cab, and to whom should I bump smack into but the enigmatic coachman himself!"

"Old Timothy!" the children yelled.

"Correct! His carriage was parked right outside the stage door of the Royale Piccadilly. What were the odds of that happening, I ask you? But no, don't answer"—for the children had already begun to figure it out—"as I expect that even the laws of mathematics are not up to the task of explaining Old Tim."

The children concurred.

"After my shock wears off, and we exchange brief pleasantries, I ask if we can hitch a ride back to Ashton Place. 'Only if you can bake!' he says. 'I can't go home without a baker, or Mrs. Clarke'll have my hide.' To prove his point, he gives me this very copy of the *Ashton Weekly Gazette*, in which a curious advertisement appears, as you may see for yourselves." Simon produced the newspaper to show the children as he recited from memory, "'Excellent bread baker needed. Experience with angry mobs preferred.' Well, I've faced the matinee crowds on the West End and lived to tell about it, but I'm all thumbs in the kitchen. On the other hand, nothing fazes Madame Ionesco, and she's as good a baker as she is a prognosticator."

"Gypsy cakes!" The Incorrigibles rubbed their tummies and swooned.

"It's her specialty, and a fine one, too," Simon agreed. "'Old Tim,' I say, 'it seems we're both in luck. We need a ride, and you need a baker.' Off we went! Along the way the coachman suggests we'd be wise to travel incognito. I ask why, and he answers, 'Because I said so! Suspend your disbelief, lad, and just do it.' That's how Flora the Bread Lady was born. One loaf, and she was a shoo-in for the baker's job, though I suspect she may have knocked out the competition with some hocus-pocus, too, if rumors are to be believed."

"And you found a job—as a chimney climber?" Alexander asked, puzzled.

"Oven elf?" Beowulf guessed.

"Smoke inspector?" That was Cassiopeia's theory.

"Nothing so fancy. I was just trying to fix the flue. It was stuck." Simon's tale was done. He put the wooden paddle back in its place. "I haven't found a job yet. We thespians don't have much experience with honest employment. I'm not sure where to begin."

"You could be Shakespeare," Alexander suggested.

"The Bard of Ashton Place," Beowulf said, trying out the title.

"Ashton's Thespians Deluxe!" Cassiopeia crowed. She and Beowulf acted out a brief swordfight in which they both met gruesome ends, much like the conclusion of *Hamlet*. They ended up sprawled on the bakehouse floor, a tragic tangle of limbs.

Simon reached out both hands and helped them up. "Someday, perhaps! But pretending to be a bard is not much of a disguise, since I already am one. And Shakespeare's long dead. It'd only draw attention if he turned up at Ashton Place."

Alexander frowned, thinking. "You need a job that is incognito."

"More incognito than Shakespeare," Beowulf said.

"You need the most incognito job there is," Cassiopeia declared. But what job would that be? It would have to suit Simon's talents and temperament, while also allowing him to be completely unrecognizable.

The Incorrigibles furrowed their brows and stroked their chins. Idly, Beowulf picked up the newspaper Simon had handed them earlier. Together the children perused the pages.

Simon poked at the rising bread loaves in frustration. "Frankly, I'm stumped. If only there was a job opening for a household navigator! That would work. Or I'd settle for being the Ashton astronomer. I know a thing or two about the constellations. I'd call myself Starry Sam, the Milky Way Man, or something of that ilk. . . ."

His voice trailed off. A troika of Incorrigibles looked up at him. Six wide eyes gleamed with insight.

"What?" Simon asked, suddenly uneasy. "You don't like Starry Sam?"

"Simawoo," Cassiopeia said as her brothers giggled helplessly, "we know the *perfect* job for you."

THE APPLICANT FOR THE JOB of baby nurse folded her large gloved hands in the lap of her brightly floral-patterned dress. She was tall, and perched with difficulty on one of the delicate antique side chairs in the front parlor of Ashton Place. "My name is Mrs. Penworthy," she said in a deep contralto voice. "Mrs. Elsinore Penworthy."

The lady smiled primly and scratched under the edge of her bonnet. The bonnet covered all her hair except for two short lengths that stuck out at each ear. It was not what one would call an elegant hairdo. It had a bit of a horse-tail look about it, to be frank. Her dress was ill fitting, snug across the shoulders and loose around the middle. However, the colorful meadow-flower print of the fabric and the shocking flounce of pink tulle that had been unevenly stitched 'round the hem surely lent the garment a festive air.

"Penworthy, eh? Write that down, Incorrigibles." Lord Fredrick chewed aggressively on his unlit cigar. Unlike Mrs. Clarke's advertisement for the baker, the advertisement Lord Fredrick had placed for a baby nurse in the *Ashton Weekly Gazette* had made no mention of angry mobs. Consequently, the household had been flooded with applicants. They formed a long line at the door of Ashton Place that stretched the full length of the curved driveway, past the formal gardens and the blooming daffodils, and onto the grassy lawn.

Such a quantity of prospective baby nurses made Lady Constance throw up her hands. "Look at them all! They keep coming, like ants at a picnic. I want nothing to do with it, if you please," she exclaimed, and waddled off to inspect her tulip garden once more.

This left Lord Fredrick in charge, though he was quick to admit he felt out of his depth. Mrs. Clarke convinced him to let the Incorrigible children assist, as they were still quite young and were bound to have more insight into what a baby might like than an older person would. Alexander had the neatest handwriting and took notes on each applicant, while Beowulf and Cassiopeia escorted the ladies in and out of the parlor.

So far there had been a wide range, from energetic young girls to calm, silver-haired ladies with long letters of reference. Most of them seemed perfectly nice. Yet, curiously, the Incorrigible children had objected to them all. "Smells like cheese" was but one example of the many disqualifying flaws they discovered. "Froggish voice," "dangerously thin ankles," "failure to smile," "too much smiling"—these reasons and more were given by the Incorrigibles to rule out one candidate after another.

By now Lord Fredrick was crabby and tired, and he had nearly given up on ever finding someone suitable.

"All right, Mrs. Penworthy," Lord Fredrick said, feigning interest, "you've some experience taking care of babies, I expect? Heaven knows I don't."

"Yes—ahem! I mean yes, my lord." Mrs. Penworthy's voice cracked like a teenaged boy's. "I do love babies so. Why, just last week I was tending the sweetest little cherub you can imagine, all dimples and velvety skin and cute little burpie-wurpies."

"But not every child is sweet." Lord Fredrick scowled. "What if the rascal's a bit wild now and then? Noisy and destructive, like a young pup, what? How would you feel about that?"

Before she could answer, Alexander loudly cleared his throat. The Incorrigibles positioned themselves behind Lord Fredrick's chair, so they could only be seen by Mrs. Penworthy. They bared their teeth into wolfish expressions, swiped at each other with pretend claws, made O-shaped howling mouths as if baying at the moon, and so on.

Mrs. Penworthy's eyes never left Lord Fredrick. "Well, Lord Ashton, sir, I'll tell you a tale, if you don't mind. When I was a wee girl, my father was the master of hounds for a small estate. 'Have extra patience with the naughty pups, Elsinore,' he always said. 'It's the wildest one in the litter who'll be leader of the pack someday.'"

"Blast! I like that answer." Lord Fredrick chewed his cigar. "Elsinore? That's in Denmark, what?"

"The capital of Denmark is Copenhagen," Beowulf interjected, pleased that he remembered.

"I wouldn't know, I'm sure," Mrs. Penworthy demurred. "I do enjoy a good Danish pastry, though." (As any globe could tell you, Denmark is the southern- most country of the northernmost nations of Europe. North of Copenhagen is the city of Elsinore, home to the castle where *Hamlet* takes place, with its wandering

189

ghosts, ill-advised eavesdropping behind the drapes, conversations with skulls, and deadly duels in iambic pentameter. No wonder the play is considered a masterpiece. Imagine how much more enjoyable it would be when viewed with a Danish pastry in one hand and a restorative cup of tea in the other!)

"Master of hounds . . . Danish pastries . . . I see nothing wrong here." Lord Fredrick turned to the Incorrigibles. "All right, give me the bad news. What's the problem this time?"

All three children shook their heads.

"What, nothing? Nothing at all?"

Cassiopeia tugged at his sleeve. "She's perfect, Lordawoo."

"Perfect? Well, well." He glanced at his pocket watch. "How many applicants are left out there?"

"Millions! Enough to keep us here past suppertime," Beowulf said, rubbing his tummy forlornly.

"Millions is hyperbole," his sister warned, though she too was getting hungry.

"I estimate two hundred and twelve," Alexander announced, after a brief mental calculation. "At eight minutes per interview, that would mean . . ." He scribbled furiously with his pencil to find exactly how many baby nurse interviews could fit into one afternoon, otherwise known as the afternoon/baby nurse problem.

"Two hundred? Blast!" Lord Fredrick stood and walked the length of the room. "I've no patience for all that helloing and chitchat about diapers! The baby's on his way and there's no time to waste. Incorrigibles, come!" It sounded like he was calling his dogs, but the children bounded over, following him to the far side of the parlor. He crouched to their level and spoke quietly. "What say you, my wolfish wards? Will Mrs. Penworthy do, or not? If she's perfect, we're unlikely to find better, what?"

"I vote yes," said Alexander.

"I vote yes, too," said Beowulf.

"I vote yes times two," said Cassiopeia. "Double yes!"

"It's settled, then." Lord Fredrick strode back across the parlor. "Congratulations, Penworthy! You've got the job."

Mrs. Elsinore "Incognito" Penworthy gave a satisfied smile and adjusted her—that is to say, his—wig. There had been no ladies' shoes in all of Ashton Place into which Simon could cram his generously sized feet. Luckily, the flounce of pink tulle (as you may have guessed, it had briefly served as a tutu before being hastily attached to the bottom of one of Mrs. Clarke's old dresses) added just enough length to keep Simon's boots concealed, as he—that is to say, she—stood tall and gave Lord Fredrick's hand a vigorous shake.

"Well," the lady crooned, with a wink that only the children could see, "that's just ducky, Your Lordship, sir!"

Lord Fredrick gazed up at his new employee, a half head taller than himself. "Incorrigibles, tell Mrs. Clarke to send the rest of the applicants away. We've found our baby nurse, by gum!"

THE EIGHTH CHAPTER

Penelope makes a daring escape.

BACK AT THE BARRACKS, THE Babushkinov twins lost no time in trying to upset Veronika with tales of all she had missed during their walk. "We saw a giant sailing ship that flew in the sky!" they boasted. "We rode in it ourselves! We sailed to Moscow and back within an hour!"

"Liars," the girl said, gazing serenely into the distance. By means of bribery and persuasion and threats, Madame Babushkinov had finally convinced her to stop acting like a coward and get out of bed. Now the child stood pale faced and determined, practicing her pliés. One hand rested on the iron bedframe, and the other arm swooped through the air as she squatted and rose, squatted and rose, over and over again.

"Lay an egg, lay an egg, lay an egg!" her brothers teased as they watched her sink low, knees akimbo.

Veronika completed her descent. "Mama does not love you," she answered on her way up. When she reached her tiptoes, she added, "Neither does Papa. They wish you had never be born!"

The boys' lips trembled, and Veronika flung her arm skyward in smug satisfaction. Their parents were not there to scold them, not that they would have in any case. The captain had gone out for a career-advancing luncheon with some officers he had met. Madame Babushkinov was off attending to her toilette, with a guard stationed outside the bath to ensure her complete privacy.

Penelope sat within earshot of the children's antics, but she scarcely heard them, for she was deep in thought. She was thinking—no, not about the Incorrigibles, or Simon, or the *korablik* or even what to have for lunch—but about a thrilling novel she had once read called *The Count of Monte Cristo*, by Alexandre Dumas. Monsieur Dumas was French, but Penelope had read the book in English, for it was extremely popular and had been translated into many languages. (Monsieur Dumas wrote another, equally popular book called *The Three Musketeers*, although there are more than three musketeers in it. Exactly how many musketeers go into *The Three Musketeers*—you may think of it as the musketeer/musketeer problem—is well worth investigating, but not just now, for Penelope's mind is occupied with *The Count of Monte Cristo*, and for good reason, too.)

In a nutshell, *The Count of Monte Cristo* is the tale of a young sailor named Edmond Dantès. He is falsely accused of treason and sentenced to the dreaded Château d'If, a prison located on a small island in the Mediterranean Sea. Dantès endures fourteen desperate years on that curséd isle, waiting for a window of opportunity to escape. When another prisoner dies, he switches places with the dead body and is buried at sea, after which he swims to freedom and is rescued by friendly smugglers. He travels incognito and assumes one disguise after another. Eventually he acquires a large fortune and reappears in society as the mysterious Count of Monte Cristo.

The rest of the book is devoted to the count's cruel and complex schemes of revenge against those who had falsely accused him in the first place, all of whom end up ruined or dead. Thus the tale ends as so many tales do, happily for some and miserably for others. Edmond Dantès's daring break from an island prison is considered one of the greatest escapes in all of literature to this very day.

Penelope had no interest in revenge, but as a person in the midst of a daring escape herself, *The Count of Monte Cristo* offered food for thought. Just as Edmond Dantès had tricked his captors by pretending to be a dead body, she had tricked the Babushkinovs into bringing her to Saint Petersburg. But now came the more difficult part of her journey, for to get back to England required passage on a ship. "I would gladly hitch a ride with friendly smugglers, as Edmond Dantès did," she thought, "but that business about being buried at sea sounds frightfully cold, and I am not much of a swimmer in any case. . . . My heavens! What is that dreadful row?"

It was Madame Babushkinov. After her toilette, the proud Madame had gone to the common room and imperiously demanded of a lowly soldier that he go and procure buttered rolls and fresh coffee for her and the children. His answer must have displeased her, for her voice cut through the barracks like a siren. "Cash for the commissary, are you mad? I asked for rolls and coffee, not a jewel-encrusted egg! Don't you know who we are? We are the Babushkinovs! Our name is all the credit we need!" It was not long before the scent of fresh rolls and hot coffee filled the air.

Penelope listened and pondered. She thought of the Count of Monte Cristo, and of that other young sailor and master of disguise, Simon Harley-Dickinson. She thought of Lady Constance Ashton and her seamstress, Madame LePoint, who could fashion a new gown in a day. Piece by piece, stitch by stitch, a plan took shape in her mind.

"All I need," she thought, "is a window of opportunity."

By midafternoon Veronika had pliéd to the point of exhaustion. She no longer complained of nerves; in fact, she seemed numb of all feeling except a kind of stone-faced endurance, like a prisoner waiting to be called to the gallows. Any joy she had once taken in dancing had left her, as had her grandiose dreams of being, at twelve years old, the youngest prima ballerina in the history of ballet. Now she simply wanted the ordeal to end. Cranky, hungry, and bone-tired, she demanded to go to her audition at once and get the whole dreadful business over with.

However, the captain had still not returned from his

officers' luncheon, and Madame Babushkinov refused to go anywhere in this strange city without him. Now she was the one overcome with nerves. Veronika's shrill, repeated demand that they leave "right *now*, Mama, right *now*!" had given her a blinding headache, or so Madame claimed. For the past hour she had been lying on her cot. "Agony," she whimpered, again and again. "Agony, agony!"

Penelope offered to go out for ice, a bottle of aspirin, a doctor, anything at all—but Madame insisted that Penelope not leave her side.

"Where is my husband?" she moaned.

"Madame, I will look for him," Penelope volunteered. "I will check every café and gentlemen's club in Saint Petersburg! Of course, that could take hours. . . ." As you see, Penelope was desperately seeking her window of opportunity. All she needed was an excuse to go out and stay out. How hard could it be?

"Yes," Madame said weakly. "All right . . ." Penelope was on her feet in a flash! "I mean no, don't leave me, Miss Lumley! What if I died right here in this horrible barracks, and Ivan was run over by an omnibus, or killed in a duel, heaven forbid? Who would care for the children then?" Madame closed her eyes and thrashed as if she were at death's door. "Oh, Maximilian, my precious baby Max! Now I will never see his sweet round face again! Those chubby hands, those dimpled cheeks . . ."

Exhausted by her own suffering, she began to snore. In despair, Veronika resumed practicing, though by now her legs were like noodles. The twins were horribly jealous to hear Baby Max praised by their mother, and decided to misbehave out of spite. Already they had discovered that the mattresses on their cots were filled with feathers, and they were plucking them out through the mattress ticking, one by one.

Penelope took deep, calming breaths, as she had been taught to do at school. "If Edmond Dantès could wait fourteen years in a cold, dark prison," she told herself, "surely I can hold steady until the captain returns. After all, how long can one luncheon last?"

BUT THE MISSING *PATER* OF the Babushkawoos did not reappear till evening. It was still light out, for Saint Petersburg is so far north on the globe that on the longest days of the year the sun sets only briefly and it never gets dark at all. These are called the White Nights, and they happen in late June and early July, but even in April the sun did not set until eight o'clock, and twilight lasted well past that hour. (Navigators, take note: Saint Petersburg is at sixty degrees north latitude. That is as far north as the lower parts of Alaska, or the Shetland Islands of Scotland, birthplace of the famously brave and rugged Shetland ponies. However, talk of ponies is best saved for later, for Captain Babushkinov has returned, and he seems to be at a rather high latitude himself!)

Yes, the captain was back, and very merry, and had a funny medicinal smell about him. He had spent the afternoon gambling, he said! Playing cards with the officers! He had lost a great deal of money! It was all to the good!

Madame Babushkinov was propped in a chair, a blanket across her lap. Her impatience had long since turned to fury. "Whose money, Ivan?" she asked in a voice like shattering glass. "Exactly *whose* money did you lose?"

"Never mind, never mind." He kissed her sloppily on one cheek. "It is men's business, and nothing for you to worry about."

"There is your business!" Madame pointed at Veronika as if accusing the girl of a crime. "What about her, you fool? She is here to audition for the tsar's own ballet, and you spend the day losing borrowed money at cards?"

"I don't even want to do it anymore!" the girl whined.

"She can't dance anyway, hee hee hee!" the boys said, tickling each other with the feathers.

"Silence!" the captain roared. He looked at Penelope. "You! Yes, you. Governess. Come here."

Penelope did so.

He lowered his deep bass voice, but it was like trying to play softly on a tuba. "Today I had luck," he said. "But it was all bad luck. I owe a great deal of money to one of the generals. My signature was not enough for him. Fool! Coward! But never mind, never mind. It is the way the world is."

He wobbled and seated himself on the edge of the nearest cot. "I must send him a pledge against my debt by midnight tonight. Ah, what have I done?" Groaning, he smacked the tops of his thighs repeatedly. This seemed to calm him, and he looked up at Penelope, a shaggy black dog with bloodshot eyes. "Governess. I need you to bring a small item of great value to the general's house. Can you do that?"

Penelope wanted to skip circles in joy, but she forced herself to speak calmly. "Of course, Captain. I will go at once."

He swiveled his massive head toward his wife.

Madame Babushkinov's lap blanket slipped unnoticed to the floor as she writhed in her chair. "Oh, no you don't, Ivan! No!"

"I will win it back, my darling! Tomorrow, you'll see, my luck will change!"

"No, no, no!" she raged, even as she wrenched the princess's ring off her finger and all but threw it at Penelope. "Fine, here it is. Take it, take it! See if I care! Ivan, you can explain to your mother how you lost her precious emerald at cards!"

"Fortune favors the bold," as the saying goes, but it also favors the patient and prepared, and Penelope was surely that. Here was her chance! On her way out, she stopped in the common room to retrieve her carpetbag, which she had earlier hidden beneath the curtained table that held the samovar. In her pocket was the letter from the Imperial Ballet. Once the Babushkinovs realized the letter was fake, and that their governess had run off, it would not take long to put *dva* and *dva* together, so to speak. The letter was evidence. Later she would burn it.

Meanwhile, she left a note of her own, saying that after her errand was complete, she would spend the night at the Saint Petersburg Home for Poor Bright

Governesses, as she feared it would be too late to return to the barracks alone.

Tolstoy was nowhere to be seen, and she was sorry not to have another chance to speak with the interesting young officer. "But he is a writer, after all," she thought, as she walked quickly—but not too quickly!—to the door. "One day I might discover a book of his in a bookshop, and read it, and that will be very like seeing him again. And who knows? They say writers sometimes base their characters on people they have met. Perhaps there will be some mention of me in his stories."

The thought of being turned into a fictional character amused her. How absurd it would feel! A moment later she was on the street, through the window of opportunity at last. "Adieu, Babushkinovs," she thought, walking briskly, the carpetbag swinging jauntily at her side. "*Arrivederci*, and farewell! But I will not say *do svidaniya*, because I have no expectation of seeing you later, or ever again."

Was it bittersweet for Penelope to part from the horrible Babushkawoos so abruptly, without so much as a good-bye? They had been her students, after all. Did she feel even a tiny tug at her heart to leave these three vile children behind?

In a word, no. She had been a prisoner in their house, just as Edmond Dantès was at the Château d'If. The Babushkinovs had treated her badly and were not one bit sorry about it. She wished them no harm, for that was not her way—but nor did she feel obliged to concern herself with the fate of that unhappy, unpleasant, and unrepentant family. "A Swanburne girl may forgive as she chooses, but she is no pushover, either," she told herself, and felt rather pleased about it, too.

But blast! What to do about this emerald ring, which could easily pay for her voyage home a hundred times over? She waited to examine it until she was ten blocks from the barracks. Then she could not help herself. She paused in a doorway to retrieve it from her pocket and hold it up to the light. The rectangular stone was the size of a domino, set in a thick gold band with delicate swirling patterns engraved on each side. If fire could be green, this was the green it would be: aglow from within and leaping to catch the light.

She returned the gem to her pocket and resumed walking. "The ring is lovely, and no doubt priceless. But I will not steal it, and not only because it would be wrong to do so," she decided. "The stone and setting are much too distinctive not to raise suspicion. If I tried to sell it, the police would be called at once.

Still, I see no harm in borrowing it for a short while. The captain said the general must have it by midnight, which gives me plenty of time."

She turned the corner of Nevsky Prospect and walked toward Theater Square. There it was! The Bolshoi Kamenny theater, home of the Imperial Russian Ballet.

Penelope had long dreamed of visiting the ballet, and knew all about it. For example, she knew that *bolshoi* meant big and *kamenny* meant stone. It had been named the "big stone theater" to avoid getting mixed up with a small wooden theater that stood nearby. "A big stone, just like the emerald in my pocket. I shall take that as a good sign," she thought. "Yet as Agatha Swanburne once cautioned, 'A plan is like a bed: made in the morning, unmade at night.' I must be prepared for whatever happens."

A well-dressed crowd had begun to gather in front of the Bolshoi Kamenny, but she avoided the main entrance and instead made her way to the alley that ran alongside the building. Thank goodness Simon had taught her how theaters work! Here she found the stage door, where the dancers and musicians and stagehands went in and out. She paused for a moment, to prepare. Her Russian would not get her far, but people in the ballet world all spoke French. Admittedly, some time had passed since she had taken French at Swanburne, but how hard could it be to recall a few simple phrases? "*Bonjour* means 'good day,'" she reminded herself. "*Merci beaucoup* means 'thank you very much.' And *fromage* is cheese, which might come in useful if I am offered a snack." The rest would come back as needed, she felt quite sure.

She knocked and waited. Moments later, the stage door opened. A man stood there, already impatient. He had the straight spine of a dancer but wore ordinary clothes and a tool belt, and his close-cropped beard was shot with gray. He did not seem particularly friendly, but perhaps he was just busy. "A stage manager! Just what I need," Penelope thought, for Simon had described the type very well. "A good stage manager is swift and efficient as a London postal worker, and I have no time to waste."

She took a deep breath and began, *en français*: "Good day, mister! I here arrive in look of job. If you please!" She smiled broadly. "I apologize big, very big. My French is old."

He lifted an eyebrow at her odd phrasing and answered in rapid-fire French that she could barely follow. "We have no openings in the corps de ballet, mademoiselle. Or among the principal dancers either, unless you are a *prima ballerina assoluta*, which, no offense, I think you are not." He gave her an appraising look. "Although your posture is not bad. Much better than your French. Good-bye!"

She wedged her carpetbag in the doorway. "Wait, wait, wait," she blurted. "The job I look is sewing. Costumes!" she added, remembering that the French word for costume was, in fact, *costume*.

"Ah, costumes! That's another matter." He glanced over his shoulder. "The wardrobe mistress always needs help. People scarcely know how to sew on a button anymore, it seems. And they call that progress! Come inside and wait. I'll see if she's busy."

"Merci, merci beaucoup," Penelope exclaimed, but he was already gone. She was not entirely sure what the man had said, but it sounded like he was coming back. He had used the word *boutons*, too. This was another good sign, for she was an excellent button sewer, thanks to a class at Swanburne devoted to that very skill.

And look where she was! She wondered—and the wondering made her woozy with hope—whether there was a performance scheduled for that night. The people waiting out front had been nattily dressed, after all.

A moment later the stage manager returned. "Mademoiselle, you're in luck. The wardrobe mistress is in a frenzy mending the costumes for tonight's performance, for they are delicate. If you can so much as hold a needle, you will be put to work at once. Follow me." He sniffed. "I hope you like feathers!"

Backstage at the Bolshoi Kamenny! It was like being inside an enormous beehive, with a constant buzz and people scurrying everywhere—costumers, stagehands, musicians, the choreographer and his many assistants. Penelope wanted to stop and soak up every detail, but the stage manager glided across the stage at a quick floating trot. It was the noiseless gait of someone who had spent long years moving silently in the dark, so as not to disturb the performance.

And there were the ballerinas, warming up. Their hair was slicked back into tight buns that sat high upon their heads, the better to emphasize their extra-long necks. Stage makeup made their eyes look enormous, and their long, knobbly-kneed legs disappeared into wide feathered tutus that bounced comically when they moved. It was as if a whole flock of Berthas had been set loose backstage! But these were not flightless birds. On the contrary, they jumped and soared as if the laws of physics did not apply at all.

"Mademoiselle?" The tap on her shoulder was sharp, the voice pointed. Penelope turned. With a wave of his hand and a few whispered words, the stage manager handed her off to the wardrobe mistress. This lady also wore her hair in a bun, but hers was pure silver. Her gaze was direct but not unkind. She had the uncompromising look of a former dancer, "or a Latin teacher at Swanburne," Penelope thought, suppressing a smile.

"You are here to work?" the woman said, in slow, deliberate French. She mimed the act of sewing. It seemed she had been warned that Penelope was not fluent.

"Yes, thank you." Penelope followed her to the far side of the stage, which was concealed from the audience by rows of heavy curtains. "These must be the wings," she said, remembering what Simon had told her about the world backstage.

"No." The woman scooped an armful of tutus from a bin and dumped them in Penelope's arms. "Not the wings. The feathers."

It was true. All of the tutus were covered with feathers. Apparently the evening's ballet was bird themed, and there were dozens of these fragile tutus on hand. With a brief demonstration, the wardrobe mistress showed Penelope how to stitch fresh feathers to the bare spots. It was simple if ticklish work, and Penelope mastered it quickly. The wardrobe mistress was soon satisfied and left her to carry on unsupervised, for the performance would begin in less than an hour and she had a long to-do list to attend to.

Penelope worked quietly, waiting. When she was certain no one was near, she put down her sewing and examined the rest of the costumes, which were hung on large garment racks by the wall and stored in labeled boxes. There were fancy dresses made of silk and velvet and chiffon, men's breeches and brocade vests, miles of taffeta and endless lengths of ribbon, and countless boxes of tiaras and leather slippers.

"What lavish costumes," she thought. "One could hardly fashion a disguise for a scullery maid or a stow-away out of these elegant fabrics. But for my purposes, they ought to do quite well." She made her selections, and soon she was back at work.

"PLACES! PLACES, PLEASE!" THE STAGE manager called. Moments later, cued by a downward strike of the conductor's baton, the music swelled and filled the theater. Like sailors hoisting a mighty sail, burly stagehands hauled thick ropes hand over hand to roll back the stage curtain, and the performance began.

For those in the audience, it was as if normal time had stopped, as they were transported by the seemingly effortless wonder of it all. For those putting on the show, it was a different matter altogether. For three long hours the orchestra played, the dancers danced, and Penelope sewed as if her life depended on it. Who could have foretold that all those years of stitching pithy wise sayings onto pillows would prove so useful? When anyone came near, she mended tutus. The rest of the time she busied herself sewing a different sort of costume. She had found most of what she needed on the garment racks, but she wanted a heavier fabric to make a warm cloak. Luckily she found a large quantity of attractive red velvet hanging at the edge of the stage.

"In for a kopek, in for a ruble," she told herself as she sliced away at it with a pair of scissors. "That is what Agatha Swanburne would say, if she were here and familiar with Russian currency. If I intend to accomplish my goal—which I do!—I must dive all the way into the pool, so to speak, and not tiptoe 'round the edge."

As she worked, she snuck awestruck glances at the stage. The Imperial Russian Ballet, laid out before her like a picnic! For years she had dreamed of seeing them perform, and naturally she had always imagined herself seated in the theater, like everyone else, but there was something magical about watching the dancers from backstage. The way they transformed into such airy, weightless beings while dancing, when offstage they were all earthbound muscle and sweaty concentration! Truly, it was a marvel.

As for the ballet itself, she was too distracted by her sewing to follow the story closely, but it involved a great many ballerinas dressed as birds doing complicated dance steps. "It rather puts me in mind of Dr. Westminster and his dancing chickens," Penelope thought as she snipped a loose thread with her teeth. The Swanburne veterinarian had a real knack for animal training and had once succeeded in teaching chickens to dance (to be fair, the chickens deserved most of the credit). "But these dancers are far more nimble than chickens, and better fliers, too," she decided. "No wonder their tutus are in constant need of mending."

Penelope sewed and stole glances at the stage, and a part of her wished it would never end, but at last the ballet was over. Now all eyes turned to the footlights, as each dancer came forward to take a bow and bask in the applause. This was her chance. Quickly she hid

behind a garment rack and slipped on the outfit she had fashioned. Her own plain dress she left behind on the rack, on the off chance there might one day be a ballet about governesses. It was unlikely, perhaps, but surely not impossible!

One glance in the backstage mirror confirmed that she was unrecognizable. "A great many *costumes* went into this one costume," she thought, pleased with both her disguise and the potential math lesson, but there was no time to solve the costume/*costumes* problem just now. For the finishing touch, she placed the princess's emerald ring on her finger. She grabbed her carpet-bag (which she had bedecked with feathers, to make it more elegant) and slipped through a door that led to the auditorium. The audience roared and clapped, and she made her way in the darkness to the back of the theater. There she blended in perfectly with the wealthy patrons of the ballet. She applauded with vigor and shouted "brava, brava," just like everyone else.

The prima ballerina was the last to come out, and received twice the applause of everyone else. Her admirers rushed the stage and handed her one bouquet after another, until her arms could barely hold all the flowers. As she bowed low, first to one side of the audience, then to the other, the great red velvet stage curtain closed majestically behind her.

There was a rather large hole at the far end of the curtain that had not been there at the evening's start.

"Whoops! I had best be on my way." Penelope tugged at the red velvet cape she now wore and drew it close 'round her shoulders as she made a hasty bee-line for the exit. It was a pity about the stage curtain, but really, what choice had she had? The weather was brisk, and she could hardly go traipsing around Saint Petersburg without a wrap. "Anyway, a bit of fabric is fair payment for my work on the tutus," she thought, "for I did sew on quite a few feathers!"

IF THERE WAS ONE THING Penelope had learned from Madame Babushkinov, it was this: people are often judged by their clothing in the same way that a book is judged by its cover.

And if there were two things Penelope had learned from Madame Babushkinov, the other one was this: when powerful-seeming people behave badly and demand to be waited upon and obeyed, very often they will get their way. For it is a rare, brave soul who will stand up to a figure of authority in high dudgeon, a fact that Penelope now hoped to take advantage of.

To that end, the costume she had fashioned was

designed not for warmth or comfort, but solely to impress. The gold satin skirt was wrapped and layered like a flaky golden pastry from a Parisian bakery. (Her inspiration had been the legendary tarte Philippe, a delicious confection, far more delicious than other desserts; in fact, it is the most delicious dessert ever invented.) The bodice was a deep-green silk embroidered with gold thread, and fitted snugly around her waist. Fur cuffs edged each long emerald sleeve, and the cape of thick red velvet fell from her shoulders like, well, a curtain. It cascaded to the ground and swirled elegantly about her feet. A tiara sparkled upon her head, and the emerald ring glittered on her hand. The ring was key. She could claim to be royalty and no one would question it, as long as she wore that ring!

"Now I shall put my theory to the test," she thought. Outside the theater, dozens of carriages were lined up at the curb. She chose the most elegant among them and lingered nearby, waiting for its owners to approach. They were a handsome middle-aged couple, very prosperous looking. The lady wore a long fur coat, the gentleman a gleaming silk top hat. He inclined his head toward his companion and spoke excitedly in Russian. The lady laughed in answer.

"A marvelous performance!" Penelope interjected as

they passed by. She spoke in poshly accented English. She did not care if her words were understood; her accent, dress, and jewelry would be doing the talking for her.

The couple looked at her, uncertain. She fluttered a hand toward them, as if waving to her subjects. At the sight of the emerald ring, their puzzled expressions disappeared and they began fawning on her shamelessly, for surely this was an English princess on holiday!

"Yes, it was magnificent," the lady replied in crisp English.

Her companion bowed low. "My lady, do us the honor to share our carriage. Let us drop you at your hotel. Where are you staying?"

In a perfect imitation of Lady Constance Ashton, Penelope let out a trilling laugh. "The finest hotel in Saint Petersburg, of course!"

"The Grand Hotel, of course! There is no other like it in the world!" the man exclaimed. He waved off their coachman so that he might personally help Penelope into the carriage. During the short ride, they pressed many invitations upon her—to parties, to the opera, to the spectacular dacha of a wealthy male friend, a very eligible bachelor!—but Penelope said no, as she was leaving town "quite soon. Family business," she explained.

"Back to England, then," the gentleman declared. Jovially he added, "The work of royalty is never done, eh?" He seemed to be fishing for some clue as to her title, rank, and connections.

Penelope merely smiled.

THE GRAND HOTEL SURELY LIVED up to its name. It was the length of a city block and could have easily been mistaken for a palace. Penelope's dazzled companions insisted on walking her through the lobby. It was good manners, true, but also they wanted to be seen with her. They kept swiveling their eyes this way and that to discover who in Saint Petersburg society might notice them with their new royal friend and start some fantastic rumor as a result.

When at last they bade her farewell at the reception desk, Penelope did not say thank you. Instead she dismissed them coolly with a nod, as if she had done them a favor by gracing them with her presence, even for a short while.

After they had gone, she addressed the clerk. Carelessly she laid her hand upon the desk to show off the emerald ring, and she spoke in the most imperious tone she could manage. "I require a room, if you please."

"You shall have our finest, my lady!" The clerk was goggle eyed at the jewel. "Under whose name shall I put your account?"

"I would prefer not to say whose name, so as not to draw attention to myself," she replied, "but if you must know, I am a close cousin of my nation's queen. You may put the room charges to her account, but I would prefer you did not gossip about it, sir!"

"Your nation's queen?" He looked puzzled. "Do you mean—"

"Queen Victoria, yes, of course!" she said, nearly yelling. "The Queen of England, though I have no wish to make that publicly known." She gave him a withering look. "I do hope you are trustworthy, sir! It is so difficult to hire trustworthy employees. My father, the Duke of—well, I would rather not mention what he is the duke of, so as not to draw attention to myself. Let me just say that my father complains about the help most bitterly! His master of hounds is afraid of dogs. His steward cannot recall the multiplication tables. It is a frightful inconvenience."

"I think I know your father," the clerk blurted. "Is he the Duke of Derby?"

"He very well may be," she snapped. "Now find me

a room at once. I have had an exceedingly long day."
It was a curious feeling, to carry on with absolutely no
concern for other people. To say there was no fun in it
would be untrue; on the other hand, she had no wish
to make it a habit. "I warn you, sir, I can be a stickler
when it comes to my accommodations. I imagine you
know the story of the princess and the pea?"

"No, my lady," he squeaked in fear.

"Well, never mind," she said, realizing her error.
Telling a story to better explain her meaning was
something a governess would do, and at the moment
she was no governess. Great royal ladies did not seek
to be understood. They sought to be obeyed.

"Have fresh flowers brought in, first thing," she
commanded. "I cannot bear to rise from bed without
fresh flowers in the room. And chocolates!"

"Yes, my lady." This kind of talk seemed not to surprise him at all. "Fresh flowers and chocolates. I hope
our royal suite will please you." He jotted it all on his
pad. "How long will you be staying with us?"

"Regrettably, I cannot stay long," she said, and she did
regret it, for it seemed a shame to spend only one night
in such a marvelous place. "I must return to England as
soon as possible. Find out what vessels sail tomorrow,
and book my passage on the first one to leave."

This was the whole point of her plan, of course. She intended to obtain passage to England without having to pay a single kopek, all by impersonating a lady of great wealth and royal relations. That those who were most able to pay their way were the least likely to be asked to was ironic, to be sure. Imagine if she had appeared at the Grand Hotel in her plain brown governess's dress and demanded a royal suite charged to Queen Victoria's account! She would have been shown the door at once.

For now, at least, the hotel clerk was convinced. "As you wish, my lady. One passage to England, first ship out. I shall confer with the harbormaster. Will you require anything else?

When she opened her mouth to answer, it nearly blossomed into a yawn. The clock that hung on the wall said it was nearly eleven thirty—an alarmingly late bedtime for Miss Penelope Lumley, but just another night at the ballet for a cousin of Queen Victoria!

"I would like a pot of strong tea," she replied, "a small box with tissue paper in it, and a trusted messenger, for I have an important errand that must be taken care of right away." The princess's ring had performed brilliantly. Now she would have it delivered to the general's house by midnight, as promised. The

Babushkinovs were late risers, and she had already told them she would spend the night at the Saint Petersburg Home for Poor Bright Governesses. By the time they realized their own governess was not coming back, she would be out to sea, on her way home, at last!

"Tea, certainly. Messenger, right away! All expenses to be charged to the account of Victoria, Queen of England. . . ." The hotel clerk muttered as he wrote it all down. "Including your passage to England?"

She graced him with a small, royal smile. "Of course. I know my cousin will be grateful for your service." At this the man blushed and stammered so much, he could barely find the key to the royal suite, but at last he did. The messenger was already waiting. Penelope stole a final glance at the emerald ring before tucking it safely into the box and handing it over, with her instructions.

"The true value of such objects is their beauty, which can never be gambled away," she thought, watching the man go. "Still, I wish the captain good luck with his angry general!"

In that moment, despite all that had happened, she finally did think of the unhappy Babushkinov family with something like forgiveness. Possibly it was because she was too tired to be cross, and would soon be leaving Russia in any case. Or perhaps kindness and forgiveness were so much a part of her nature that they kept popping to the surface, like one of those cheerful yellow bath duckies they have nowadays. They can be held underwater by force, but their true nature is to float, and they will always find a way to do so when given the chance.

"Yes, I wish them all the best of luck." She fought back another yawn and was grateful she had any sort of bed to sleep in that night. "May they learn that their family can be as happy or unhappy as they choose to be!"

THE NINTH CHAPTER

A messenger is blamed, but
fairly.

AND THAT IS HOW MISS Penelope Lumley, once a Poor Bright Female and later a lowly governess in a grand house, attended the Imperial Russian Ballet from a seat closer than any royal box, and spent a night in the finest suite of the most luxurious hotel in Saint Petersburg. Saint Petersburg, the capital of all of Russia! A city known for its opulence!

The sleepy pretend princess was escorted to her rooms by a fleet of crisply dressed bellboys and hotel maids. They offered to hang up her clothes, close the drapes, open the windows, turn down the bed, pour champagne, run a hot bath, and so on, but Penelope dismissed them all with a bleary-eyed wave.

Alone at last in the royal suite! In other circumstances she could have spent hours admiring the fine antiques, the priceless art, and even the jewel-encrusted eggs lined up proudly in a gilded cabinet: a royal chicken coop for some very unusual chickens. So much of the decor was plated in gold, it was as if King Midas himself had been a guest here and carelessly laid his hands on everything within reach.

At the moment, however, Penelope's only wish was to wrestle herself out of that absurd outfit and into her own plain flannel nightdress before nodding off. She laid the gown neatly over a stunning Louis XV gilt wood armchair that would nowadays be in a museum. She removed her tiara and placed it on the head of the gold-leafed marble cherub that served as one of the bedposts. "I shall wear my royal costume again in the morning, to board whatever magnificent ship bound for England the clerk has booked passage on," she thought, giving the cherub a fond pat on the cheek. The stone child's face looked a bit like Cassiopeia when she was sleeping. "And I must remember to be rude and bossy for the whole voyage. Truly, acting a part is a great deal of work! Perhaps it grows easier with practice. I will have to ask Simon about it—*yawn!*—when I get home."

In this sleepy but optimistic spirit, she climbed into the high, wide bed, slipped between sheets of pure satin, and laid her head on a pillow stuffed with eiderdown. This was no princess-and-the-pea type situation. The mattress was soft as a cloud, and the bed's exhausted occupant slept so deeply and so well that no dreams dared disturb her.

But alas, and woe! The fulcrum of fortune has a way of seesawing from one condition to its opposite with no warning, like a sudden squall on an otherwise balmy day. It was all because of the messenger. (Those of you who are familiar with the saying "Don't blame the messenger" may protest. However, facts are facts, and no one ought to object if just this once the messenger is blamed, for indeed it was his fault.)

In a nutshell: Not everyone is as honest as our dear Miss Lumley. The messenger's curiosity about the contents of the little box got the better of him, and he peeked. Once he saw the gem inside, his promise to deliver the box to the general's house by midnight was forgotten. The messenger had some urgent gambling debts of his own to pay, and he knew of a broker who bought valuable items for cash, no questions asked.

This broker would not mind being awoken at midnight if there was some quick and profitable business at hand!

Straight to the broker the messenger dashed. Midnight came and went. At one o'clock in the morning, a square-jawed private arrived at the barracks, roused Captain Babushkinov, and informed him that the furious general had challenged him to a duel. Pistols at dawn!

The captain was mightily upset. He was upset that his sleep had been interrupted, and more upset to learn about the theft of the ring, but he was most upset about the duel. To get shot was a bad outcome, and so was shooting a general, so the thing was bound to end badly no matter what. Madame Babushkinov insisted that the police be called. She had an eye for jewelry and was able to describe the stolen ring in perfect detail between bouts of tearful yelling, "That thief of a governess! Thank goodness we still have our good name, which no one can ever take from us!"

The always-fascinating sound of grown-ups fighting soon woke the Babushkawoos. The twins could not follow what was going on but challenged the amused private to a duel by hurling their nightcaps at his feet. He had made their mother cry: an insult that could not go unanswered!

Veronika eavesdropped more carefully, for she assumed all the shouting must have to do with her. Once she understood that no, it was because her governess had been exposed as a criminal, it was as if a weight had been lifted from her, and she began to think more clearly than before. Quietly, and unnoticed by the others, she looked everywhere for the precious letter from the ballet. It was gone. She alone put *dva* and *dva* together, but she said nothing, for the grown-ups were still arguing about the ring and the duel.

Yet the discovery that there was no audition, had never been an audition, and would never be an audition was such a jolt to her system that it caused her to have what is known as an epiphany. (The exact nature of her life-changing insight was Veronika's business alone. Perhaps someday she would write her own book about it, just as that young Tolstoy fellow would write his. For now, it is enough to know that the girl smiled, yawned, and stretched like an ordinary child, not a dancer. Then she went back to bed, where she slept more soundly than she had in many months.)

As for the ring, the shady characters who dealt in stolen items were well known to the Saint Petersburg police, and officers were dispatched to interview them all. It was now nearly three in the morning, and the particular broker we are concerned with was snoring in bed, but a policeman pounding on the door got him up again. He denied knowing anything about a ring with a green stone, a red stone, a polka-dot stone, or any other type of stone, and made outraged protests about the late hour, the absurd accusation, the mud trampled on his clean floor by the policemen's dirty boots!

The officers looked around, opening drawers, emptying closets, and making a dreadful mess. Eventually they left, with a threat to return in the morning and search the whole place twice as thoroughly in the daylight.

Now painfully awake, the broker drank a strong black coffee and rued his change of fortune. A stroke of good luck had brought him a midnight visit from a debt-ridden messenger with a valuable ring. The desperate fellow had been glad to accept a tenth of the jewel's worth. Money was exchanged, and now the ring belonged to the broker. If he sold it for even half its value, what a profit he would make! But the tide of luck had already turned. There was no longer a chance of selling the ring for even a single kopek without ending up in jail, not with the police already searching for it.

What should the broker do? In such a predicament,

many would fall prey to a mixed-up way of thinking called the "sunk cost fallacy," which is best explained by telling a brief story. Imagine you have been sent to sell your family's cow at the market, but instead you trade the cow for a handful of beans. (If you happen to also imagine that your name is Jack, and you are a character in a fairy tale involving giants and magic beanstalks, that is entirely your business.)

Here is where the sunk cost fallacy comes in. "Fallacy" means a mistaken belief, and "sunk cost" means money that is already spent. Thus, the sunk cost fallacy is the mistaken belief that the money you once paid for something has anything to do with what it might now be worth. In other words, a fistful of beans does not become valuable simply because you paid a cow for them. The cow is a sunk cost, and the beans must be taken on their own merits. Perhaps they are magic, perhaps not. Perhaps a beanstalk will grow to the clouds and an adventure with giants will ensue. Or perhaps you will slurp a last bowl of watery bean soup and long for the days when your family owned a cow, from which you could get milk and soothing lowing and soft-eyed companionship, at least.

The broker in stolen goods was a criminal, but he was also a businessman, and he knew all about the sunk cost fallacy. The money he had paid for the ring mere hours before? Sunk as a shipwreck at the bottom of the sea! The dream of great profits that had danced through his head as he slept? Gone and forgotten! He wasted no time whining about his losses, or imagining there was some way to recapture the ring's value. Now his only wish was to avoid getting carted off to jail. He put the ring in its box, woke up one of his own servants, and ordered the man to take the box back to the messenger who had brought it to him in the first place.

"But he'll be asleep," the servant groggily objected. He was none too pleased to be sent out at that hour himself.

"I don't care if he's dead! Wake him up," the broker ordered, "and tell him to retrace his steps. He must take this worthless rock back to wherever he stole it from. Right away! Before we all end up in Siberia!"

The broker's servant did as he was told. The hotel messenger was not asleep at all but pacing his room in his nightclothes. He had rid himself of his debts, which was good news. The bad news? He was so racked with guilt about stealing the ring that he had already decided to flee Saint Petersburg at dawn and make a new life for himself elsewhere.

But now the accurséd box had returned! The sight of it struck fear in his heart. "It is an albatross 'round my neck!" he protested, but he also did as he was told. With his coat hastily thrown over his nightclothes and his feet in slippers, he raced back to the hotel and left the box at the front desk, addressed to the mysterious young lady in the royal suite, the unnamed cousin of England's queen.

The next day he failed to report to work, and the day after as well. On the third day, the Grand Hotel replaced him with another, more trustworthy employee. (What became of the poor fellow is another story, and would make a fine Russian novel, full of bad choices, pointless suffering, and lives ruined for no good reason. For now, it is enough to say that his brush with thievery taught him much about crime and punishment, and the dangers of thinking that doing a wrong thing "just this once" makes it somehow less wrong. As Agatha Swanburne once said, "A conscience is like a treasure map. You must follow it to the very end, if you wish to profit from it!")

WHAT A NIGHT IT HAD turned out to be! The back-and-forth of the emerald ring was enough to put one in mind of the children's game called hot potato, which

232

has nothing to do with cooked spuds or even warm globes. Broadly speaking, a "hot potato" is an item that no one wants. The princess's emerald ring had become just such a potato. As a result, neither the Babushkinovs nor the general and the square-jawed private who worked for him, nor the Saint Petersburg police, nor the broker in stolen goods, his servant, or the hotel messenger whose fault it all was got much sleep.

However, Miss Penelope Lumley snoozed through the whole business and knew nothing about it. Before dawn she rose, put on her royal costume, and packed up her feathered carpetbag. Then she waited, ready to board whatever ship of luxury the hotel had found for her, and the sooner, the better.

At six o'clock sharp, there was a knock at her door. There stood a fresh-faced bellboy. Her first thought was that he looked barely older than Alexander Incorrigible.

"I have your flowers, your grace," the boy said, out of breath. The bouquet was so large he could barely carry it. "And your chocolates."

In all her weary playacting, she had forgotten about ordering these things, but their arrival reminded her to get "back in character," so to speak. She stepped aside so the boy might come in and set down the vase.

"Thank you—that is to say, tut-tut! The Cockney flower girls of London sell nicer flowers than these!" The boy gave her a receipt to sign for the items. In her haste, she signed *P. Lumley.* She realized her error at once but thought it best not to make a fuss over crossing it out, as it would simply draw attention to the name, and she would soon be safely at sea in any case.

After handing him his fountain pen and the receipt, she popped a whole chocolate in her mouth all at once, as she had often seen Lady Constance do. "Now, young sir," she said with difficulty, for it turned out to be a gooey one, with a sticky caramel center. "I wish to know what time my ship leaves."

But the capable young man was already holding the ticket. "It's right here, your grace," he said.

"Hmm," she replied, trying to sound displeased. She examined the ticket: first-class passage on the *Royal Amsterdam,* the finest Dutch clipper ship to sail the northern waters, leaving promptly at ten o'clock! She could hardly have asked for better.

"Royal Amsterdam, hah! A mere tugboat," she scoffed. "I will endure it, I suppose. But I need a carriage to take me to the dock."

"Already arranged, my lady!"

"Is that so?" She forced herself to frown as she

swallowed the last of the chocolate. "In that case, have a hearty breakfast brought to my room. A bowl of hot porridge would hit the spot, with a spoonful of jam— why, what is that in your hand?"

"This package was at the front desk for you." Proudly he held out the little box. "I'll see to your breakfast right away—"

"Wait." Penelope's fingers went cold as she opened the box. There was the emerald ring, with the tissue paper carelessly crumpled around it! "This was to be delivered to a general's house last night," she said, handing it back to him. "Clearly it was not. I should not have trusted that messenger!"

The cheerful bellboy clicked his heels together in the Russian fashion. "Shall I deliver it somewhere for you now, your grace?"

"I'm afraid it is too late. And no time for breakfast, either. Blast!" Hot porridge would have been lovely, but not today. No doubt all the police in Saint Petersburg were looking for her, or soon would be. She grabbed her red velvet cloak and feathered carpetbag. "I shall need that carriage at once."

"Your grace, the ship doesn't sail until ten."

"Too late!" She was already striding down the hall. The bellboy scampered behind. "But it is the only luxury passenger ship to leave today."

"Never mind luxury!" she retorted. "I don't care what kind of ship is it. I must leave the city, now. What is the very next vessel to leave Saint Petersburg?"

The boy looked as if he might cry. "I'm sorry, I don't know, your grace!"

Poor child! She took pity on him and dropped her imperious tone. "Of course you do not. How could you? You are not the harbormaster, after all. However, you are an excellent bellboy and will no doubt achieve great things in life, if you apply yourself! For now, just get me to the street, but not through the hotel lobby, where we will be seen—is there a side door? Through the kitchen, perhaps?"

The bewildered bellboy did as she asked. Before long they had slipped out to the street through a service door. The boy put his fingers to his lips and whistled sharply to hail a carriage. The first to stop was not one of the fine carriages that picked up the hotel's wealthy guests, but a simple horse-drawn wagon, more suited to delivering goods to the kitchen. At the moment, the wagon was full of beets.

Penelope clambered up next to the driver, as it was the only place to sit. "Take me to the waterfront, right away," she said. At the driver's blank look, she made swimming motions, to no avail.

The puzzled driver spoke to the bellboy in Russian and made concerned gestures toward his cargo. After a brief negotiation, the bellboy prevailed. He turned to Penelope.

"He wants to know which dock, your ladyship?"

"Wherever I am likely to find a ship putting out to sea right now." The boy translated. By now the sun had risen, and Penelope's fear made her impatient. "Let's go! *Ah-deen, dva, tree!*" she said to the driver. Obligingly he started the horses at a trot.

"But your grace! The box!" The bellboy broke into a run and chased after the moving wagon. With a strong overhead toss, he threw the box at Penelope. Countless games of playing hot potato with the Incorrigible children had honed her reflexes. Without thinking, she caught the box with both hands.

"To be found with this emerald is the last thing I need!" she exclaimed, and tossed it back to the bellboy.

Determined, the boy threw it to the driver, in whose lap it landed. The annoyed driver shoved it at Penelope and kept his eyes on the road.

"Very well, but we must hurry." She grabbed the reins and gave them a hard shake. "Hey-a, hey-a!" she called to the horses. "Now, *gallop!*"

Obediently the horses took off. Penelope was nearly knocked out of her seat. But there was a traffic jam not far ahead, and the driver cursed in Russian as he pulled the sweating team to a hard stop. An angry general waving a pistol was being pursued through the intersection by an even angrier pair of little Russian boys, who were in turn being pursued by their parents: a hysterical, well-dressed woman and a tall, imposing captain with a bandage tied 'round his head, though the wound was clearly no more than a scratch.

"It is the Babushkinovs!" Penelope cried. She jumped down from her seat into the wagon itself, to hide among the beets. Alas, the wagon was a rickety wooden affair. The force of her landing was enough to split the boards in two.

"Beets!" Madame Babushkinov cried in horror as the spilled beets tumbled in a river of red across the road.

Penelope hung on to the railing with one hand and wedged her feet on either side of the split. The little box was in her other hand. Thinking quickly, she threw it high in the air. "Hot potato!" she cried, to get their attention. The twins' heads whipped upward, searching.

"I have it!" yelled Boris.

"I have it!" yelled Constantin, shouting over his brother.

The twins raced to be first to catch the box, but the beets were rolling underfoot. At the same moment, the two boys flailed and tripped. Distracted by their cries, their mother also lost her balance on the sea of beets and ended up sprawled on her backside in the road, as the soaring emerald ring reached the top of its flight, paused, then dropped fantastically from the sky and landed in her lap.

Penelope kept low and out of sight in the broken wagon. The spilled beets had stopped all the other traffic, and in the chaos and distraction, her driver had found an opening and gotten them through.

She peeked between the wooden slats at the scene they were leaving behind. Madame Babushkinov held the ring aloft in triumph, as the confused general and her equally confused husband stood nearby. "Ivan Victorovich, look!" she cried. "Your mother's ring, dropped from heaven itself! We have been saved! Saved by the beets!"

THE RICKETY WAGON TURNED DOWN one street and then another. Penelope was still hanging on in the back and could not see where they were going, but they were surely heading toward the sea, for the smell of the cold salt air grew stronger by the minute.

She drew a deep breath. The sea air was nourishing and gave her hope. "My costume has been spoiled by all this rolling around in a beet wagon, and I no longer have the ring," she thought, "but a first-class ticket for the *Royal Amsterdam* will serve as proof of my wealthy connections. With it, I will easily convince some captain or other to take me on as a passenger."

The wagon stopped. "Phew!" the driver exclaimed, holding his nose. Even the horses tossed their heads and snorted in distaste.

"If you mean that something smells fishy around here, I quite agree," Penelope said, climbing out. The whole place stank of fish. A look at the vessels preparing to set sail revealed why. These were no luxury schooners. The beet-wagon driver had taken her where the fishing boats berthed, for those were the very first boats to leave Saint Petersburg each day.

"There has been an unfortunate misunderstanding," she said to the driver, "for these are all fishing boats, yet I am a passenger, not a fish, obviously. I wonder if you might possibly take me to a different dock?"

The driver glared and let out a stream of angry

words in Russian. His meaning was along the lines of "Listen, Princess Whoever-You-Are, I've brought you where you said you wanted to go. Now I expect to be paid for the ride, plus the cost of fixing my broken wagon. And don't forget about my lost beets! That's a sunk cost I can never get back!"

Penelope understood not a word, but the fellow's tone was plain as day. And it was clear from the way he kept slapping one open palm with the back of his other hand that he wanted money. She gave him a winning smile. "Please submit your bill to the Grand Hotel of Saint Petersburg, to be charged to my account—"

"*Nyet!*" he roared, and took a threatening step toward her.

"My good sir, you shall be paid, I promise—but not just yet," she said, and bolted. The driver shouted and shook his fist, but he could not give chase without leaving his horses, and after losing his beets he had no wish to lose his animals as well.

Penelope ran in a zigzag, ducking behind crates and heaps of coiled rope as she made her way to the ships. At the far end of the dock, a Norwegian trawler was being loaded with provisions. "The Incorrigibles would use their noses to discover what these wooden casks contain, and so can I, if I concentrate," she thought, sniffing her way along. "I smell fresh water, salt, hard-tack, and sauerkraut. And all these empty barrels were once filled with"—she sniffed deeply, to sort it out from the general fishy smell of the dock—"not sole, not flounder, but herring, if I am not mistaken. . . . Empty barrels! Eureka!"

She glanced about to make sure no one was watching, but the crew was hard at work, preparing to set sail. She pried the top off an empty barrel and began to climb in. "One leg at a time, and never mind the dress, which is already ruined," she thought. "But, hmm! There is something inside this barrel after all . . . perhaps if I give a small kick to dislodge the contents . . ."

"Ah!" cried the barrel, or rather, the man it contained. Penelope withdrew in a flash. The fellow stood with effort and blinked his eyes in the early-morning light, for he had been hiding in the dark for an hour already. He stared at Penelope in horror.

"Albatross!" he wailed. "The albatross has returned!"

"I know you." Penelope gave him a hard look. "Aren't you the messenger from the Grand Hotel who was supposed to deliver that small box to a general's house? There has been a great deal of trouble because of you."

"Yes, it is all my fault!" the messenger replied in

despair, for indeed it was the same fellow. "I was in terrible debt, sick with worry, and when I saw that precious jewel I lost my head. I never should have peeked! What a fool I was, to think that committing a crime would improve my situation. Now I must flee Saint Petersburg or else die of shame." His eyes filled with tears, but it might have been from the overpowering smell of herring. "I have always had bad luck. I was born to cold, unhappy parents who preferred my brother to me. Later I fell in with the wrong companions—"

Penelope interrupted him. "This is no time for a Russian novel, sir. The ship will soon set sail, and two stowaways on board is one stowaway too many. I must ask you to leave."

He started to protest but soon gave up, since it was all his fault to begin with. Sadly he climbed out of the barrel, like a hermit crab being evicted from a favorite shell. Fishy tears rolled down his cheeks.

The man was pessimax personified. Penelope could not help feeling sorry for him. "Take heart, sir. Your luck is about to improve. Look." She reached into her carpetbag and produced a ticket.

He read it, and his eyes grew wide. "First-class passage on the *Royal Amsterdam*?"

"It will be more comfortable than traveling in—ugh!—one of these barrels, I assure you." With a grunt, Penelope climbed in. "The ship leaves at ten o'clock. Let your actions be blameless until then! As Agatha Swanburne once said, 'Anyone can be good for a minute. Multiply by sixty and the hours will take care of themselves.' Now, if you will hand me my carpetbag, thank you! And be so kind as to fasten the lid. . . ."

The messenger whose fault it all was bowed low, amazed—how quickly one's life could change! He placed the lid on the barrel and ran off, clutching the precious ticket.

AND THAT IS HOW MISS Penelope Lumley, so recently a guest in the royal suite of a hotel as grand as its name, gave away her first-class ticket on the *Royal Amsterdam* clipper and became a stowaway on a Norwegian fishing ship bound for who knows where, traveling in the least grand, dirtiest, and most herring-scented accommodations imaginable.

It had been a rough ride to board the ship—the barrel had been tipped on its side and rolled across a wooden ramp to the deck, then righted and lined up with all the others. During the ordeal, she had imagined herself as Edith-Anne Pevington from the

Giddy-Yap, Rainbow! books she had loved so much as a child. Edith-Anne's knack for breaking wild ponies to the saddle was demonstrated many times in the series, but there was always a great deal of bucking and kicking to endure. Once or twice the fictional heroine was tossed off, to land with her face in the fictional dirt. It was not exactly like being rolled in a barrel, but it was close enough to keep Penelope from panicking till the banging and tumbling were over.

Now, somewhat recovered, she considered her options. "It is only a matter of time before I am found out. Better to announce my presence than wait to be discovered," she decided. "But first we must get far enough from shore that they would not consider turning back. Fishermen are honest, hardworking folk. I expect they will treat me fairly, once they learn I am 'along for the ride,' so to speak."

And so she waited, for an hour, or perhaps two. It was woefully uncomfortable. Worse, some feathers from her carpetbag had come loose and were floating around the barrel in time to her breath, threatening to make her sneeze. She fought the urge for as long as she could, but as Agatha Swanburne once said (the wise founder had a terrible head cold at the time), "Sooner or later, every sneeze will have its day, *ah-choo!*"

245

"Ah—ah—ah-choo!" Penelope managed to wriggle one hand over her mouth, but it was too late. A moment later the lid of the barrel was pried off, revealing a circle of blue sky that was instantly eclipsed by a man, peering in. His pale complexion and round face would have made him a dead ringer for the man in the moon, if the moon had wispy blond hair, bright blue eyes, and a puzzled expression.

He blurted some strong words of surprise in his native tongue. Soon a whole constellation of faces appeared, all looking down at Penelope.

"Good morning," she said.

"God morgen!" the moon-faced man replied. The rest laughed.

Penelope tried to stand, but her legs had fallen asleep. As she flailed, several strong arms reached into the barrel to help. With their aid, she rose like a jack-in-the-box, swaying unsteadily as her eyes adjusted to the light.

"Good morning!" She spoke more confidently now that she was upright and could breathe properly. "I am on your boat quite by accident, for which I apologize. We shall have to make the best of it." Before her stood a dozen men with fair, red-cheeked complexions and eyes in a permanent squint. They were dressed in work

pants and thick knitted sweaters and caps. A few wore bibbed overalls made of oilcloth. All were blond and tall and broad shouldered as Vikings.

"I would like to speak with your captain." She reached up to nudge her bent tiara back in place. It had taken quite a beating in the barrel. "Tell him that a close relative of England's queen is aboard this . . . this . . ." She glanced at the weatherworn decks, the mended sails and seaweed-encrusted ropes, and of course the stink of fish was everywhere, but she thought it best to be polite. "This fine, seaworthy vessel."

The men must have understood at least some of her meaning, for they began talking excitedly among themselves. *"Kaptein, ja! Kaptein Strøm!"* they agreed. Two lifted her out of the barrel as if she weighed no more than the air, and they gently guided her with their rough hands and tattooed forearms as she took one wobbly landlubber's step after another, to the captain's cabin.

CAPTAIN ROLF STRØM WAS A man of few words who worked fiercely hard for a living. He knew the value of money, which is to say he knew exactly how many tons of herring he and his men had to draw from the sea every week in order to make a profit. The idea of trying to get something for nothing offended him to the core, and he made this very clear.

"Stowaway!" He pointed at Penelope. Then he ran his finger across his throat.

Penelope gulped, adjusted her rumpled velvet cloak, and tried once more to convince the captain, through pantomime and whatever words in English or French he seemed to recognize, that she was not a stowaway precisely, but more of an accidental passenger, and that the Queen of England would pay generously for her safe passage home, but Captain Strøm was not born yesterday, as the saying goes. He knew a liar when she was sitting in front of him, wrapped in a filthy piece of stage curtain and balancing a broken costume crown on her head.

"We no go to England," he said. "We go where fish go."

"A small detour?" she begged.

"The fish," he said, leaning back in his chair, "do not catch themselves."

His reply had the pithy wisdom of Agatha Swanburne, and who could argue? Luckily for Penelope, back on land Captain Strøm was the doting father to a houseful of tall, strong-limbed daughters, and it was not in his great Nordic heart to toss her overboard. He would provide his accidental passenger with a private bunk, as she was the only female on board, but otherwise she would enjoy the same creature comforts that he and his crew did. Which is to say, none.

Her bed was a thin blanket spread across a wooden shelf. Her tattered dress was no match for the blustery winds at sea. She was given a spare set of cabin boy's clothes that were only a little too large for her: a pair of wide-legged cotton duck trousers, and a thick knitted sweater and cap, just as the crew wore. If not for these, she would have been chilled to the bone.

"The way royal ladies are expected to dress is terribly inconvenient," she thought, once she had changed into this warmer and far more comfortable uniform. "I wonder how Queen Victoria manages it? I do hope she gets a day off now and then, and can run about playing with the dogs on the lawn in sensible footwear and a warm hat."

After a bit of practice walking in trousers, which she rather liked once she got used to it, she ventured on deck. "Alf!" one of the sailors barked. Soon others did the same. "Alf! Alf!" Worried, she glanced at the sky to see if the moon was full—was this ship also under some sort of wolf curse? But it turned out the first mate's name was Alf. Everyone was afraid of the *kaptein*, who said little, but all the sailors liked Alf. He was one of the few aboard who had learned a bit of English during his travels, although his favorite word seemed to be "Nope." He greeted Penelope with a friendly smile.

"Nope," he said, by way of greeting. He managed to introduce himself and the others and compliment her on her uniform. "Nice pants," he said, patting his own, for now Penelope was dressed like the rest of the crew.

"Alf," she said, once she realized they could converse, "can you tell me the name of this ship?" The other men had gone back to swabbing out the dories, stacking them neatly one inside the next. There the little rowboats would sit like Russian nesting dolls, until morning came and it was time to fish once more.

"Nope," he said, and added, *"Eikenøtt."*

To Penelope's ear it sounded like "I cannot." She frowned, for to give an answer of "I cannot" when asked a direct question struck her as rude. "I beg your pardon," she said firmly, "but if I am going to be sailing among you, surely you can tell me the name of the ship."

Alf explained her question to the others, who performed their answer as a charade. They made little squirrel faces, nibbling away with imaginary buck teeth, while holding their paws—that is to say, hands—in front of them.

"Eikenøtt," Alf said, gesturing to his men. "What *ekorn* eat."

"Ekorn?" Penelope repeated. "Do you mean squirrels and acorns?" It took a bit more nibbling, whisker stroking, and tail twitching to establish that by *ekorn* the fishermen meant squirrel, while *eikenøtt* seemed to be the Norwegian word for acorn.

"Acorn! That is a curious name for a ship," she said, but the name pleased her all the same, since it reminded her of home.

That night she struggled to find a comfortable position in which to sleep. Imagine the luxurious cruise she might have taken if not for that foolish messenger! All those tasty chef-prepared meals, the well-appointed stateroom, the soft, silk-sheeted bed! Instead, here she was on the good ship *Acorn,* in a bunk that was as small and hard as a nutshell and not nearly as cozy as a squirrel nest in the treetops would be.

But then she thought of Nutsawoo, and her heart swelled. Any discomfort would be worth getting back to Ashton Place. As soon as she was able, she vowed to give his tiny, not-too-bright head as many head scratches as he—or she—wanted, and some tasty *eikenøtts,* too.

The Tenth Chapter

*Nothing is more sealike than
the sea.*

DEAR OLD NUTSAWOO! NO DOUBT you too have wondered about the goings-on in the treetops of Ashton Place, as that dimwitted rodent prepares for the great adventure in store. To raise children is no joke, for one never knows how they will turn out. Some children are raised by wolves and still manage to acquire kind hearts and excellent table manners. Others are given every advantage—doting parents, a splendid dacha in which to spend the summer months, a scholarship to the best schools in Saint Petersburg—and yet grow up to be shady brokers in stolen goods, or hotel messengers of dubious morals. As Miss Charlotte Mortimer once told her favorite pupil, "No one's fate is written in India ink." It is up to each of us to decide what sort of person we wish to become.

Which raises the questions: Was Nutsawoo eagerly looking forward to having a nestful of baby squirrels to raise? Was the expectant rodent determined to be the very best squirrel parent possible? It is pleasant to think so, but frankly it is hard to tell what is in a squirrel's mind, unless it is autumn, in which case the answer is *eikenøtts, eikenøtts,* and more *eikenøtts.*

As for that other parent-to-be, Lady Constance Ashton, normally she was the sort of person whose thoughts flew out of her mouth willy-nilly whether anyone was listening or not, but on the topic of her own impending motherhood, she had said little. Still, anyone whose life is in the midst of great change needs a trusted friend to confide in. In the days since the hiring of Mrs. Elsinore Penworthy, the two ladies had formed a deep womanly bond. On sunny afternoons they strolled arm in arm through the daffodils, which were already at the peak of cheerful yellow bloom.

"I wonder why the daffodils blossom first and the tulips come after," Lady Constance observed on one of their walks. "Is it the same every year? Or do they take turns? If I were a tulip, I think I should tire of always being second."

"Perhaps the tulips prefer to come last," Mrs. Penworthy replied. "In the theater, it's the star of the show who takes the final bow. And it's the last bite of cake that's the sweetest, don't you think?"

"Quite so, Mrs. Penworthy! Dessert *is* the best part of any meal." When feeling playful, Lady Constance liked to draw out her friend's name in a singsong voice that started in a high pitch and dropped to a low one, and she did so now. "Mrs. Penworthy! Do you think I will be a good mother?"

"Of course you will, dear," the tall, broad-shouldered baby nurse replied. "You'll take to it like a duck takes to water! Speaking of which, look at this dreadful mud puddle from all that spring rain we've had. You musn't step in that; it'll ruin your pretty shoes. Let me give you a lift, won't you, Lady C?"

"Certainly—whee!" she cried merrily, as Simon effortlessly scooped up her pregnant bulk and carried her over the puddle as if she weighed no more than a feather. "You are so wonderfully strong, Mrs. Penworthy! I expect it's from so many years of carrying babies around."

"Sure, Lady C, that's the reason why," the baby nurse said, chuckling. And so their stroll continued.

That Mrs. Penworthy was really Simon Harley-Dickinson in disguise was known only to the Incorrigible children, Mrs. Clarke (whose closet had supplied much of his—that is to say, her—wardrobe), and Old Timothy, who always seemed to know the truth of what was going on at Ashton Place. Otherwise the sprawling household went about its business and took the newcomer at face value. Lady Constance certainly did. When the weather was too cool or wet to walk outside, they sat in the baby's room, knitting. Lady Constance had never knitted before. Nor had Simon, but his knowledge of sailor knots was vast, and he quickly realized that knitting was simply rows of knots hitched together on needles. Soon he was an absolute whiz at it. While Lady Constance dutifully knitted a baby hat, one slow stitch at a time, Simon whipped together sweaters, scarves, and mittens for everyone in the household, blankets for the baby's crib, and baby clothes galore.

The Incorrigible children were thrilled when they found out, for *learn to knit* was on the to-doawoo list, and now that Master Gogolev was gone, they had all the free time in the world. (Poor Master Gogolev! As you might imagine, he never recovered from his terrifying encounter with the Ghost of Librarian Past. His nerves were shot. He could no longer drag himself upstairs to the nursery; in fact he could scarcely get out of bed. Finally, and with some pointed encouragement from Mrs. Clarke, who had had quite enough of his cease- less demands and complaints, he asked Lord Fredrick if he might take a long restorative holiday abroad, at a spa. "All right, but stay away from tar pits—that's my advice," Lord Fredrick had said in reply. Gogolev left on the next train. What became of him afterward we may never know. Perhaps someday he was once again able to enjoy a piece of toast without weeping. Perhaps his horror of librarians also faded in time. We can only hope, for after all, few things are more enjoyable than a snack of tea and toast while curled up with a library book.)

As for the Incorrigibles' desire to join in the knit- ting: at first Lady Constance protested, for she still held strong opinions about what a bad influence the wolf children would be on her own child. Mrs. Pen- worthy did not argue the point, but merely said, "Well, for now that's not a worry, since your wee little Ashton isn't born yet. And the children do so want to make presents for the baby. Presents! Isn't that sweet?"

"I suppose so," Lady Constance answered, unsure. The three Ashton wards did seem harmless at the moment, as Alexander and Beowulf helpfully wound tangled skeins into neat balls of yarn, while Cassiopeia used her abacus to calculate how many stitches to cast on for baby-sized booties and bibs. Mrs. Penworthy actually seemed to like the Incorrigibles, and Lady Constance trusted her new friend's opinion more than anyone's, except Fredrick's, of course. Too, Lady Constance was terribly fond of presents, and she imagined her baby would be as well, for who doesn't like presents?

In this quiet way, a change in the lady's thinking took place. Not all at once, with shouted arguments and a big to-do, but in the more usual way people change—bit by bit, starting with a tiny, acorn-sized willingness to try something new, followed by patient repetition, until what once was so uncomfortably foreign and strange no longer feels strange at all. Soon it was commonplace to find the five knitters peacefully gathered in the baby's room, needles *click-clack*ing away.

During these days Madame Ionesco kept to herself. Simon said it was partly because she was working baker's hours—she baked bread all night and slept during the daytime—but mostly to do with her "preparations" for the first full moon in May. "It's highly mysterious, I know, but she won't say more than that," he told the children. They longed to see their spooky friend, but all in good time. For now, there was a fresh basket of superb bread every morning, no Gogolev moping about, and countless baby presents to knit. Best of all, their dear friend Simawoo was close by, in two equally lovable versions if you counted Mrs. Penworthy, which of course they did.

If only Lumawoo would come back! Then everything would be perfect.

THE *ACORN* WAS BUILT FOR fishing, not travel. It went out empty and came back when the hold was full, after weeks or even months at sea. Everyone aboard worked, and the work lasted all day, every day, from the hour when the pink light of dawn crept over the horizon to well past nightfall, when the stars shone softly in the half-lit sky and moonlight danced over the water.

Penelope expected that she too would be put to work. She did not mind, for she had been raised to be useful. She could mend all those knitted sweaters, or patch a torn sail. She could embroider pocket handkerchiefs for the crew, although these down-to-earth fellows might be just as glad to wipe their noses on their sleeves. "I could give lessons in any number of subjects," she thought, "but not poetry. There are simply too many poems about shipwrecks, which would hardly be suitable, given the circumstances."

But when she asked Alf about a job, he only said, "Nope!" It was just as well, for she was so seasick at first she could barely stand. By the third day she had gotten her sea legs, which meant she felt queasy only part of the time. That afternoon she ventured on deck for some air, and Captain Strøm himself approached her. They had not spoken since their first interview, which Penelope chalked up to him being busy and perhaps shy, never mind the fact that she did not speak Norwegian.

He towered over her, taller even than Captain Babushkinov. The skin across his cheekbones was cracked and reddened from a life spent outdoors, and his eyes were blue as glacier ice.

"Pay," he said, and held out his hand.

There is a brutal honesty at sea. There are things that float and things that sink, and no amount of talk can change one to the other, or persuade a sail to fill when there is no wind. Three days aboard ship had already weakened Penelope's capacity to lie. She mumbled her threadbare story about being the cousin of

England's queen, but her heart was not in it, and she fell silent.

Strøm stood before her, implacable as the tides. "Pay," he said, "or fish."

"Fish?" she said weakly, for the idea of baiting a hook made her queasy all over again. "But surely there are other jobs I could do . . . and the Queen of England will cover any expense. . . ."

"Queen, ha ha!" he said, and strode away. Moments later he returned with a fishing pole, which he placed in her hands like a scepter. "Queen of fish!"

PENELOPE SOON GREW TO LIKE fishing. In fact, she found that she liked nearly everything about life aboard ship. It was orderly and full of purpose, much like the Swanburne Academy, if Swanburne had been a boat full of Norwegian fishermen instead of a school full of Poor Bright Females. She found comfort in the tidiness of the ship: the casks of salt lined up like obedient dogs, and the empty, scrubbed-out dories that were hoisted aboard at the end of each day's work and neatly stacked, waiting for the dawn to come.

Everyone had a task to do and a place to be. Each morning the men set out in the dories to cast their nets into the sea. Near sunset they returned, manfully pulling the oars as the dories rode low in the water, heavy with glistening, still-wriggling fish. The day's catch was heaved on board and cleaned. Then the headless, gutted herring were shoveled into the ship's hold and packed between layers of salt, to preserve them.

There was no spare dory for Penelope, and she would not have been strong enough to row her own little boat through choppy seas in any case. Instead she sat on the deck of the *Acorn* with her fishing pole and cast her line over the side. Her prey was not herring, but dinner: a nice halibut, a tasty haddock, or even a scrumptious sole would do. Anything to break up the monotony of herring, salt tack, and sauerkraut at every meal.

After a few false starts and pricked fingers, she learned to bait her hook with scraps left over from the previous night's cleaning. She failed to catch any-thing, but she was never bored, for no two days were alike. Some mornings the fog came in low and thick, and swirled 'round the hull like smoke. Other days dawned so clear the air shimmered and played tricks on her eyes. Once she could have sworn she saw fig-ures standing on tiptoe on the glittering surface of the water. "Mermaids!" she cried, but it was only a pod of dolphins, balanced upright on their tails. Their smooth, long-nosed heads nodded in time to the music of the sea, once to the right and once to the left, as if taking a bow. They leaped over the swells with the grace of a corps de ballet and plunged into the depths once more.

Now and then a great jellyfish floated by, like an open umbrella made of glass, pulsing its way along just beneath the surface. Farther off, whales blew jets of water from their blowholes like smoke from the smokestack of a Bloomer steam locomotive. Only once did a whale come close enough for Penelope to gaze into its unfathomable eye. It was an especially large type of whale called a sperm whale; from nose to tail it was as long as the *Acorn* itself. (Fans of whales, books, and books about whales may already be familiar with *Moby-Dick*, by Mr. Herman Melville. This famous story of a sea captain obsessed with a whale is packed with symbolism, suitable for use as a doorstop in a pinch, and well worth reading, too.)

Penelope learned to scurry up the rope rigging like a squirrel. From there she could sometimes see other boats dotting the horizon, like toys in an enormous bathtub. She learned to stand clear when the boom swung across the deck as the boat changed tack by

angling into the wind till the leeward side of the sails became the windward side, or the other way 'round. She learned to clean a fish with a curved knife sharper than any sewing needle and save the fish heads for bait.

She even learned to navigate, a little. The *Acorn* tacked a zigzag route through the water, searching for where the fish were plentiful. It was the movement of the sun, arcing from east to west over the course of a long Nordic day, and the whirling of the stars during the brief, dim nights, that kept Penelope knowing her right from her left, so to speak.

She saw the northern lights, too! Ribbons of pink and green, yellow and purple and blue swirled in the night sky in a miraculous display. Why the sky glows with a whole rainbow of colors near the poles of the earth is a fascinating question, but for once Penelope did not wonder why. She simply stood in awe. The aurora borealis! How she longed for the Incorrigible children to see it! But perhaps they would get the chance someday.

Breakfast and lunch she ate alone, for the men were out in the dories and Captain Strøm stayed at the helm, poring over the sea charts. At dinner they all gathered at a long wooden table belowdecks. There she learned the fishermen's way of saying grace before a meal, which Alf translated for her:

We give thanks for the fish in the sea,
And more thanks for the fish in the hold.
Most of all, thanks for the fish on the plate.
Down the hatch they go!

They all slapped their bellies at the last line. This was the cue to begin eating. After dinner the men would sing, accompanied by tin whistles and the bittersweet pluck of mandolin strings. The shanties the crew sang during the day were rhythmic work songs, good for keeping time as they hauled rope and shoveled herring into the hold, but the songs sung after dinner were full of longing and woe. Penelope could not understand the words, but she imagined they told tales of lost loves, shipwrecks, and fish that got away.

Each night she sat in the corner on an upended bucket, eyes closed. The music washed over her and filled her with the kind of sadness that satisfies the heart the way a good meal satisfies the belly. "A touch of melancholy is to be expected aboard ship, as sailors spend most of their lives far from home. It is a hard life and a lonely one, and yet . . ." She thought of Simon, and his great love of the sea, which she had now begun to understand. ". . . it does have its charms."

In this way the days passed. Soon Penelope had spent more than a week at sea. From the sun and stars she knew they were heading in the right direction, at least. From the moon she knew she was running out of time.

One night she awoke with a start. She had dreamed that the man in the moon had Edward Ashton's face and followed her everywhere she went. It took a few deep calming breaths and some basic astronomy for her to recover, for it happened to be the night of the new moon, when the last sliver of waning crescent is snuffed out and the moon is invisible to the eye.

"For tonight at least, there is no one watching and nothing to fear," she told herself. "Yet if tonight is the new moon, it has been two weeks and a day since I left Plinkst. And there are only two weeks left till the first full moon of May, when Lady Constance is due to give birth. How will I ever get back to England in time?" There was no going back to sleep after that. Near dawn she finally dozed off, but by then it was time to get up and get to work.

Thus preoccupied with worry and hazy minded from lack of sleep, Penelope gathered her fishing pole, bait, and bucket. The dories were still neatly stacked. The sun was above the horizon, and the weather was fair enough, if breezy, but the men had not gone out to fish. Some were doing chores on deck or in the galley, but most were down in the hold, packing the salted herring into empty barrels.

She might have wondered why this was so, but her mind was still on the moon. Penelope settled in her usual spot, pole in hand, and watched her cork fishing float dance on the water's surface. If a fish bit the hook, the float would get pulled under. Her job was to wait for this momentous event to occur, after which she would do her best to reel in the fish. That was the idea, at least. So far the float had only gone down when her line tangled in seaweed, or because a sea crab had nibbled at the bait until there was only a thread of gristle left. Then she had to start over by putting a fresh fish head on the hook and casting it out once more.

Before long Alf appeared at her side. He glanced into the bucket of seawater she kept at her feet, in case she caught anything.

"Not yet," she said, in answer to his quizzical look, "but I am beginning to feel quite close to catching a fish. Today might just be the day!"

"Nope." Alf jerked his head toward the helm. "Strøm," he said. All the men referred to the captain as Strøm. Two words would be one word too many for a man so silent.

Penelope put down her pole and made off at a trot, for by now she knew that walking was no way for a sailor to obey a summons from the captain. Strøm was at the wheel, gazing outward. He stood with ease, as if the ship was in a dead calm, but the seas were choppy from the playful wind.

"Look," he said, pointing south.

She peered. A faint haze blurred the horizon. Land!

"Is that . . . England?" she asked in hope.

"Nei." His crinkled eyes narrowed to icy-blue slits. "Queen of fish? Hah! Good-bye!"

The breeze gusted and salt spray blew in her face. "I realize my fishing skills are not up to professional standards, but surely I will improve with practice," she said. It was not easy to talk while trying to keep her balance. But if Strøm could stand there without holding on, so could she.

He turned his trouser pockets inside out, showing them to be empty. "No pay," he said, as if to remind her how she got herself into this mess. Then he pantomimed reeling in a fish and finding nothing on the hook. "No fish." He waved at Penelope. "Bye-bye!" he said.

"This is . . . an unfortunate misunderstanding," she said, tottering. The weave and bob of the ship made her stomach churn. Without thinking, she reached out to steady herself, but in doing so she fell upon the wheel with both hands.

"Whoops!" she cried, but it was too late. Unwittingly she had pulled the ship hard to port. The salt casks toppled and rolled, and the men shouted and cursed as the boom swung wildly across the deck, knocking them over like bowling pins.

"Alf!" Strøm roared. Seconds later Alf appeared, sporting a fresh bruise on his head.

The *Acorn*'s captain let out a rare stream of angry words. He pointed at Penelope and made a gesture with one thumb that seemed to indicate being tossed overboard. Alf nodded, looking grim. He led Penelope back to her bunk and told her to collect her things.

"I wonder how one says 'jetsam' in Norwegian, for I fear that is what I am about to become!" she thought. "Or perhaps they will make me walk the plank, as pirates do. Dear me, I ought to have learned to swim when I had the chance!" Penelope's few possessions—including her broken tiara, her ruined princess costume, and her papier-mâché seashell—were already in her bag. "If the Count of Monte Cristo could be buried at sea and live to tell the tale, then so can I! Once in the briny deep I shall paddle with all my might, and wait for another ship to come by. Perhaps I will meet some friendly smugglers before too long."

Luckily, Strøm was no pirate; in fact, he would have been deeply offended at the idea. While Penelope fretted, the *Acorn*'s captain set course for the not-so-distant shore, where he planned to sell off some fish and buy provisions, as well as get rid of his accidental passenger. Whether she was a royal relation or not he did not know, or care. But when it came to fishing, the girl had bad luck, and that was something he could not allow, not on his ship, not with a half-empty hold and a crew of men to feed.

Once the ship was anchored, Alf and Penelope climbed into a dory, and he rowed her to the shore. The rest of the crew was too busy shoveling herring into barrels while singing rhythmic sea chanties to even say good-bye.

Alf sang under his breath as well, in time to the strokes of his oars. At the dock he lashed the dory to a post with rope. Penelope could not help but admire the quick, expert way he tied his sailor knots. How the

Incorrigible children would have enjoyed seeing it!

He offered a hand to help her climb out, but she had acquired enough sailor's pride to insist on doing it herself. Once she was on land, the ground under her feet felt weirdly still.

"Where are we?" she asked.

"Frankenforde." Alf hopped back into the dory to get her bag. He was so light-footed the little rowboat hardly moved.

"Frankenforde," she repeated, trying to imagine where that might be. "I don't suppose that is in England, is it?"

"Nope. Germany."

Her heart sank. Germany! It was better than Russia, but still so very far from home!

Alf held the damp, sea-stained carpetbag at arm's length. Its fluffy coating of white feathers was flattened with salt spray, making it look—and smell—convincingly like a large white seabird, or the remains of one. "Nope, nope, nope," he scolded as he handed it to Penelope. Everyone knew that a dead albatross was bad luck aboard ship. No wonder little princess stowaway never caught anything!

If Penelope had expected Alf to help her get her bearings before leaving her alone in a strange country, she would have been disappointed. Once rid of her and her unlucky charm, he turned and strode off with purpose. The first mate's next stop would be the fish market, to see what price could be gotten for the *Acorn*'s herring.

"Alf, wait!" she called, hurrying after him. His rolling sailor's gait made her think of Simon, and she felt a pang of despair—would she ever get home to Ashton Place?

"I am truly sorry for all the trouble I have caused," she said, breathlessly trying to keep pace. "Is there any way to get Captain Strøm to reconsider bringing me to England? They do eat a great deal of herring there."

"Nope," he said, still walking. And that was the last time she saw Alf.

THE ELEVENTH CHAPTER

A tiny bookshop has what
Penelope needs.

UNLIKE MISS PENELOPE LUMLEY, EDWARD Ashton had no need of disguises and trickery to get from one place to the next, for he had money, and plenty of it. He hired expert drivers with carriage horses fleet-footed enough to win the Derby. He paid triple the usual fare to book passage on a ship that was already packed snug as a tin of herring. Privately he paid still more to the captain to make sure they would travel at full sail, no matter the weather.

Once ashore, he bought a first-class ticket for the

sleek new steam engine trains that now crisscrossed Europe (whether this could be considered progress or not was a matter of opinion). He had boarded the train in France, near Calais. Already he had passed into Germany. During the same days Penelope had spent aboard the *Acorn*, fishing and pondering the vastness of the sea, Edward Ashton too had been on the move, and he had covered a great deal of ground.

"By now I expect the governess has found a way out of Plinkst," he thought, gazing out the train window at the scenery flashing by. It was a lush and mysterious landscape, a dense wood of dizzyingly tall fir trees that covered the rolling mountains like a living blanket of green. "She is misguided and naive, but the girl has pluck. She would move the Black Forest itself to reach the wolf children before the first full moon of May."

The image of Penelope reunited with the Incorrigibles made his pulse race—how often he had imagined doing them in, and in such a gruesome variety of ways! But in the end it would not matter how they perished.

What mattered was that they *all* did. All five of them.

The wheels slowed, *clickety-clack, find the fifth, clickety-clack, find the fifth,* as the motorman applied the brake and the train made its way 'round a steep mountain curve. If only he could slow his mind so easily! Too often it spun like a cyclone, the faces of the governess and her three wolfish charges whirling behind his eyes until he could no longer see what was before him.

He drew his black cloak snugly around, as if making himself into a shadow. "There was no time to deal with the girl in Russia, as I had intended—but she will come home of her own accord, like a well-trained dog. The wolf children are already in hand. The fifth lies elsewhere, with its parents. This time I will not—I cannot!—fail."

The guidebook full of clues that had led him to Switzerland had been nothing but a red herring. All that precious time wasted, searching for the Lumleys where they were not! But no matter. Now, thanks to that idiot Gogolev, his luck had changed. A far more valuable book had come into his hands—really, what were the odds?—and the truth had been revealed.

Imagine, a clue of such magnitude hidden in plain sight, right on the opening pages! Melancholy poems, indeed! He had not felt so—well, optimistic—in years.

"'I wander through the meadows green,'" he murmured to himself, and smiled.

For now he was certain: his long-lost prey was in

Germany, in a small coastal village named—but surely you can guess where he was going.

He had not arrived yet, as the connecting train from Gooden-Baaden had been delayed. A flock of furious pheasants was blocking the tracks and stubbornly refused to move. This was unexpected, as pheasants are usually quite docile birds, and tasty, too.

But rest assured: he was on his way.

Willkommen in Frankenforde!

It was an attractive sign, as signs go. The words (which Penelope correctly understood to mean "Welcome to Frankenforde!") were written in graceful looping letters on a panel of wood, with a painted border of green leaves and small white flowers.

"A town that strives to make such a good first impression must surely be a friendly place," she thought. "Curious! I thought edelweiss only grew in the mountains. But the pictures are charming, nevertheless."

As you see, she was trying to keep her spirits up. It was not easy. Optoomuchstically speaking, she had escaped Russia and now merely needed to hop, skip, and jump to that happy land where Victoria was queen. Yet the hard, pessimax truth of the matter found her stranded and penniless in a midsized European nation where she did not speak the language, wearing boy's clothes and smelling of fish. She was nearer to her destination than she had been, but oh! England! Home was still so very far away.

She racked her brains for all she could remember about European geography. What stood between her and Ashton Place? Was it the Alps, the Black Forest, the beautiful blue Danube? "At least there are no scorching-hot deserts in the way, as there might be in Africa," she thought. "What luck! Not a single deadly cobra lies in my path!" You see how desperate she was to look on the bright side. But it was only a modest stroke of luck not to have to trudge across the burning sands of the Sahara, when she still had half of Europe to get across, and the English Channel, too.

"Think, Penny! An atlas would come in useful. Some money, too. And food," she realized, for she was terribly hungry, and the closer she got to town, the more her mouth began to water. Either it was her imagination, or Frankenforde smelled deliciously of cake.

She hoisted her carpetbag from one hand to the other and resumed walking. She followed the scent just as the Incorrigible children would. Soon she found herself in the village square, in front of a perfectly charming bakery with a large, street-facing window. What glorious desserts lay within, so close and yet so utterly out of reach! It reminded her of the line from Mr. Coleridge's strange poem about the ancient mariner and the albatross.

Water, water, everywhere,
And all the boards did shrink;
Water, water, everywhere,
Nor any drop to drink.

"Cake, cake, everywhere, and not a slice for me," she recited, using her poetic license to make the poem fit her own circumstances more neatly. She pressed her nose to the glass and stared at the muffins and biscuits, the trays of tarts, and the magnificent Black Forest cakes, thickly frosted in snow-white icing, with crowns of cherries and shaved dark chocolate on top.

Then she caught a glimpse of her reflection, bedraggled and wide-eyed. Reluctantly she backed away from the glass. "I look like a runaway cabin boy," she thought. "If I am seen lurking around, I am likely to be turned over to the police."

What to do? She had no money, no plan, no hope, and no Black Forest cake! The situation was bleak. She turned to go. But where?

Ring-ring! Ring-ring!

A bell jingled as a customer left the establishment next to the bakery. Penelope had been so distracted by her own misery that she had not even noticed the shop next door. She looked in the window, and her carpetbag slipped to the ground.

"Books!" she exclaimed. And not just any books. Here was a whole series of books, lovingly displayed in an artful tableau of a pony paddock, with miniature carved and painted pony figures grazing on green velvet grass, and little white fences made of whitewashed twigs lashed together with thread. The titles were all in German, but there was no mistaking the illustrations of Edith-Anne Pevington and her beloved pony, Rainbow, on the covers.

Penelope's heart swelled as if she had received a thousand birthday cards all at once. *"Eine Gewitterwolke für Regenbogen,"* she said, pronouncing one of the titles as best she could. "That must be *A Stormcloud for Rainbow*!" The sad-faced pony and gray skies gave it away. (Fans of books about ponies know that *A Stormcloud for Rainbow* is the most melancholy tale in the series. This is not saying much, as the Giddy-Yap, Rainbow! books incline toward the cheerful.

280

However, in this episode Rainbow falls into a funk after losing an important competition and questions the meaning of everything a pony holds dear. Having red ribbons braided through one's mane, prancing obediently through obstacle courses, and taking jumps at a trot—what was it all for? To win a trophy? To please Edith-Anne Pevington? Was that all there was to a pony's life?)

Penelope smiled, then beamed, then laughed aloud, for even the grimmest Giddy-Yap, Rainbow! book had joy to spare. "I will go into this bookshop, just to look," she decided. "It may have an atlas, if the travel section is well stocked. Perhaps all is not yet lost." Just like that, hope was restored. It was a sliver of hope, mind you, thin as the thinnest crescent moon, but sometimes a sliver is all a person needs. The bell jingled softly as she entered.

Ring-ring! Ring-ring!

The shop was tiny, but like all the best bookstores it gave the distinct impression that whatever book one needed was somewhere within its overflowing shelves. A colorful globe—a real one, mounted on a wooden stand that let it spin as the earth does—led her to the travel section. There she found a whole shelf of guidebooks, to cities near and far, and past and present, too. "One for Istanbul and one for Constantinople," she marveled. "And here is one for Rome, and one for ancient Rome. Truly, it is the Eternal City."

There were maps an arms'-breadth wide that folded like accordions until they could be slipped into a pocket, and dictionaries that translated words from one language into a dozen others. There were memoirs by Arctic explorers, fearless mountaineers, and deep-sea divers who braved the briny deep wearing those new-fangled diving costumes. These were heavy suits with helmets into which air was pumped, allowing a person to breathe underwater. What an invention!

And there on its own small desk, propped at an angle on a wooden stand, just waiting to be opened, was a perfectly splendid atlas.

Penelope put down her carpetbag and wiped her hands on her sailor pants before touching the beautiful volume. She leafed through the maps until she found Frankenforde. Then she turned page after page, examining every bit of terrain that lay between her and where she most longed to be.

At first she thought she must be mistaken. She flipped the pages back and forth. How could there still be so many miles of mountains, rivers, lakes, and forests to march up, down, around, and through? And this before ever reaching the English Channel! That would be a mighty swim, indeed.

"It is too far!" she blurted. Then she began to cry in earnest, for the truth was as plain as the difference between the right foot and the left, the North Pole and the South, the new moon and the full: with scarcely a week left, there was no possible way she could get back to England in time to save her beloved Incorrigibles.

Whether Edward Ashton achieved his murderous schemes or the curse upon the Ashtons put a gruesome end to them all hardly mattered. She had failed, and she would never see the children again.

Nor would she see Simon, or Miss Mortimer or Mrs. Clarke, or even that dear scamp Nutsawoo!

She wept in that tiny bookshop in Frankenforde, and rubbed the dirty sleeve of her fisherman's sweater across her wet cheeks and leaky nose. It was a storm-cloud for Rainbow indeed. Her shoulders heaved as she tried to quiet her sobs. What she longed to do was howl with grief, long and loud. But that would hardly be good manners in a bookshop.

"Weltschmerz?" a kind voice asked, just behind her. Penelope turned. It was a woman, a sales clerk, no doubt. She must have been alerted by all the sniffling and shuddering. Perhaps she had come to prevent her

unhappy customer from dripping hot salty tears on the books.

The woman gazed at her with great sympathy and held out a clean pocket handkerchief.

"Thank you very much," Penelope said, taking it. She wiped her eyes, and blew her nose, and could not help noticing that the handkerchief had the letter L embroidered upon it. "How odd," she mumbled through her sobs, not caring if the clerk understood her. "At my school we learned to embroider pocket handkerchiefs in just this way. I have lost all mine during my travels, unfortunately, else I would show you how similar they are. For my last name too begins with an L. . . ."

She looked up to find the sales clerk staring at her, open-mouthed. The woman's gray-green eyes brimmed with tears.

"Penelope?" Her voice was no more than a whisper. "Penelope Lumley? Of the Swanburne Academy for Poor Bright Females?"

"Why, yes." Sheer surprise stopped Penelope's crying at once. She stared at the woman's face. It had a familiar look to it—there was the same elfin chin as Cassiopeia, the poetic mouth of Beowulf. And the woman wore her hair just as Miss Mortimer did, in a pretty chignon at the base of her neck. Only the color was different. It was not blond, like Miss Mortimer's, but a once-vivid auburn that had been softened by time, with strands of silver running through.

"Oh—how unlikely this is!" the woman said, finding her voice. "And yet we must embrace the unexpected and not lose hope, as Charlotte never fails to remind me. Penny, my dear Penny—you must have found the clue I left for you! How clever you are!"

"Clue? What clue?" Penelope felt woozy. The ground rolled beneath her feet as if it were her first day aboard ship.

The woman reached out to steady her, and let her hand rest on Penelope's arm. "Penelope. Do you know who I am?"

"She means to say—do you know who *we* are?" A man appeared at the woman's side. He looked at Penelope with the same clear-eyed gaze as Alexander Incorrigible, though his eyes shone.

Penelope took a deep, calming breath and looked from one eager, misty-eyed face to the other. "If I am not mistaken," she said, with all the professionalism she could muster, "you are the Long-Lost Lumleys."

WHAT A HEARTWARMING SCENE BURST into bloom! There were enough hugs and glad tears and cries of

"Who would believe it?" and "Did you ever?" to bring a hundred sentimental West End plays to a happy end. But it was strange, too, for Penelope had not seen her parents for such a very long time.

And they also admitted that they found it strange, for the Penelope who stood before them was a young woman (albeit an oddly dressed one), and not the small child they had last seen many years before.

Penelope's feelings were so mixed between joy and something far more bittersweet, one might easily have mistaken it for Christmas Day. There were so many questions to ask, and answer! But there was one question Penelope needed settled on the spot. Even though she believed she already knew the truth, it felt both urgent and necessary that she hear it straight from the Lumleys' mouths, so to speak.

"Excuse me—that is, I must ask you—about, well . . ." Her lower lip trembled, and she could say no more.

Mater Lumley gazed at her, soft eyed as a cow. "I expect you want to know where we have been all these years, and why we left you at Swanburne and did not come back?"

"And why you did not hear from us, year after year, not even on your birthday?" Pater Lumley added. They both looked very sad.

Penelope shook her head. Of course she did want to know these things, but all that could wait until later. "What I most wish to know is this—" she began. Her mother took her by both hands.

"I know we have a great deal to explain, Penelope," Mater Lumley said. "We did what we did for your safety. Yet it must have been horribly difficult for you. I am so sorry."

"It was difficult for us, too, but we are adults, and made a choice. You are—you *were*—a child, with no say in the matter. I am sorry, too." Pater Lumley's voice was rough and soft at the same time.

"Well, the past cannot be changed," Penelope said, after a moment. Which was true, yet it meant a great deal to hear these words of apology from her parents. She felt her spirit grow lighter, as if a package she had been carrying for a long time could finally be put down. "Until someone invents a time machine, that is! And we are together now, which is more important. But the most important thing of all . . ." She paused, unsure how to broach a topic so near to her heart.

"Is a meal, no doubt! You must be starving. Come." Mater Lumley stood and took her by the hand. Pater Lumley reached for the carpetbag.

"Here, let me carry your—albatross!" he said, smiling. "Hmm, why so many feathers? Were you trying to fly back to England?"

The question she so desperately longed to ask withered on her tongue, as the very mention of England upset her all over again. Mater Lumley whispered something to her husband. He nodded, then went to the front door and turned over the GEÖFFNET sign to GESCHLOSSEN, to say that the bookstore was closed.

Mater Lumley led Penelope through a short hallway at the back of the shop and up a flight of stairs to the apartment above the store. It was a lovely, sunny place, with trailing green plants in the windows. The walls were lined with books and paintings, and there were embroidered pillows on every chair. "Just like at Swanburne," Penelope said, which made her weep afresh, for had any Swanburne girl ever failed so miserably at her duties?

Mater Lumley was a wise woman. She made no attempt to cheer Penelope or pepper her with questions or advice. Instead she brought her a cozy blanket and went to the kitchen to put the kettle on. By this time Pater Lumley had joined them upstairs. As they waited for the water to come to a boil, he assembled a truly excellent sliced apple, cheddar, and mustard sandwich, one that would have put Old Timothy's best efforts to shame.

Mater Lumley made Penelope a cup of tea, with milk and two sugars, just the way she liked it, and Pater Lumley put the sandwich on a pretty plate with a leaf-and-flower pattern all 'round the edges, much like the sign that had welcomed Penelope to Frankenforde. Then they both sat quietly and waited, for as anyone who has ever tamed a wild thing knows, if one remains calm and friendly and offers a tasty treat, even a creature who has suffered a great shock will soon calm down enough to make friends.

So it was with Penelope. Before long her heart settled a bit, and with a nod of thanks, she reached for her food. One bite, and she was ravenous. After she had devoured it all, Mater Lumley produced a thick slice of Black Forest cake from the bakery next door. By the last forkful Penelope had declared it the best meal she had eaten in her life (and Penelope had once dined at the Fern Court in London, run by the world-famous Chef Philippe, so this was high praise indeed.)

Now the words came in a flood. She told her parents all that had happened, from the day of her arrival at Ashton Place to her terrible banishment to Plinkst, her daring escape from the Babushkinovs, her time at sea, and now, this unexpected reunion in Frankenforde. By the time she was done telling, it was evening. More sandwiches were served, with soup this time, and more tea and cake. The sunny apartment was now cozily dark and lit by the hearth fire Pater Lumley carefully built and tended.

Her parents had listened quietly all the way through and gave no sign of surprise, not even when Penelope explained that Edward Ashton was alive and determined to satisfy the curse upon the Ashtons by delivering Penelope and the Incorrigibles—all of whom seemed to be descended from Agatha Swanburne herself, though Penelope still did not know exactly how—to an untimely and gruesome end.

"In doing so, he thinks he will save his side of the family tree from extinction. He told me so himself," she said miserably. "But time is running out. The exact words of the curse are: 'In the fourth generation, the hunt begins—and ends.' One way or the other, the curse will end when Lady Constance's baby is born."

"And not a moment sooner, either." Pater Lumley frowned in concentration. It was an expression that would be familiar to anyone who had observed Penelope deep in thought. "No wonder Ashton's efforts have failed. The spirits Beyond the Veil have a taste for the theatrical. They'll want to be on hand for a spectacular event. A grand finale, if you will. When is the child expected?"

"The first full moon of May. Scarcely a week from now." Penelope stared glumly at her hands. "I will never get back to England in time. It is impossible!"

Her parents exchanged a look, the kind of look in which something is decided without a word being spoken.

"We must not lose hope," Mater Lumley said gently. "As my grandmother said, 'When the impossible becomes merely difficult, that's when you know you've—'"

"Your grandmother! Do you mean Agatha Swanburne was my great-grandmother?" Penelope interrupted.

"Indeed she was." Mater Lumley rose from her chair. She stretched and yawned. "It has been a remarkable day, and there is much to ponder, but even the most extraordinary days of our lives last no longer than the ordinary ones, and are 'rounded with a sleep,' as Shakespeare wrote."

"Yes, in *The Tempest*. Marvelous play! Yet I have always wondered why there are so many stories about shipwrecks, when so few of us are sailors." Now Pater

Lumley stood. He too yawned and stretched. "I will soon be rounded with a sleep myself. Let us go to bed, and leave the harder questions till tomorrow, when we are rested and can think better."

Her parents were right, of course, and not only because Shakespeare said so. Still, Penelope did not want the day or the conversation to end. "But Mater Lumley . . . Pater Lumley . . ." She stopped to stifle a yawn herself, for they are highly contagious, as the Lumley parents clearly knew! "I want to ask so many things! About our family tree, for example . . ."

Mater Lumley smoothed back her hair with a hand, an elegant gesture that made Penelope think of Miss Mortimer. "I am sure you have many questions, my long-lost girl, but late bedtimes will do none of us any good. On the other hand . . ."

Pater Lumley chuckled and went to stoke the fire, for clearly they would be up a little while longer.

"On the other hand, you have gone a long time without answers," his wife finished, taking a seat once more. "Tonight, three questions only. The rest can wait till tomorrow."

Three! Penelope frowned. How was she to winnow down her countless questions to a mere troika? Luckily she had read enough of those wish-giving, genie-in-a-bottle stories to know not to ask a yes-or-no question, for those were always a waste. "All right," she said, after considering it. "My first question is: what happened to Agatha Ashton and her descendants after Pax threw her out?"

Mater Lumley smiled. "The adventures of Agatha Ashton could fill a book! There are countless tales of her world travels, the remarkable people she met, and the things she learned. Too many to share now, though someday I will tell you them all." At Penelope's disappointed look, she went on. "But when Agatha was done traveling, and had gained the kind of wisdom that is won only through broad-minded experience, she returned to England. There she met and married a man named Theodore Swanburne. They had a daughter named Theodora. She too grew up to be a fascinating woman, a scientist with a special interest in the nature of time. They say she even tried to invent a time machine!"

Penelope's eyes grew wide, but she knew better than to ask a second question by accident!

"She very nearly succeeded, too. Or so she often claimed. Theodora married a fellow scientist, Dr. Samuel Mortimer. He was a widower with a little girl of his own, not quite two years old. Sadly, his wife had died of a fever not long after the birth. The child's name was, and is, Charlotte."

"Miss Charlotte Mortimer!" Penelope exclaimed. "So that is how Agatha Swanburne became Miss Mortimer's grandmother."

"Yes. Theodora was her stepmother, and she could not have asked for a better one. A few years later, Theodora and Samuel had another daughter."

"And here she sits. Your mother, Susannah." Pater Lumley kissed his wife on the cheek and gave the fire another poke.

Penelope shook her head in wonder. Imagine, her mother and Miss Mortimer, children together!

Mater Lumley drew her lap blanket 'round her; she was the very picture of coziness and comfort. "Charlotte and I were as close as sisters could be. We still are, though circumstances prevent us from seeing each other as often as we would like. Dreamy Susannah, she used to call me! Even as a child I was fond of poetry. Charlotte was more of a practical type."

"She is an excellent headmistress," Penelope said in all seriousness, but for some reason the remark made her parents laugh.

"Well, I have no doubt of it!" her mother said. "You already know what became of Charlotte. As for me, I grew up and fell in love with a kind and talented man." She glanced warmly at her husband. "And here he is. Hans Lumley. Your father."

"Hans Lumley," Penelope repeated softly. She had a sudden impulse. "May I have some paper, and a pencil? I would like to draw our family tree."

Pater Lumley chuckled as Mater Lumley answered, "Of course, but that is your second question."

Blast! Genies could be tricky, and so could parents, it seemed! At least she had one question left. A large sheet of drawing paper and a sharpened pencil were easily found among her father's art supplies. Penelope drew a circle with her own name right in the middle, and drew lines and boxes all around. "Hans Lumley is my father," she said, writing it in. "My mother is Susannah Lumley, who has a half sister, Charlotte Mortimer." She looked up. "That makes Miss Mortimer my aunt."

"Correct." Mater Lumley got on the floor next to Penelope to help. "My mother, Theodora, is your grandmother. She is still alive, though we see her rarely; she is quite an explorer! Her mother, Agatha Swanburne, was your great-grandmother, and Agatha's twin brother, Pax Ashton—"

"Was my great-grand-uncle." The sudden onslaught of relatives made her head spin. "Edward Ashton is his son. That means Edward Ashton and I . . ."

"Are some sort of cousins. We shall have to let Cassiopeia and her abacus figure out which kind." Mater Lumley laid a hand on her arm. "Are you all right, Penny? You look pale. Shall I find some smelling salts?"

"I am quite well." Penelope stared at the paper, already covered with marks. After a moment's hesitation, she wrote Edward Ashton's name down beneath Pax's, for they were father and son. Then she drew a faint line between her name and his. *Cousin*, she wrote.

The pencil hovered in the air. "And what about the Incorrigible children?" she asked.

"Is that your third question?"

"Yes." For this was the question Penelope had wanted to ask all along.

Mater Lumley held her gaze a long time before she spoke. "Hans and I are the Lucky Lumleys, indeed. We have been blessed with four children."

"Four clever, good-hearted, auburn-haired children," Pater Lumley added, from his seat near the fire. "And from what Charlotte has told us, you have been a perfectly wonderful big sister, Penelope. We are so very proud of you all."

Penelope had long known the answer, in her heart. But hearing her own long-lost parents say it aloud was like a spring thaw at the South Pole. A lump in her heart that she had not even known was there began to melt, and the water flowed, mostly from her eyes.

Mater Lumley hugged her and spoke in her ear. "It is too much to explain now, but know that we did all we could to protect you. We hid you in plain sight at Swanburne, in the care of family and friends. There you escaped Edward Ashton's notice for many years—thanks, in part, to the hair poultice! That was Charlotte's idea. We were not quite so lucky with the younger three. Edward Ashton snatched them away to serve his own terrible schemes, although I believe he will fail in the end. As you see, providence has cared for all four of you very well, so far."

"Old Timothy was a great help, too," Pater Lumley remarked. "The man makes a decent sandwich, if I do say so myself!"

One would have thought Penelope would have run out of tears by now, but she wept again with joy and grief and wonder, until she had soaked her own pocket handkerchief and several of her parents', too. "We are all one family," she said, gazing at the family tree written out before her. "I am an Ashton, and a Swanburne, and a Lumley, *and* an Incorrigible!" She blew her nose. "But Edward Ashton believes there is a fifth."

Mater Lumley's eyes grew wide. "I beg your pardon?"

"The wolf's curse said there were five murdered cubs to be avenged. Edward Ashton believes his efforts have failed because he has only found four of us. He is convinced that you have had another child."

"Well, that is unexpected!" Mater Lumley's voice stayed lighthearted even as her cheeks went pale. "It is bad news that he thinks so, Penelope. We must act quickly. For he will be searching for us, now."

A dreadful feeling rose in Penelope then, sharp and cold as a plunge into a frozen sea. It was the iced-over, heartless feeling that enables some people to do terrible things for what they believe are perfectly justifiable reasons.

But then she thought, "This must be how Edward Ashton feels all the time," and she took a long, deep breath, and then another, and waited until the feeling passed. Her nose filled with the aroma of good tea and excellent cake and her mother's lavender-scented perfume, mixed with the pleasant burning-wood smell from the fire that her father was tending even now. It was the smell of family, and now that she had breathed deeply of it, she knew she would never be without it again, no matter what.

She stood, determined. "I must get back to England, and to the Incorrigibles," she said. "There is a fortune-teller there, an expert on curses and all things supernatural, who may be able to help us yet—but there is not much time." She looked from one parent to the other. "I know it is far. But there must be a way."

Her parents exchanged a glance. "There is a way," her father said.

"Well, what on earth is it?" Penelope blurted, annoyed. Honestly, they were being as enigmatic as Old Timothy!

"What on earth, indeed!" her father said. Now he was smiling. "The answer is plain as the paintings on the wall."

"Paintings?" She looked around at the art-filled apartment. "What do paintings have to do with it?"

Mater Lumley cocked her head to one side just as Cassiopeia Incorrigible would have done. "My dear Penny," she said, eyes twinkling, "I hope you are not afraid of heights."

THE TWELFTH CHAPTER

"Made happy by the verdant scene."

PARENTS! THEY COULD BE MYSTERIOUS and maddening, or so Penelope was quickly learning. Over her protests bedtime was declared, for she had used up her three questions and that, as the elder Lumleys said, was that.

Her father fashioned a cozy nest out of blankets, and her mother offered one of her own nightdresses to wear, and an embroidered pillow that read, *The difference between a dream and a plan is a to-do list.* It was an experience common to most childhoods, though new to Penelope—that of drifting off to sleep as her parents spoke quietly in another room, trying not to be over-heard. The comforting, murmuring sound was like the lap of waves against the hull of a watertight ship, and she slept as well as she ever had in her life.

She awoke to find her cabin boy's trousers and warm knit sweater on the foot of her bed, neatly folded and smelling of fresh soap and wood smoke. They must have been washed and hung near the fire overnight to dry. She bathed and dressed quickly, for she wanted to look at those paintings in the morning light. Plain as the paintings on the wall? Afraid of heights? Whatever could Pater and Mater Lumley have meant?

Her parents were already up. The kitchen smelled marvelous, of coffee and shaving soap and lavender water, and a hot breakfast cooked by one's own mother. Penelope peeked into the pot on the stove—porridge with jam, excellent!—but turned her attention to the walls.

"Don't you like porridge?" her mother asked.

"I do, very much. But first I intend to examine these paintings." She stood in front of the nearest one with a look of deep concentration on her face.

Pater Lumley chuckled. He had finished his meal and was now at the kitchen counter, making sand-wiches. "I'll offer a hint if you like."

"No, thank you." Penelope's eyes were fixed on the

painting. "I took several art appreciation classes at Swanburne and did rather well, I am proud to say. If there is some hidden meaning to be found, I will find it."

She finished looking and moved on to the next painting. Then the next. "They are landscapes," she said after examining a dozen. "Lovely ones, too. But there is nothing symbolic. No mythological figures, either."

"Hmm," her father said, cutting the sandwiches into perfect triangles. Mater Lumley sipped her coffee with a look of private amusement.

Penelope folded her arms and squinted, then made a telescope out of her cupped hands, but to no avail. "To see past the obvious, I must look the way the Incorrigibles sniff," she thought. She concentrated afresh, wholeheartedly, and without distraction, and drew all the powers of her attention together as if weaving many thin strands into a mighty rope, strong enough to hold a ship at anchor.

"Eureka!" she exclaimed at last. "Although they depict a variety of landscapes, each of these paintings uses the same point of view." (As the art critics among you know, point of view simply means where the painter has imagined him or herself to be in relation to the picture. For example, a picture of a person in a barrel might be drawn as if one were outside the barrel looking in, or inside the barrel looking out. It is the painter's artistic license that makes such feats possible, just as poetic license lets poets write convincingly about terrible shipwrecks and storms at sea without getting the least bit wet.)

"Point of view, eh?" Pater Lumley wrapped the sandwiches in clean napkins, ready for a picnic. "Tell me more."

"See? The painter is in the air." Penelope stepped closer and gestured at the canvas. "One might even call it a bird's-eye view. The green meadow stretches out below like a carpet, and those little dots of white—is that edelweiss?—are like points of light." She turned to him. "Did you once live on a very high mountain?"

"Yes, but there is more to it than that," he said, with maddening mysteriousness.

Her mother interjected. "Eat your porridge, Penny. We will be leaving very soon."

Penelope was hungry and glad to obey. Her parents made quick preparations together without needing to say a word, as if they had done it many times before. Soon there were two good-sized rucksacks packed full and propped against the wall, each cleverly designed to strap onto a person's back. Mater Lumley opened Penelope's feathered carpetbag, placed the sandwiches inside, and fastened it shut.

Mater Lumley looked at her husband. "We should go as soon as Penny is done with breakfast," she said quietly. "I have that cold, prickly feeling down the back of my neck. He cannot be far."

Pater Lumley nodded. "Time to pull down the curtain," he said, and disappeared outside.

Penelope finished swallowing and wiped her lips with a napkin. "What curtain?" she asked. "Where are we going? 'He cannot be far. . . .' Do you mean Edward Ashton? I think you must."

"Three questions, all at once!" Mater Lumley answered in mock dismay. "Well, all right. The third question you have answered yourself. As for the second: we are going where we are urgently needed, and faster than you can imagine."

"England!" Penelope exclaimed. "And the curtain?"

Mater Lumley moved the rucksacks to the top of the stairs, as if that brought them one step closer to leaving. "Your father and I live in Frankenforde only part of the year. We stay as long as it takes to sell enough books and paintings to tide us over the rest of the time. He has devised a way to make sure no one bothers the shop while we are—elsewhere. It involves a curtain." She smiled. "Your father has a knack for stagecraft, I think!"

Naturally Penelope wanted to ask where "elsewhere" might be, and how on earth they were going to get to England so quickly, and whether by any chance her theatrically inclined father had ever heard of a young playwright named Simon Harley-Dickinson, but Pater Lumley had bounded back upstairs, and there was no more time for questions.

"All done," he said. He put on an extra-warm coat, as if he expected to be going someplace cold, and strapped on a rucksack.

Mater Lumley did the same. To Penelope she said, "There is a coat and hat in your carpetbag, and food and water. It's a bit heavier than it was, but I know you can manage it. This way, Penny—no, not through the shop. We will slip out the back door."

Moments later, they were in an alleyway that connected to the back alleys and rear yards of all the shops and houses in Frankenforde. Penelope followed her parents through countless twists and turns. They reached the edge of town without once setting foot on the street or in the square, and without being seen by anyone.

Beyond the village was the forest. There was no path in sight. Only a silent, shadowy maze of tall trees, blocking out the dim light of dawn.

Her parents did not hesitate.

What choice did she have but to follow?

AND SO, LIKE A CHARACTER in an old fairy tale, Penelope marched bravely into the dark German woods. Unlike most young people in fairy tales, she had both her mother and father to guide her. Even so, her parents each made a *shh!* gesture when she attempted to speak. The woods were quiet; apparently they needed to stay that way. But her mind was full of questions.

"To say we are going to England is all very well, but how? It must involve being high up, since Mater Lumley asked if I was afraid of heights," Penelope mused. "Curious! I wonder if we will scale a mountain, with crampons and a pickax? Or perhaps the trip will involve a magic carpet, or heaven forbid, a flying broomstick! Imagine trying to hold on to one of those at high speed!"

This train of thought may sound childish, but bear in mind that Penelope had muddled through without her parents for many a year. Now they were here and had taken charge, which left Penelope "off duty," as they say. Frankly, it was a relief to be able to think like a child for once, and although she did not wholly believe in magic, who knew? Perhaps things worked differently here in Germany, home of the Brothers Grimm and their peculiar tales about frog kings and golden geese, cottages made of candy and people no bigger than a thumb, little girls in bloodred capes and, of course, any number of tricky and dangerous wolves.

The Lumleys marched until they reached a lake. "If it were winter, we would skate across," Mater Lumley remarked. Pater Lumley strode to a large rock outcropping not far from the bank. Hidden among the rocks was a small rowboat and a pair of oars, which he proceeded to drag to the lake's edge. Penelope hopped in with a sailor's ease.

It was good to be on the water again. The wind was against them, but Pater Lumley was a strong rower. Within half an hour they reached the opposite shore. This time they hid the boat in a hollow among the roots of an enormous tree. Thick green moss grew over the hollow like a stage curtain; one would never know the tree had such a hiding place within.

"You have done this many times," Penelope said to her mother.

"Countless times, yes. This is my favorite place in the world." Before them was a meadow, as lush and green as a fairyland. The trees that circled it stood tall and straight, like kindly protectors. There was a special quietness about the place, punctuated now and then by the high trill of birdsong.

Mater and Pater Lumley walked with purpose into the meadow. Penelope scampered after them.

"'I wander through the meadows green,'" Mater Lumley recited softly as she walked.

"'Made happy by the verdant scene,'" Penelope interrupted. "'Wanderlust!' It is my favorite poem. Did *you* write it?"

Pater Lumley took his wife's hand. "Yes, she did. And all the other poems in that volume, too."

Mater Lumley turned to her. "I gave that book to Charlotte for you, Penny. I called them melancholy poems because we were apart, but they are also full of the joy I always feel here, in this meadow. It is the place that renews my hope."

"And now here I am, standing in the meadow green." Penelope's mind whirred. "Wait—you said you left a clue for me. Was it in the book of poems? If so, I never found it."

"It was the tides of fate that brought you back to us, then," Pater Lumley said.

Mater Lumley frowned. "Where is the book now?"

"With the Incorrigible children. I gave it to them when I was sent to Plinkst."

She looked relieved. "That's all right, then. You will see them soon enough, and if they have solved it, I'm sure you'll hear all about it. Next time we are together, we will have a good chuckle over it."

"What do you mean, 'next time we are together'?" Penelope asked, but her parents did not answer.

"Here we are," Pater Lumley said, hands on hips. Both her parents turned their faces to the sky.

There, like a strange, giant flower blooming in the middle of the tender spring grass, was an enormous balloon. It floated serenely at treetop height and was tethered with ropes to a circle of stakes that had been hammered firmly into the earth. Beneath it hung a large basket, woven out of reeds. It was not unlike the basket Margaret used to carry the clean laundry up and down the stairs at Ashton Place, except that it was big enough to hold a passenger or two.

"Is this yours?" Penelope asked, awestruck.

Pater Lumley shook his head. "No, but we have a balloon of our own, even larger than this one. It is on its way but is not here yet."

"If this is not your balloon, whose is it?"

"Why, it's mine, governess! Mine, all mine!"

A man stood up in the basket. He was a tall fellow

with white muttonchop whiskers. He wore a pith helmet that had been painted to match the balloon's bright patchwork of colors and patterns, with a small, brave flag flying on top.

"Admiral Faucet!" she gasped. "What are you doing here?"

"Piloting a balloon, obviously!" he bellowed. Nimbly he climbed down a rope ladder to the ground. "The balloon business is booming, or ballooning, if you don't mind the pun. It's both profitable and full of derring-do, which makes it an entirely suitable enterprise for a brave explorer like myself. I remember you, governess! You taught those three wolf children the Ashtons keep as pets. Excellent trackers, as I recall. We all went chasing after that big bird that got loose in the woods. What a marvelous pursuit that was!"

"You mean Bertha, the ostrich. I remember it all too well." Her tone was chilly, for Admiral Faucet (he pronounced it Faw-*say*) had made a poor impression on her the last time they had met. She turned to her parents. "I do not know what dealings you have had with this man, but he is not to be trusted."

"There's no need to hold a grudge," the admiral interjected. "I've learned my lesson. No more wooing rich widows for me! No more crackpot schemes about ostrich racing! I'll stick to good honest ballooning from now on."

He stooped to retrieve a fancy carved walking stick that was propped against one of the balloon's anchoring stakes. Clearly he did not need it for walking, but it proved useful for making grand gestures. "So you know Hans and Suzie too, eh?" he said, twirling the stick toward her parents. "I see a bit of a family resemblance, not that it's any of my business. Anyway, we balloonists tend to stick together. It takes courage and skill to brave the heavens, and good old Hans and Suzie know as much about it as anyone."

Penelope flinched to hear her parents referred to so casually, but they did not seem to mind.

Admiral Faucet slapped her father on the back. "I keep telling Hans here to open an aerial show and sell tickets. 'Touch the Clouds with the Lighter-Than-Air Lumleys! Paint the Landscape as Seen from Above!' Why, they'd make a fortune!"

"We prefer a more private existence than you do, Faucet," Pater Lumley answered.

"The Incognito Lumleys, that's you two, to a T. It's a rare treat to find you at sea level, I must say." Admiral Faucet turned to Penelope and jerked a thumb at her parents. "These two could draw you a map of alpine villages so remote, the only way to get there is by balloon! Unless you're a goat, of course, and even those Swiss mountain goats don't go as high."

Penelope had always been a whiz at puzzles. Quickly she put all the facts together. "So that is where 'elsewhere' is!" she said to her parents. "It explains why all those paintings are painted from above. You live in the sky. And Edward Ashton has been searching for you on land, all these years."

Admiral Faucet pounded his walking stick on the ground. "Edward Ashton! The lying scoundrel. I'll not soon forgive him for the nasty trick he played on me. Any foe of his is a friend of mine, and I mean it." He glanced at his pocket watch. "Time's flying, and so must we! Now, which one of you is going to England?"

Penelope looked at her parents, her heart sinking.

"The admiral and his balloon will take you to England," Mater Lumley said gently. "We will follow just as soon as we can."

"But—but—but why can't we all go?" Even as the words tumbled out, she knew how childish she sounded.

"Not possible." Admiral Faucet rapped his stick on the side of the basket. "My balloon's a compact model. It'll only hold two people of average size." He hoisted his trousers around his ample middle. "I'm a bit larger than average, and you're a wee thing, so we'll be all right. I've got our provisions weighed to the ounce."

Pater Lumley handed him the carpetbag. "Here you go, sir. Seven pounds, five ounces, exactly."

"Sounds like a bouncing baby baggage, har har!" The admiral hoisted the bag in his hand for a moment before loading it inside. "Even a few pounds over capacity and we won't fly right, or at all," he explained. "And we've a long way to go! Over land and sea, hup, hup, hup!"

Mater Lumley spoke reassuringly. "The admiral is an experienced pilot, Penny. Do as he says and you will be quite safe."

Penelope forced herself to look up. The balloon was so small, and the sky was so large! She would simply have to keep her eyes shut the whole time.

"What's the matter, governess? Afraid of heights?"

That question again! Penelope squirmed. It was not so much that she was afraid of heights. It was that she was afraid she *would* be afraid of heights, once at high altitude, and by then it would be too late. "Buck up, Penny!" she scolded herself. "You never minded looking out the nursery window at Ashton Place, and that was on the third floor!" Granted, there was an elm tree

right outside, with spreading branches full of dancing leaves and friendly squirrels. That cozy view never
prompted the sick, panicky feeling of being unmoored
from the earth that the phrase "touch the clouds" had
stirred up in her.

"I will go," she said, with far more confidence than
she felt.

Admiral Faucet scowled. "Better be sure, governess.
Balloon travel is not for the faint of heart. Once you're
up, you're up! There's no changing your mind, for I
can't very well put down in the middle of the English
Channel. And the basket is small, so we've got to get
along peacefully. No whining or complaining."

Penelope stood straight and tall. "Admiral, may I
remind you, I am a Swanburne graduate. There will be
no whining or complaining from me."

"I should think not!" Mater Lumley said. Both her
parents laughed at that, but it was the kind of laughter
meant to keep things cheerful when sadness is right
beneath the surface. Penelope knew the sound well.

Admiral Faucet wet a finger in his mouth and held
it up to check the wind. "Not bad, not bad. We'll be in
England by week's end, give or take." He climbed back
up the rope ladder that dangled from the side of the
basket. "All aboard! Governess, say your good-byes.

315

The sun has been up for an hour, and the wind is fair. Time to go!"

Her parents each gave her a quick, tight hug. Pater Lumley offered a hand to steady her as she set foot on the rope ladder.

"I am not afraid," she said, and climbed into the basket without help. It was small, but not nearly as small as a herring barrel, and much sweeter smelling, too. The thought that she had already survived worse cheered her somewhat.

Admiral Faucet added more coal to the small stove that heated the air and made the balloon rise. At once the balloon stretched taut, straining at the ropes.

"Ready for takeoff," he called to the ground. The Lumleys skillfully untethered the ropes, one by one. Mater Lumley dropped the last rope. With a sideways lurch, the balloon began to rise.

Penelope held on for dear life. "Good-bye!" she called, leaning over the basket's edge. Her parents were growing smaller by the minute.

"We will see you soon, Penny dear!" Mater Lumley called, waving furiously. "Soon! I promise!"

"That is what you said the last time!" Penny yelled back, but her voice was swallowed by the wind.

THE TOWN OF FRANKENFORDE LOOKED even more picturesque than usual in the rosy glow of early morning. Some townspeople were already astir, for just as certain professions are the cause of late bedtimes (actors come to mind, and theater critics, too, alas!), other jobs demand an early start. Bakers, for example.

As Madame Ionesco herself could tell you, a baker must work in the dead of night in order to have plenty of fresh-baked treats ready for the morning's customers. For who does not like a tasty apple strudel with their morning coffee? Or a thick slice of gingerbread, spicy and sweet, still warm from the oven? Or even a scrumptious *Berliner Pfannkuchen*, filled with marmalade and dusted with powdered sugar?

Edward Ashton was a man obsessed—a man who had resolved to commit murder. A man who had loosed the reins of his mind to gallop in pursuit of evil and was now unable to gather them up again! But he was also a man who had been traveling for days without rest or food. He had arrived in the village an hour past dawn. He knew his prey was near, but the mesmerizing aroma from the bakery nearly made him faint. "Breakfast, coffee—and then the Lumleys," he told himself. With a trembling hand he opened the bakery door.

Ring-ring! Ring-ring!

317

A ruddy-cheeked woman in a flour-dusted apron appeared behind the counter, protesting mildly that the shop was not yet open, she was still icing the Black Forest cakes, could he come back in *zehn Minuten, bitte*? Ashton ignored her. He growled his order in German and paid for his coffee and *Berliner Pfannkuchen* (think of it as an extra-yummy jelly doughnut). He stood at the counter and shoved the food into his mouth like a starved animal, scattering crumbs over himself and the floor.

The woman pressed her lips together. She grabbed a broom and swept all around him, right up to the edge of his shoes, but he did not move.

"Where is the bookstore?" he asked, waving the book of melancholy poetry around. "I know it is nearby. I have the address right here."

"Sometimes there is a bookstore in Frankenforde, and sometimes there isn't," the woman answered, still sweeping.

"No riddles!" he snapped. "Just tell me where it is."

"When there is a bookstore, it's next door," she answered curtly, and disappeared into the back. It was a perfect example of why one must always use good manners when making a purchase in a shop. The baker was hardly inclined to be helpful after that rude, wild-eyed fellow made such a mess in her bakery—and while she was in the middle of icing her Black Forest cakes, yet!

"Bookstore, next door, bookstore, next door . . ." Edward Ashton left the bakery, muttering and flicking the ends of his black cloak in annoyance, the way a cat will flick the tip of its tail when the mousie is just out of reach. He looked to the right, then to the left. On one side of the bakery was a shoemaker. On the other side was a shop that sold little Tyrolean hats. There was no sign at all of a bookstore.

He walked the length of the street, and all four sides of the village square. No matter who he asked, the answer was the same: the bookstore was next door to the bakery, sometimes! And sometimes it was not.

His breath quickened with frustration and rage. What had he missed? Back to the bakery he went. He looked in the window and rested his forehead against the cool, smooth glass. Pastries, biscuits, the freshly iced cakes—each a work of art. "Once I find the bookstore," he thought, "I will treat myself to a slice of that superb Black Forest cake." Absently he licked the marmalade off his fingertips. He would search the town again, a hundred times, a hundred times a hundred if need be! Perhaps the Tyrolean hatmaker could give him better directions. Indeed, he had always had a fondness for that style of hat. He resolved to go ask him and, if the fellow was not in yet, to wait.

On his way to the hat shop he passed the bakery's other window. This one held a dazzling display of birthday cakes, in many styles and flavors. Upon the largest of the cakes the following words were written in a flowing cursive, in English:

Happy birthday
To our children
Wherever you might be.

The penmanship was quite good, considering it was all done in icing. Ashton sniffed, doggishly. He frowned, and sniffed again. He reached out to tap the window, only to find it was not glass at all, but an enormous canvas drop, a painted curtain, like the backdrop for a play.

Fury rose within him as he tried to fight his way behind the canvas. It was not easy, as Pater Lumley had rigged an ingenious system of knots 'round the curtain's edge to keep it steady in all weather. With a roar of frustration, Edward Ashton pulled a knife out of his boot and slit the canvas from top to bottom, coincidentally slicing the painted birthday cake in two.

Behind the gaping curtain lay the bookstore's actual window, with the Giddy-Yap, Rainbow! books on cheerful display. The store was dark, the door was locked. The sign read GESCHLOSSEN. Closed.

Pony books and birthday cakes! The Lumleys had been here, all right. But they were already gone.

"I am too late!" he said, and crumpled to the ground. If only those blasted pheasants had not held up his train!

His mind raced. Horses, trains, boats—all were easy to intercept. He must think and act quickly. Like a man in leg irons he staggered to his feet. "They cannot get away from me again!" he said, sheathing his knife. "Never, never, never!"

By now the square had filled with people. A few regarded the strange, muttering man with suspicion, or pity. One or two may have noticed the ripped curtain, with the halves of the painted birthday cake now flapping in the breeze. But most ignored the strange scene and minded their own business. This is what busy grown-ups tend to do, especially in the morning when there are jobs to get to and errands to run. At such times, small children are the only ones who have time to notice things properly.

"Mama, schau!" just such a child cried, pointing upward. *"Ein Luftballon!"*

It was then that Edward Ashton looked up at the sky.

The Thirteenth Chapter

A ship that flies in the air.

"Hang in there, governess! Takeoff and landing are the bumpiest parts of the journey. Once we achieve altitude, we'll have smooth sailing, never you fear."

Penelope made a small, miserable noise to acknowledge Admiral Faucet's remark. It was not the sickening sway of the rising balloon that had sent her to the floor of the basket with her knees clutched to her chest. No, it was watching her parents shrink to the size of squirrels, then toy soldiers, then mere specks, that had made her curl up in misery, taking one deep, calming breath after another. Frankenforde as seen from above could fit in a nutshell with room to spare, and the Itty-Bitty Lumleys would be no more than grains of sand within it.

"It is the coming and going that is hard," she thought, sniffling back her tears. "But better they should be the Here-and-Gone, See-You-Later Lumleys than go back to being Long-Lost! And think what it will be like for the Incorrigibles—that is, my brothers and sister, the three littlest Lumleys!—to meet their parents once more."

This happy thought got her feet under her. Soon she braved standing up. At first she kept her eyes downcast and concentrated on getting her flying legs, so to speak. When she finally lifted her face, the rush of fresh air (and really, what air could be fresher?), the canopy of sparkling blue sky all around, the sheer storybook magic of being in flight washed all fear from her, and she spread her arms wide and laughed aloud.

Admiral Faucet chuckled. "I knew you'd come 'round. Enjoy the view while you can! Your parents—now don't deny it, I've got eyes to see with, miss!—asked me to travel incognito as best I could. We'll have to sacrifice scenery for secrecy."

Penelope looked up. "A brightly colored balloon floating across a clear blue sky? What secrecy can there be in that?"

He added more coal to the stove, for the stronger the fire, the hotter the air and the faster the balloon rose. "You'll see. Lucky for us it's springtime. April showers bring May flowers, as the proverb goes. There'll be no shortage of stratocumuli and nimbostrati to hide behind."

"I beg your pardon?"

"Clouds, governess! It's higher than I typically fly, but with enough hot air, there's no reason we can't get above the clouds. It's quite a sight! You'll want to put on your hat and coat, though. It does get chilly up there."

It was all as the admiral described. When the balloon pierced the fog of the low-lying clouds, the air grew cold and damp. They were briefly blinded as the mist swirled all around, but soon they popped through to the other side. Above, the sky was bluer than the clearest day imaginable. Below, the tops of the clouds formed a thick layer that churned like an ocean of cake frosting. Penelope was tempted to reach out and catch some on her finger, just as she used to scrape the last bit of icing from the bowl when Cook let her help in the kitchen. But she knew better, for clouds are made of water droplets and ice crystals, not sugar and butter and cream. And leaning out of a balloon in flight is never advisable.

Brrr! The temperature had dropped thirty degrees already. Now she understood why her parents had packed her a warm coat and hat. Admiral Faucet made tea by heating water on the same stove that heated air for the balloon, and they each helped themselves to a sandwich. Occasionally the admiral glanced at a small compass he carried in his pocket, or added more fuel to the fire. Otherwise he left the balloon to its own devices.

Penelope cradled the warm tea between her hands. "Admiral Faucet, I am curious. How do you keep this vessel on course?"

"On course? You mean how do I steer the blasted thing?"

"Yes."

He laughed merrily. "You can't steer a balloon, governess! That's the fun of it. It's just a big bag of hot air. It blows where the wind takes it. If you have a particular destination in mind, it's up to you to find the wind that's heading your way."

"You make it sound as if there are different winds to choose from," she said, not wholly convinced.

"That's because there are. The wind blows in all directions. Which one you catch depends on your altitude. It's much easier than steering, when you get used to it. Just decide where you'd like to end up, and choose the wind that suits you best. Now, hand me another one of those sandwiches, would you?"

NOTHING PASSES THE TIME LIKE a good story, of course, and the admiral was nothing if not a talker. Alas, all his tales tended to be about himself and his globe-trotting adventures, and there was a sameness to them that soon wearied Penelope. Eventually she pretended to nap, so as not to have to listen anymore. "Imagine what Miss Mortimer would say," she rued. "A Swanburne girl on a long journey without a single book to read!" And only yesterday she had been in a bookstore, too. Grimm's fairy tales would have been suitable, given her recent experience in the German woods. *The Arabian Nights* and its flying carpets would also have served nicely. If only she had thought to borrow one of them!

Luckily, the workings of one's own mind are highly portable, as they weigh nothing and take up no room in a suitcase. Penelope decided to occupy herself by making lists of questions for her parents. "At three questions a day, in a week I ought to be able to ask quite a few. Twenty-one, to be exact," she thought. "The seven-times table is tricky, but the three-times table is easy as falling off a—whoops!"

"Scared you, did I?" The admiral chuckled as he lowered himself back into the basket. He had climbed up the rope rigging of the balloon to mend a small hole with a piece of rubber and some spirit gum. "That was easy! Just like patching a bicycle tire. Hans taught me how, but I've never done a repair on the fly before."

"Admiral Faucet, have you seen my parents' balloon?" It had just occurred to her that the admiral might have answers to some of the very questions she had in mind.

"I surely have. It's a magnificent vessel, much larger than this one. Looks a bit like a gondola! It's nicely camouflaged, too." He frowned. "I wonder why it was delayed? I hope nothing tragic happened." At her stricken face, he changed his tone. "Don't worry. No news is no news, as they say. I expect you'll see them soon enough. Unless . . ."

"Unless?"

But he caught himself. "Unless nothing. Personally I like to look on the bright side of things, and I recommend you do the same. One thing I've learned flying a balloon, governess—when your spirits are lighter than air, it helps keep the ship afloat, if you catch my meaning!"

ON THE THIRD DAY THEY got caught in a thunderstorm. That was the most frightening part of the trip. No matter how hard Admiral Faucet maneuvered the balloon to rise above the storm, it remained stuck in the thick of it, bullied about by the winds.

"We've got to lighten up!" he yelled. All nonessentials were tossed overboard. They saved one sandwich each, but the rest went over. Penelope held on to the papier-mâché seashell as long as she could. She even considered tucking a note inside, like a letter in a bottle, in case she was never heard from again. But she had already tossed the carpetbag that held her pen and paper, and so the seashell went over empty. (Whether the carpetbag was mistaken for an albatross as it fell we may never know. However, the papier-mâché seashell was carried by the wind quite a long way before landing—improbably, but not impossibly— in the scorching sands of the Sahara. Decades later, it was found by scientists, who marveled at the appearance of this perfectly preserved ocean mollusk in the middle of a desert. It was the cause of much scientific debate, until the small children of one of the scientists pointed out that the shell was made of shredded paper, water, and flour, just like the stuff they played with at school. That sparked an entirely different debate about not poking around Daddy's office unsupervised, children being seen and not heard, and so on.)

Penelope and Admiral Faucet survived the storm, but the loss of the sandwiches was a great disappointment. Nevertheless, by minding their altitude and choosing their winds wisely, the two brave balloonists made their way across Europe. It was on the morning of the fifth day that the admiral declared them safely across the North Sea.

"How do you know?" she asked. The sky and clouds all looked the same to her.

"Go see for yourself!" Faucet was tall and could easily peer over the basket's rim. Penelope had to go right to the edge on tiptoes to get a good look. Far below, through the tattered clouds, the chalk cliffs of Dover glowed white as old bone, and the dark water of the English Channel was flecked with whitecaps.

"Home sweet home! Now we just need to find Ashton Place," he said. "Do you think you'd recognize it from the air?"

She tried to imagine a bird's-eye view of the estate. "It is surrounded by a large forest," she ventured.

"So's half of England. What else?"

"The house is extremely large. And neoclassical in design," she added.

"So's Buckingham Palace," he retorted. "Think, governess!"

She thought hard. What would be an unmistakable feature of the landscape that would be visible from high above? "I know!" she said. "There is a new train line that runs to Ashton Station, pulled by a red Bloomer steam locomotive. If we locate the train from the air, it will lead us to the exact forest and large neoclassical house we are aiming for."

He pulled on his muttonchop whiskers. "A red locomotive, moving fast along shiny new tracks. And it blows a trail of smoke behind it? Like a man running after the omnibus while clutching a lit cigar?"

She nodded.

"That should be easy to spot. And you're sure the choo-choo's red?"

"As a rose," she said. Happiness swelled within her. Could they really be that close to home?

The admiral let some air out of the balloon to get them below the clouds. They followed the snaky line of the River Thames inland from the North Sea, passing directly over London. How incredible to see that marvelous city from above! The people were like so many ants at a picnic, swarming here and there in pursuit of crumbs. Was Simon down there somewhere? Was Madame Ionesco? Penelope could only wonder, for of course she had no way of knowing all that had happened while she was away.

Farther inland they flew, over the tranquil patchwork of fields and farms that marks the English countryside to this very day (and, one hopes, for many years to come). The meadows were dotted with creamy white sheep. "Like little clouds floating on the grass," Penelope mused. She might never have thought this had she not spent time among the clouds herself, which is a perfect example of how travel broadens the mind.

Ashton Place was only a day's journey by train to London. They must be getting close. Fearlessly she leaned over the edge of the basket, searching the ground below. "There it is!" she yelled. There was no mistaking the curve of iron tracks slicing through the fertile earth. And there was the Bloomer rolling along, a gleam of apple red trailing white smoke behind like the tail of a kite. She listened for the grating chug of the wheels and metal-on-metal screech of the brakes as the train rounded each curve, but it was still too far away.

It did not matter. The train's silent, serpentine progress gave them a line to follow. The admiral proved deft at finding the wind he needed to keep the Bloomer in view. Before long a dense and mysterious forest spread beneath them. Then came the many colors of the garden beds, their bright spring bloom like a rainbow along the grand curved driveway Penelope knew so well and had feared she might never see again!

"I'll put down in a clearing in the woods, if I can," the admiral said, frantically letting air out of the balloon until they were skimming the treetops. "This way our arrival will be a real surprise. We'll come up with a careful plan of attack and take things step by step. Hup, hup, hup! Eh, governess? Governess?" He looked around the tiny basket. "Blast, where did the governess go?"

THE THIRD-FLOOR NURSERY AT ASHTON Place was open for business. Mrs. Penworthy had volunteered to act as the children's temporary governess, since they had no other and the baby nurse had time to spare for another day or so, until the baby was born. Great heaps of knitting were folded and stacked all around. There were all the sweaters, mittens, hats, and scarves one might expect, along with some more, well, *unusual* projects.

For example, there was a knitted map of England that used blue yarn for the water and a mix of greens and browns for the land, with the occasional white knot stitch thrown in to represent a sheep. This was Alexander's doing, as you might have guessed.

Beowulf had knitted a carrying case with a strap, perfect for those times when one gets the urge to paint *en plein air* and needs to carry one's portable easel, paints, and brushes outdoors.

As for Cassiopeia, she had knitted a collection of eye patches for playing at pirates, and a holster to fit a toy dagger that Beowulf had gnawed for her out of a fallen tree branch. He had painted it to give the impression of a gleaming metal blade, sharp enough to split an eyelash, but it was actually smooth-sanded wood and quite safe to play with.

At the moment, Cassiopeia and her brothers were merrily swashbuckling 'round the nursery, slashing at imaginary foes. Mrs. Penworthy had declared the day's lesson to be Making Things Up, Pirate Edition. This was enjoyable for the children and of great practical use for Simon, for he had been struggling to write a play about pirates for some time now. Watching the children pretend was giving him ideas. (The bards among you know that writing is nine-tenths pretending on paper and one-tenth spelling and punctuation marks. The correct use of apostrophes is important, and choosing the right words is more important, but pretending will always be the most important part of the whole business, and who does not like to pretend?)

"I like that slicing and dicing, Cassawoof." Simon took notes with furrowed brow. "But if all the characters are made to walk the plank in the opening scene, the play will be too short. Can't we kill them closer to the end?"

In reply came a muffled *whump . . . thud!* Then a creak, as of a bending tree branch, followed by an "Ouch!" Simon stared at his pages and sighed. "All right. Walk the plank it is. But where do we go from there?"

"Simawoo," Beowulf said. Like his siblings, he wore a knitted eye patch. At the moment he was staring at the nursery window, rubbing his free eye as if to get it to work better. But Simon was deep in concentration, his gleam of genius fully engaged.

"All right, let me think! All the pirates are thrown overboard. Who's left? Maybe—I know it's improbable, but it just might work! Maybe the cabin boy can take over the ship *and* the plot. . . ."

"Simawoo?" Alexander ripped off his eye patch and

turned his spyglass to the nursery window.

"A cabin boy. Hmm!" Simon frowned and tapped his pencil against his chin. "Cabin boy, cabin boy. I could call it *Cabin Boy on Holiday*. Say, that's not bad!"

Tap-tap-tap-tap! Someone—could it be that missing scamp, Nutsawoo?—was tapping on the glass of the nursery window.

"Simawooooo!" the children howled in unison. It was a strange, strangled howl, a mix of joy and confusion and disbelief, and it ended abruptly as all three Incorrigibles hurled themselves at the window and fought to be the first to open it.

The spring breeze blew the curtains into the room like billowing sails, and the nursery filled with the scent of clouds, and sky, and apple, mustard, and cheddar sandwiches. There was the faintest whiff of herring, too, for it would take more than one washing to get that smell out of a thick knitted sweater.

"Well," said Miss Penelope Lumley, who stood, wobbly but secure, on the spreading branch of the elm tree. Her hard landing made the branch sway to and fro, but she had sea legs enough to manage it, after all the traveling she had done. "Isn't anyone going to say hello?"

The children stood, frozen. "Excuse me, Lumawoo

Bird, as seen from the Nursery Window," Alexander inquired in a shaky voice. "Are you real? Or pretend?"

"We have been making things up," Beowulf explained. "So it is not easy to tell."

"For example." Cassiopeia took out her dagger and recited, in a foot-stomping iambic pentameter, "'Is THIS a DAGger WHICH I SEE beFORE me?'"

"Shakespeare!" Penelope cried, full of joy, and clambered inside. (She was correct, of course. The famous line about the dagger is from one of Shakespeare's tragedies. Alas, the play cannot be named within these pages. To do so is the worst kind of bad luck, for this particular play is thought to have a curse upon it. To learn more you must ask your nearest thespian, but be sure to inquire about the "Scottish play" and under no circumstances say the title even if you do know what it is. To hear that accursèd name would make any professional actor flee in terror, as if being chased by a thousand theater critics!)

Luckily, Penelope knew not to say the name of the Scottish play, as Simon—oh! Simon Harley-Dickinson! Would she see him soon again, too?—had explained it all to her long ago. "Your dagger is a pretend dagger, Cassiopeia, but it is a real pretend dagger, and very well made from the looks of it. And I too am as real

as real can be! Oh, look at you all! It is so good to be home!" Then she noticed Mrs. Penworthy. "Pardon me, ma'am! I am not a burglar, I assure you."

The baby nurse had already leaped to his—or her—feet, but did not move toward the intruder. "Hold on, now," Simon said warily. "Is this a cabin boy I see before me?" He could hardly trust his eyes either, as he had been making things up about cabin boys, and now one seemed to have flown right in the window. With a squirrel aboard, no less! For the long-absent Nutsawoo was there too, chattering and skittering joyously from one of Penelope's shoulders to the other. The dim-witted creature knew exactly who had dangled from a rope ladder hastily lowered from a balloon and landed in the same spreading elm branches that the fluffy-tailed, beady-eyed menace called home.

Penelope removed her knitted cap and shook out her shining auburn hair, which matched the Incorrigible children's hair as perfectly as one sock matches its mate. "I am Miss Penelope Lumley," she said to the nurse. "I once was—and, I hope, will be again—the children's governess."

The Incorrigible children threw themselves upon her. They barked and howled and yapped with joy. After all, they had promised Lord Fredrick to practice being barky, and the Incorrigibles always kept their promises.

"Why so wolfish?" Penelope said lovingly, as she hugged all three. "Clearly I have been away too long. But madame, you surely do look familiar. . . ."

"That's Mrs. Penworthy!" the children exclaimed, although they could hardly speak for laughing.

Simon grinned and pulled off his wig. "Well, well, well," he said, for even a bard can find himself at a loss for words when his heart is full. "I can't imagine a better plot twist than this!"

PENELOPE DISENTANGLED HERSELF FROM THE children's hugs and turned to her friend.

"Simon, I am overjoyed to see you, and eager to know how you are. I am also curious about that costume you have on! But first things first: Have you located Madame Ionesco? Is she nearby? Does she know how to undo the curse?"

"Same to you, on all three counts!" Simon scratched his head. "As for your questions: I have, and she is. And yes, I think she might, but I don't know the details. She told me she wouldn't say a word about the curse until all four wolf babies had arrived. What's that about, I wonder?"

"But we are only three! One-two-three, one-two-three, one-two-three . . ." The Incorrigibles counted and spun in a circle until they got dizzy and fell down, giggling.

Penelope looked at their dear little faces. What a surprise they had in store! "There is a great deal to explain," she said, "but it is a long and complicated story that is best saved until there is time to tell it properly. Four wolf babies, indeed! Well, never mind that. I have reason to think she will reveal herself now."

To Simon she added, "Where can we find the good Madame?"

"The bakehouse. She's been baking bread like mad."

"To the bakehouse!" the children cried with enthusiasm, for surely there would be something good to eat once they arrived. This appealed to Penelope, too, who was by now quite hungry.

"Yes, we must go at once." She looked down at her sailor outfit. "I have no other clothes to wear, but perhaps it is just as well to travel incognito. If anyone asks, I am your cousin, Alf, a cabin boy on leave."

Simon pulled his wig back on. "Alf it is. And I'll go back to being Mrs. Penworthy. Now, don't laugh! At the moment I'm the baby nurse and substitute governess.

And I intend to do a good job of it, too, until the real one is ready to return." He waited until the children were busy putting Nutsawoo back outside, then quietly asked, "But what do you know about Edward Ashton? He's not here now, though Mrs. Clarke told me he'd spent a few days as a houseguest not two weeks ago. Looked like he'd been through the wars, she said, and seemed to have gone a bit unhinged."

"He has been looking for my parents," she said. "Have no fear. He can search the globe over, but he will not find them."

"Your parents? Wait a minute—is there more to this plot twist than meets the eye?"

Cassiopeia ran back from the window and hurled herself atop Simon's shoulders. "Giddy-yap, Mrs. Penworthy!" she yelled. "Gallop to the bakehouse, on the double!"

"Mind the hair, Cassawoof," he admonished, for she had grabbed the two pigtails as reins and was yanking them this way and that. To Penelope he said, "It's plain by the look on your face the answer is yes. To be continued, Alf the cabin boy!"

"Yes, we shall save the rest for later," she said, eyes a-twinkle. What a marvelous secret she had, and how much fun it would be to tell it! She took Beowulf by

341

one hand and Alexander by the other. Despite everything that had already happened, and all that was yet
to come, at that moment she thought she had never
been so happy in her life. "To the bakehouse!"

As you recall, the soothsayer kept odd hours. She
was not in the bakehouse, but Simon knew where she
slept, in a little shed not far off. The path that led to
it was flanked by a garden, now planted with strange
herbs of the type a spell-casting soothsayer might
need, for professional purposes.

Penelope was eager to hear Madame's solution to
the Ashton/curse problem (for indeed, the curse had
divided the Ashtons in two). "It ought not to be difficult for a weird woman of her skill," she said to Mrs.
Penworthy as they walked. "We simply need a way to
undo the curse, without committing . . ." She stopped,
not wishing to say "murder" in front of the children.
"Rhymes with birder," she said instead, in a low voice.

"Sheepherder!" the children yelled, for they missed
nothing. Children rarely do, especially when older
people are trying to slip something past them.

"What a racket! What are you trying to do, wake
the dead?" It was the spooky Madame herself, cackling
merrily in the doorway to her shed. "'Murder' is the

word you're looking for, cookie. We'll have none of that creepy talk around here. The dead hate that word, for obvious reasons. Hey, wolf kids!"

"Madame Ionesco!" The children were thrilled to see her at last, and gave her many hugs.

"Thank you for the Gypsy cakes," Alexander said, ever polite.

"You like the bread, huh? Me too. When the dough rises, it looks like a big balloon." She gave Penelope a meaningful wink as she ushered them inside. "You just made it, Lumley! I was getting worried."

"'A Swanburne girl may arrive early, or in the nick of time, but she is never late,'" Penelope said.

"That's pithy," the Madame said approvingly. "Well, you're all here, finally. Now we can talk. Sit down already!"

There was nothing to sit upon in the shed but upended dough buckets, but they sufficed. Simon leaned forward, all eagerness. "Does that mean there's a way to undo the curse without committing—" He glanced at the children and dropped his voice. "Rhymes with birder?"

"Blurred her?'" Alexander offered.

"Preferred her?" Beowulf suggested.

"Maybe you misheard her," Cassiopeia crowed.

"Bloody murder!" the soothsayer yelled, impatient. "Yes, yes! I've got it all figured out, more or less. What do you think I've been doing back here?"

"Baking Gypsy cakes?" Beowulf said, full of hope.

"Besides that. I've been working on the curse." She too found a bucket to sit upon; luckily Simon turned it over quickly, before she fell in. "A curse is like a contract. Two parties sign on the dotted line. Neither one of them can change it. Unless!"

"Unless?" They all said it at once.

Madame Ionesco swung her legs until they kicked the bucket, so to speak. "Unless both parties agree to the change. It falls under Amendments and Modifications, page six hundred forty-two in the *Soothsayer's Almanac of Curses and Spells*, Third Edition. I had to do a lot of research, I hope you realize."

"Thank you for your hard work," Penelope said, meaning it.

"I'm just saying, don't be surprised at the bill. Anyway, if both parties agree, you draw up a new contract to replace the old. One signs, the other signs, and abracadabra! You're done."

Simon looked skeptical. "Hang on, Madame. In this case, one of the parties involved was Admiral Percival Racine Ashton, who's long dead, correct?"

She rolled her eyes. "One of the deadest. You should hear him! What a bore. I wouldn't want to get stuck next to him at a party."

Penelope was thinking hard. "And the other party was the sacred wolf of the island of Ahwoo-Ahwoo. Surely she's dead by now as well?"

The fortune-teller shrugged. "Dead, alive. It's hard to say. Those magic animals are kind of in-between to start with."

Simon paced 'round the tiny shed, ducking his head occasionally because of the low ceiling. "So how do we get a long-dead admiral and a hard-to-say-if-she's-dead magic wolf to tear up an old contract and sign a new one?"

Madame Ionesco cracked her knuckles as if preparing for a fight. "Dead is the least of our problems. It's the negotiation I'm worried about. We'll find out when the full moon comes."

"That's tomorrow." Simon turned to Penelope. "At least we won't have Edward Ashton to worry about."

"Perhaps," she said, for she knew how sharply fate can swerve between one day and the next. "We shall find out tomorrow."

"Tomorrow, and tomorrow, and tomorrow," the children agreed. It was another line from that Scottish play whose title cannot be spoken. Perhaps someday Madame Ionesco could remove that curse as well. If so, she would surely go down in the history books as a hero to all in the theatrical firmament. However, as both Agatha Swanburne and her great-granddaughter were fond of saying, "First things first." It was one of their pithiest sayings, and one of the wisest, too.

ONLY ONE DAY LEFT TILL the first full moon of May! Lady Constance seemed untroubled. She no longer took long walks in the garden. Instead she passed the time in her private parlor with various companions, Mrs. Clarke or Margaret, or of course Mrs. Penworthy, but most often now it was Fredrick who sat by her, pouring tea and rolling skeins of yarn as the mother-to-be knitted in slow motion, by the window. Her constant prattle had given way to a dreamier state. Row by row she knitted a baby's bib, but she would stop every few stitches and stare into the thin air, as if thinking thoughts too deep to be understood by anyone, most of all herself.

"Fredrick," she said during one such interval. "What is that object in the sky?"

"Do you mean the sun, dear?"

She answered calmly but firmly. "No, I do not mean

the sun. The sun is not an object in the sky, like a kite, or a ball tossed into the air. The sun is a burning source of light and heat, like a candle, only it is very large and very far away. I imagine you are surprised I know that, but I do, for I have been taking books from the library now and then. And reading them!"

"Is it a bird, then?" Fredrick guessed. "Sparrow, perhaps? Nuthatch? Warbler?"

"I am not playing a game, Fredrick. Honestly! Come see for yourself."

Lord Fredrick got up and parted the curtains. "Well, blast! It looks like a full moon to me. I could swear it's a day early. But what's it doing in the garden?"

She stood up to get a better view. "Why, the moon *is* in the garden! How odd. It was in the sky a moment ago. It must have . . . landed."

Fredrick grew agitated. "Blasted almanac! I checked and double-checked. The full moon's not till tomorrow, so what's it doing here now? Yap. Woof." He tried to make himself yap and bark, but they came out as ordinary words. "All clear. There must be some sort of mix-up."

"I should say so. For not only has the moon landed in my garden, it seems to be shrinking quite rapidly. Waning, is that what it's called? Yes! The moon is

347

waning, right before our very eyes." She pursed her pretty bow lips. "It looks like a soufflé that has begun to deflate. Oh, now I am desperately craving a soufflé for lunch! I know we just had breakfast, but I am eating for two, after all."

"This is most disturbing. I'll have Old Tim find out what's what." Fredrick rang the bellpull as he shouted, "Timothy! Timothy!"

Penelope, the children, and Simon had arrived back at the house at the same time Lord Fredrick was yanking on the bellpull. The enigmatic coachman nearly knocked them over as he dashed up the stairs. "Coming, sir! Out of my way, cubs! Ahoy, sailor. Pardon me, Penworthy!"

"That's Mrs. Penworthy to you, you old rogue! Allow me to introduce my cousin, Alf, a cabin boy on leave . . ." But Old Timothy was already gone. "Wonder where Old Tim's going in such a rush," Simon remarked as they made their way to the third floor. "Some sort of horse emergency, perhaps? Anyway, Alf, I'm still trying to figure out the bit about four wolf babies. What did Madame Ionesco mean by that, do you suppose?"

Penelope brushed the question off. "Why, I expect it is like *The Three Musketeers*, by Mr. Alexandre Dumas.

There are four musketeers in it, despite the title. Poetic license, perhaps?"

"Hmm. I don't see the connection. And if I read my cabin boys right," he added slyly, "you know something you're not saying."

Penelope blushed, for she had no wish to deceive Simon, of all people. She let the children enter the nursery ahead of them so she could speak privately. "You are quite right, of course. I have news that is going to come as a great shock to the children. I want to make sure to tell them in just the right way, at just the right time." Frankly, she had no idea how the Incorrigibles would react. Would they be glad to have a big sister or disappointed to lose a governess? And what about Mater and Pater Lumley? Doubtless the children would be full of questions about their parents, very few of which Penelope could answer, as she had hardly had the chance to ask any questions herself.

Meanwhile, Nutsawoo was urgently *tap-tap-tapping* at the window. The children struggled to open it, but the top latch was stuck.

"Nutsy, what's the matter? We don't see you for weeks, and now you're all demanding." Simon strode to the window and got it open again. What he saw made him blurt a few words that were perfectly suitable for a sailor, but not often heard from a baby nurse—at least, not while children were present.

"What's the moon doing on the ground?" Alexander asked, quite reasonably.

"Fall of Rome? Fall of moon!" Cassiopeia loved all the phases of the moon, but the full moon was her favorite.

"Moon balloon!" Beowulf declared, after a moment's careful observation. It could have been the start of a poem, but it was also an accurate description of what he saw.

Penelope ran over to look. "That is no moon," she said, overjoyed. "It is the Long-Lost Lumleys!"

The Fourteenth Chapter

Moon plus moon equals
two moons!

WHAT PENELOPE HAD TOLD SIMON in the nursery was true: On the one hand, she was eager to share the strange and happy truth of the Lumley family tree with the Incorrigibles. On the other hand, she waited. She wanted to tell them at just the right time, in just the right way, using just the right words. Yet, as fans of the Scottish poet Mr. Robert Burns well know,

> *The best-laid schemes o' mice an' men*
> *Gang aft agley.*

(To "gang aft agley" means to often go astray, much like Mrs. Penworthy's wig, which was easily knocked askew.)

These curious words are from the poem called "To a Mouse," but the sentiment does not apply solely to rodents, or to wigs, for that matter. What they mean is this: whether one is a man, a mouse, a governess, or an Incorrigible, the great plot twists of life will arrange themselves as they see fit, regardless of how much fretting and planning one does in advance. This is not cause for alarm. Quite the opposite; it is a comforting reminder that worrying serves little purpose. Worse, it takes up valuable time that could be better spent reading novels, taking walks in a shaded park, having friends over for tea and biscuits, and any number of equally pleasant pursuits.

Out to the garden the five young people ran. The balloon had crashed right in the middle of the daffodils. The wicker basket was large and shaped like a gondola, just as Admiral Faucet had described. The balloon itself had been cleverly camouflaged as a full moon. Now it was almost completely deflated and lay in a heap on the ground. Beneath it were three figures, struggling to get out from beneath the fabric.

The Incorrigibles had personal experience being

covered by bedsheets while pretending to be ghosties, so it was all one big man-in-the-moon costume to them. They knew just what to do, and they ran full tilt to help this troika of newcomers wriggle free.

"One! Two! Three!" the children yelled, and lifted the crumpled balloon up, up, and away.

None of the three were strangers to Penelope, of course, although she was surprised to see Miss Charlotte Mortimer among them! The children also knew and loved Miss Mortimer, for they had met her at the Swanburne Academy. She embraced them fiercely. "My dear children! Just who I wanted to see!"

Pater Lumley stepped forward from the wrecked balloon. Mater Lumley did, too, and took her husband's hand. They had the strangest expressions on their faces.

"Alexander. Beowulf. Cassiopeia. We are your parents," Pater Lumley said. "I am sorry we have been away so long."

Luckily, the Incorrigibles were prepared. As they had been taught to do by their governess, they used their very best socially useful phrases. Truly, their manners were beyond reproach.

"How do you do?" Cassiopeia said grandly, with a curtsy that touched the ground.

"Greetings, noble parents. It is a pleasure to make your acquaintance." Beowulf tipped an imaginary hat and bowed with flair.

"We welcome you to Ashton Place, respected ancestors!" Alexander proclaimed, then clicked his heels together three times, in the Russian style. Beowulf did the same, and Cassiopeia performed a ballerina twirl on tiptoes. The children seemed quite pleased with themselves.

"Well, I'm glad that's all settled," Mater Lumley said, and laughed.

Penelope laughed, too, for it was just what she had said to the children upon first meeting them. "Allow me to introduce Simon Harley-Dickinson," she said, pushing him forward.

"*And* Mrs. Penworthy," Alexander added, for complete accuracy.

Simon shook Pater Lumley's hand and bowed to both ladies. "It's a true pleasure. Forgive my costume. There's a long story attached—"

Miss Mortimer placed a hand on his arm. "And we are eager to hear it, Simon, but it will have to wait until later. We have a more urgent problem. It seems our balloon had a stowaway."

"Edward Ashton," Penelope blurted. It was not a

question. She knew her adversary too well.

Simon wheeled around, searching. "Blast! I was hoping we'd seen the last of that scoundrel."

Miss Mortimer looked grim. "Yes. It is because of Edward Ashton we landed so abruptly. He's gone quite mad, I fear. There is a great deal to tell you. But not here. Not in the open."

Penelope glanced over her right shoulder, then her left, but saw nothing but trees, brave yellow daffodils, and the fallen moon balloon. Still, she trusted Miss Mortimer's judgment. "We had best go to the house, then," she said, leading the way. "Mrs. Clarke will find us a safe place to talk, and a hot meal, too. I expect she will be happily surprised to see me, and overjoyed to meet you."

Pater Lumley turned to the Incorrigibles. "Come along, children. Follow your sister."

Confused, the boys looked at Cassiopeia, who was behind them. The little girl shrugged. Then all three heads swiveled to Penelope.

"*Sistawoo!*" they howled, full throated. No need for bows and curtsies, handshakes and socially useful phrases now! They pounced on her like a trio of cubs, yapping and laughing till they were breathless with joy. It was all they could do not to lick her face, although, to be frank, she would not have minded one bit.

(Which only goes to prove—although no further proof is needed—that sometimes "just the right words" are no words at all. No disrespect to Shakespeare, Tolstoy, or *Moby-Dick* is intended by this, for every poet knows it already. As the proverb tells us, "Speech is silver, silence is golden." And nothing more need be said about that!)

ON THE WAY TO THE house they passed Old Timothy, heading toward the garden. His pace was remarkably slow. He stopped often to sniff the flowers, and there were plenty to sniff, since it was the first week of May and nearly everything was in bloom. He ambled, he strolled, he sauntered, and seemed in no rush to get to his destination.

"Good day, good day," he remarked. "What a fine day for a group of strangers with no prior knowledge of each other to meet by chance on the garden path, as it were."

The Incorrigibles thought he was joking. "But you know who *we* are!" they cried.

"Do I, though?" He gave them a stern, cockeyed look. "Most people don't know the first thing about who they are, never mind the rest of humanity! How am I, a poor old coachman, supposed to keep track of all those names and faces? All I know is that Lord Fredrick called for me all urgent like, and told me the full moon had dropped from the sky and landed in the flower beds. He saw it and Lady Constance saw it, too, or so he claims. I know it can't be true, and therefore it isn't true, but I promised I'd have a look nevertheless."

"But *why* can't it be true?" Beowulf said, giggling. It was fun to provoke the enigmatic old fellow.

"Because!" he roared. The children jumped back. "Because the full moon isn't till tomorrow! That's a simple fact of time and space, and no amount of yapping can change it. Now step aside, all you perfect strangers, and I'll be on my way as if we've never met."

"But we *have* met!" the children crowed.

The coachman lowered his voice. "If I tell Lord Fredrick that a moon balloon full of visitors fell from the sky, it'd raise questions, wouldn't it? And questions tend to want answers, don't they? And the poor man has enough on his mind as it is, with tomorrow being the first full moon of May. A fact you people ought to bear in mind! If you exist! Which I'm prepared to say you don't. Now good day, and we'll not speak of this again."

"Quite right. Good day to you too, sir!" Miss Mortimer said, deeply amused.

"Wait. Almost forgot." He reached inside his coat. "Funny, the random rubbish birds steal for their nests and then drop along the way. Here, sailor boy; you take it. It'd prop open a window in a pinch." He handed Penelope the object in question and went on his way, calling over his shoulder, "Can't have flotsam and jetsam in the flower beds, no sirree!"

Penelope was speechless. It was her book of melancholy German poems in translation! The children recognized it at once. "We lent it to Master Gogolev when he was writing poems," Alexander explained. "Then he was gone, and the book was, too."

Beowulf sniffed the binding. "It used to smell like Lumawoo. Now it smells like an unhappy person with no friends."

"Master Gogolev must have given it to Edward Ashton," Pater Lumley said to his wife, who had gasped in surprise at the discovery. Now she looked rueful.

"He should have asked first," Cassiopeia said crossly.

"Yes, he should have," Penelope agreed. She was amazed to have the familiar and much-loved book back in her hands. "But it no longer matters, for the book has found its way home, as we all have." A torn strip of

black fabric—from Edward Ashton's cloak, perhaps?—
was tucked inside as a bookmark. She opened to the
marked page, and read aloud.

"I wander through the meadows green
Made happy by the verdant scene."

"'That book is how Edward Ashton found us in Frankenforde. The clue is on the first page," Mater Lumley
added, in answer to Penelope's questioning look.

Penelope flipped to the beginning. "'Published by
Degrees,'" she read, "'at fifty-four North and twelve
East, Globus-Strasse.'"

"Globus-Strasse means Globe Street," Alexander
translated, for he still remembered some German from
his earliest years.

"And 'published by degrees.'" Simon stroked his
chin. "Hang on! Fifty-four degrees north and twelve
degrees east. Those are numbers of latitude and longitude. If I had my maps handy—"

"You would discover that they point to Frankenforde." Pater Lumley patted the young navigator on
the back of his floral-patterned dress. "Good thinking,
Simon. It's the rare baby nurse who could figure that
out so quickly!"

Miss Mortimer frowned. "Susannah, if I had known about this—"

"You would never have given her the book. I know. It was a risk I ought not have taken." Mater Lumley turned to Penelope. "I left the clue for you, Penny. I had hoped one day you would figure it out, and find comfort in knowing where we were, at least."

"Geography was never my best subject," Penelope sheepishly admitted. "All those midsized European nations and their capital cities, imports and exports and what have you! I could hardly keep them straight."

Simon adjusted his wig, which had gang agley once more. "I'd have spotted it straight away, if I'd seen it. Serves me right for not reading more poetry."

Miss Mortimer hustled them along. "There will be plenty of time for poetry, if all goes well. Now, let us get inside and put ourselves in Mrs. Clarke's care. Gossip travels quickly in a house such as this. It is best for us to remain incognito for a little while longer, at least."

THE EXPRESSION ON MRS. CLARKE'S face was a sight to behold.

"Miss Lumley, my word! You've come home at last! Well, nothing should surprise me ever again, and that's the truth. Here's Simon trotting about in my old clothes, and you drop in from the sky—the very sky itself!—dressed like a sailor boy, and the servants are gossiping about a moon falling in the daffydils, and look who turns up!" She paused to dab her eyes; she was already on her third pocket handkerchief. "It's your long-lost ma and pa, and now you tell me these three precious children are Lumleys, too! I don't know what to say, except providence is kind, and we oughtn't ever lose hope, for there's no telling what the next hour will bring, is there?"

They had gathered in a cozy downstairs room off the kitchen that only the servants used. Most great houses of the day would not bother with such a room, but at Ashton Place Mrs. Clarke was in charge, and she wanted her staff to have a comfortable spot to take tea breaks and put their feet up when they were tired. She had decorated the room herself. It was a riot of floral patterns, soft carpets, and comfortable furniture strewn with pillows, nothing like the formal, antique-filled rooms upstairs.

Trays of hot tea and buttered toast were brought out, and pitchers of milk and biscuits for the children. Once they were settled, Mater Lumley, Pater Lumley, and Miss Mortimer promised to tell the tale of how

361

they had ended up crashing their balloon in the garden (you may think of it as the tale of the moon balloon landing, although nowadays "moon landing" has come to mean something quite different, as the astronauts among you are well aware).

Mater Lumley helped herself to more tea, and a biscuit, too. Then she began. "Penelope, even before you surprised us by showing up in Frankenforde, we had arranged for your aunt Charlotte—yes, children, Miss Mortimer is your aunt as well!—to fly our balloon from its hiding place in a remote part of the Alps to the meadow green outside the town."

"I had done it before, several times," Miss Mortimer said. "And always on the night of the new moon, to avoid having too many moons in the sky at once. This time we could not wait. Years from now, I expect, grandparents will tell their grandchildren stories of that strange day when there were two moons in the sky."

"Moon plus moon equals two moons!" Cassiopeia said, clearly thrilled at the notion.

"Indeed it does, Cassawoof! I was delayed—rather embarrassingly!—when I made a right turn at the Danube River instead of a left. Such a beautiful sight! I grew distracted while admiring it and got quite turned around."

Now Pater Lumley picked up the tale. "Charlotte arrived not long after Penelope and Admiral Faucet took off in his balloon. Quickly we prepared to leave. We had released all the ropes but one when Edward Ashton himself came crashing out of the trees and into the meadow."

"But how did he find you?" Penelope asked. "That meadow was so tucked away and private."

"He did have the exact latitude and longitude, though," Simon answered.

"Yes, and he may have seen the first balloon rising from the forest. Or perhaps he was just lucky," Pater Lumley went on. "He was wild and incoherent, and soaking wet, too—he must have swum across the lake. Even as our balloon rose from the ground, he seized that last anchor rope and tried to stop us, but we got away. Or so we thought."

"Unbeknownst to us, Ashton had climbed up the rope and lashed himself to the bottom of the gondola. Imagine riding in the open air like that, all the way to England! But we did not fly nearly as high as you and Admiral Faucet did. Our balloon is—or should I say was—well camouflaged," Mater Lumley said. "Your father painted an excellent moon face, didn't he, children?"

"Moon balloon!" the children agreed. They tossed biscuits into the air and caught them in their mouths. It was a joyous reunion, after all.

Miss Mortimer tossed and caught one, too. "I thought our ship of the air was not flying quite right," she said after she was done swallowing. "I blamed it on the extra sandwiches we packed. Still, we made it to England swiftly, thanks to favorable winds."

She leaned forward, as a good storyteller does when the most exciting part is about to be told. "It was not until we were quite close, but still high above the forest that surrounds Ashton Place, that Edward Ashton made himself known. He hauled himself up the ropes. Before we could subdue him, he smashed a pair of thick spectacles he must have had with him and used the broken glass to poke our balloon full of holes. Like Swiss cheese."

Cassiopeia turned to her brothers. "See, the moon *is* made of cheese!" All three patted their tummies. That would be a great deal of cheese, for sure.

"We lurched and nearly tipped," Miss Mortimer went on. "Ashton dangled from the ropes above. 'Thanks for the lift,' he said, and jumped."

"He jumped from the balloon in midair? But surely he was killed!" Penelope exclaimed.

The three balloonists shook her heads. "He had made himself a parachute out of his own dark cloak," Miss Mortimer explained. "I think we must assume he survived."

"He must have dropped the book of poems during his fall." Penelope looked thoughtful. "Come to think of it, there has been no news of Admiral Faucet since I too jumped ship. I hope he is all right." In answer to Simon's surprised look, she said, "I held a low opinion of the admiral before our trip, but there is something about sharing an adventure that makes friends of the most unlikely companions."

Miss Mortimer nodded in agreement. "I expect the admiral landed safely. His vessel was in good condition, the weather was fair, and he is an experienced pilot. But balloons are unpredictable and easily blown off course. He could be in a different part of England altogether."

"I'd bet the moon itself he's all right. That Faucet fellow has a knack for survival, and self-invention, too." Simon turned to the rest of them. "Speaking of survival, and moons—our soothsayer friend Madame Ionesco warned us to expect real theatrics from Beyond the Veil tomorrow. The first full moon of May means closing night for the curse upon the Ashtons, as we theater folk say. I wish there was something we could do to prepare."

Miss Mortimer paused to take a deep calming breath, which made Penelope even more worried than before. "Does the fortune-teller have a plan?" the headmistress asked.

"After a fashion," Penelope replied. "It involves some complex negotiations with parties no longer living."

"We don't want anyone to commit murder," Beowulf explained. The Incorrigible children were now curled in their blankets, still listening.

"I am glad to hear it, Beowulf." Miss Mortimer tucked her legs beneath her on the sofa. Everyone was getting sleepy, it seemed. "We must be vigilant about Edward Ashton, for he is unhinged and capable of anything. As for the spirits Beyond the Veil—I fear there is nothing we can do to prepare for them. We will put our trust in your friend the soothsayer."

"When it comes to the supernatural, Madame Ionesco is as reliable as they come. I realize that's not saying much. But I think the old girl can pull it off," Simon declared. Still, an air of doubt had entered the room.

"We must hope for the best," Pater Lumley said firmly. "The main thing is that we are together now. We are safe for the moment, and there is nothing to do but wait."

"No matter what happens tomorrow, we have these hours together, at least." Her words sounded grim, but Mater Lumley was smiling. "And you must have so many questions for us. All those questions you have saved for later! Now you may ask away. We truly have all the time in the world."

THERE WAS SO MUCH TO ask, and to tell.

Penelope and the Incorrigibles heard about their parents' years in remote alpine villages, on the run from danger with baby Penelope in tow. "The hunt was on for us, but it was our children Edward Ashton wanted, even before you were born," Mater Lumley explained. "We used fake names and disguises and stayed on the move. We succeeded in keeping you a secret, Penny dear. He never knew you existed. But it was only a matter of time. You were getting older. You needed safety and stability, an education, and other children to play with. We had to face facts."

Thus, the Lumleys had made the heartbreaking decision to hide Penelope in plain sight, as it were, at the Swanburne Academy. They dared not visit but kept a close eye on their daughter through Charlotte.

"We hoped Ashton would give up, but he had his spies watching us, always. Some awful baroness . . . an earl of something or other . . . ," Mater Lumley said.

"Baroness Hoover, and the Earl of Maytag." Penelope shivered at the names.

"Yes. Many times we slipped away at the eleventh hour. We missed you dreadfully, Penny, but there seemed no way to contact you without putting you in danger."

"And thanks to the hair poultice, you appeared to be one Swanburne girl among many," Miss Mortimer interjected.

"You were a needle in a haystack, to be sure!" Simon teased. Penelope shook her head. That poultice! How she had disliked it! But now she knew the reason for it, at least.

Pater Lumley went on. "We grew ever more skilled at traveling incognito and hiding our whereabouts. To our great delight, we were blessed with three more children. We discovered ballooning, which changed everything, or so we thought. We allowed ourselves to feel safe, so safe that we began to think we might soon bring you home again, Penelope. But then came that day—that dreadful day!—when the three littlest Lumleys disappeared."

It was quite an experience for the Incorrigibles to hear this spellbinding story, especially since it was about them. However, their bellies were full of milk and biscuits, and they had made a marvelous pillow fort on the floor to snuggle in, so they listened the way they might have listened to any bedtime story: wriggling and poking one another and looking as if they were not listening at all.

Mater Lumley dabbed her eyes with a pocket handkerchief. "We had made a brief landing in a field near the village of Heidiheim, to replenish our water jugs from the stream there, and to purchase some goat's milk and cheese from a farmer we knew well. Our backs were turned for only a moment, and the children were gone."

"Maybe we went to pick flowers?" Cassiopeia suggested.

"Or for yodeling lessons." Beowulf gave it a try. *"Yodle-odle-odle-awoo!"*

"I think we were looking for hot chocolate," Alexander said.

"Those were terrible days." Mater Lumley shook her head. "But we had loyal spies of our own. Charlotte, of course. And Old Timothy."

"Enigmatic Old Tim! He had me fooled for ages," Simon said. "He'd make a swell actor."

"I always liked him," Beowulf said with sleepy

conviction, which made everyone laugh.

"With their help we learned that the children had been spirited away to England and left in the forest of Ashton Place. Imagine! Our own dear children, lost in the woods! It was like something out of the Brothers Grimm. Of course we were frightened. But Timothy found clever ways to care for them, as did some rather unusual wolves."

The children yapped softly at the mention of the wolves. Pater Lumley patted Alexander's head, which was nearest to him. "The wolves were a reminder that the strange curse upon the Ashtons was a mystery bigger than mere reason could overrule."

"Like one of those tragic plays from ancient Greece," Simon offered. "Every time you try to flee your fate, it only makes things worse."

Mater Lumley nodded. "Yes. We worried that any attempt at rescue could backfire. And we dared not provoke Edward Ashton to action, for we feared what his action would be."

"Murder!" cried Beowulf.

"Most foul!" Cassiopeia said with feeling.

"As in the best it is," Alexander concluded. It was one of the ghost's lines from *Hamlet*, and the children said it with such spirit that everyone felt moved to applaud. The children bowed and snuggled back into their pillow fort.

"We had no choice but to trust in providence," Mater Lumley continued gently, addressing the children. "Penelope was happy at Swanburne and under her aunt Charlotte's care, and you three were having a wonderful time with the wolves. What better protectors could you have? We believed you were safe, as long as Fredrick did not find you. For years, he did not."

"But then he did find them," Penelope said quietly.

"Yes. Thank goodness Old Timothy made sure no one was harmed."

"That Lord Fredrick brought the children home to live as his wards was something no one expected," Pater Lumley said. "We still don't fully understand why Fredrick took them in, though of course we are glad he did."

"I can explain that." Penelope straightened, for she too was slumped with fatigue. It was long past her bedtime by now. "As a child, Lord Fredrick was cruelly teased for barking and howling when the moon was full. The Incorrigibles' wolfish behavior reminded him of his own, but they had no shame about it. He hoped to learn that from them."

Alexander sat up. "He wants us to woofy up the baby, too," he said.

"What?" Penelope exclaimed. This was the first anyone else had heard about it, and all heads turned.

"He asked us to." Beowulf crawled out of the pillow fort and sat on his haunches. "To bark and howl and teach the baby to be woofish."

Cassiopeia popped out as well. "We have been practicing. Listen!" The Incorrigibles proceeded to bark and howl with all their might. Mater and Pater Lumley were amazed.

"What excellent howlers! You'll have to teach us to do it, too," Pater Lumley said, ruffling Beowulf's hair.

Miss Mortimer had been listening hard to all of this. "It seems we may have underestimated Fredrick," she said to Mater Lumley. She turned to Penelope. "As soon as the children were found by Lord Fredrick, the Ashtons placed an advertisement for a governess. You know what happened after that! Meanwhile, your parents had taken to spending most of the year in the air. I visited as often as I could, and helped transport the balloon to its various hiding places, mostly high in the Alps." She gave a sad smile. "The good ship *Chanteloup* served us well."

"Shantaloo?" Penelope repeated, recognizing the

name. "Miss Mortimer, did you name your cat after the balloon?"

The headmistress smiled. "*Chanteloup* is French. It means 'song of the wolf.' I named my cat after my favorite poet."

"And I named our balloon after *my* favorite poet," Pater Lumley said, a playful twinkle in his eye. He wrote it down so the children could see how it was spelled. Only then did they recognize the word.

"That is *our* favorite poet, too!" Beowulf said.

Penelope had already figured it out. She held up the book so the children could see. "See? It is right on the front."

"Chanteloup was my nom de plume," Mater Lumley said modestly. "I started using it when I wrote my very first verse. I was only sixteen at the time."

"Tell us, tell us!" the children cried.

"Oh, I think you know it already." Mater Lumley laughed, and began to sing.

> *"All hail to our founder Agatha!*
> *Pithy and wise is she."*

Penelope's own mother had written the Swanburne school song! Really, what were the odds? "To think I have been singing it all these years . . . ," she began, but she became choked up, and all conversation stopped while her parents took turns hugging her.

"I have a question," Alexander said shyly, when things had settled once more. "What are our Lumley names? I think I might remember mine, a little."

Mater and Pater Lumley exchanged a glance. "What do you remember?" Pater Lumley asked.

"Was it . . . Sam?"

Mater Lumley's hands flew to her heart. "Yes, it was! We called you Samuel, after my father and Charlotte's. But you have become Alexander Incorrigible now, haven't you?"

He nodded eagerly, for he did want to keep his own name.

"Then of course that is who you are."

"I don't remember my Lumley name," Beowulf confessed.

"I don't either." Cassiopeia looked worried, for to learn to spell a second name when she was not yet on solid ground with the first would be asking a great deal.

Pater Lumley gathered his two youngest children onto his lap. "Beowulf is your Incorrigible Lumley name. And Cassiopeia is yours."

Mater Lumley put her hand on Alexander's head.

With the other she squeezed Penelope's hand. "You are all Incorrigible Lumleys, through and through."

Mrs. Clarke had been quiet all this time, taking in every word as her knitting needles silently flew. Now she paused in her work. She rummaged in her pockets for another clean pocket handkerchief, wiped her eyes, and blew her nose with gusto. Yet when she spoke, her tone was chatty, as if it were some other kindhearted housekeeper who had just been overcome with tears for the twelfth time that day.

"I wonder what name Lord Fredrick and Lady Constance have picked for the baby," she chirped. "They haven't mentioned it. I suppose we'll find out soon enough."

"Too soon for my taste!" Simon blurted, but he was not the only one who thought it. Who knew what the next day would hold?

The good housekeeper tried again to say something cheerful, for she was one of those people who believe too much silence makes a room gloomy. She glanced outside and remarked, "It's always so dark before the moon rises, isn't it?"

No one could argue with that.

The Fifteenth and Final Chapter

*The night of the full moon
comes at last.*

While the Lumleys slept, the moon rose. It was full and round as a loaf of Gypsy cake, and bright enough to cast long, dancing shadows on the grass.

Beyond the Veil, the spirits stirred. In the bakehouse, the dough for the morning's bread rose. It is safe to say the soothsayer got very little sleep that night.

But she was not the only one awake.

At the grand house known as Ashton Place, something else began to stir, too.

Imagine a tulip bulb that has spent long months asleep in the cool, dark earth. One day, whether through happenstance, the hands on the clock, the phases of the moon, or some secret primordial plan, the moment comes when it is finally ready to sprout.

On the outside, very little changes. At least, at first.

Inside, however, great events begin to unfold. . . .

LADY CONSTANCE WAS NO STRANGER to complaining, but this was something altogether different. She had spent the night waking and dozing and waking again. Unable to sit still, she wandered the halls like a restless ghost. Every hour or so she asked for snacks, but left most uneaten.

As the day of the full moon dawned and blossomed, her restlessness turned into something more, well, cowlike.

"Mooooo!" she said, after demanding more tea and of course, chocolates. *"Moooooo!"* When she was done mooing, she looked surprised. "Fredrick, is there a cow in here?" she asked. He had not left her side for hours.

"Not that I can tell, dear." Lack of sleep made him even more bleary-eyed than usual. "But you yourself just made the most heartfelt mooing noise. Are you all right?"

"Was that me?" She dabbed her forehead with a napkin from her tray. She was looking quite pink all of a sudden. "For a moment, it felt as if something was getting ready to burst! What I imagine the tulip bulb must feel like, when the tulip begins to grow. A most peculiar type of discomfort. Never mind, it's gone now." She patted his hand and went back to nibbling her chocolate.

But before long, that bursting-into-bloom feeling came again, and that was when Mrs. Clarke took over the proceedings. "You, my lady, are getting ready to have your baby," she announced.

"*Mooooooo!* Am I? Is that what this noise is all about?" Lady Constance patted her belly. "Well, I shall miss being 'round as the full moon. It is amusing to waddle like a duck, and I have grown used to it. But the baby will be amusing, too. *MOOOOO!*" This one came more sharply, almost as a surprise. A drop of sweat trickled down her forehead. "Mrs. Clarke, look." She was a little out of breath. "It seems I may have begun to perspire. Can you imagine such a thing?"

Lord Fredrick had no idea what to make of it. He took the housekeeper aside. "I say, Mrs. Clarke, is she turning into a cow?"

"It's all quite normal, Your Lordship. It only means the baby will be here soon." Mrs. Clarke's tone was reassuring, but she had a businesslike look about her, for there was much to be done.

Dr. Veltschmerz was sent for. He arrived within the hour but declared the situation well in hand and went out for a stroll and a cigar. Margaret ran in and out, bringing fresh towels and water and tea and buttered toast, clean pocket handkerchiefs, and whatever else Mrs. Clarke ordered.

As for Lord Fredrick, in Miss Lumley's day, it was the custom for a father-to-be to wait out these sorts of occasions at his gentlemen's club, where he could smoke a pipe, drink a glass of brandy, talk politics, and so on. However, Lord Fredrick was much too concerned about Constance and the Bouncing Baby Ashton to set one foot outside his wife's bedchamber. He hovered like an anxious mother hen and spent as much time mopping his own brow as he did his wife's.

Interestingly, the person Lady Constance most wanted by her side was Mrs. Elsinore Penworthy. Margaret was sent to fetch the baby nurse, galumphing downstairs in a flash, wig only slightly askew (or agley, if you prefer the old Scottish word). Lady Constance lit up like the dawn to see her dear lady friend.

"Mrs. Penworthy—may I call you Elsinore?—take my hand, if you please! *Moooo!*" By this point, her cheeks turned bright red each time the feeling came. "My word! This is going to be rather a large tulip, I think!"

Simon—that is to say, Mrs. Penworthy—squeezed her hand gamely. "Just imagine how lovely it will be when it blossoms," she crooned.

FIRM IN THEIR RESOLVE TO enjoy each other's company fully until fate might decree otherwise, Penelope and the children were giving Miss Mortimer and Mater and Pater Lumley a tour of the nursery when the news came. The grown-ups had oohed and aahed over the excellent globe and the well-stocked bookshelves, the watercolor paints and the abacus, the wooden building blocks, and all the knitted gifts the Incorrigible children had begun, if not always finished.

Miss Mortimer was especially charmed by the large, sunny window. "What a fine-looking elm tree, with such graceful, spreading branches," she remarked. "And those sweet springtime sounds of the warblers and nuthatches are like music to the ear. . . ."

"Eeeeeeeeeeeek!" It was Margaret, who had arrived at a gallop and now stood squealing with excitement in the doorway. "There you all are! Mrs. Clarke told me to run quick as the wind and tell you four things: the baby's on its way, the doctor's come and gone, Mrs. Penworthy's looking after Lady Constance—"

"Mrs. Penworthy!" Penelope exclaimed. She would not have taken Simon for a midwife!

"Well, she is the baby nurse, after all. . . . Drat, now I've lost track. How many was that?"

"Three!" the children cried.

"One more then, let me think. . . . Oh! The baker! That was it. She wants you to send for the baker, right away."

"Yes!" Mater Lumley glanced anxiously at her husband and seized a cardigan from the pile of knitted things, as if preparing to go out. "We must fetch the baker, now."

He nodded and threw a scarf around his neck. "No having babies without the baker, no sirree!"

"Certainly, the baker must be summoned at once," Miss Mortimer said with urgency, and pulled on some mittens.

"The baker, the baker!" the children yelled, and ran around frantically dressing themselves in knitwear from head to toe.

Margaret, who was not privy to all the complexities

of the situation, seemed puzzled by this sudden out-cry for baking expertise. "'Scuse me," she chirped, "but what's the point of a baker when a lady's having a child?"

"I am surprised you do not know, Margaret." Penelope's words poured out lickety-split, for now that the big moment had arrived, she too was overcome with nerves. "Having a baby is hard, hungry work, and a snack is bound to come in useful. And no one knows better than a baker how to take loaves and muffins and pies and buns out of the oven, and having a baby is like that, very much like it indeed. Now run to the bake-house, children, quick! Tell Madame—that is, Flora the Bread Lady—to come to the house right away." (And that is how the phrase "having a bun in the oven" came to mean "soon to have a baby." It was Miss Penelope Lumley who first came up with the metaphor, you see, though she is rarely given credit for it.)

Mater and Pater Lumley accompanied the children to the bakehouse, for safety's sake. So far there had been no sign of Edward Ashton, though Old Timothy had been riding the grounds since dawn, looking for him.

The Lumleys soon returned, with Madame Ionesco

and as many baskets of fresh bread as they could carry. They marched straight upstairs to Lady Constance's private parlor. Penelope and Miss Mortimer were already there. Lady Constance was in her bedchamber, along with Lord Fredrick, Mrs. Clarke, and Mrs. Penworthy. Margaret ran in and out as required, but otherwise the door that led from the parlor to the bedchamber stayed closed.

"Make sandwiches. This is gonna take a while," the soothsayer said to Pater Lumley, putting him in charge of the bread, but there was one special loaf she set aside for Lady Constance. "I put a little spell on that one," she confided to Penelope. "The new-mommy spell. It'll make things easier for her. All right, I'm going in. Nobody leave!" she admonished them all. "These things take time. I need all hands on deck. You kids know what that means?"

"Aye aye, Madame Gypsy Cake!" the children answered, saluting. Madame Ionesco gave them a wink and disappeared behind the bedchamber door.

"Moooooo!" The cowlike lowing sounds came at intervals, and an impromptu waiting room sprang up in the parlor. Extra chairs and small tables were brought in. Fresh tea trays were delivered on the half hour and the empty cups whisked away. Pater Lumley

made sandwiches by the dozen, and everyone agreed they were excellent.

Mater Lumley taught the children card games. Penelope showed them how to play *durak*, the game she used to play with the Princess Popkinova. Muffled voices and strains of the occasional sea chantey could be heard from the bedchamber, and those who were tempted to eavesdrop (which was, frankly, everyone) bravely fought the urge.

As morning turned to afternoon, Mrs. Penworthy—that is to say, Simon—popped out of the inner room for a breather. He looked flushed and so nervous, one might almost imagine he was having a baby himself.

"I've seen many an opening night, but this is a new twist for me!" he said to Penelope, as he gave his scalp a good scratch under the horsehair wig.

She offered him a sandwich of thin-sliced cucumber and cream cheese. "When I assisted at the births of calves and lambs back at the Swanburne Academy, Dr. Westminster always said we should keep calm and trust nature to take its course."

Simon looked unconvinced. "That's all very well on the farm. It's different when the cow wants you to hold her hand, sing songs, and tell stories the whole blessed time! I'm running out of material."

The bedchamber door opened and Lord Fredrick stepped out. "Penworthy! There you are. Constance is calling for you."

"Right-o, sir. Once more unto the breach!" Simon gave Penelope a helpless look, adjusted his dress, and strode back in.

"I like that Mrs. Penworthy," Lord Fredrick remarked to Miss Mortimer, as he helped himself to a ham on rye. "A nice, sturdy woman, what? Constance thinks the world of her. I don't suppose you know this, but there have been some strange twists and turns in the Ashton family tree. Makes me a bit anxious about the baby. I suppose that's normal, but when your family's got a curse on it—it's a long story, I'll tell you later, if you're interested. . . . Well, it just makes it all the more stressful."

Miss Mortimer knew all about it, of course. "Fredrick—if I may call you that—don't be afraid. We are here to help make sure things go well."

"Yes." Pater Lumley came and stood by her. "It's true we have only just met, sir, but you can count us as your friends."

Mater Lumley went so far as to lay a hand on Lord Fredrick's arm. "Your wife and child will be just fine. I am sure of it."

"All right, good to hear. No harm in being optimistic, I suppose!" He looked around and took in these visitors as best he could: the calm couple in European clothes; the elegant English headmistress; the slender chap in the sailor suit who looked like he could be Miss Lumley's twin brother, the resemblance was so strong. "Blast! I'm not quite sure how all of you ended up here in my house. But I daresay it feels perfectly at home having you about. The more the merrier, I suppose!"

"*Moooooooooo!*"

"That's my girl! I'd best get back inside." He grabbed another sandwich, a sliced apple, cheddar, and mustard. "Mmm, very good, very good! Yes, I oughtn't worry. Things are going well."

LORD FREDRICK WAS QUITE CORRECT. Inside the birthing room, nature was taking its course. Outside, the Lumleys stood watch over their cousins, the Ashtons. The task of removing the family curse remained in the spooky hands of Madame Ionesco, but first things first. If Edward Ashton had planned a final act of treachery, the time to attempt it was now. So far, however, he was nowhere to be seen.

Hours passed before Madame Ionesco next emerged.

386

"Cutie," she said to Penelope, who had by now dealt so many games of cards her fingers ached, "tell the cook I need soup. But not just any soup. The Russian kind. It's red. Made of beets. Very tasty."

"You mean borscht," Penelope said. "Is it good for a lady in labor?"

Madame grinned her semitoothless grin. "Who says it's for her?" Back into the birthing room she went.

The borscht was prepared and delivered, and afternoon turned to evening. It might have been coincidence, but as the sun set and gave the soon-to-rise moon full rein over the sky, Lady Constance's mooing turned to a different kind of sound altogether.

"Ahwoooo!" she howled, quite musically. *"Ahwoooo! Ahwoooo!"*

"That's it, my dear!" Lord Fredrick could be heard cheering her on. *"Ahwoooo, ahwoooo!"*

Helpfully, the Incorrigible Lumleys joined in, too.

"Ahwoooo!"

"Ahwoooo!"

"Ahwoooooooo!"

But even all that noise was not enough to conceal the thunder of hooves at a gallop, coming ever closer to the house.

Penelope leaped to her feet in alarm.

"Noooooooo!"

This howl of protest came from the window. There, tottering on the edge of the railing that circled the parlor's private balcony, was Edward Ashton. "Time is running out! Five cubs to be avenged!" he yelled, pounding on the glass. The French doors opened, and he toppled into the parlor.

"Come here, you rascal!" It was Old Timothy. He scrambled up the vine-covered trellis that led to the balcony quite nimbly for an old bowlegged coachman. "You won't get away from me again!" Pater Lumley jumped to assist as Old Timothy seized his prey by the collar. "The old schemer was hiding in the woods. I flushed him out of the bushes like a hound flushes out a fox. A merry hunt it was, wouldn't you say, Eddie, old boy?"

The intruder was weak from his ordeals and winded from the climb, and it took little effort to subdue him. Pater Lumley cut down the long tasseled cord of embroidered gold silk that served as a bellpull and lashed Edward Ashton to a chair.

"Apologies for the intrusion, ladies and gents. If not for Dr. Veltschmerz blocking my way, I'd have had this scoundrel bagged before he got past the tulips. But

don't worry. I'll deal with the gloomy doctor later." To Penelope he added, "I found your friend Faucet, too, while I was searching the woods. He's bruised from a rough landing but in good working order otherwise."

The door to the bedchamber opened. Lord Fredrick stood framed within it. His face was damp with perspiration, but he showed no sign of barking or howling or scratching. The full moon's attention was elsewhere, it seemed.

"Blast! My wife's in the middle of having a baby. Can you keep the racket down out here?" Then he saw what was going on, or thought he did. "Quinzy, is that you?"

"Fools! Don't you understand we are all doomed?" Edward Ashton moaned.

"Doomed, what nonsense! Get hold of yourself, sir," Lord Fredrick ordered. "There are children present, for heaven's sake."

"Children, yes! But how many?" Edward Ashton fixed the Incorrigibles with a piercing stare. "One, two, three. One, two, three." He lifted his head and glared at Penelope. "Four! But where is the fifth?"

"Is that why you chased us all over Switzerland? Searching for another little Lumley to put in your murderous sights?" Remarkably, Pater Lumley laughed. "That was a lot of trudging through the Alps for nothing, then!"

"I don't believe you!" Ashton roared, straining against the knots.

"I am sorry to disappoint you, Edward," Mater Lumley said, in a voice both calm and steely. "But these four remarkable children are all we have."

Edward Ashton tried to stand, but the cord was too snug. "But—no! It makes no sense." His eyes darted from one auburn head to the next. "Five cubs to be avenged, the old sailor said. All must be destroyed, or the Ashtons will come to a gruesome and permanent end!"

"Edward, you really ought to read *The Three Musketeers*," Miss Mortimer suggested. "It has four musketeers in it, but nobody seems to mind."

"And stop all that gruesome end talk, or I'll stick a real bag over your head." Old Timothy was still breathless himself, and mopped his brow with a handkerchief. "Now listen up, everyone. There's something I ought to warn you about. Those wolves that live in the forest—"

Mater Lumley interrupted. "No need to warn us about the wolves, Timothy. From what we've been told, they are friendly as can be."

The old coachman tugged at his collar. "Normally, that's true. . . ."

"Wait!" Lord Fredrick cried. "Listen!"

Waaaaaaa!

Waaaaaaa!

There was no mistaking the mewling newborn cry.

"Hooray, hooray!" the Incorrigibles shouted, for they knew what the sound meant.

"No! I have failed!" Edward Ashton writhed and struggled as the rope held him fast. "We will all perish!"

"No one's gonna perish, you big crybaby." It was Madame Ionesco, emerging from Lady Constance's bedchamber. "Where's the new daddy?"

Miss Mortimer gave Lord Fredrick a nudge. "I believe the soothsayer means you, Fredrick."

"I suppose you're right! Here I am, soothsayer! What news? Do we have a baby, then?" He tugged at his jacket and smoothed his hair as if he were about to meet the tsar himself.

"Not exactly." Madame Ionesco smiled her semi-toothless smile. "You better come see."

OLD TIMOTHY STAYED IN THE parlor to keep watch over Edward Ashton. Reverent and wide-eyed with curiosity, the rest tiptoed into Lady Constance's bedchamber.

Penelope looked around. "Where is—" She almost said Simon by mistake. "Where is Mrs. Penworthy?"

Madame Ionesco chuckled. "Oh, that one fainted half an hour ago. The squeaking girl went to get smelling salts—not to worry!" A quick peek 'round the far side of the bed revealed Simon out cold on the floor. He snored manfully and seemed quite comfortable.

And there, sitting up in bed in a rose-pink bed jacket, was Lady Constance. Her eyes were bright, and her face was flushed with pretty pink circles on each cheek. Her butter-colored hair had been combed into a simple ponytail. She looked rested and radiant and very, very pleased with herself.

"Poor Mrs. Penworthy!" she said with a merry laugh. "You would have thought she had never seen a baby being born before! I shall tease her about it for months. I was quite brave, though, wasn't I, Madame Ionesco?"

Madame squeezed her hand. "You were terrific."

"Constance, you devil!" Lord Fredrick had reached the wicker cradle, and he grinned from ear to ear. "Well, this is a surprise! That's not a Bouncing Baby Ashton at all." He puffed out his chest. "That's *two* babies. Hi-dee-ho! Two! A ready-made family!"

"I had no idea," Lady Constance said modestly. "But I *was* rather large."

The babies were alike as two peas in a pod, and nestled against each other just as they had in the womb, snug in the blankets that had been knitted just for them. "One's a boy and one's a girl," Madame Ionesco said, "but don't ask me which is which."

"It's their birthday!" Beowulf pointed out. At once the Incorrigibles began to sing.

> *"For these are jolly good babies,*
> *For these are jolly good babies,*
> *For these are jolly good babies,*
> *And so say all of us!"*

The newborns slept through the singing—as well as the hip-hip, hoorays!—that followed, but the noise did manage to rouse Simon. "Good morning!" he exclaimed, sitting up. "What am I doing on the floor?" Then his head cleared. "Wait a minute. The baby!" Then his head cleared a bit more, and he switched to his Mrs. Penworthy voice. "I meant to say, the baby! Did I miss it?"

"No. You missed *two* babies!" Cassiopeia crowed with glee.

There was a crash of broken crockery in the parlor, as if a tea tray had been upended.

"Clumsy old Tim! Sounds like we'll be needing a mop," Mrs. Clarke said, not at all cross. But the door was flung open, and Edward Ashton burst into the bedchamber brandishing a knife.

"Hey!" Pater Lumley exclaimed. "Those were my best balloon-tying knots! How did you get loose?"

"They were superb knots, sir," Ashton replied. "Impossible to untie. Which is why it was so kind of you to leave a knife within reach."

He raised his right arm. In his hand was the bread knife that Pater Lumley had used to make sandwiches. The blade was still streaked yellow with mustard, or perhaps it was the gold threads of the bellpull cord, or both.

"Where is Old Timothy?" Penelope cried.

"Out cold." Ashton nodded at the housekeeper. "Mrs. Clarke, my apologies for breaking a good teapot on the coachman's exceptionally hard head."

"Never mind the teapot, you brute! Poor Tim! At least you didn't commit—" But then Mrs. Clarke caught herself. "Rhymes with birder," she finished.

Edward Ashton's face twisted. "I have no wish to

394

harm that old man. Despite what you think of me, I am no monster."

"You're no hero, either," Simon snapped. "Barging in with a knife and scaring the daylights out of us all! You ought to be ashamed."

"I do not pretend to be a hero. But I will save my family. It is regrettable I can only save half." He turned to Mater and Pater Lumley, who did not flinch, even with the tip of the bread knife wobbling in their direction. "You say you have four children. Are you quite sure?"

"Of course," Mater Lumley said. Her husband nodded.

"Five are needed to undo the curse." His voice grew sharp. "How many are missing, wolf children?"

"One," Cassiopeia squeaked, for although she was frightened, she could never resist a math problem. "One is missing."

"Not anymore." There was a terrible look on Edward Ashton's face. "For now there is a fifth."

"And a sixth, too!" Lady Constance must have still been under the influence of the special bread Madame Ionesco had provided, for these terrible goings-on seemed not to trouble her at all. "Not that I'm boasting, mind you! That would be ill-mannered."

Ashton's face registered surprise, for he had not yet looked inside the cradle. "Do you mean they are twins? How unexpected. But it changes nothing. It is only fair—there must be some sacrifice on Pax's side as well, it seems. So be it! I must . . . be strong! I must . . . do . . . what I have sworn . . . to do!" He swayed on his feet, bread knife high in the air.

Penelope understood his mind at once. "Monster! They are your own grandchildren! Would you sacrifice them, too?"

"Of course not, governess." His dark eyes glittered. "I need only one."

"Children—stand back!" Penelope yelled, lunging toward the madman. "He means to harm the babies!"

WHAT HAPPENED NEXT HAPPENED ALL at once, in the blink of an eye. It was one of those moments when people's true natures are revealed, for when there is no time to think, one can only act from the heart. (Of course, to write it all at once would turn the page into an inky blotch, which would be as difficult to read as invisible ink. Instead, imagine the following events happening in concert, the way the instruments of an orchestra commence playing together at the swoop of the conductor's baton.)

"That's Cook's best bread knife! You hand that back right now!" Mrs. Clarke bellowed, reaching for Edward Ashton's upraised arm.

"Ahwoooo!" With a howling battle cry, teeth bared and fists raised, the Incorrigibles rushed to the defense of the babies by forming an Incorrigible pyramid in front of the cradle. Cassiopeia stood with one foot each on the shoulders of her brothers.

"Stop this instant!" Penelope cried, as she flung herself between Edward Ashton and the Incorrigibles.

"Blast! That's no way to behave in front of my wife!" Lord Fredrick leaped forward to seize Edward Ashton from behind.

Simon Harley-Dickinson, still on the floor, sprang to his feet and shouted, "Oh, no you don't!" He put his head down and charged at Edward Ashton like a furious bull charging at a matador's red cape.

Alas, due to his poor eyesight Lord Fredrick missed his target and ended up sprawled on the carpet. Mrs. Clarke got hold of Ashton's free arm, but madness and fury had roused his last surge of strength, and she was dragged behind him as he lurched toward the cradle. Simon's head caught him square in the belly, which caused him to double over, groaning. His knife-wielding

arm buckled and somehow—it was good luck for Ashton, but bad for Simon!—hooked itself 'round Simon's neck, with the gleaming knife edge pressed against the young bard's throat.

No one dared speak, except for one person.

It was the person who had been bravest of all that day. Clearly she had bravery left to spare.

"You leave Mrs. Penworthy alone!" Lady Constance Ashton yelled. Unable to get out of bed, she hurled the very last chocolate on her tray at the attacker.

The chocolate hit Ashton in one eye, knocking him sideways. That was all the chance Simon needed. He twisted free. With a blind sweep, Ashton slashed the bread knife in Simon's direction but caught only the horsehair wig, which was now impaled on the blade.

By this time Miss Mortimer and Mater Lumley had made it to the front ranks. They seized Ashton firmly, one on each side, as Pater Lumley grabbed Ashton's forearm with both hands. Still the madman's white-knuckled grip held firm. The wig dangled comically from the knife's tip.

"Fools!" Edward Ashton cried. "Fools! Let me go! If the curse is not ended, we are all doomed, don't you understand? Doomed! Doomed!"

Lord Frederick squinted. "Bit dramatic, there, don't

you think? Here, I'll take that off your hands." Lord Fredrick reached out for the bread knife, but his father only tightened his grip.

Miss Mortimer spoke in that stern headmistress tone that no Swanburne girl had ever found the will to disobey. "Edward, release that knife at once."

But Edward Ashton was no Swanburne girl. He growled and snarled like a caught animal, and it was all they could do to hold him.

"I'll take care of this, Charlotte." It was Old Timothy, swaggering in the door like a captain on the deck of his own ship. He rubbed the fresh bump at the top of his skull and winced, but he seemed otherwise unharmed. "You can put the knife down now, Eddie," he said, in the same soothing tone he might use to calm a frightened horse. "There's a good lad. Now give that to Old Tim, ta-tum, ta-tum, ta-tum," he murmured as he reached one gnarled hand fearlessly toward the blade.

It was uncanny to see how Old Timothy's cooing voice acted upon the villain. Edward Ashton's face lost its twist of rage and went slack, and his grasp on the knife softened with each ta-tum. It was if the coachman's words were a time machine that brought the trembling madman back to days long past, before years of murderous intrigue had twisted little Eddie Ashton's spirit into one fueled only by vengeance and fear.

Old Timothy never let up his hypnotic murmuring. "Good boy, Eddie, just let it go . . . there'll be a treat in it for you, just hand the knife over to your old friend Tim . . ."

Through it all Madame Ionesco stood swaying, eyes closed, humming softly to herself. One would have thought she was hardly paying attention. But the moment the knife dropped into Old Timothy's hand, her eyes flew open.

"I'll take that, Timmy boy," she said, extending a hand. Old Timothy gave her the bread knife. Mrs. Penworthy's horsehair wig was still upon it.

"Go ahead with your singing and soothsaying, folks," Old Timothy said. "I know when a horse is broke to harness, and this one surely is. I'll make sure he doesn't cause any more trouble. Come along now, Eddie. I'll bring you someplace you can rest."

Meek as a lamb following his flock, Edward Ashton took Old Timothy's arm. No one doubted that the enigmatic coachman had the situation well in hand this time, but Pater Lumley went with them, just in case.

After they were gone, Lord Fredrick rubbed his eyes. "Blast! That fellow looked like Judge Quinzy to me, but you all kept calling him Edward. Now I've got the strangest feeling. Is there something I'm missing?"

Before anyone could explain, a howl unlike any that had so far been heard that day echoed throughout the house.

"AHWOOOOOOOOOO!"

Then came an ear-piercing scream, like a thousand unoiled door hinges all swinging at the same time. Whatever Margaret had just seen had frightened her terribly!

Thump-thump, thump-thump!

Heavy footfalls trotted menacingly up the stairs. The Incorrigible children sniffed.

"Mama Woof?" Cassiopeia said. She sounded uncertain.

Alexander shook his head. "Not exactly," he said.

"I smell ghosties," Beowulf added, with a gulp of fear.

The door opened.

This was no ordinary wolf, nor even a highly unusual wolf, but something far more strange and powerful.

It was Mama Woof on the outside, but it was not Mama Woof on the inside.

The children could tell this at once. Mater and Pater Lumley could not, but good manners were good manners, after all.

"My dear Mother Wolf," Mater Lumley said in a shaking voice, "if I could have written you a thank-you note, I would have. We are so grateful for the excellent care you took of our children—"

The giant beast threw back its head. "*AHWOO-OOOOOOOO! I am the sacred wolf of Ahwoo-Ahwoo!*" Its voice shook the room, a thunder of rage and grief. "I have come for justice! Blood for blood! A pelt for a pelt!"

Everyone looked at Madame Ionesco.

"Sometimes you have to wake the dead. Sometimes they wake up by themselves." The soothsayer shrugged. "Saves me a lot of work, frankly."

The wolf swept its glowing eyes 'round the room and took in each terrified countenance. "Murderer!" This was aimed at Lord Fredrick. "I know you by your face, Ashton! And by your companion. That cabin boy who shadowed your every step."

"I beg your pardon?" Lord Fredrick replied, bewildered.

Simon stage-whispered in his ear. "Freddy, she thinks you're the long-dead Admiral Ashton who committed the rhymes-with-birder of her cubs, and that Miss Lumley here is Pudge, the cabin boy."

"And I thought *my* eyesight was poor," Lord Fredrick whispered back. "Ought I play along?"

"If it were me, I'd give the performance of a lifetime." Simon looked up. The enormous creature towered over them all.

"All right." Lord Fredrick tugged at his collar. "What should I say?"

Madame Ionesco rolled her eyes. "Apologize, Fred! Do it like you mean it!"

"Right!" Lord Fredrick cleared his throat. "Well, Sacred Wolf of Ahwoo-Ahwoo—may I call you Wolfy?"

"No!" the beast roared.

"All right, I'll just get to it, then! On behalf of the entire Ashton family, past, present, and future, I'd like to say I'm sorry. Really, awfully sorry about that business with the wolf cubs. It was a dreadful thing to do. We've all learned a great deal, and you won't be seeing any more bad behavior from us. On my word, I am truly sorry." He broke character. "Blast! I feel even worse about it, now that I'm a father myself."

Madame Ionesco nudged him in the ribs. "And . . . go on . . . the curse . . ."

"Yes, yes, almost forgot!" He gulped. "I sincerely hope you'll undo this curse you've put on us Ashtons. I do appreciate your consideration, what?"

The wolf growled, long and fierce.

Madame Ionesco listened hard. "Okay. I think she's saying maybe that's a good start. . . ."

"I can speak for myself!" the wolf roared. "Sorry doesn't bring back my cubs! Why should I undo the curse?"

"To make peace, doggie." Even the soothsayer looked frightened. "Let bygones be bygones."

"Put the past behind us, so to speak," Lord Fredrick added.

The wolf's fur bristled all along its back. "No! Nothing can undo the past!"

Madame Ionesco turned to the others and shrugged. "So sorry, guys. Not gonna happen. It's been a pleasure. I hope your gruesome ends come quick and easy. I know it's not what we hoped for, but you win some, you lose some."

"Wait! Nothing can change the past, it's true." Penelope stepped forward till she was face-to-face with the frightening beast. "The past is over. A sunk cost, if you will. All the pains and losses, the mistakes and misdeeds—none of these can be undone."

The wolf's eyes glowed like torches in the dim room.

Penelope took a breath and went on. "However, the terms of the curse are clear. They say that only one side of the family can remain, or both will perish. I would argue that only one side does remain."

She turned and gestured to the Incorrigibles. "For here we have Alexander, Beowulf, and Cassiopeia, and me, Penelope. We are the four Lumley children, the great-grandchildren of Agatha Swanburne."

Miss Mortimer's gentle smile and her mother's encouraging look gave her confidence, but so did the words of Agatha Swanburne, and the wisdom gleaned from every story of bravery and pluck she had ever heard or read. She turned toward the cradle. "And here we have the great-grandchildren of Agatha's twin brother, Pax. It was four generations ago that the family tree split in two. The curse foretold that we would always be at war with each other. That in order to survive, one side would have to throw the other to the wolves, so to speak. Yet here we all are."

"Brothers and sisters," Alexander said.

"Sisters and brothers," Beowulf chimed in.

"And pets!" No doubt Cassiopeia was thinking of Nutsawoo.

The wolf pulled back its lips in a snarl, revealing its deadly teeth.

Mrs. Clarke gasped, but Penelope was no longer the least bit afraid. "Lord Fredrick. Is it true that you told the Incorrigibles that your own children were to be raised alongside them, like siblings?"

"Yes, I did. Simpler that way, what?" He turned to his wife. "You don't mind, do you, dear?"

Lady Constance yawned prettily; what a long day she had had! "I do like simple things, Fredrick," she replied sweetly. "The simpler the better!"

"Yes, as Occam's Razor reminds us." Penelope stood by the Incorrigibles. "And moments ago, when the lives of Lord and Lady Ashton's newborn babies were threatened, it was these three brave children who ran to protect them, was it not?"

"You did also, Penny, dear," Miss Mortimer interjected. "All four of you hurled yourselves into harm's way to save those innocent newborns." She looked at the wolf and spoke imploringly. "The descendants of Agatha Swanburne stood ready to sacrifice themselves for the descendants of Pax Ashton. Surely that makes them one family again."

The spirit-wolf's eyes narrowed to slits. "My cubs were slain for their pelts and perished on the blood-stained sands of Ahwoo-Ahwoo. I demand blood for blood! A pelt for a pelt!"

There were twin whimpers from the cradle, as the babies briefly roused and then sank back into their newborn dreams. Penelope racked her brains, but she had said everything she could think of to say. Was this what was meant by a hopeless case? When you had done your best, and it was still not good enough?

Yet even a hopeless case was never without hope; this she believed to her very bones.

Madame Ionesco frowned. "Blood and a pelt, hmm! You drive a tough bargain, doggie. All right. Bring me that bowl of borscht, would you, big sister?"

By now the soup was cold, but Penelope knew better than to question the mysterious Madame. Carefully she lifted the tray and carried the bowl of rich red soup to the soothsayer.

Madame Ionesco dipped one finger into the soup, took it out, and licked it. "Not bad," she said. "Maybe add a little more dill next time."

The bread knife that held the horsehair wig lay at the foot of the bed. Madame placed it next to the soup and offered the whole tray to the wolf. "Here you go, doggie. Blood and a pelt. Just like you ordered."

"That's not blood. That's borscht," Simon blurted.

"Tell that to a beet." Again, Madame Ionesco turned to the wolf. "Just try it," she urged. "It's not bad."

The great beast nuzzled the horsehair wig with her nose and sniffed at the soup. Finally she took a slurp. Her ears swiveled in surprise.

"*Grrrrr!* It's good," the creature said, and lapped up the rest. When she had licked the last bloodred morsels of borscht from her whiskers, the wolf swept her shining eyes 'round the room.

"*Ahwoo, ahwoo!*" the wolf intoned. "Most unexpected! I came to witness the extinction of the curséd Ashtons, a family split in two. Yet now I cannot tell which side is which. Each of you was willing to sacrifice yourself for another."

"That's because we are siblings." Alexander stood proudly next to the cradle.

"Brothers," Beowulf said, joining him.

"And sisters, oojie woojie woo!" Cassiopeia cooed at the babies.

"And I am a mother!" Lady Constance giggled. "I can hardly believe it myself."

"And I'm a father, it appears!" Lord Fredrick said

happily, and patted his wife's hand.

"I am a big sister, and some sort of cousin," said Penelope, looking at the children. "And a daughter," she added. Mater Lumley smiled.

"And a niece, don't forget!" put in Miss Mortimer.

"I'm not sure what I am, exactly, but I do feel part of the family, if you don't mind my saying so," Simon offered. Shyly he took Penelope's hand.

"I'm just the soothsayer—don't mind me!" Madame Ionesco chuckled.

"Does this mean that only one side remains?" Penelope clutched Simon's hand in hope. "Have the terms of the curse been fulfilled?"

The wolf's cold yellow eyes softened to a burnished gold. "Two sides have turned to one. Not through violence, but through compassion and kindness. The tree that was split down the middle has grown together once more."

A powerful wag of the wolf's great furry tail pushed aside the drapes, and the cool blue light of the first full moon of May shone brightly upon them all. *"Ahwoo!"* the beast sang, full throated. It was a song of forgiveness. *"Ahwoo, ahwoo!* As there is one nose, one tail, and one moon in the sky, the Ashtons are again one family. Live long together, and live in peace. The terms of the curse have been fulfilled."

With that, the shimmering spirit of the Sacred Wolf of Ahwoo-Ahwoo detached itself from Mama Woof. It floated upward and hovered near the ceiling, then burst into countless sprays of gold that glittered in the air like fireworks. A moment later, it was gone.

"Hooray!" cried the Incorrigibles, who understood that something marvelous had happened. Simon and Penelope hugged each other, and Mater and Pater Lumley embraced all their children in turn.

Lady Constance beamed and yawned, for she had had a very long day indeed. Her husband held her hand in one of his own, and used the other to rock the cradle that held the future of their new and no longer curséd family.

Mama Woof seemed dazed by the experience, but thanks to the nourishing borscht and some tasty sandwich meats offered by the children, she was soon quite herself again.

"That's a good girl." Madame Ionesco scratched the enormous beast on the muzzle as if she were a much-loved pet. The wolf did not seem to mind at all. "Not what you expected, eh? But people change, doggie. People change."

Truly, the first full moon of May had turned out to be a day worth celebrating. No doubt Cook would have baked a cake for the occasion, had she known how well things would turn out. However, there was still one small betrayal left to settle.

Simon rubbed bashfully at his head, which was far easier to do now that that itchy horsehair wig was off. "Whoops! I guess I owe you an apology, Lady C," he said. "As you can tell, I haven't been completely honest with you."

Lady Constance merely laughed. "No need to apologize, Mrs. Penworthy! Many a lady has resorted to artificial means when her own natural beauty was in need of a boost, as the Americans say. I have dabbled in a bit of rouge and lip tint myself now and then. But not to worry. My dressmaker, Madame LePoint, knows the finest wigmakers in Paris. She can have a new wig made for you that is far more flattering." Her little nose wrinkled. "Your old one did you no favors, if I may speak frankly, one lady to another! It had a bit of a barnyard smell about it, too."

Simon, amazed, looked at Penelope, who was desperately trying not to laugh.

"Well, thanks very much! You're awfully kind, Lady C," he said, and curtsied as daintily as he could. The

Incorrigibles nudged each other and looked pleased, for they enjoyed having both Simon and Mrs. Penworthy around, and now it seemed that he—that is to say, they—would be able to stay on as the baby nurse after all. It made perfect sense to the children, for they were used to thinking with their hearts.

Throughout all this, Lord Fredrick only had eyes for his wife. "You certainly don't need any rouge today, my dear," he said. "I can see you clear as day. You look radiant."

"Do I?" There was no mirror handy, but none was required; the truth of it was reflected on her husband's face. "Well, I *feel* radiant, so there," she said merrily. "I believe motherhood suits me, Fredrick!"

EPILOGUE

By morning, Edward Ashton had disappeared.

Old Timothy had locked him in the barn overnight. This was ironic, since the barn was where the Incorrigible children had been put when Lord Fredrick first found them in the woods. Yet it was not an unkindness on either occasion, for the barn was cozy and filled with clean hay and friendly animals. Old Timothy had stayed till Edward fell asleep. The man had shown no signs of violence, or even resistance. The former lord of Ashton Place seemed reduced to a muttering simpleton.

But when Old Timothy returned in the morning to deliver breakfast—it was an excellent breakfast, too, as Mrs. Clarke herself had prepared a tray of hot porridge, jam, butter, and a basket of muffins, saying as she did so, "If a bloodthirsty wolf who's been dead for ages can put the past behind her and move on, what excuse do the rest of us have for holding a grudge, I ask you?"—he was gone. A hollow in the bed of hay showed where he had slept, but the spot was cold. It seemed he had been gone for hours.

"We ought to start a hunting party, what?" Lord Fredrick said when told. By this time it had been explained to him who "Quinzy" really was, a revelation that Lord Fredrick took rather well, given the circumstances. "But a peaceful one, please! No weapons. He is my father, after all. Perhaps he's just hiding in the woods."

Everyone who could be spared went outside to join the search. This included Admiral Faucet, who had made his way to the house early, in time for a good breakfast and a much-needed shave, as well as a round of apologies for some past misdeeds, all of which were promptly forgiven.

The children ran around the grounds and sniffed, but the scents of madness, meanness, and vengeance were nowhere to be found at Ashton Place.

Old Timothy checked the stables, but no horses were missing.

"That means he must have escaped on foot," Beowulf deduced. "But which one? The right foot, or the left?"

Alexander swiveled his spyglass upward. "Maybe not. Look!" High in the sky, a multicolored balloon lurched one way and then the other.

Admiral Faucet spluttered, "My balloon!"

"No worries, Faucet old chap. I'll buy you a new one," Lord Fredrick offered. "I'm still awfully rich, you know."

"Much appreciated, sir! But I'm more concerned with the fellow inside. In the first place, he doesn't know how to fly it. In the second place, after my rough landing in the treetops, that balloon's in bad shape. I'd wager it's leaking hot air like, well, a faucet. It might stay up for a day or so, but that's it. And with the wind blowing the way it is . . ." His voice grew ominous. "He'll crash in the ocean for sure."

The question of whether they ought to rescue Edward Ashton from certain death in a broken balloon might have posed an ethical dilemma, had there been any chance of saving him. But already it was too late. The stolen balloon rose quickly—too quickly, according to Faucet—and the howls of its lone passenger could no longer be heard, as the balloon shrank to a tiny smudge of rainbow in the sky. It blew topsy-turvy in an eastward direction, borne by fate and the prevailing winds toward the wide, unforgiving sea.

As you might expect, Lord Fredrick's feelings about this were mixed. "Even a terrible father is a father," he said later, when they had all gone back inside to visit with Lady Constance and the babies. "Not having one is a pity, no matter how you slice it. I had one, lost one, found one, now I've lost him again. It's upsetting. And now I'm a father, too! I hope I have more of a knack for it than old Edward."

Lady Constance and the twins were being well cared for by Mater and Pater Lumley, Madame Ionesco, and Mrs. Penworthy, too. Her pony-scented pigtails had been replaced to great advantage with Simon's own unruly shock of hair, which tumbled quite naturally over her—his—intelligent forehead.

Pater Lumley put his arm around Fredrick's shoulders. "All parents make mistakes. You'll make some, too." Mater Lumley offered a clean pocket handkerchief, which Lord Fredrick put to good use.

Lady Constance looked upon her husband with

417

sympathy and gestured for him to come sit next to her. "I have news that will cheer you, Fredrick! I have thought of names for the babies. The little girl I would like to name Fern. Ferns are pleasant to be among and come in many varieties, so I am told. Therefore, I think the name will suit her no matter what sort of person she turns out to be."

Penelope nearly clapped her hands in delight, for she was very fond of ferns.

"And Fredrick, dear, if it is all right with you, I think we ought to name the boy Edward. After your father."

"What?" he exclaimed.

"The worst of him was not very nice, true, but nobody is perfect! We can name our son Edward after the best of your father, in honor of the father you would like to be. I have complete faith in you, Fredrick!" Constance chirped.

Lord Fredrick cheered up a great deal after he heard that. In any case, Fern and Edward needed diaper changes, again, and as the newly blesséd Ashtons would soon learn, there is little time to worry about how to be a good parent when one is busy being one.

Penelope, who still felt remorse about the unpaid hotel and taxi bills she had left behind in Russia, was doubly committed to making sure the good fortune-teller's expenses were settled promptly. "Madame, I know your services do not come cheaply," she said, taking the weird woman aside. "If you would give me an invoice, I will take the matter up with Lord Fredrick as soon—well, as soon as he is done changing diapers."

"Oojie woojie woo!" the lord of Ashton Place cooed as he put Fern—or was it Edward?—back in the crib.

Madame Ionesco patted Penelope's hand. "No charge! It's a baby present, times two."

Lord Fredrick straightened. "I'd best write down the birthday so I don't forget. Everybody likes to get a card on their birthday, what? Hand me my almanac, would you, Old Tim?"

But the almanac was nowhere to be found. "Where is that book?" he said, turning in circles. "It's uncanny. The blasted almanac still won't stay put!"

Madame Ionesco chuckled. "Sorry, poppa! I've been meaning to tell you. There's a little spell on your alma-nac. In Romanian it's called . . . well, in Romanian, it's complicated. Loosely translated, it's the other-sock spell."

"Socks? What's that got to do with it?" Lord Fred-rick asked.

"I bet I know!" Simon exclaimed. "It's the spell that makes people lose the other sock, isn't it?"

Madame Ionesco grinned. "You got it, baby nurse!" To the others she explained, "Long ago in soothsayer time—which is not like the clock on the wall, by the way!—one of my fellow fortune-tellers mixed up her abracadabras with her presto changos, and the other-sock spell got loose. Now we can't get rid of it. You can't put a genie back in the bottle, know what I mean? Anyway, Fred, somebody—it might have been me!—put the other-sock spell on your almanac."

He tipped his head to the side in a doglike expression of bewilderment. "Is that why I'm always misplacing it?

"Yup. Also, you need glasses, honey."

Penelope was grateful for this insight about socks, for she too struggled with socks that went missing on laundry day, and this despite having an exceptionally well-organized stocking drawer. "But why put a spell on the almanac?" she asked.

The fortune-teller shrugged. "Feeling ashamed is no good for the digestion. Freddy was using the almanac to try to keep his howling a secret. The sooner he got caught, the better. And Old Timothy helped, too, didn't you, you enigmatic cutie?"

The coachman looked smug. "His Lordship would

circle the dates of the full moons, and I'd sneak in and change them."

Lord Fredrick shook his head. "You're a tricky one, Old Tim, though that's no surprise. Well, I can't be cross about it, or anything else, really. Not today!" His blurry gaze met that of his new babies. "Oojie woojie woo, you little yappers," he crooned. "Oojie woojie ahwoo-ahwoo, what?"

The babies' lips pursed into two round O's.

"Look, Fredrick," Lady Constance said, all aglow. "I think they're trying to howl!"

ONE WOULD THINK THERE HAD always been babies at Ashton Place. Everything had changed, and yet it all came to seem quite normal as the days went by. An abundance of knitted sweaters and scarves began to appear on the household staff, which gave a cozy feeling to the grand house. Meanwhile, Penelope had returned to wearing her comfortable brown governess dresses, although she did ask that Madame LePoint alter them slightly. A fortnight in sailor pants had made her accustomed to having pockets, and she saw no need to give them up. Soon this too became the fashion at Ashton Place, until even Lady Constance began requesting pockets on her dresses. They came in useful for holding rattles and pacifiers and, of course, the occasional chocolate treat.

However, there was another curious alteration at which no one could cease marveling. After the night of the curse breaking, the portraits of Admiral Percival Racine Ashton and the Honorable Pax Ashton that hung in Lord Fredrick's study were never the same. They lost their long noses and pointed, wolfish ears. The expressions that had once been so cold and offputting took on a warmer, more familiar look. One could almost call them kindly.

And the portrait of Agatha Swanburne, long in residence in the headmistress's office at Swanburne, now hung next to that of her twin brother, Pax. Miss Mortimer supervised the installation personally. Penelope, Simon, and the Incorrigible Lumleys gathered for the special occasion. Madame Ionesco was there, too, as the spooky change in the paintings pleased her to no end.

"Agatha belongs here, at home." Miss Mortimer stood back to admire the rearranged gallery of Ashton ancestors. From a certain angle, it looked as if Agatha and Pax were glancing at each other, a twin twinkle of merriment in each oil-painted eye. "And there is another, rather intriguing portrait of her at the British Museum that deserves to be more widely seen. I've

arranged to have it moved to Swanburne as a permanent loan, courtesy of the meweezum. Drat! I mean
museum. Now you've got me saying it, Cassawoof!"

Cassiopeia grinned at hearing her baby word for
museum come out of Miss Mortimer's mouth.

"And both portraits of Agatha were painted by Pax
himself?" Penelope asked, looking at the signature—
a large, swooping A. It was how all the Ashton men
signed their names.

Miss Mortimer nodded. "Yes. Pax painted portraits
of his sister his whole life long. As cruel as he was to
her, he never forgot her."

"Since we're on the subject of art appreciation,"
Simon said, "what's up with Edward Ashton's portrait?
The rest have gone positively cuddly, but his looks the
same as ever."

"I know what it means," Penelope said firmly. "It
means he's still alive."

"Hang on. I'll see if I can find out." Madame
Ionesco squinted at the portrait and mumbled a few
words of soothsayerese. The dead duck on the mantel-
piece let out a single protesting *quack*, but the portrait
of Edward Ashton remained unchanged. "Hmm! You
might be right. But don't worry, honey. He won't bother
you anymore. I don't think."

"Is that another prophecy?" Penelope asked with hope, for the good fortune-teller had never been wrong yet.

The soothsayer shrugged. "Call it my opinion. The dead are predictable. But the living? Please. You never know what they'll do next."

PENELOPE WAS DEEPLY RELIEVED TO think that Edward Ashton was no longer a threat to anyone, even if it was only Madame Ionesco's opinion. But where was he?

No one knew. Admiral Faucet maintained that no one could have survived the journey across the sea in that tattered balloon, especially a person with no balloon-flying experience.

Still—oddly—some weeks after the birth of Fern and Edward, and all the dramatic events of that strange, moonlit night, a letter arrived from Europe. It was addressed to Lord Fredrick, and it was from his mother.

After some pleasantries about her croquet game (she had been practicing a great deal and had improved tremendously, she said), she wrote:

And now, Freddy, allow me to share news of a more personal nature. I have made a new friend, a gentleman who goes by the name of Ward.

He reminds me of your father—those dark eyes!—and yet I know it is not him. Your father was so sharp minded, so unflappable. Poor Ward is like a child most of the time. He plays croquet, not well, and sings sea chanteys. He has a horror of dogs, imagine! I pity him, but there is something easy and familiar about his company, too.

Freddy, you know how stubbornly I believed your father was still alive and would someday return. But I have come to see that my belief was nothing more than a wish. It is Ward, so like and yet so unlike your father, who has cured me of my false hopes. Perhaps that is why I feel so attached to him.

My dear son, you have always had a good heart, and I imagine that fatherhood comes quite naturally to you. I look forward to meeting my grandchildren as soon as the croquet tournament season is over. Ward sends his regrets, for he is not inclined to take a trip to England; he says he has traveled quite enough in his life and is utterly fatigued by it. The only place he might someday return to is the Alps. He longs to hike there in the summer months, he says, when the edelweiss is in bloom, for he sometimes has a strange feeling he left something there, something important, and that if he could only find it, he would be quite himself again. Did I mention he was enigmatic? Sometimes he reminds me of that old coachman of yours.

Your loving mother (now a grandmother, too!),
Mrs. Hortense Ashton

Mrs. Clarke came upon the letter while straighten-
ing Lord Fredrick's desk. To read it without permission
could be considered a kind of eavesdropping, but it
was there in full view, and she was only human, after
all. Wisely, she decided to keep its contents to herself.
"After all, a letter from one's mother is a person's private business," she reasoned. "And I've no intention of
starting any wild rumors, especially ones that might
trouble the sleep of poor Miss Lumley! Surely she's
had enough excitement already."

Still, it was a credit to the British postal service that
a letter from so far away could arrive at Ashton Place
so quickly, especially given the vast quantities of mail
they were suddenly called upon to deliver. For Ashton Place was positively buried in congratulatory notes
and baby gifts. Lady Constance delighted in each one,
and she personally wrote countless prompt thank-you
notes while the babies gurgled in their cradle.

"I am setting a good example for the children," she
explained to Margaret, who could scarcely believe
her eyes. "One is never too young to learn good manners! By the by, there is a letter here addressed to Miss

426

Lumley—will you bring it to her? This mark on the envelope has been made to resemble the royal seal. Someone must be playing a joke on our governess, ha ha!"

Margaret did as she was asked, and naturally she too thought the letter was a joke. Penelope knew otherwise. After a few deep calming breaths to quell her shaking hands, she managed to slit open the envelope and unfold the letter within.

My dear Miss Lumley (or shall I call you cousin?),

I am writing with regard to a bill from the Grand Hotel in Saint Petersburg, Russia, which was sent to my particular attention at Buckingham Palace. Am I right in deducing that these charges were incurred by you? A night in the royal suite, flowers, chocolates—I am fond of chocolates myself, so I cannot object—and an entire wagonload of beets! You must have developed a taste for them while traveling abroad. Personally, I prefer a dish of good English peas.

I have been to Saint Petersburg only once, to attend the wedding of an old school friend of my husband's. The tsar insisted on giving us tickets to the ballet, as he is absurdly proud of it, but to be frank, Albert and I are more the types to enjoy a good cricket match and a beer, followed by an early bedtime. In any case, we were starving; we skipped the ballet and went to dinner instead.

But about your bill: I ought to tell you that my steward was quite cross, as he had no record of approving such an expense. He brought it to my attention during our weekly budget meeting. (Yes, even the Crown must keep to a budget! Castles tend to be drafty; you cannot imagine the amount of firewood we go through.) I recognized your name as the young governess who had written to me in such a heartfelt way a year or so ago, expressing your concerns about the poor. A Swanburne graduate, as I recall?

"I assure you," I told the steward, "Miss Lumley is not the sort of girl to run up an extravagant hotel bill and send it to her queen unless she had a very, very good reason to do so." I can only imagine what sort of predicament you must have been in, and I do hope that things have worked out happily for you and yours.

I have instructed my steward to pay the bill in full, and you may put the matter out of your mind. However, if there should come another occasion when you have need of the royal purse, I encourage you to ask permission first. Failing to do so sets a poor example for the little princes and princesses, never mind the members of Parliament.

As ever, your devoted Sovereign,
Victoria, Queen of the Realm

Penelope was surprised to read this, for how on earth did the Grand Hotel learn her real name? But then she remembered how she had signed for the flowers and chocolates by mistake.

This letter was not the only mail she had received. The previous day, a whole sack of mail had been delivered, thanks to the Princess Popkinova! The old woman had had all the mail addressed to Penelope packed up and forwarded from Plinkst to Ashton Place.

What a mountain of correspondence it was! Several months' worth of daily letters from the Incorrigible children and Simon, and quite a few letters from Miss Charlotte Mortimer and Mrs. Clarke, too. Simon lugged it up to the nursery for her and grunted mightily when he put it down.

Penelope hoped Svetlana had not had the burden of dragging the heavy mailbag back to the post office. "Yet who knows," she said to Simon, for she had told him all about the Russian girl. "A trip to the post office may have been a window of opportunity for her to escape from Plinkst herself. I wish her well! Though I expect I will never know what becomes of her. It is a strange feeling, to meet people who make such a vivid impression, and then not know how things turn out for them."

Simon nodded. "Just like going to the theater. Once the curtain comes down, the story's over. Then everyone gets to imagine their own version of what happens next." His eyes took on their characteristic gleam. "Think of us, for instance. How do you imagine we'll all turn out?"

"Us? You mean you and me, and the children, and everyone else here at Ashton Place?" She thought for a moment. "Well, I expect Lady Constance and Lord Fredrick may well turn out to be better parents than anyone could have expected. And I would not be surprised if Fern and Edward grow up to be the best of friends, and are as sweet and clever as two children could be."

"A bit woofish, too, I'll wager!" Simon smiled. "And there's no harm in that, is there?"

"Certainly there is not," she said. "As for the Incorrigibles . . ." She closed her eyes for a moment, to better imagine it. "Alexander could grow up to be a navigator, and perhaps serve in the Royal Navy. Beowulf is so sensitive and creative. . . ."

"A moody poet, perhaps?"

"I think painting is his true calling. Perhaps someday

there will be an entire gallery at the British Museum devoted to his art. And Cassiopeia has a fierce sense of justice, don't you agree? And the courage to stand up to figures of authority in high dudgeon. I would not be surprised if she sat on the bench someday."

Simon laughed. "Just so. The Honorable Cassiopeia Incorrigible Lumley. I can picture it, clear as day!"

The thought of little Cassiopeia in a white wig and judge's robes, dispensing justice with the fair, firm confidence of a true Swanburne girl, made Penelope grin from ear to ear. It was an amusing game, to imagine what might become of each of them!

"All right, what about Madame Ionesco?" Simon asked, leaning back in his chair.

Penelope pretended to gaze into a crystal ball (it was really the nursery globe). "I foresee the spooky Madame will have very good fortune indeed. Her Gypsy cakes will become an international success!"

Simon paused. "And Edward Ashton?"

The question drained the laughter from her. "He will have to sort out his own fate. I will not imagine a future for him, but trust that the scales of justice will weigh in suitably."

Hmm! Whom had she left out?

"Mrs. Clarke will live on happily and dote on the

babies. Margaret and Jasper may well start a family of their own someday. Old Timothy—well, he is quite an enigma! Whatever the future holds for him, I expect there will be a touch of mystery about it."

Simon held her gaze.

"And what of you? And me?"

Penelope blushed but did not look away.

"The Incorrigible Lumleys—that is to say, my brothers and sister—will still be needing a governess. I expect I shall stay on at Ashton Place in that capacity for some time yet. But in years to come, who knows? I might like to try my hand at writing poetry, or books of stories. Like Giddy-Yap, Rainbow!, perhaps! Or something altogether different."

He nodded approvingly. "Say, I like those pony books, too! And don't forget about the bard of Ashton Place, Mr. Simon Harley-Dickinson. What's his fate, I wonder?"

"Hmmm . . . I shall have to check my crystal globe." She gave the nursery globe a spin, closed her eyes, and imitated Madame Ionesco once more. "Your pirate play will be a smash hit in the West End. The crystal ball don't lie, honey. Your show is a hit! Or was. Or will be."

He bowed to his imaginary audience. "Thank you, thank you!" This prediction was music to Simon's ears.

Pleased, Penelope kept up the Ionesco act. "You will

have a long voyage ahead!" she intoned, waving her hands over the globe.

His face changed. "A long voyage!" he exclaimed. Clearly he was no longer playing. "Wait, are you sure you're not just pretending to be a soothsayer?"

"Simon, do you mean you are setting sail once more? So soon?" To say her heart sank was an apt metaphor, considering the subject. She swallowed hard and tried to sound brave and cheerful. "Although . . . I suppose, knowing your love of seaborne adventure, I ought not expect you to stay on dry land for long."

He fidgeted in his chair. "Funny you should mention the sea," he said. "Penelope, I've been thinking."

"About what?" she said, her voice squeaking like Margaret's.

"About, well . . ." He cracked his knuckles, pushed his hair off his forehead, tugged at his collar. "All right, I might as well spit it out. I've been thinking . . . about Bertha."

This was not what she had been hoping to hear. "You mean Bertha the ostrich?" she replied needlessly, to hide her disappointment.

He leaned forward, excitement shining in his eyes. "The very one. The big bird's got to get back to Africa somehow." He took the globe in his own hands and turned it from one hemisphere to the other. "What do you say we take her home? From rainy England to the sun-bleached sands of the Sahara!"

Either time had stopped or her breathing had, or both. A trip to Africa with Simon! What fun it would be—and yet . . .

"Bertha surely deserves to go home, as much as any of us do," she said carefully. "But if I may be frank—"

"You may, of course!"

"Thank you—well, I have only just gotten home myself. And I confess, I have grown weary of train schedules and troikas, seasickness and hot air balloons."

He stroked his chin. "You've got travel fatigue, and no wonder. So you'd like nothing more than to stay put for a bit, then?"

"I would." She gestured at the heap of mail. "As you see, I have a great deal of correspondence to catch up on, and the children have hardly had a proper lesson for months. But Simon, if *you* want to take Bertha home to Africa, by all means . . ."

"I do," he said quickly, "and at the same time I don't. On the one hand, it would be a grand adventure. But on the other hand . . ." He sat up, scratched his head, and then wrung his hands in a nervous gesture that would not have looked out of place on Nutsawoo. "Well, as we've just established," he finally said, "*you've* just gotten home, which is a powerful argument in favor of *me* staying put. And then there's Fern and Edward to consider. I am the baby nurse, after all. I can't just pick up and leave. I've got important responsibilities! Or Mrs. Penworthy does, which is the same thing."

Penelope started to laugh.

"Now, don't laugh, it's all quite serious!" he said, though he was laughing, too. "And I'd like to get to know your parents. They've got heaps of stories to tell, and I do love a good plot twist." His voice softened. "I expect you'd like to get to know them better, too. You've all been apart a good long while, to say the least."

Indeed they had, but no more. Mater and Pater Lumley had declined Lord Fredrick's invitation to live in the grand house at Ashton Place but had happily accepted his offer of a small cottage on the grounds. They would run a bookstore, give painting lessons, and assume Madame Ionesco's bakehouse duties when she was off prognosticating, for they had surely learned a thing or two about baking while in Frankenforde. The Incorrigible Lumley children would live in the cottage with their parents, but the nursery would also remain theirs to enjoy, and they would be free to come and go as they wished.

As for Penelope, she was too fond of her lovely room to leave it altogether, but she also rather liked waking up in her parents' cottage, to the smell of coffee and shaving cream and lavender water, and it seemed right that she too should come and go between them as she wished. After all, at sixteen she was nearer a grown-up than a child, but she had missed a great deal of what most people think of as childhood, and now she could have her fill. Happily there was no rush, about any of it—the brave adventure of growing up, or the sweetness of being a well-loved child, safe under her parents' roof. Truly, she had all the time in the world.

Simon was giving her the most tender, cow-eyed look. "I am grateful that you understand my position," she said. It came out rather formally, for a lump had formed in her throat, and she was trying not to cry.

"Oh, I do understand," he assured her. "I absolutely do. And I think—that is—I hope you understand mine. Meaning, if you'd rather stay put for a bit, then I would, too."

She looked down at her hands, now folded neatly in her lap. His rested carelessly on his knees. The question of what it would it be like to hold hands took shape in her mind at the exact moment his hand reached out and took hers.

"I believe—yes, I do understand." Then she smiled, and so did he, and all nervousness left her, for it seemed a decision of sorts had been made between them. But all she said was "Do you think Bertha will mind waiting just a bit longer to go home?"

He withdrew his hand and sat up straight, grinning. "Not at all. In fact, I think she's rather excited about the new babies. Nutsawoo's babies, I mean."

Yes, Nutsawoo! The long-lost scamp had become a frequent visitor once more, usually with an adorable troika of squirrel babies scampering behind, and another grown-up-sized squirrel, too.

"I'm sure Bertha will want to see Nutsawoo's family grow up a bit before we set off," Simon continued. "Why, I saw her just this morning acting as a stepladder for the little ones to get to the high branch of the elm!"

"An ostrich serving as baby nurse to a litter of squirrels?" Penelope chuckled. "What are the odds of that happening, I wonder?"

"It's unexpected, sure. But what isn't?"

At that moment the Incorrigible Lumleys came racing in. They had taken to having parents as readily as ducks take to water, as the saying goes, and had already enjoyed a hearty breakfast prepared by their father. He had artfully arranged the plates to resemble Mama Woof, with fried eggs for her yellow wolf eyes, crisp bacon strips for whiskers, and two halves of buttered brown toast for her alert, upright ears.

During their meal they had enjoyed some cheerful poetry read aloud by Mater Lumley. It was a lovely poem by Mr. William Wordsworth, called "I Wandered Lonely as a Cloud," although nowadays most people simply know it as "Daffodils," as that is what the poem is about.

> *I wandered lonely as a Cloud*
> *That floats on high o'er vales and Hills,*
> *When all at once I saw a crowd,*
> *A host, of golden Daffodils. . . .*

After both meal and poem were consumed, the Incorrigibles said thank you very much, asked to be excused, cleared their dishes from the table, and set out in search of adventure. This is the proper way to manage having parents. After all, once they have been loved, fed, clothed, and educated, most children are well able to fashion their own entertainments, and the wise Mater and Pater will let them. (Interestingly, it is when children know their parents are close at hand that they feel most able to bravely set off into the world. There is a bittersweet irony in this, whose full meaning only becomes apparent when one has children of one's own.)

The Incorrigible Lumleys began their day's to-doawoos by visiting Fern and Edward in the babies' room, and offering some brief lessons in yapping, woofing, howling, burping, wiggling, napping, and other essential skills. Then they ran upstairs to the nursery and went straight to the window, to check on Nutsawoo's family. Squirrels are no geniuses, mind you, but the squirrel babies already knew how to line up on the branch of the elm to beg for treats. Naturally, the children were happy to oblige.

After that, they said good morning to Penelope and clambered onto Simon as if he were a tree suitable for climbing. Only then did they see the great pile of correspondence.

"Our letters!" they cried, and scrambled down again. Simon made a comic show of being capsized, but as he had often proved, he had sea legs enough to weather storms far worse than this.

Penelope gazed upon the littlest Lumleys with a look that was equal parts loving big sister and exceedingly fond governess, and indeed, the two feelings were so thoroughly mixed together there was no telling them apart. "They are your letters, indeed. What an impressive collection! I am eager to read them, each and every one."

"Mine have maps," Alexander explained.

"Mine have math problems!" Cassiopeia said, and ran for her abacus.

"Mine have poetic meter. A villanelle, actually," Beowulf added modestly.

Penelope ruffled his hair. "A villanelle, my word! Aren't you clever!"

"And what about *your* letters, Simawoo?" Cassiopeia asked, full of mischief.

Simon shoved his hands into his pockets and shifted bashfully from one foot to the other. "Most of what I wrote's what I'd call personal, but I did include some thrilling excerpts from my pirate play. It's quite a tale, if I do say so myself." He plucked one of his own letters from the towering heap. "Shall I proclaim it aloud in a grand voice and wave my arms too much, like one of Leeds' Thespians on Demand?"

The children cried, "Yes, yes!" but looked at Penelope for a final decision. She was their governess, after all.

"Please do, Simon." She settled into her chair, and the Incorrigibles gathered 'round her just as they always had, for they all loved a good story, and that was one thing that would never change. Penelope reached contentedly for her tea. "I would like that very much."

Finis

Acknowledgments

IT TAKES MANY LOVING HANDS to make a book. I'm grateful to my editor, Donna Bray, and to the countless individuals whose dedicated, skilled work has made it possible for this story of a plucky young governess and three children who were raised by wolves to find its way to readers around the world. As the Incorrigible children would say: Thankawoo, to each of you, from the bottom of my heart.

Many of my readers have come to know the Incorrigible Children of Ashton Place books through the wonderful audiobook recordings by Katherine Kellgren, starting with *The Mysterious Howling* in 2010. As I wrote each book in the series, more and more I came to look forward to "Katy day": the day that Katy, after devouring her advance copy of the manuscript, would call me, full of boundless enthusiasm and insightful questions. Writing books can be lonely work, but Katy had a superhuman gift of jumping into an imaginary world with both feet and a wide-open heart. I was always so grateful for the company. Over the years we became dear friends.

The last time I spoke with Katy was in late December of 2017, after Christmas, shortly before she died of a difficult illness that she had been bravely fighting for a long time. We spoke of many things, friendship and love and poetry among them. She asked me to read to her, and as I ran to pull a favorite book of poetry off the shelf, she said no, she would like to hear this book, *The Long-Lost Home*, which she would not be able to record as she had the others. I started from the beginning, and when we reached the spot where the Swanburne school song is sung, she joined in and sang along with me, remembering every note and word.

This book is dedicated to Katy, to the art and music and poetry and people she loved, and to wonderful storytellers everywhere.

31901063268272